FULL BLAZE

A Firehawks Novel

M.L. BUCHMAN

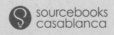

Published by Sourcebooks Casablanca, an imprint of Sourcebooks, Inc.
P.O. Box 4410, Naperville, Illinois 60567-4410
(630) 961-3900
Fax: (630) 961-2168
www.sourcebooks.com

Printed and bound in Canada.
MBP 10 9 8 7 6 5 4 3 2 1

Praise for *Pure Heat*

"Meticulously researched, hard-hitting, and suspenseful...Buchman writes with beauty and simmering passion."

—*Publishers Weekly* Starred Review

"Strong, competent female characters and compelling technical and regional details are juxtaposed with a tender romance... A natural for all military romance fans."

—*Booklist* Starred Review

"Buchman's adept use of source material will blow the readers' minds and leave them awestruck that a wonderful love story can be so seamlessly woven in among technical details."

—*RT Book Reviews* Top Pick, 4.5 Stars

"If you are looking for an action-packed romantic read set in a world filled with danger, *Pure Heat* is one you will want to pick up."

—*Fresh Fiction*

"A heavy hitter and worth every minute spent reading. It's a tightly written, well-thought-out plot with a fascinating dynamic between the hero and heroine... A believable feel of authenticity made this book hard to put down."

—*Long and Short Reviews*

Also by M.L. Buchman

To the lady who has walked through the fire
with me for much of two decades.

Chapter 1

CAL JACKSON STARED UP AT THE WALL OF FLAME EATING ITS way toward him through the forest. He was always tempting fate one step too far. Now he was way past the second step, as well as the third. He was standing in the foreign land of totally screwed. In his seven years of fighting wildfires and five more photographing them, he'd never been this far over the line. Not even close.

He'd ridden the edge a lot since he was a testosterone-laden teen. It had earned him his fair share of cold slaps from ticked-off women, but maybe more than his share of warm and friendly nights. It had also led to numerous interesting opportunities to travel for both work and play, so he'd learned to take that risk without really thinking about it.

He tried not to take that second step very often; it was his warning that he was pushing the limits. But dancing along the edge of that step was what had won him so many of his awards. Though the Pulitzer for photography and "best of" for World Press Photo still remained out of reach, he'd bagged a lot of awards including the cover on *National Geographic*. And *Time*, twice.

Out here, way past the second step, the Grindstone Canyon Fire was in full-throated roar. The sound throbbed against his body with bass notes that actually shook his inner organs. He'd stood close beside the tracks when two-hundred-car freight trains had flown past at full speed. This was louder. Nor did it conveniently pass by and Doppler into the distance; this train of fire had him clear in its sights.

The air was growing so hot that it hurt to breathe. His acute sense of smell for smoke, burning pitch, and carbon had long since been overwhelmed by the saturation of them in the air. He'd embedded tight with a crew of hotshot firefighters who were fast losing ground against the wildfire despite their best efforts. It happened that way. Fighting fire was a delicate back-and-forth dance between flame and attacker, almost like a hip-hop advance and retreat, attack and counterattack by both sides of the…hoedown.

Hoedown? Where had he come up with that? Third foster father. Yuck!

In one way the comparison was appropriate, as it was with the rakes, Pulaskis, and even hoes that a hotshot crew used to battle the flames. Not hoedown, but rather… His brain was trying to work out what hip-hop dancers called that battle of dance, power, and sensuality—that had to be about the stupidest damn thought to have as his last on earth.

The Grindstone in southern California was probably the last big fire of the year in the United States. The Pacific Northwest was already getting rain, and Colorado had snow, though that hadn't slowed down the Fern Lake Fire back in 2012. He'd won two awards and gotten national headlines on that one for his piece on fighting wildfires when the supply tanks and rivers froze and the helicopters couldn't get at the water to fight the flames.

The Southeast had just been soaked by a really

serious trio of hurricanes. So this year California was last in the hot seat, and the fires above Santa Barbara were doing their best to take back the hills for Mother Nature. It had started in the same area of Rattlesnake Canyon Park as the lethal Rattlesnake Fire of 1953 that killed fifteen firefighters. Though this time it was started by lightning rather than a psycho arsonist.

You'd think he'd have grabbed a clue from the historical setting, though he'd been no better with history than most of the subjects in school, except fighting and photography. With maturity, he'd added "fire" as an adjective to both of them. He now knew fire history as well as any hotshot walking the hills, except for this time when it should have warned him. There hadn't been a bad burn here in more than sixty years, so it was due.

The hotshot crew he'd been with had been in the heat for a week, driving ahead and then retreating—dancing that careful strategic dance against the fire. Less than two minutes ago the crew had taken off down a narrow track leading across a cliff face and onto a rolling slope that led down into the distant valley. Their escape route was clean. He'd hesitated an extra fifteen seconds to get a shot of a massive fig tree, over eighty feet tall, being ripped up by fire-generated winds and tossed aside like a matchstick. Fifteen lousy seconds.

The problem was that the fire had cast the flaming tree down right across his escape route. The tree not only lay across the path, but it was catching all of the surrounding material on fire as well. The crew looked at him helplessly across the gap.

The notch canyon that separated them was too far for a rope cast, and the vertical walls that plunged down to either side of his position required a level of mountain-eering skill that included hammers and pitons, neither of which he was carrying. He carefully eyed a ledge about ten feet below, but could think of no way to get down to it. Far too narrow a landing to risk a jump. Yet.

He could see the crew boss on the radio, but with the fire's roar, Cal couldn't hear him even though his own radio handset was in its pouch right against his shoulder and the volume was turned up to full.

The smoke blotted out the boss just as he was about to make a hand sign of some sort. A glance upward into the smoke canopy told him that no helicopters would be able to save his sorry behind. The mushroom cloud of smoke—looking like a nuclear blast, it was so intense— rose ten thousand feet above the California landscape would block any line of approach.

The ravine to the south was clogged with fire, and the one to the north was now fully lit by the thrown tree, its branches ablaze like a thousand-armed candelabra. The two ravines met to the west. The only way out was east—and there raged the beast.

The narrow ledge of his final demise was covered in a few dogwood and valley oak trees, tall grasses, and dense manzanita brush. When the fire rolled over this site, it would burn hot. Hot in the same way it had burned over the nineteen-man crew in Yarnell, Arizona, the air so superheated it had burned right through their foil emergency shelters. It had done that despite the circular clearing they'd cut around themselves. And he didn't even carry a chain saw to try to make a clearing. All he had were his cameras.

He backed to the edge of the precipice and then turned

once more to look at the flame. He wasn't even conscious of his actions as he lifted his new Canon Mark III camera, found the frame, shot the photo. Zoomed back. Found the next, shot it. The beast was close. He'd only once been so close to the heart of the firestorm. During his days as a member of a hotshot crew, they'd have been long gone before the heart of the fire rolled this close. The camera was actually heating in his hands, prickly hot to hold.

Too close! That was it. He dropped the camera into his bag and pulled out his old workhorse 6D body with the 28 mm wide-angle lens. No way he'd risk a lens change with all of the dust and ash in the air.

There! He could see the image coming together that would make a cover photo. Another prizewinner was almost here. Just a few more seconds… If he could just…

A metal shape zipped by the lens, fast. He didn't see what it was, but some instinct had him pressing the shutter. He flicked back to the image.

On his viewfinder a winged drone a half-dozen feet in length, painted black with gold-and-orange flames, had flown between him and the fire. It had a bold "MHA" emblazoned on its side.

Some comfort that was. All it meant was that someone from Mount Hood Aviation was going to have the award-winning photo of the journalist who burned alive while clutching his camera like a damned idiot. All because he'd had to take that third step and now couldn't wrench back from it.

Cal was going to make a lousy Cinderella, no pretty gown rising from the ashes for him. But he was sure going to end up as a cinder. Another thirty seconds and he'd have to take his chances inside the foil shelter, though he'd sworn he'd never do that again.

Maybe his life was supposed to pass before his eyes right about now, but he hoped not. He'd beaten the first sixteen years of his life down with every ounce of a firefighter's willpower until they didn't exist. The time since had been mostly good, but with the way his luck was running today, he'd get to see those early days before he'd named himself Calvin Jackson.

Some idiot part of him started to raise the camera again, but then he stopped. His cameras were going to cook right along with him, even if he threw himself over them like a Marine covering a grenade to save his buddies. For once he just looked at the wall of flame. Its heart so hot it glowed gold as the fire swarmed up tree trunks six stories tall with a single breath, sheathing each tree in a cloak of flame just six inches and fifteen hundred degrees thick. The roar deepened as if gathering its breath. So loud that—

The sharp blast of a voice over a loudspeaker not ten feet behind him so startled Cal that he almost stumbled off the ledge. Completely masked by the roar of the fire and with hundred-foot flames less than thirty yards away, a helicopter had come to hover behind him. It wore the same paint job as the drone.

A glance up showed the rotor blades shimmering in a lethal arc just a few feet above him and no break in the smoke-cloud cover. The hotshot crew was still invisible across the ravine. But far down below, right off the narrow spit of cliff he was perched upon, he could see the terrain. The pilot had flown up through a hole underneath the smoke and ash cloud.

"Get aboard, you bloody git!" the speaker screamed at him. He wouldn't have heard it if it weren't less than ten feet away and aimed right at him.

The chopper hung just out of reach, hovering with its open side door toward him. Over his shoulder he could see that the spinning rotor disk was within a foot or so of a stout oak tree. They couldn't fly any closer to him. The chopper didn't even have skids to grab on to like they always did in the movies, just wheels.

The cargo bay door was an open four-by-four-foot square of salvation, hanging a half-dozen feet away over a hundred-yard drop. He stuffed both cameras into the padded bag, snapped it shut, and chucked the bag through the door toward the rear so it wouldn't go out the other side, which was also open. Then, squatting to make the leap while the chopper bounced in the roiling air currents, he jumped into space.

He landed mostly inside the door. Far enough to drag himself the rest of the way. He spotted a rope line, made sure it was secured to something, then snapped the D ring on the front of his safety harness onto it so that he was now secure.

"Good to go," he shouted to the pilot. There was no way he could be heard. The freight train was screaming toward them, barely ten yards from the rotor tips.

The pilot, flying alone, risked a quick glance back, but was skilled enough for the chopper to remain rock stable despite the turbulent environment.

Cal only had long enough to get the impression of a narrow face and mirrored shades wrapped in a large, earmuff pilot's headset. Seeing he was aboard, the pilot rolled the chopper hard left and dove down through the dwindling smoke hole. He caught the camera bag as it skidded across the deck plating.

A glance up at the cliff showed a tongue of flame now reaching out to grab where the chopper had hovered only moments before.

Now that he was safe, the adrenaline rush kicked out hard. He'd fought fires from California to Alaska, and he'd photographed them in Brazil, Russia, and a dozen other places. He'd never before had his hands shake so badly that he couldn't even open the bag to make sure the cameras were okay. All he could do was clench it to his chest and let the shakes run through him.

—✳✳✳—

"Yeah, Ground Command. This is Hawk Oh-two, I got him. You can release your crew to the next site."

Jeannie Clark clicked off her mike and the one-word acknowledgment came right back. She was bummed. She'd finally found a flaw with her beautiful new Firehawk. Well, almost new. The machine had done a couple tours in Iraq first, but it had been totally renovated, repainted, and reconfigured with a big belly tank for dumping retardant on wildfires. It was new to her. Her boss and MHA's lead pilot, Emily Beale, had only just certified her in this type last month. And the chopper was also new to Mount Hood Aviation's "Hoodies," one of the country's premier firefighters-for-hire contractors. It was only the second load-rated Type I helicopter in their inventory.

Until recently, she'd only been certified in the midsize Type II Twin Huey 212 and the tiny Type III MD500, both much-lower-capacity crafts. The Firehawk was built on the Sikorsky Black Hawk frame and could lift a massive thousand gallons of retardant or water, about four and a half tons. That could make a serious dent in a blaze except when Mama Nature was really kicking up her heels with Papa Fire. That was what her Australian friend Dale always called them, as if they were part of his Aboriginal Dreamtime creation mysticism. She'd looked up the expression and it wasn't, but she'd kept using it even after coming to America. People always looked at her cross-eyed when she used it, so she now kept it to herself.

The thing was, with her MD500, she could have scooted right onto that cliff edge instead of hovering out in space. Had to give the guy some points—at three hundred feet up a cliff, he'd jumped right out with no hesitation. That said something about guts, or desperation. She'd half expected him to freeze and die there. Even three more seconds and she'd have had to bug out and leave him there to burn.

She continued to maneuver hard and fast, trying to get down and out of the smoke-clear hole before it totally closed. Driving straight out through the ash wall that surrounded her on all sides had two bad things going for it. First, you couldn't see squat—even radar got dicey in some of the heat and ash plumes. Second, her air filters would ingest enough ash to clog them up good. Then she'd have to go back to base and wait while they were serviced. Assuming her engines kept running long enough even to do that. Doing an autorotate landing into the suburbs of Santa Barbara wasn't her idea of a good time.

Still, she might have to return to base because Mister Brainless Got-himself-trapped was hurt.

"You okay back there?"

In answer he squeezed between the pilot and copilot seats, stepping carefully over the center console despite the lunges of the chopper due to her maneuverings. He also was smart enough not to bump the cyclic control between his knees as he slid into the seat and buckled up. Only once he was buckled in did he release the line attached to his harness and toss it toward the rear. That spoke of training.

The acrid scent of char and smoke was a slap to her face, it radiated off his black-smeared yellow Nomex fire suit. He was dressed like a hotshot right down to the foil shelter on his hip, but all he carried was a padded bag clutched tight against his chest.

She pointed a finger toward a dangling headset without taking her hands off the dual controls of cyclic and collective. Especially not with the cliff still a bare two rotor widths away, 107 feet and four inches, give or take the odd boulder.

His hands were fumbling as he pulled on the headset. Adrenaline letdown. She'd seen it before, had it herself when a tree had exploded below her MD500 a few months ago and taken out the tail rotor. Crash landing in the middle of the New Tillamook Burn had been a wild ride. He finally got the headset pulled on, once he figured out he had to remove his hard hat first.

"What the hell is in that bag," she asked him over the intercom, "that you had to throw it in before yourself? Are you berko, Yank?" Didn't the guy have any idea about personal safety first?

"Did I?" He glanced down at the bag as if it might know the answer. Then he pulled its strap over his head, tangling it in the headset's cord. Took him a bit to straighten it all out before he answered.

"It's my cameras." He turned to face her and did that standard freeze double-take.

When Jeannie glanced over, he was grinning at her. Oh crap! She knew that look. Another smoke jock thinking, "What's a woman doing flying a big nasty helicopter like this? And how far can I get with her?" The answers were: she'd busted her ass for years to get here, and he would get absolutely nowhere. She was half sorry that Steve's drone had found a safe way in to him and she'd rescued him.

"Pretty damn stupid of me, now that you mention it." His voice was deep and wry over the intercom.

Well, okay, he got another half a point for not saying the expected. Add that to the one he'd earned jumping into space to reach her chopper, and he was still nowhere. In her personal system, it took at least ten points to get a date, though this guy might need twenty.

"Huh. It's not like I wasn't already wearing the strap across my chest. I never really understood a buddy's story until this moment. He told me about being at a forward air base in Iraq when he heard a shell coming in. Says he knew he was dead and it was too late to move, so he chucked his bag out of their foxhole to save the pictures he'd taken."

Damn, but he had a nice voice for storytelling, all deep and warm. No way that was worth another point. Couldn't be.

"Ralph figured they might even support his wife awhile after he died, if the cameras were recovered. But the damn mortar round missed their barricaded position and landed square on the bag. Blew six grand of cameras and lenses and a month of dangerous work to smithereens; didn't do anything else other than make a hole in the dirt. Guess I thought the same thing on some level."

Jeannie shook her head and paid attention to the smoke wall. It was thinning near the ground, but the air at the lower edge of the plume still had a mind of its own. And they were getting down into power-line territory. Power lines loved the taste of fresh rotor blade and always threw a little power party over roasted downed chopper.

Married. Figures. How many jerks went voluntarily and died on Everest or in some godforsaken hole, leaving behind a family while in pursuit of their sport? Military was different. If you were in the service, like her brother Randall in the Royal Australian Air Force, and the RAAF said, "Go there," you went. It's what you'd signed up for.

This joker wasn't even fire crew; he was a photographer. He'd literally jumped off the cliff without a safety net, and he'd saved his camera bag first.

"Calvin Jackson, at your service. Everyone calls me Cal."

"Got a twin brother named Hobbes? Did people call you Calvin and Hobbes? Are you the evil one?"

"No brother." For a just a moment his voice was hard and clipped, then he asked, "And you are?" His voice was abruptly all smooth in that way guys always thought was so charming.

"Smart enough to be your worst nightmare, mate," Jeannie replied. She'd met a hundred guys like him, maybe a thousand. Wife at home, chatting up the pretty pilot in the field. She could see them homing in on her from ten thousand feet away. Ever since her days flying in the Australian bush. She'd wing into some remote cattle station, with emergency supplies or a doctor aboard, and every puppy-dog lonely cowhand would start circling around the Sheila pilot.

That silenced him.

Before he could find a new tack, she cut him off. "Are you okay? Or do I have to stop this run to get you to some medico?" She managed to clear the bottom of the plume before she reached the Santa Barbara suburb crammed up against the base of the foothills. One of the engine crews waved while spraying down houses against the flames approaching from another draw. She rocked her cyclic left and right to return the wave as she flew out.

"I'm fine. Do what you need to do."

"You mean what I was doing before I had to fly up and rescue your sorry behind for your wife's sake?"

"Yeah, that. Except I'm not married."

Jeannie headed for the nearest swimming pool, a lot of those in this high-end neighborhood, then glanced over at him. Cal had settled in comfortably, looking out the window like any normal rubbernecking tourist, not like some freaked-out survivor of a close brush with death. Good recovery time. His smoke-smeared face actually highlighted his light brown eyes and bright smile. The man was several points worth of handsome and clearly knew it.

He turned to meet her gaze.

"Biding your time? It's not going to work on me," she informed him.

"Damn, and I had such hopes what with not knowing your name and all."

Okay, she'd give him another half point for funny. She had a weak spot for funny, not that she'd ever admit that to this man.

Cal alternated between watching the nameless pilot and admiring her skill.

She was very easy to watch. While the heavy gear covered her frame, what he could see was exceptional. Fine-fingered hands that rested lightly on the controls. She flew with no hesitation, absolute confidence in what she was doing.

It was her face that was so captivating. Not some pretty girl, though she was beautiful. Her face had character. He'd bet that behind her mirrored shades her eyes were dark. They'd be dark, thoughtful, even penetrating, staring right through any bullshit. Her face wasn't merely narrow. The features were delicate, sophisticated. He liked that; it looked good on her.

Her hair, which he hadn't noticed at first because of the high-backed pilot seat, was great. It was thick, dark brown, and streamed down behind the earmuffs of the headset in a wind-tousled cascade past her shoulders.

She leaned over to look out the bubble window built into the door.

He did the same on his side. The upper half of the door was a Plexiglas window that bulged outward enough for him to stick his head into it and look straight down. They were hovering twenty feet or so over someone's swimming pool. Lawn furniture skittered away in every direction beneath the downward blast of the rotor wash.

But they weren't descending any farther.

He glanced over at her and noted a dark red streak down the back of her long hair, reaching down past her shoulder blades, heart-of-fire red. He had the recent experience to remind himself of how accurately she'd reproduced the color. It looked like a home dye job by a woman skilled at doing things for herself, but it was also cute and worked on her. She was craning her neck to look toward the stern.

He looked back out his window and down. A six-inch snorkel hose hung twenty feet down into the pool. Even as he watched, he could hear the pumps kick on. Despite being at the other end of the hose, they vibrated the airframe against his feet on the deck plates. A swirl of water formed around the jet pump as it drove water up the snorkel hose. The chopper felt as if it was settling or perhaps stabilizing as it sucked up the load.

"How much can you hold?"

"A thousand gallons at this altitude. Minus a hundred for the foam tank I have rigged in the stern and minus thirty more for you." She said it matter-of-factly, but he could hear the insult.

He didn't feel the least bit guilty—too damn glad to be alive. This time when he looked over, he noticed more than the color of her hair. Her position, twisted to look out and down at the pool, revealed a trim waist despite the heavy jacket she wore. He took another bet with himself that in addition to warm brown eyes, she'd have a light form, making an even nicer package. And she made her living floating like a vapor through the air.

It reminded him of the old song about the girl with the light brown hair.

"I dream of Jeannie with the dark red hair," he sang lightly.

———

Jeannie jerked around to stare at the photographer chap.

"How did you know my name? And it's 'with the bright blue hair.'"

"Because it, uh, used to be blue? No, because it never was blue." He laughed at the joke. "Sure. How did I miss that? Didn't know your name. I just liked how you fit the song, floating on the smoke of the fire."

The jet pump whined as it sucked air. Turning once more to the window, she descended to get the lower end of the snorkel back in the water and watched the fill gauge. Five more seconds to full. She shut off at 920 gallons. And—done. Retracting the snorkel onto the hose reel and rising back into the air, she made sure that she stayed clear of chimneys, tall trees, and power lines.

No one had ever gotten that right. Her hair had never been blue. She'd put in the red streak after her first flight against fire. The woman who'd certified her in Australia had said Jeannie was so good that she must have a fire-red streak down her back. She'd showed up with it the next day and flown that way ever since.

The thing about the blue had always been her little joke, a line to keep guys at a distance. And it had always worked to make them look foolish or confused, occasionally ticking them off, which worked just as well. But not Cal Jackson. He'd done it with fewer clues than most. That had to be worth another point, though she gave it up reluctantly.

She called Mark Henderson, flying air attack command in the Beech Baron up at seven thousand feet. "Air attack, this is Hawk Oh-two with a full load of water and foam…and a passenger. Where do you want me?"

She listened to the directions and grinned at the cooing sound in the background. His one-year-old daughter would be curled up in her tiny car seat flying copilot beside him—the team's most junior member.

The hotshot crew that Cal had been with had repositioned to cut a firebreak across a feeder of fire reaching north along an overgrown greenway. The residents hadn't dead-limbed trees or cleared brush, despite warnings, even though the greenway reached deep into the rich-people suburb. The ever-growing urban-forest interface was always risky, but an untended one was just asking for what you deserved. And then they wondered why their homes burned. Jeannie was instructed to follow Emily Beale in Hawk Oh-one to give the hotshots a hand.

"I can drop you back in with your hotshot crew, if you want," Jeannie told Cal over the intercom. "We're headed over to give them a hand."

"I'm fine where I am, if that's okay with you. They're probably tired of me anyway."

"Great. So now I'm saddled with your deadweight?" She climbed to six hundred feet above ground level, turning to a heading of one-two-zero, and spotted Emily setting up for her attack run a half mile ahead.

"I know it's a burden, but I'm easy."

"Well, I'm not." What idiot part of her brain decided

to add sexual innuendo to this conversation? It wasn't the sort of thing she ever did.

She heard a camera-shutter click sound over the headset. She looked over, right into a big, fat camera lens barely two feet away. She heard another click.

"Cut that out!" Even as she opened her mouth, she heard a third click.

And then he laughed aloud. "Oh, we gotta frame that one."

Turning away, she lined up on her attack run, then checked in on the hotshots' frequency for final guidance. Her best option would be to just ignore the man in the copilot seat. She wished that was easier to do.

Cal had enjoyed flustering her. She was so smooth, so professional. In addition to the lovely Australian accent, like Nicole Kidman's when she wasn't covering it, Jeannie's voice had all the markers of higher education. He flipped through the three photos on his viewfinder's screen. The last one was funny: her mouth open, the anger obvious, and the camera reflected in the mirrored shades clearly illustrated the reason for her ire. He should blow it up and laminate it to the side of her chopper some night.

The head-on shot of her still and quiet a moment earlier was far better, though. It captured the serious pilot, the frank gaze of a professional, a very pretty professional, doing her job. Though that shot had the mood spoiled by the dual reflections of his camera.

It was the first shot that stopped him. That was an amazing photo. The same intentness, now in profile — she had an exceptionally pleasant profile—high forehead, nice nose, and womanly lips above a well-defined chin and a splendid length of neck. But the wide-angle lens had captured her hands on the controls of a vastly complex machine. Beyond the window, the wall of smoke and flame hung so close he could feel his nerves starting to return.

He'd never been afraid of fire. Respected it? Immensely. But afraid? Not until he'd almost been burned to death for the second time in his life.

He lowered the camera and inspected where he had come to rest.

As a hotshot for seven years, he'd been delivered by helitack any number of times but he'd only gotten to ride up front a few times. Those trips had been in a much smaller and simpler chopper. The Firehawk was a monster. A dozen smoke eaters could cram in the cargo bay along with their gear. The controls up here in the front were arranged in a giant T. A long console between the seats offered a bewildering array of electronics. It was set up with three columns of gear, some of it radios, but a lot of which he didn't recognize.

Then the broad top of the T spread sideways just below the main windshield. It presented each seat with two large glass squares like laptop screens, with a half-dozen control buttons on each of the four sides. A quick glance showed that his two screens and Jeannie's two were each showing different information. Terrain map, radar with tiny blips that must be other aircraft, and the other two completely cluttered with images of dials and gauges that he couldn't begin to interpret.

Overhead, above the windscreen, was another bank of controls mounted in the ceiling with levers for two engines and a bunch of switches and circuit breakers. As far as he could tell, it would require a serious college course to even understand what half of the labels meant, never mind how to use them.

Taken all together, it meant only one thing to him: *Way out of your league, Cal.* He was good at two things: fighting fire and photographing the fight. Those were the only skills he'd ever found, and the only real pleasures. Jeannie was from a whole other level of the world that he didn't get to play in. He rarely even had the opportunity to watch it from the outside.

Between his knees, the cyclic control wiggled back and forth, mirroring Jeannie's smooth control movements with her right hand on her own stick. A lever between the left side of his seat and the door rose and fell slightly. A quick glance revealed that it too was matching her left hand's actions.

What he really liked was the view. In addition to his bubble window in the door and the broad windscreen above the console, the chopper also offered a wide view through a window that formed the lower front corners of the helicopter's nose down around his feet. The numerous windows offered an unprecedented view of the fire.

He stayed with the wide-angle lens, wanting to capture the feeling of the view from the safe bubble of the chopper. They bounced and twisted through the air currents, rising heat creating updrafts and microbursts that were keeping Jeannie busy.

Then with the long lens, he snapped the hotshots, tiny blots of yellow before a wall of smoke and fire that appeared to stretch on forever. When you were in it, tasting the fire, hawking and spitting to clear the ash from your tongue and cursing the loss of even that much moisture, all you saw was your part of the battle—a couple dozen yards, sometimes only a couple of dozen feet. Here, above it but still in it, the fire took on a different character. The battle looked hopeless, the tiny twenty-man hotshot team and the massive forest ablaze around them.

Yet that was how the battles were fought, up close and personal. And other than the smokejumpers, the hotshots were the ones closest to the front. Engine companies, dozer teams, and locals worked where their equipment could go. Where they couldn't go, the hotshots hiked in. And where the hotshots couldn't go, the smokies jumped out of their airplanes and parachuted in. Above the ground teams flew helitankers and fixed-wing air tankers, raining water, water with foam, or retardant down from the heavens, depending on what the ground team needed and what was available.

Just past the hotshot crew he could see the lead chopper start its dump. Retardant. The dark red cascaded down like a heaven-born waterfall. Jeannie had said a thousand gallons, a couple of hot tubs worth all at once. Didn't sound like much when he thought of it that way. Though he knew from working previous fires that a thousand gallons had a huge impact on holding a line.

With his telephoto he watched the trees the lead pilot was hitting just outside the fire's flank, trapping it into a narrow band that could then be cut off with a firebreak. They'd steer the fire to its own destruction when it ran out of places to escape to and reignite.

The retardant would coat the unburned timber and block oxygen from the surface. No oxygen, no fire. They left a red stripe across the forest for hundreds of yards, clearly marking what had and hadn't been hit.

Jeannie swung to the east of the first retardant drop over the burning flank of the trees. He felt the motorized vents open, could feel the helicopter lighten, become more jittery in the heat-wracked winds.

"Hey, you can't see it." He tried looking out the side window, but the water and foam was, of course, pouring out directly behind them as they flew forward. Even the bulge in the window wasn't enough to see anything.

"You got it in one, mate," Jeannie answered him. "We dump blind." But she was making minor course corrections even as she flew.

"Then how?" He flapped a hand like a snake to indicate her course changes.

"Following inside the Major's line. Best pilot I've ever met, just unbelievably good, so whatever the Major does, I do. Always works out."

"The Major?"

"Ex-major, former Army. But when you meet her, there's no question. She's in total control." Jeannie flicked a switch on the handle of her cyclic control and he heard the drop doors shut beneath their feet.

She. He'd fallen in with the helitanker girls of Mount Hood Aviation. Cal had heard about them and dismissed the stories as exaggerated because they were told by men about firefighting women. Women were a rare breed in wildfire, so the grunts either gunned for them, placed them on impossible pedestals, or, more typically, did both.

This particular female pilot had done a damn neat bit of flying to save his behind. And she said that her teammate was unbelievably better. So maybe the pedestal was deserved in this case.

"Can't see when I drop, but I'm not above peeking." Having said that, Jeannie spun them around in a move so slick it left his head spinning. She continued to fly in the direction she'd been going, but now they faced backward so that they could see where she'd just flown.

Even as Cal reoriented himself to flying backward, he could see the results. The water, mixed with foaming agent, had expanded in volume by more than ten times to cover a broad area. Jeannie's load had dropped over a swath of crown fire, flames jumping from the top of one tree to the next.

How many times had he stood beneath a crown and raged as the fire passed him by, high overhead, totally out of his reach to fight it? He could see the line where the foam had cooled the upper fires, knocking them back to earth, down to where the hotshots and other fire teams could fight them on the ground. He'd often appreciated it from the ground, but he'd never seen it from above.

"Sweet!"

"Thanks."

They shared a smile. Then she shifted the controls. In one smooth motion they went from flying backward to flying forward the way they were facing, headed once more for the swimming pool.

"Where did you learn to fly like this?" Cal had seen a lot of pilots, but Jeannie had a smoothness he hadn't seen before. "It's like you're wired into the gear. And the way you stayed stable in the currents off the ridge when you saved my sorry ass… You must have some kind of mystic communion with the world's winds."

Jeannie was grinning. "I'm a cyborg, wired straight into my sweet machine. Do you always run your mouth like a 'roo gone mad?"

"A 'roo?"

"A kangaroo."

"So you're from Australia?" Cal did his best to appear clueless.

"What, didn't my accent give me away?"

"Might have if I hadn't thought you were a Kiwi." Of course he'd recognized the Strine in her speech. It was like Scottish, always sounding so sexy to his American-trained ear. But that didn't mean he couldn't tease her about it a bit.

"A Kiwi?" Her voice rose enough to hurt his ears over the headset that blocked most of the rotor noise. "A Kiwi? I sound like a goddamn islander? Wherever you got your ear, you should demand a goddamn refund."

"I asked for one, but when I was on the Black Saturday bushfire, they weren't issuing Strine hearing aids to bloody Yank hotshots."

The chopper actually jinked sideways as Jeannie twisted to look at him. She recovered instantly, he was glad to see, and continued her descent toward the same swimming pool they'd used before.

She lowered and started the snorkel before speaking again. This time her voice was whisper soft.

"You fought Down Under on the Black Saturday fire?"

"Sure, didn't you?" He tried to make it funny.

She nodded, but didn't say anything.

And suddenly he was sorry he'd teased her. More

than a million acres, four thousand homes and businesses, and 173 lives. The flames had moved at over sixty kilometers per hour across the land. Even cars weren't fast enough to escape the flames on some of the rutted back roads that the Australians called tracks.

Jeannie sucked another nine hundred gallons into the belly tank, while the furniture that hadn't been blown aside before was slammed up against the fence. After that, they fell into a quiet routine as she flew.

On one of the trips, he had her call the hotshot ground crew. "They'll want to know about that tongue of fire to the west. They can't see it from the ground yet, but if they move fast, they can cut it off." And by the time they returned with the next load, the hotshots had done just that. It was a new perspective up here, one that they mostly enjoyed in silence.

They made three more trips before she needed to get more foaming agent and fuel. He kept taking photos, but nothing matched that first portrait of her. The image was burned into his brain. He'd take a picture of Beale's helicopter, for that was the ex-major's name, spilling retardant…and think about Jeannie's profile. He'd hear the tank doors opening for their own drop…and think about her smooth accent.

Cal Jackson never went soft on any woman, yet somehow she'd slipped past his guard in just their first hour of meeting. Hell, in the first ten minutes, if he was willing to admit the truth. Which he wasn't.

When they returned to the helispot to fuel up, he hopped off and left her to fly the next round alone. First, he'd been running with the hotshots for more than forty straight hours before he'd been trapped, and he was falling asleep in the seat now that the last of the adrenaline was gone.

Second, he needed a little more distance from Jeannie of the deep-red hair.

Chapter 2

JEANNIE DROPPED DOWN BESIDE BEALE'S CHOPPER. Normally she liked this time of day. The sun setting especially red and gold because of all of the dust and ash in the air. She'd logged more than seventy thousand gallons dropped and one hotshot photographer rescued. She liked the way the two Firehawk choppers looked side by side in the farmer's field that they'd converted to a helispot—a fancy name for some tanker and fuel trucks, a food truck with some rickety picnic tables, and a row of tents.

Her old MD500 was already in. Vern Meany was getting the hang of her. The pair of MHA's Huey 212s were landing just as she was. Not a coincidence. The U.S. Forest Service contract said no flights between thirty minutes before sunset and thirty after dawn. Only Emily Beale was night-certified, but even she tried not to fly that shift, because she had to be grounded to rest a minimum of ten hours straight out of every twenty-four. One emergency night flight could screw up the morning runs.

The advantage of the helispot was that it was less than five minutes flying time from the near edge of the fire. The disadvantage was a lack of any form of amenities. What she really needed was a hot shower and some time to get over being pissed at Mr. Cal Joker.

"What? Weren't you on the Black Saturday fire? Hell of a lark."

Her family's home and all of their belongings had gone up in that fire. They'd lost several acquaintances and one good friend whose husband had never recovered from the loss. Jeannie had done her best to fight the fire, but half the time her chopper was needed for rescue more than protecting homes. And then they were grounded most of the remaining time due to the high winds and dense smoke.

Her parents' agri-flight company had literally gone up in the smoke. They'd managed to fly out two of the crop dusters, but that meant they'd had to leave the cars behind to burn along with a half-dozen aircraft they'd been repairing for other pilots. And the home that had been in their family for generations…gone.

That was what had driven her back to the United States. She'd first come here for her master's degree in fire science, flown a couple summers with California Department of Forestry and Fire Protection and one with Mount Hood Aviation, then gone to fly in Australia after graduation. But there was more to learn. When MHA had called with a year-round gig, she hadn't been able to turn down the offer.

But Mr. Asshole Photographer had sure taken any joy out of the day. His mother should have thrown him away and kept the bloody stork.

Once the Firehawk was settled, Jeannie began the shutdown checklist. Cycling down electronics and engines and finishing up the logs for the day was normally a soothing, meditative action. But her pen wouldn't write; it took her a while to scrounge up one that wasn't dried out. The setting sun was streaming straight into the front windshield, making it wholly impossible to read the gauges in the shadow. And her pretty chopper had a hundred smoke smears on the seat, the headset, the door, the cargo bay, the…all from the jerk who wouldn't stay safe with his hot-shot crew.

After nearly breaking the plastic clipboard with the log sheet on it, Jeannie set it down very carefully. She slowly removed the headset that felt as if it had become permanently implanted into the sides of her head and hung it over the collective. Now she could hear the soft pings of the metal cooling in the turbine engines.

Jeannie leaned her head back against her seat, closed her eyes, and did her best not to scream.

The right-hand door on her side of the chopper creaked open, letting in the smells of smoke and cooking dinner. Of the achingly dry grasses—they had to worry about not igniting them with the service truck's exhaust even though the hay harvest was done.

"Hi!"

She opened one eye and spotted Calvin Jackson standing just to her right and wearing one of his smarmy grins on his handsome face.

She didn't plan.

She didn't even think.

Jeannie blessed being left-handed as she shot out a fist and clipped him sharply on the chin. With it coming all the way across her body, she got some good power behind it. He tumbled backward, landing hard on the ground at Emily Beale's feet. She had come up behind Cal without Jeannie noticing.

Jeannie looked at Emily, waiting for her reaction. Behind her mirrored shades, the fierce blond tilted her head down to look at the man groaning at her feet, then back up at Jeannie.

"Nice punch," was all she said.

"Uh, thanks." Jeannie's hand hurt like hell. The guy must have a steel plate embedded in his chin.

Jeannie had to reach over with her right hand to pull the ignition key—her left hand was zinging too much to grip at the moment—and then she climbed down and closed the door.

She stepped over Cal, stopping shoulder to shoulder with Emily but facing in the opposite direction. "Okay if I finish the shutdown later?"

"Get some ice on your hand. I'll ask Denise and her service crew to finish it for you."

Jeannie nodded, managing not to look down at the evil Mr. Calvin Jackson, then headed for the food truck to get an ice pack and a cold beer.

—⁓—

"You certainly didn't make a friend today, did you?"

Cal lay on his back, the short-cut grass prickling like hell. His head hadn't stopped spinning, so he didn't try getting up just yet.

He blinked open one eye against the pain. A pretty blond looked down at him through mirrored shades. He'd bet she'd be even better right side up, but it wasn't worth the risk of standing to find out.

She waited quietly.

"I kinda thought that I had, but apparently not so much." He levered himself up to sitting position and leaned back against the chopper to wait out the head whirl. He was right. Once the blond steadied a bit in his

vision, she was a stunner. A stunner with a wedding ring
and a serious dose of attitude.

"If you damaged her hand, I won't be pleased."

He opened his mouth to protest on behalf of his chin,
then thought better of it. "You must be the ex-major she
was talking about."

"Which means I know many ways to hurt you. What
did you do to her?"

"Nothing. She saved my life today, damned amazing
bit of flying. She's really, really good. I liked her too. But I
was mainly coming over to thank her again for saving me."

At that the major stopped her "looming in the gathering darkness" thing. She was tall, slender, and poised
like a fighter. There wasn't a chance in hell he was ever
going to mess with her.

A big man strolled up close enough for Cal to see
him clearly. Cal hadn't noticed when the sun had disappeared beyond the trees, though it still lit the sky with
the blood-orange of an ash-filled sky. The guy was the
antithesis of the woman: dark-haired, broad-shouldered.
He had a big, easy grin, a rolling gait, and a one-year-old
girl tucked in the crook of one of his massive arms.

"Trouble here?" He handed the girl off to the woman.
Then he abruptly changed moods and took over doing
the badass looming thing.

"Just trying to figure that out myself," was the woman's soft reply as she settled the baby more comfortably.

Cal looked around, but didn't see help coming from
anywhere soon. He was on his own here, a feeling he
knew all too well from his youth. But he was no longer
a small boy easily bullied and beaten.

He struggled to his feet, only having to brace himself

briefly against the chopper before his head finally settled.
If he'd had more than two hours sleep in the last forty-
eight, he'd be fine, but he was still more light-headed than
the day after a serious bender. He recognized the guy's
aggressive stance, so he matched it, even though the guy
towered above his own six feet. He sure hoped he wasn't
about to get slammed a second time. Unlike Jeannie's,
this guy's fist looked as big as Cal's head.

"I'm just a photographer. Got cut off from my hotshot crew and—"

"Cut off. How?" The big guy's voice was deep. "Who
was your escort?"

"No one. I'm not some newsie." Cal had escorted
plenty of reporters around a fire when he was a
hotshot—he'd hated it. Without proper training, civilians were always getting into trouble, doing the wrong
thing at the wrong time, asking stupid questions when
the priority was working some serious hustle on cutting
a fire line. Or getting the hell out of Dodge as he should
have done earlier.

From experience, Cal knew that was what the guy
would be thinking he was. He only knew of two wildfire
photographers in the whole country with red-card firefighter certification, and he was one of them.

"I've been embedded with them for over a month.
I earned my damn red card a decade ago and spent
seven years in the crews before I picked up the camera.
I hesitated for a photograph and there was a bad fall. I
wasn't more than a hundred feet behind and got cut off.
Shit! And now I've got you two on my case and Jeannie
punching me for reasons I can't fathom."

There was a silence. A long-held balancing act.

Cal didn't back down.

"Harrumph," was the big guy's only comment.

The woman watched Cal for a moment longer, offered him the barest of nods, then cooed at her daughter and just walked away.

The big guy watched his wife's departure for a long moment before turning back to face Cal. Now he wore a smile.

"What?" Cal closed his fists, just in case the smile was a feral one of the moment before attack.

The big guy held out a hand, taking Cal's fist and shaking it when he didn't respond. "Emily's a pretty good judge of people. And I've been married to her long enough to know better than to second-guess her."

"So, I'm... What? I'm suddenly magically okay?"

"Well, she didn't throw you off base for messing up Jeannie's hand with your chin." The guy slapped him hard enough on the arm to send Cal staggering aside.

"Is your wife really that fierce?"

"You have no idea. So don't get all cocky, but she's going to leave it up to you to fix whatever you messed up with Jeannie. She's very protective of her crew. I'm Mark Henderson, the Incident Commander—Air for Mount Hood Aviation. In my official role as ICA, I've already chatted with the hotshot crew boss. He said you were a good man in a tight spot, not given to mistakes or panic, and just got caught out. So you've got no problems with me, as long as you have none with my wife."

Cal rubbed his chin one last time. "I still don't know what the hell I did wrong."

A blond in a stained MHA coverall pulled her service truck up beside the chopper.

"Good punch, eh?" Henderson was being amused.

The woman pulled out a flashlight and a clipboard with a checklist on it, then climbed up into the chopper pilot's seat, leaving the door open.

"Straight left." Cal returned Henderson's smile. "So fast I never saw it coming."

"She has an older brother," the woman informed him in a no-nonsense tone.

"Hey, Denise."

"Hey yourself, Mark." The blond smirked down at Cal.

"Her brother's in the Royal Australian Air Force now, but apparently he used to tease the hell out of her when they were kids. Guess she learned to fight back when someone deserved it." She turned to her task and apparently he dropped completely off her guy-even-exists radar.

Great. Now he was being told he'd actually deserved something that...he didn't deserve. Cal wondered just what planet he'd landed on where stunning women with blond hair down to their butt fixed twenty-million-dollar helicopters and wholly discounted perfectly innocent hotshots.

"C'mon." Mark rested a hand on Cal's shoulder. "Let's get some dinner." They headed toward the food truck and the picnic tables scattered around it as Denise started to work on her checklist.

Cal fell in beside him, half thinking he shouldn't go anywhere near wherever Jeannie went. But he didn't have a lot of choice with Henderson's meat-cleaver-sized hand on his shoulder.

"First time I tried to kiss my Emily, she slammed me face-first into a mess-hall table on an aircraft carrier.

Could have had my ass court-martialed. Should have. I was her commanding officer and way out of line. Married me instead. 'Course I had to follow her halfway around the planet and back to convince her that was the right thing to do."

"I didn't try to kiss Jeannie." Hadn't even really thought about trying until this very moment. She was too smart and focused for him anyway. And unless he wanted to be on the receiving end of another serious punch, it was something he wouldn't be trying anytime soon.

"You're not stupid, are you?"

Cal looked over and up at Mark. There weren't all that many people he had to look up at. Now it was Mark he wanted to strike at unexpectedly, feel that satisfaction of fist against bone. Cal had found a way out of high school at sixteen. Junior year he'd forged an ID and joined a fire cleanup crew while still underage. He'd been motivated and it took less than six months to make hotshot—one long, hard fire season. He'd done that fair and square.

No one got to call him stupid and get away with it. But he was playing in a different arena here than as a foster kid in a crappy high school or even in a hotshot crew. He bit his tongue hard before finding a reply he could live with.

"No dumber than average."

"Then why didn't you try to kiss her?"

What the hell?

"You mean other than I've only known Jeannie for a couple of hours? And while I'm as much of a hound dog as the next man, I do happen to respect the women I chase."

"Right. Aside from that." Mark's deep voice was dismissive of such trivia.

Cal thought about how much he'd been impressed by Jeannie's flying, by her beauty, and most of all by that quiet expression he'd captured with his camera.

That was when he clued into what Mark was really asking him. Not why hadn't he tried to kiss her, but why wasn't he acting as if she was the most attractive woman he'd ever met.

When she actually was.

There was a thought to shock the shit out of him. But it was true, and he must be showing it.

Was he that obvious, even if he hadn't seen it himself? Well, he'd certainly engaged her emotions, though his sore jaw said they were the wrong ones.

Jeannie, of the bright blue hair that was actually dark red, wasn't some firefighter-bar groupie only marginally contained in a tight tank top. Lord knows there were enough of those around to keep almost any man happy. No, Jeannie was a seriously skilled professional, flying one of the newest, best, and most expensive pieces of firefighting equipment in existence. Only the biggest air tankers and a few other choppers could do more or cost more per hour to operate. She was not a girl in a bar, and for one of the first times in his life, he wasn't sure just what the attraction to that had been.

"I'll…have to get back to you on that."

"Good lad." He'd apparently just passed some test. Mark clapped him on the shoulder as if he was trying to use Cal for a pile driver. "Let's go meet some people."

"I let Denise know to work on your bird."

"Thanks, Emily." Jeannie turned from the chow-truck line to face her boss. She went to tickle Tessa's cheek, but her left hand still stung badly when she moved it. She reached out with her right and earned a giggle for her efforts.

"Did you break anything?"

Jeannie flexed her hand carefully, but was able to show full range of motion. "No, it just stings. The guy has a jaw like a brick." She selected the meat loaf and mashies option, and Betsy dished it up for her.

"I'll have the same. Smells great," Emily told MHA's main cook. "Could Jeannie get a bag of ice on the side?"

Betsy produced one in moments and handed it over. "Trouble on landing?"

"She was massaging somebody's jaw for them," Emily offered before Jeannie could make up some excuse.

"You go, girl!" Betsy shot her a thumbs-up. "Anybody we know? Wait… The new guy. Handsome as could be. Sat by himself out at the farthest table for much of the afternoon, real quiet. Punched him, did you? You must like him."

"What? No! Not even close. I—"

Emily took her own tray, which came complete with a couple jars of baby food for Tessa, and guided Jeannie away to a picnic table.

"Seriously, I—" Jeannie set her tray down awkwardly with only one hand.

"Ice on hand," Emily ordered her. "Food in mouth. You need the calories after today."

Jeannie did as she was told. But there was no way she liked this Calvin guy. Even if, she did a little mental

math, he had somehow slipped past ten points. Fighting
the Black Saturday bushfires, he may have even snuck
up close to twenty without her noticing.

Damn him!

—⁓—

Cal landed at a picnic table lit with a battery-powered
lantern and the orange glow of the tail end of sunset. To
the west, the suburbs and trees hid the horizon, though
there was still a hint of pink. The last thing the sunlight
hit was the massive smoke cloud rising to the east above
the Santa Barbara hills. It glowed red at the top from
the sun and red at the bottom from the thirty-percent
contained fire. In between was dark and turbulent.

He felt bad about not still being out with the hotshot crew. As if he was letting the team down by not
being there, even though he only wielded a camera.
He didn't swing a Pulaski or wield a chain saw much
anymore, not unless things got really tight, so he tried
to help out by running for drinking water, breaking
down the cases of supplies that were airdropped in
each night, and generally trying to help the team
stay upbeat despite the grinding slog that was hotshot firefighting.

He also often served as scout. It let him range off to
either side of wherever the hotshots were digging in and
trying to stop the beast. He could swing up to a mile
left or right along the line and search out problems, find
possible advantages for the next attack, and pin down
the ever-important escape routes.

That was what the lone survivor of the Granite
Mountain hotshots on the Yarnell Fire had been doing,

looking ahead over the next ridge just as he was supposed to be doing. It was impossible to imagine the survivor guilt he must still be feeling years later, one man of twenty.

Cal also liked the photographic possibilities that working as scout offered. Shoulder to shoulder with the crew boss, long view of the beast eating another ridge, air drops of retardant, foam, and water. Even shots of the temporary camps as the hotshots crashed for four hours of sleep in a cluster around a pallet of food and water that had been parachuted in. They often slept sprawled on the ground, removing only their packs and hard hats before passing out.

It was so very human. That was what he liked about doing the photography. The walls of fire sold the best: a couple million dollars of mansion wrapped in a cloak of flame, a humble garden shed surviving due to the fire's vagaries. But the people fighting the battle past all reasonable limits were what so intrigued him.

Cal didn't feel as bad about not being still in the fire when he looked at the meal spread before him on the picnic table. It was hard to feel sad while facing the massive double burger, including all the trimmings, and the giant bag of chips open in the middle of the table. It was the first meal he'd had in days that didn't come out of an MRE pouch. Meals-Ready-to-Eat didn't have much going for them other than calories, though those certainly counted.

Jeannie, he noted, was sitting several tables away with the other pilots. Two blond women, one of them the scary ex-major, three guys, and Jeannie. The tables between them were filled with smokies and a couple engine crews who had been rotated out for sleep and food before being shoved back into the fray. He shifted a little to the left so that he had a clear sight line to her.

"Got your ass caught out in the wind?" TJ aimed a pickle wedge at Cal's chest like a sword. He was an old guy in his fifties or sixties who had obviously done his time in the smoke before moving behind a radio.

"Had better days," Cal admitted. He'd also never been punched by a beautiful woman before. Slapped? Yes. Flattened? Hell no.

"TJ knows all about better days," Chutes, another old-timer, told him.

"Aw, don't dig out that story." But the smile was easygoing.

"How far back do you two go?" Cal asked, then bit into his burger. Oh God, that was so good. The smoke and char finally where they belonged, rather than in the air he breathed. Whoever cooked these was damn good.

"The Bronze Age, if you let them get started," said Henderson, coming over with his own mounded plate of fried chicken.

"That's why they put TJ behind a radio." Chutes nodded toward his pal. "Couldn't trust him to jump anymore. He'd shatter like a china doll."

"Spent a decade more in the smoke than you," TJ fired back.

"Which is two decades after you should have gotten out."

Their back-and-forth was easygoing and had a familiar rhythm that Cal had no problem falling into. They'd said "jump." So Chutes and TJ had both been smokejumpers. Chutes now oversaw all of the parachute loads that were dropped to the action crews in the field, as well as commanding the smokejumpers' parachute loft. Apparently he didn't have any other name.

The fifth guy at the table was Steve Mercer, who Cal had met after Jeannie dropped him off…and before she'd hit him. A glance revealed her laughing with the other pilots. Once he saw her, he could pick out her laugh from the others. It was a great laugh, sparkly but from the gut. Man, he was in trouble on this one. *Think about something else, anything else.*

"I got a great shot of your drone," he told Steve. "Right up against the nastiest wall of fire you can imagine."

"Cool. I have one or two inside my truck." Steve jerked a thumb over toward the service van and drone launcher. "But only in free flight above the fire. Don't have much excuse to fly in low and hot like that. And when I do, there's rarely time for a picture."

"Well, there wasn't really time, but I got it anyway."

"Is it true that you threw your camera bag aboard Jeannie's chopper before jumping in yourself?"

"She-it!" Chutes drawled out. "You do crap like that, you're gonna fit right in with this motley crew."

There was a new thought. Maybe Cal could talk his way into embedding with MHA for a while. Their heli-aviation team had a reputation for being one of the best. He glanced over at Jeannie's table. As he turned back to face the crowd at his table, he caught ICA Henderson watching him with a small smile on his face.

Okay, you caught me. Cal acknowledged Henderson's knowing smile with a nod.

He turned to the other guys at the table.

"So, what would make you MHA guys of any interest to me as a wildfire photojournalist?" This was ground he was comfortable on. And it was always good to turn the question around like that rather than asking if he could come aboard. Everyone wanted to think they were interesting. On a fire crew it was easy, since most of them were. And the woman he couldn't stop glancing toward definitely ranked as very interesting.

Henderson's smile grew and Cal decided that he agreed. "Camera in the Fiery Sky" could be the new series title. Cal definitely liked the idea of doing more flying with MHA.

Jeannie waited until dinner was breaking up. She tried to anticipate in which direction Cal would leave and moved to place herself in the shadows. It was well after dark and the temperature was dropping from the earlier southern California scorch to merely intolerable. Maybe they'd make some headway on the fire tonight. It wasn't a monster yet, but it was big and showing definite attitude.

With MHA's actions, they were holding it to a Type II fire. Barely. They really didn't want to call out a Type I Incident Management Team unless they had to. That would mean they were in a whole new world of hurt in terms of the fire's complexity and threat.

All through dinner, Emily Beale hadn't said a single word about Jeannie flexing her sore hand or having punched Cal Jackson with no apparent provocation. Well, Jeannie had to admit that even her own justification was looking pretty lame in retrospect.

She couldn't help noticing that Cal sat with ICA Henderson and the old guard. Of course his hotshot background would buy him an easy seat with the two former smokejumpers, so that shouldn't surprise her.

What did surprise her was how aware of him she was.

At first she'd caught him watching her tentatively. She'd pulled off her LA Dodgers baseball cap, letting her ponytail slip out of the back hole, and resettled the hat. With her hair down, she could safely keep an eye on Cal without appearing to. She wasn't fooling Emily, but she'd never expected to do that.

Something had changed with him, shifted somehow during the meal. She'd missed when he went from being the outsider to being one of the crew, but he now huddled forward more confidently, laughing more easily. She'd seen his nerves so bad that he'd totally snarled himself in the headset cord, so he couldn't fool her. But Jeannie suspected that this was more his natural state. His recovery from a near-fatal experience had been surprisingly rapid, as would only happen with a man who'd learned to trust himself in dangerous situations.

But she didn't trust him. And why not? That was what she'd spent all of dinner trying to puzzle out. He'd fought the Black Saturday bushfire. He'd made light of it, but maybe he'd done that because the thing had been so grim.

With a cloud of dust and a burst of blaring rock-and-roll on their radio, a smoke-smeared wildfire engine crew arrived at the well-lit food truck, driving their heavy-duty, ash-colored vehicle right up beside a picnic table. They flocked about with a frenetic energy that couldn't last long before exhaustion took over. Hopefully it would hold out long enough for them to consume some calories before their imminent collapse like zapped bugs. Cal and the others vacated their table to make way.

She'd guessed Cal's trajectory almost correctly and only had to shift a little until she was sitting on the front bumper of Steve's black drone-control van directly in Cal's path.

"Cal."

He stumbled to a halt not five feet away. She could see him as a fairly clear silhouette against the mess area's yellow camp lights, but that was all.

"Uh, hi. Jeannie?" He had identified her only by her voice and on a single word. Why was she enjoying that? She didn't want to be liking that, not from him. Then she heard that humor of his come to the fore as he answered his own question. "She of the stout left punch?"

"You calling me stout, jackaroo?" She liked bantering with him. He was quick.

"Just your punch. The rest of you, not a bit. And I've never worked a cattle station, Australian or otherwise."

But he didn't move in for "the kill." For the sweep-the-girl-off-her-feet kiss that so many guys thought was charming. Of course, she had punched him, so maybe it was just survival instinct, something he'd already proved he possessed.

"I admit"—his voice was droll, all she had to judge him by at the moment—"that I found that particular, narrow aspect of stoutness to be, well…"

"Flattening?" she offered.

"I was going with 'daunting,'" he corrected, "but 'flattening' works. May I?" His silhouette waved an arm toward the other end of the bumper.

At her nod, he didn't move at all. Right. She would be near enough invisible in the dark. "Sure. Just keep your chin to yourself, mate."

"Good advice." Cal sat on the other side of the cable winch mounted at the center of the bumper.

"So, I'm guessing you've somehow talked Henderson into letting you fly with me."

"Damn, Jeannie. Where's your bottle? You magic too? How did you figure that out? And all he gave me—at least I think, he plays his cards pretty close—was permission to ask you."

Jeannie considered what that would mean. Much of wildfire flying was tense and incredibly busy. A fixed-wing air-tanker pilot only spoke with three people during a flight: the air commander circling high above, the guide plane that led them into the fire, releasing a puff of smoke to mark where to begin the drop, and the tower at the retanking base. And on a smaller fire, the first two were the same person.

The helitankers talked to the air commander, the other helitankers—because it was rare for there to be only one whirlybird on a fire—ground commanders, ground teams… The list of frequencies she had to maintain was almost as crazy as the ICA's. The Firehawk had several extra radios, and she was always switching between them. Thankfully, they were all on tap using the four-way switch under her left thumb and the microphone push-to-talk switch under her right index finger. About the only people she didn't talk to were the air tankers, their guides, and any airport tower… She just stayed out of the fixed-wingers' way.

But much of flying helitanker was the constant

shuttling from supply point to flame and back, hopefully on a short-circuit loop, depending on where the water or retardant was. It could get hard to hold focus flying alone for a fourteen-hour day.

She remembered how much she'd enjoyed flying with Emily during the training and checkout rides as she moved up from the MD500 to the Firehawk. She had already been carded in the Twin Huey 212s, so she was used to dual turbine engines and belly tanks. The added complexity in the Firehawk had been mostly related to how much faster you could get into trouble. It boasted twice the load capacity and half again the speed of the Huey, and blew her poor little MD500 out of the water. But she'd also enjoyed Emily's company while she gathered the required flight hours.

Mark Henderson could offer Cal Jackson permission all he wanted, but Jeannie could simply say no and she knew Emily would back her up to the hilt. And even Mark knew to stay out of his wife's way.

Jeannie could feel herself growing more confident every day she flew with Emily, as if the woman were an elixir of self-assuredness.

"We'll see," she finally told the figure waiting in the dark. "And thanks."

"Thanks? For what, putting my chin in the way of your fist?"

She hadn't really noticed it over the headset, but in the growing silence of the settling camp, his voice was unique. There was a depth, a strength that was terribly attractive. She really liked his voice. It was the kind you wanted close beside you in the dark.

"No, I want to apologize for that. What I wanted to say was thanks for fighting the Black Saturday bushfires."

She could feel him shift on the truck bumper. Lit from below, the ash cloud of the Grindstone Canyon Fire above the Santa Barbara hills was just enough light behind him that she could make out his movement as he leaned against the truck's radiator grill to look up and out at the sky.

"That was ugly."

That statement encompassed the total scope of his comment. Cal went silent and continued his inspection of the dark sky. This time there was no joking, no sense of humor about it. The grim statement said that she had indeed misjudged him. He wasn't being flippant about fighting fire. Somewhere in his past, he too had seen what it could do.

Chapter 3

SOMEONE KICKED CAL. HARD.

He grunted and rolled away. It was dark, pre-dawn maybe.

Cal had been in enough fights as he bounced between foster homes that there was no hesitation. Pivoting on an elbow tucked against his side, he swung out his feet in a wide arc.

A high cry and his attacker fell to the ground with a grunt.

Cal rose to get the position advantage and banged his head hard against the underside of the truck he'd been sleeping beside. That dropped him back to the ground and filled his eyes with blazing splotches of light.

He knew he wouldn't be stable if he tried to stand after that hard a blow to his head, so this had become a ground war.

Finding his attacker by their gasping breath, he rolled right on top of...

"Ow! What the hell?" *Jeannie!*

"Jeannie?" He had her pinned beneath him in the darkness.

"Cal?"

"Why the hell did you kick me?" His head was really starting to spin now.

"I tripped on you. Why did you kick me?"

"I was sleeping." He slowly became aware of her

body warm against his. He'd slept under his jacket, which had been fine until the morning dew settled damp and chilly. Jeannie wasn't damp and chilly. Everywhere they touched, a warmth radiated out of her.

"You slept here? In front of Steve's truck?" He could feel her breath brushing against his cheek.

"As good as anywhere." He breathed in deeply. The morning was quiet, just the two of them wrapped in a breathless cocoon of dark and silence.

"You smell incredible." He buried his nose in her hair and inhaled again. "Really incredible."

"You're slaying me with your poetry." She shoved against him. "And your body weight."

"Oh, sorry." He sat up slowly, unsure of the whereabouts of the truck bumper. There, close behind him. He reached out a hand and helped her sit up, making sure she didn't clip the heavy steel. His legs were across hers, and he was sort of sitting in her lap. They were so close that they were practically in each other's arms... They *were* in each other's arms. The back of her leather jacket lay against one of his palms as he held her upright, the thin T-shirt material covering her rib cage beneath his other.

―――

Jeannie knew it was dumb, but she let herself stay in Cal's arms a moment. It felt so good to be held. She'd lost half the night to nightmares of her family cattle station in flames. Seeing generations of history and hard work burning, as if she'd actually seen it consumed by the flames rather than being fifty kilometers away dropping a load of foam while it happened.

Cal's hands on her felt good, strong, safe. She could feel her pulse against his palm. Reaching out into the dark, she found his chest. Like any wildland firefighter, apparently even one who wielded a camera, he was immensely fit.

Safe.

That word circled back again, washing off the blackened layers of last night's fearful sleep. Then she had an evil thought. If simply being held by Cal Jackson felt this good, what would it be like to kiss him? Maybe if she were a morning person, her common sense would have awoken by now. But she wasn't. She was a night owl with an early alarm clock.

So, with her common sense having hit the snooze button, Jeannie leaned in the last few inches and kissed him.

Cal actually hesitated. Actually had the decency to pull back, to make sure it was something she meant to do.

But the first brief meeting of lips was enough. It told her what she needed to know. Jeannie left one hand on the center of his chest. She ran the other up his shoulder, into his ever-so-soft hair, and pulled him back to her.

This time he didn't hesitate. Neither was he all tongue and hard pressure. He tasted her lips, then her tongue, as if they were the finest treat. His hand didn't lunge up and grab her breast. It simply wrapped around her ribs, holding her tight against him. Such amazing hands.

She'd noticed them on the flight yesterday, even as he took her photograph. Big hands that held the camera so delicately, as if it were porcelain, but with the confidence of long familiarity. That was why she'd turned away to concentrate on the flight, because she could really spend some time getting to know those hands.

Jeannie wasn't promiscuous; she enjoyed a good joke and a good tease as much as the next girl. It almost always stopped there. But Cal's kiss could convince her that she'd really been missing something. Nerve endings all down her body insisted on telling her just how happy they were with this wake-up call.

Cal broke it off first. Easing back. Pulling away. Coming back for just the gentlest brush of lips. Then easing another inch away.

Her head was spinning from far more than the fall when he'd swept her feet out from under her.

"Whoa there, Helitack. Just whoa there." His breathing was ragged.

She liked the nickname. Jeannie typically flew in a helitanker role, but every now and then, especially with the big Firehawk, she transported a crew into position for a helicopter-launched attack, a helitack.

Jeannie brushed her lips across his once more and could feel his pulse race skyward. Had she ever had that effect on a lover? Sure, when they were at the top moments of sex. But just from a kiss? Not that she could recall.

Then she could feel her own ribs heaving against his palm and she knew she was no better off.

"Damn, Hotshot. That kiss was aces."

"Right back at ya, Helitack. What brought that on? No, wait. Don't answer that. I don't want to know. It's a dangerous weapon, and I don't know if I'd survive if I knew how to wield it—not if it makes us do that again."

Jeannie turned, able now to see him faintly in the slowly breaking day. She shifted until she knelt, straddling his knees. Against his mild protest, he didn't put up much of a fight, she draped an arm over either shoulder and leaned in to kiss him again. Just to see if her first reaction was real or imagined.

Overbalanced, he tipped back against the truck.

"Ow! Shit!" He jerked the hand from her ribs and moved it to the back of his head.

"Sissy!" She hadn't knocked him against the truck that hard. She ran her fingers through his hair until she found his fingers and then the massive lump.

"Easy," he hissed. "Undercarriage of the truck. Thought you were attacking me, and I tried to stand up under the truck."

She eased back until she was sitting across his calves and helped him upright.

"Remind me to be more careful if I ever wake you up again. You wake up nasty, Hotshot."

"While you just kick people in their sleep."

"Completely intentional, I promise. I'll make sure to do it next time too. I'll just dodge away faster. Truth be told, I don't wake up gracefully either, at least not before noon. But why sleep here?" She stood. She really needed some coffee and then to prepare her bird for the day. Maybe some food before she actually flew, if her stomach woke up soon enough. And if it stopped flip-flopping about from the overwhelming power of Cal's kiss. She helped him to his feet, then bent down to retrieve his jacket while his eyes slowly uncrossed from the vertigo of standing up.

"No beautiful helitack gals offering me a share of

their bed. Besides, I like sleeping under the stars. Slept out on a lot of fires."

She gazed upward. The lightening of the eastern sky didn't brighten the day much. All it did was add definition to the massive ash cloud.

"No stars," she commented. She looked down to see him rubbing the back of his head once more and wincing.

"Damn truck just made me see plenty of them."

"A lot of smoke up there."

With the unerring compass of a firefighter, he turned to face the ash plume without even needing to scan the horizon. He gazed at it for ten long seconds, assessing the pattern and flow of the clouds. They didn't need to exchange any words; they both knew how to read it.

The lower reaches of the smoke cloud weren't just dark, they were black with hot ash. Mid-level billowed with fast-moving heat clouds. The high plume, lit white by the morning sun behind it, rose until the jet stream flattened its top. All that taken together meant that the fire was on the move and had found plenty of fresh fuel in the night. New territory burned and new areas were under threat.

"C'mon." He took her hand and pulled her toward the food truck. "We've got to get you up in the air."

That simple. Like any true wildland firefighter, what he cared most about was beating the fire.

That he had also just, without hesitation, stated that she was a major asset in the battle was rather startling. No gender question. No age question. No competency doubts. All that crap about pretty women and big helicopters that was usually thrown across her path didn't exist for Cal Jackson.

She stopped him for just a moment before they got to the food truck, though it was hard because she could smell the brewing coffee.

He looked down at her, waiting for her. Giving her room to think her own thoughts, rather than telling her what she was supposed to be thinking.

Well, she finally knew the answer to Cal's question from last night.

"Us," she told him. "We've got to get us up in the air."

His hesitation and nod before he turned once more toward the food truck were thanks aplenty.

Chapter 4

EXACTLY THIRTY MINUTES AFTER OFFICIAL LOCAL SUN-rise, to the second, the choppers of Mount Hood Aviation roared aloft as a unit into the gray sky. Emily flew the other Firehawk to Jeannie's right. The pair of 212s and the MD500 fell behind quickly. They were less than halfway to the front line when Jeannie spotted Henderson's plane climbing into the morning sky.

"Good morning, sports fans," he called over the command frequency. "We only lost a dozen homes overnight because the local engines kicked some serious butt. Any bets on the insurance companies screaming about their incompetency?" He didn't wait for an answer. "No? Now it's time to punch this sucker out. Firehawks Oh-one and Oh-two, I want you working the flank two miles east of where you left off last night." He read off coordinates that Cal scribbled down on a handy pad of paper.

Jeannie toggled her number two screen to a terrain map and pointed a finger at the right keypad. "Punch in the coordinates there," she instructed Cal over the intercom. It saved her engaging the autopilot and removing her hand from the controls.

He keyed them correctly the first time, and together he and Jeannie leaned in to study the terrain. Rough but not impassable for the ground crews.

She toggled the feed to a new overlay.

"What's that?" Cal inspected it carefully.

"Steve's drone imaging. He has a feed to Emily, Mark, and me. He managed to set up an auto-sync on the terrain map of his latest data stream from the drone's infrared camera. You can see the fire clearly. But notice the small dots."

"Looks like a smoke team."

"Good eye. That's—"

"I've got two good eyes," Cal cut her off and aimed a powerhouse smile at her that left her heart rate distinctly elevated.

She'd definitely noticed his light brown eyes. A nice match to his wavy, light brown hair. *Focus, girl.* "That's your hotshot team. Depending on where Steve is flying, the information can be out-of-date, but it at least gives us an idea."

"Fire's moving north-northeast."

Jeannie couldn't see how he could tell that from the tiny terrain map. When she glanced over, he wasn't looking at the map any longer. Instead, he had his camera with its long lens aimed ahead.

"Cheater," she muttered to herself. Then she saw what he'd seen. The plume was still visible from their side of the fire, but it was sending up black smoke. It was being blown away from them and had found fresh fuel. Now it was headed back into the mountains. The problem was that the fire had burned south into Parma Park. So, when it turned east once more, whole hillsides of mountainside homes would suddenly be at risk.

Throughout the long day of flying, Jeannie kept being surprised by what Cal could see. Always a beat ahead of her own observations, sometimes several. And his cameras were kept busy as well.

At one of the refueling stops, he shifted into the rear of the chopper, saying, "Gotta get away from the Plexiglas." She rigged a monkey line for him, a three-meter strap that let him move freely about the rear cabin without falling out the wide-open cargo bay doors. He wore one of the headsets so they were still able to talk.

Every now and then he'd ask her to fly a little sideways on a drop or track a hundred yards farther north on a return flight. When she could safely comply, she did.

Most of their talk was about the logistics of fire. And he was good about dropping a conversation in mid-syllable if a call came in from outside. It was easy and friendly, but it didn't tell her much more about the man she'd so wantonly kissed. Kicked, then kissed. And now she was awake enough to kick herself for it.

She never dated within her own crew. Jeannie had made that mistake once years before when she'd been living in Katherine in the Northern Territory and flying supplies out to the cattle stations while still piloting fixed wing. Jeannie actually did owe Jeoffrey some gratitude. The awful collapse of their relationship had been part of what motivated her to leave Katherine and go to America for her fire science degree, which had ultimately gotten her into flying fire-attack rotorcraft.

When Cal hadn't been part of their crew, uh, yesterday… How had he done that? Just yesterday he'd been a complete unknown. And now she'd kissed him and he was wandering about her chopper as if he'd always been there. She could feel the tiny shifts when he crisscrossed the cargo bay. Was aware of him in a way that was really upsetting her. She didn't want any of this.

One thing Jeannie knew that Cal would just have to

learn: once she knew what she wanted, there was no stopping her. And what she wanted was *not* Cal Jackson. At this point in her life she cared about flying and fire and her new Blackhawk. That was plenty.

The decision made her feel easier about this morning's kiss. It had been merely a pleasant aberration. She tried to engage Cal in a friendly conversation over the headset; that would prove that she could be pleasant without jumping into bed with a man.

Cal didn't cooperate. His replies were brief, often monosyllabic, occasionally no more than grunts.

Jeannie was starting to get pissed again, so she decided to ignore him and focused on the problems around her. And there were plenty.

The Grindstone Canyon Fire had long since gone beyond Grindstone Canyon. Now that the fire was moving back into residential neighborhoods, the battle on the ground had shifted from wildfire engine crews on twisty logging roads to include a lot of local engine companies defending homes. Now that they had roads, the fire districts' big, pretty red engines could access the fire's leading edge.

The city had already killed the electricity to the entire hillside. The number of secondary fires caused by sparking wires from burned-over power poles and torched houses was a major concern. Even more than the evacuation orders and the house-to-house searches by the police, the loss of electricity had finally convinced the residents it was time to leave. Maybe it was the loss of their air-conditioning. It didn't matter in the end.

What did matter was that suddenly the roads were clogged with panicked drivers trying to salvage their belongings into their sports cars, then racing downhill. At the same time, the news vans raced uphill. The resulting congestion blocked the big engines from getting where they were needed among the narrow, twisting roads.

That doubled the load on MHA. Several big air tankers were up. Making neat seventeen-minute laps from the airfield, the pair of red-and-white BAe-146s were dropping beautiful long swaths of bright red retardant on the ridges. Their four jet engines and three-thousand-gallon capacities made them powerful allies. They were also maneuverable enough to navigate the steep hills reasonably well. They couldn't get down into the terrain like the rotorcraft, but they were still amazing to watch.

Sometime during the morning, the cooler sea breeze was replaced by the Santa Ana winds. They weren't heavy yet, but they were predicted to be. And since this fire was already in the Santa Barbara suburbs, the fire teams had to kill it fast. That wind change—along with the fire's invasion into residential areas and the complexity that added—had escalated it from a Type II to a Type I fire during the morning. Rick Dobson, MHA's Type I Incident Commander, one of only seventeen in the country, was flying in from Utah in a King Air and issuing a constant stream of instructions to Henderson and Carly Mercer, MHA's fire behavior analyst.

Thankfully, that increased their loads, but not hers. Her job was to fly and dump. Normally she clung to every word Carly said, trying to figure out how the woman saw what she did. Nicknamed the Fire Witch, Carly was another of those people who made Jeannie feel smarter simply by working with her. For all of

Jeannie's flying and fire science degree, Carly knew things that could never be taught. Of course, she'd been raised by a smokejumper father and, after a fire had caught him, by her smokejumper uncle. Fire was in her blood. Jeannie knew it would be in Carly's kid's blood, when she got around to having one. For now, Jeannie concentrated on listening to Carly and flying as much like Emily as she could.

She lined up her latest load of water over the backyard of a house clogged with ornamental trees dying from the long summer. The moment before she released her load, right where the ground crew really needed it, her radio crackled on the command frequency.

"Firehawk Oh-two, abort water drop. Repeat, abort drop. We need an emergency evac." Henderson read out a set of coordinates.

"Pisser!"

Cal stuck his head up between the seats and looked at her. She was too angry to turn around as she flew toward the coordinates, pushing her Hawk ahead hard at almost two hundred miles per hour. The fading protests of the ground commander only made her angrier.

"What?"

"Some damn idiot didn't pay attention to the evac order, so I have to go do a rescue while we lose two more homes. Probably some idiot who—"

"Got caught on a cliff edge with his tail out in wind?"

"Crap, Cal. Sorry."

"That's okay." He knelt at the back edge of the center console and looked out the front windscreen with her.

She heard the click over the intercom from his headset microphone as he took a photo that must be capturing something interesting, but she'd be damned if she knew what.

"They're just people in extraordinary circumstances doing what people do. Is it worth the energy to get pissed at them?"

She ducked the Hawk below a particularly low-hanging pall of smoke and then climbed quickly to fly over the big power line that ran along the edge of Parma Park. Jeannie would have to dump her load before she could pick up any people. But she'd like it to be somewhere at least marginally useful.

"I mean people just—"

"Look," she cut him off before he could make her feel worse. "I don't appreciate you making me feel stupid. Just because you're right, it doesn't give you that right."

"Yes, ma'am!" She caught his smart salute in her peripheral vision. "Whatever you say, Captain, sir."

"Careful, or I'll ground your pretty behind along with whatever…" She tapered off as the problem came into sight. A policeman in a cruiser, trapped a hundred feet from a wall of flames that cut across the road. Behind him was a cul-de-sac that led nowhere. His only other option was to retreat into the unknown woods on foot.

Cal was gone from beside her, probably back to one of the doors for a clear photo.

As she roared up to hover and observe the scene, the cop waved a rather desperate hand. Then a mother and two kids clambered out of the rear seat. The flames were reaching toward the car, and he was running out of street to back up on really fast. In another minute there wouldn't even be room to land.

Cal started to say something, but she saw it already.

With a quick twist that elicited a yelp and a curse from Cal, Jeannie lined up the Hawk. She couldn't douse the whole road and open an escape route, but a thousand gallons would buy them the time they needed for a rescue.

"You okay back there?" She started her run and triggered the vent doors and the foam pump for a half-load drop.

"Fine," he grumbled. "Just warn me next time you're gonna do that. I'll put on my hard hat."

"Sure thing, Hotshot. Got it on now?"

"Yes. In self-defen—"

"Good!" She carved a hard turn, doubling back beside the initial part of her drop without wasting time to close the tank.

"Ow! Crap!"

She kept her smile to herself by keeping her gaze straight ahead. Then she hammered down toward the trapped cop and family.

Cal made some loud noise as they landed, but he didn't explain it and she was too busy watching her rotor tips and the mailboxes, fence posts, telephone poles, wires, and everything else that adorned the street as she settled into place. She actually ended up with one wheel on the road and the other over a thirty-foot drop-off.

"Help 'em up, Cal!" She had to concentrate on keeping the Hawk level and stable without actually landing it.

The officer herded the family over with their heads ducked down. In moments they were loading up. She could hear Cal giving calm directions and snapping them into seats.

Jeannie also kept an eye on the flames, but they were

holding to the other side of the line of her dousing. For now. No way she'd actually stopped them.

"Okay!" Cal reached up between the seats and grabbed his two-way radio that he'd left charging on the console. She could see him slip it into the shoulder harness of his Nomex fire suit. "Climb about five feet and hold."

"What the hell?"

"Just do it, Magic Girl." His voice was practically a caress.

Then he was gone.

Others had tried that nickname on her because of her name, and she'd quashed them but good. She wasn't some dreamy, damned buxom blond living in a 1960s sitcom. So, why did she like it so much when Cal said it?

Not knowing why, she climbed five feet and held. The fire was still cooperating at the moment. She felt, more than heard, the loud click. A light blinked on her console, showing the cargo hook was engaged. Jeannie spotted Cal ducking out from beneath the chopper, trailing a lifting harness.

Over his radio, he called to her. "Hover about fifty feet over the cop car."

She spotted him running forward along the unpaved road with the other end of the heavy harness dragging after her. By the time she was in the air over the car, she'd recovered enough from her shock to run the calculations. The car probably only weighed a ton and a half. Add in Cal, the cop, and the family, and her Firehawk could still pick them all up clean and easy.

She stuck her head out into the Plexiglas bubble on her door's window and looked down. Cal was fast and efficient despite the pounding downdraft of the Firehawk's rotor. In under thirty seconds he had attached all four cables to the corners of the car and yanked each one before checking it again visually. Competent. It reminded her of how his hands had felt while holding her. Very competent.

He spun a single finger over his head in a motion to start hoisting.

"Get aboard!" She moved to land near the car, but there wasn't room because of a pair of telephone poles. He waved her off and made the hoist motion again.

She didn't like the idea of having someone climbing into the cop car while it was an underslung load, but it was clear that even if she did land, he wouldn't be climbing aboard.

Stubborn idiot!

She continued to climb, taking the slack out of the cable.

"Ten feet. Five," Cal called over the radio, continuing to wind his finger in the air.

Jeannie eased her rate of climb down to a creep and felt the cable go taut as the chopper took the load. She waited five seconds, about all she was willing to give Cal to get aboard as the flames were once again on the move.

"You in?" she radioed.

"Go for it," he called, and she did. Climbing upward she could see the car spin sideways as the load came on the cable and it straightened out. When she had the load twenty feet in the air, she spotted Cal. Still on the ground.

He'd backed up a dozen paces and had his camera out.

"Calvin Jackson! Even your cartoon self isn't this stupid!"

"It's a good shot. Keep going!"

"You're gonna be trapped."

"No. The hotshots are just over that ridge to the north. I checked the images on Steve's fire map. I'm clear all the way up. Keep going." And he continued to shoot the images.

"Drongo!"

"I'll assume that was foul. You wanted me back with the hotshots anyway, Magic Girl. Over and out." He signed off, waved once, and turned toward the hills that only a hotshot could climb over. That was when she noticed that he'd also slung on the pack that had been hanging in the chopper's cargo bay. He was completely gone from her chopper, which hurt like hell.

She climbed away, looking for a place to set down the cop car, its owner, and the people that the officer had risked his life to save.

⁓

Cal ducked under the trees before turning back to watch Jeannie fly away. The only way she'd go was if he left her no choice.

He pulled out the telephoto and captured a couple more amazing shots. "Mount Hood Aviation chopper saves family and police car." Hell of a headline, and he'd sell the images for the cover story. The car going up into the sky, the cop's smoke-stained face looking down in relief and amazement. The horror written openly across the woman's and kids' faces as they watched the fire, now recovered from its dousing, roar over their small cabin. He snapped a shot of the cabin tucked back in the trees as it went up in flames. No power lines. Weekender place left primitive. They'd probably never even heard the evac order, so they owed the cop their lives.

He shot another one of the chopper with the car dangling beneath, backdropped by a distant wall of flame, except it didn't look distant because he'd used the telephoto and been far enough away to flatten the depth of field.

He waited there under the edge of the trees, perhaps longer than he should have. But he so liked watching Jeannie fly. When she was out of sight, he turned and began climbing the ridge.

He really had to cut it out. He glanced at his watch. Twenty-four hours. Twenty-four lousy, stinking hours, and he'd spent far too much of it thinking about the woman whose kiss was more powerful than her punch.

This wasn't any Cal Jackson that he knew. It was part of the reason he'd left the cockpit for the cargo bay and ultimately the chopper for the woods—he'd needed the distance. Sitting so close that he could touch her had become almost unbearable without doing so. He actually was a morning person, no matter how nasty he woke up when kicked. Despite the bump on the head, he'd been very, very wide awake by the time she'd laid that kiss on him.

He circled an outcropping, took a slug from his water bottle, and kept clambering up through the young alder and black cottonwood.

The woman tasted of warm winter fires and moonlit nights. Jeannie of the dark-red hair streak, of the magic touch and the amazing body—he'd had a chance to confirm that before she geared up this morning—was horribly distracting. Women weren't supposed to be distracting. They were supposed to be fun. Splendid, shared, mutual fun. Love-'em-and-leave-'em types. Jeannie was the kind of woman who was all about being dedicated and forthright. Commitment would be high on the list of qualities she'd look for in a man. She was precisely the kind of woman that Cal avoided like a Type I fire...except he'd made a career of rushing into Type I fires.

So why was he trudging up this hillside back to his hotshot team to get away from her?

Well, it had been a hell of a set of photographs. It also would make good advertising for MHA in the newspapers. Henderson would be okay with that. Actually, if Cal played it right, he could probably get the shots and his article to go national. That could be fun and pay for a couple more months of his present lifestyle at a single go.

Run it with one of the photos he'd taken of Jeannie yesterday. Not the quiet one of her profile. He wasn't willing to share that one with anyone else. But the frank, no-nonsense expression as she stared at the photographer, anonymous behind his camera in her reflected image. He started composing the story as he crested the ridge and looked at the vista of what was going on around him. He enjoyed writing the story himself in addition to providing the images. He'd learned to tell fire stories like a good ghost story around a campfire, and they sold well that way. The personal story behind each picture, bringing the whole experience alive for the reader comfortable in their armchair.

He could see that the Grindstone Canyon Fire was indeed living up to its name, gearing up to grind the hill-dwellers down into powdery ash. From here atop the ridge he had a fairly good view of what was going on. The heart of the fire was still up in the rugged hills to the north and east, the plume still massive. In the daylight it showed more black than gray or red. So thick, it was obscuring the heart of the fire itself.

With a smaller fire, you could always see some way into it. You could fly in from the backside, hike in through the black where it had already burned. Or in a savannah fire, it would be a thin, though hot, boundary line. The Black Saturday bushfire had rarely been more than a few hundred meters from leading edge to trailing edge. The problem was that the leading edge had been so hot—with a constant supply of fresh fuel—despite moving so fast, that by the time the trailing edge arrived, everything in its path had been destroyed. With the variable winds, the Grindstone Fire was expanding in every direction at once, finding thick reserves of forest and the occasional home as it burned.

To the northwest of his current position, Cal could see a couple of trees swaying in ways that had nothing to do with the winds. Sure enough, in a few moments, one of them tipped slowly to the side and quickly disappeared from sight. A minute later, another followed. That would be his hotshot crew cutting a firebreak in hopes of protecting western Cielito. They were about a half mile away over some rough ground, but no sign of the fire itself. The towering smoke plume beyond the ridge said that it was definitely coming though.

In all the other directions, far below, he could see

the streets and highways of Santa Barbara. With the
shifting wind, the city was darkly shadowed at eleven
in the morning. Most cars on the roads had their head-
lights on.

"Welcome to the dark side," he told them. There was
a whole "glamour" aspect to firefighting that had never
really made sense to him, not that he was complaining.
Sure you had cool machines and you had to be fit to be
a firefighter. The glamour aspect made for firefighter
calendars and women who actually cooed at you in bars
like pigeons flocking to bread crumbs.

The reality that he struggled to capture with his
camera was hard work, blazing heat, and itchy protective
gear that always seemed to rub you raw in some spot or
other. The air parched dry by the heat, choking you with
ash. It all wore you down, along with the brutal amount
of physical effort. The number one cause of firefighter
deaths wasn't burns, it was heart attack. Even in younger
men, at some point the load was simply too much for the
heart to bear. Firefighting was about working mere feet
from excruciating death until you were so tired that you
began hallucinating.

And he loved it. In and around fire was the first and
only place he'd ever belonged.

Cal sat down on the ridge and pulled out his water
bottle and an energy bar. He found a comfortable boulder
to lean against so that he could watch the whole show.

A roar from behind him had Cal ducking. A red-
and-white air tanker, its four jet engines spinning
just above idle, swooped over his head like the Star
Destroyer at the opening of the original *Star Wars*—
barely five hundred feet above the ridge. It followed

a small black-and-flame-painted twin Beech airplane
for approximately a mile. That would be Henderson
and his daughter.

No, it wouldn't. Unless the man didn't match Cal's
first impression of him, he'd never put his daughter at
risk. Lead planes had been known to go down when
they went too low and got caught in a bad microburst
downdraft. Only three or four that he knew of over
many years, but that didn't sound like Henderson. It
also sounded like something his wife would skin him
alive for.

Cal changed frequencies on his radio and scanned
the sky. Henderson's voice directed the lead plane to
alter course a hundred feet west. Who was he kidding,
tweaking a jet-borne flight of retardant a hundred feet?
Cal spotted Henderson's plane far above at the Incident
Air Commander altitude, well clear of the fire.

The small lead plane jinked a little west, forcing the
big tanker to bank left, then right to pick up the new
line. The lead released a puff of smoke. Three seconds
later, the big jet-engine air tanker reached the tiny white
puff and released its load. Retardant spilled out in a long
billowing cascade of brilliant red for more than a quarter mile. It was so beautiful that Cal could never tire of
watching it.

Damn! He hadn't pulled out his camera at all. Hadn't
even thought to. He already had a hundred shots just like
this, but it bothered him that he hadn't taken one picture
since he'd begun climbing the ridge.

Odd to just be the observer. It wasn't how he watched
the world. He watched it through a lens, and he actually
felt a little naked without the added distance. Playing

with the sensation, he snapped the clasps on his camera case shut. A bit of a chill went up his spine, and he didn't know why.

Another roar as the next big air tanker came by low overhead. He didn't jump this time, had already spotted the little lead plane circling back from the first tanker's run to a new alignment.

He fished his tablet computer out of his camera bag, transferred over the block of photos from the last hour, and began tapping out the article between glances up at the occasional air tanker and to make sure he still had several escape routes if the fire changed its mind and headed this way.

He had a good start on the article and had picked out the photos that he'd most likely use when he heard something that didn't fit. Beyond a long ridge, the fire was still clawing across the land toward the firebreak being cut by the hotshots. On the other side of the ridge lay only the black where there had so recently been a house and a cop car. A high whine, only a little louder than a kid's radio-controlled plane, abruptly Dopplered by him across the back of the ridge.

Steve's drone. The little black bullet with its red-and-orange flames painted down the side zipped by not a hundred feet away. Last night at dinner, Steve had promised to show it to him, but they hadn't had a chance. Something Cal would definitely have to make time for.

At just ninety miles per hour, it was slower than the big air tankers riding close to stall speed to make their drops, but it looked sleek and bullet fast. The drone circled overhead once more. This time, as it passed by, it waggled its wings at him.

Cal raised a hand to wave back at Steve. Apparently the resolution on the cameras was pretty good and there was a chance he'd see the gesture. Working with MHA would be something pretty cool. Between the drones and the Firehawk and…and Jeannie. Damn the woman. Didn't she have the decency to stay out of his thoughts for even five minutes in a row?

He took another bite of his energy bar and went back to working on his article.

Cal recognized the next craft to arrive the moment he heard it—the heavy beat of a Firehawk helicopter climbing the ridge behind him. A glance over, and there was Jeannie's chopper rising from the depths like the god Neptune. She topped the ridge and settled it on a flat spot not a hundred yards away. Damn, but he enjoyed watching that woman as she shut down the chopper, climbed down, and headed in his direction carrying a small plastic sack. Even her walk was a wonder to behold.

"What is it with you and that camera?"

Cal looked at her in surprise, then realized he was watching her through the viewfinder. Probably meant he'd taken several shots as well. He slid the zoom back, knocked down the exposure, and caught her bright in the foreground with a slightly hip-thrown walk like a lioness on the prowl, her silhouetted machine behind, and the distant fire. Her stonewashed jeans, freed from the Nomex pants, clung pale blue and as tight as leggings. He clicked the shutter. If that picture came out, it was another he'd never show to anyone. He lowered the camera without checking it, half afraid that he'd blush if he did.

"What brings you up here?"

"Lunch." She held up the sack. "I asked Steve to make sure you got out okay, then figured you deserved something better than an MRE. I'm required to take thirty minutes down time, so…" She pulled open the bag and started inspecting the contents, while handing him a sandwich.

Roast beef on whole wheat with a bunch of fixings. A part of him wanted to lean in and kiss her in thanks, and also because she looked so amazing. Most of him decided it was better to back away and unwrap his sandwich.

Jeannie found her own sandwich, sat, and leaned beside him against the boulder.

"Hell of a view you picked out here, Hotshot."

"Yeah, I was thinking of building my McMansion right here when I really hit it big." The part he didn't say was that any place with Jeannie in front of it would be a hell of a view.

———⁓———

Jeannie laid her head back against the boulder, closed her eyes, and simply enjoyed the quiet. Her body had been vibrated for six hours straight by the pounding of the big Hawk's rotors. It was another, albeit minor, problem with her new bird. Long flights made you feel as if you'd been wrapped up in an eggbeater for the entire flight. Even though the headset blocked most of the sound, the deep bass notes were driven directly into her body. She'd asked Emily about it and been told that Emily now felt odd when her body *wasn't* buzzing slightly from the sonic bombardment.

She took another bite and enjoyed the layered flavors

of horseradish and mustard, of roast beef and ripe tomato. One of the many things she liked about working for MHA was that they really tried to take care of the crew. Betsy in the food truck worked just as hard as the retardant and refuel grunts who scrambled to match the mage-like efficiency of Denise's chopper service crews. They really made it a joy to fly with Mount Hood Aviation.

Jeannie had gone back to the helispot for a refuel and a load of retardant. Within three minutes, the bird was all set, Denise had spot-checked the air filters to make sure they weren't ash plugged, and Henderson had delivered a double sack lunch.

Wait a sec. Henderson had…

"I'm gonna kill him!" Jeannie jerked upright and twisted to look down through the smoke haze toward the helispot invisible five miles away.

"Kill who?" Cal mumbled around a mouthful of sandwich.

No way in hell was she going to explain to Cal Jackson that they'd both just been set up by Mr. Ever-so-smooth, soon to be Mr. Ever-so-toast Henderson. No, better than killing him herself, she'd get Emily to do in her husband. Unless she was in on it? Emily had been playing with her daughter over by the food truck while they were taking their own required break…

"Arrggghhhh!" She liked Cal. She'd been looking forward to having lunch with him as soon as…as soon as Henderson had planted the damn idea in her head. As soon as Emily had her husband plant the…

But Emily Beale didn't strike her as the matchmaking sort. If it wasn't that…then MHA was interested in Cal Jackson for himself, though she wasn't sure why. And they were using her to recruit him. They had some amazingly skilled firefighters already on staff, some of the best in the business. Why did they want another hotshot?

"What's so special about you?" Crap! She hadn't meant it to sound like that.

"About me? Not a thing."

It didn't sound like false modesty when Cal said it. For some reason his tone put her at ease far more than any glib answer could have. He already was special, or she wouldn't be having these problems with him inside her head. And Henderson had seen something that she hadn't in two half-days aloft with Cal. What was it? Maybe if she just stepped back for a moment and stopped trying so hard, she'd figure it out. She wasn't very good at stopping; she preferred to be doing.

"What brought that on?" He eyed her over a bag of chips.

She wasn't going to be answering that question anytime soon. New subject. She dug her own bag of chips out of the sack along with a Coke.

"You're a photographer. That's your only job?"

"Sure. Made a good living doing it for the last several years. Do you want a résumé, Magic Lady? Or maybe my bank balance?"

Crap. This was getting worse. Maybe she should just try the truth.

"I'm just trying to figure out why MHA is trying to recruit you so hot and heavy."

"They are?" He blinked at her like an owl suddenly caught out under the midday glare.

"And you apparently didn't know this." If she'd just screwed up some master plan of the air attack commander…she really didn't care.

"There has to be something else about you." Then she thought of the operation at the start of this summer during the New Tillamook Burn and almost blurted out, "the second contract." She'd been warned never even to admit to its existence when questioned, let alone volunteer information. MHA's secret special-mission contract to assist the CIA on covert assessments under the cover of fighting wildfires must be behind this. But there was no way she could ask Henderson or Emily, and she certainly couldn't mention it to Cal. That meant she was on her own to figure it out.

"Well, how about you show me some of your photographs and we'll see what we can figure out."

"Is that an invitation?" He made his leer comic, or she might have dumped her soda over his head. But that would be a waste of a perfectly good soda.

"Guess again. Any chance I ever saw any of them?"

"Well, I'm one of the only two red-carded wildfire photographers there are. The other is a lady who does it as a summer hobby, when she isn't teaching at Cornell. Here." He dug a tablet computer out of his camera bag where he'd stuffed it to protect the screen from falling mustard. He tapped at it for a few seconds, and turned it to her. "This isn't my best, but a lot of folks have seen it."

It was the cover of *National Geographic*. A distant shot of a fiery snake of luminescent orange leaped up into the sky from the heart of a small country church turned torch-red by the fire. The firenado, truly a twirling, wind-driven vortex of superheated flame, stretched a dozen times the church's height before disappearing into the blackest cloud imaginable.

Jeannie had read this issue. Most wildland firefighters in America had read this issue, and probably around the world. She still owned a copy and pulled it out every so often. The pictures and the story had so captured how she felt and thought, and what she'd experienced while doing her job.

"Did you write the article too?" She was about to feel very humbled.

He shrugged. "Mostly. They assigned me an amazing editor who slapped it into its final shape." He tapped the computer screen, then stroked his index finger across it.

Fern Lake. The firefight in the snow. A close shot from just over a firefighter's shoulder. Him warming his hands for a moment by holding them toward a thirty-foot wall of flame, his Pulaski fire tool propped momentarily against his hip, a puff of freezing breath turned white against the brilliant orange backdrop. She knew this one too.

The emotional punch of his images was right to the gut every time.

—•—

Cal didn't quite know what to do with Jeannie's reactions to his photos. They were good images, especially the one from the Fern Lake fire. That was more him somehow. The cover shot was pretty; the firefighter was powerful.

Jeannie had almost bowed over the tablet as she slowly stroked from one photo to the next through most of the Fern Lake folder. The emotions on her face were unreadable, especially after her hair slipped forward and masked her face from view. He couldn't gauge her reaction. Finally he couldn't stand to wait any longer.

"Told you I had two good eyes." He added a laugh that she didn't join. It should have worked. Cute, funny, just what the moment called for. He fell back into an uncomfortable silence and tried to eat another bite of his sandwich, which had gone leaden in his gut.

She finally handed back his tablet after sweeping through the entire *National Geographic* folder as well, both the published and unused pictures. She ate in silence for a long time before speaking.

"Those are amazing." When she looked at him, her eyes shone with wonder. The last thing he'd ever expected to evoke in anybody.

Jeannie offered to have him back aboard for the afternoon.

Cal was tempted. Really tempted. Which was exactly why he opted to finish his interrupted hike and rejoin the hotshot crew as they readied for the imminent battle at the firebreak that they'd been cutting for the last several hours. With no dozer able to reach them, it would be their will and their skill with chain saws and Pulaskis against one seriously angry fire. The aircrews would be backing them up, but they fought a clean battle from hundreds of feet up in the sky. Down here the fight was dirty and personal.

As he hiked across the terrain, he could see Jeannie and Beale circling in, time after time. Retardant, foam, water, all depending on Henderson's calls and the overall incident commander's plan of attack. He enjoyed the sound of her voice over the radio accompanying him on his hike through the woods. It was as if they were walking together.

The big fixed-wing air tankers must be reinforcing the line elsewhere. It was a battle with many fronts, and he was glad to be in on just one small part of it. Soon he'd be sweaty, exhausted, and sleep deprived just like any hotshot. And he couldn't wait. Maybe that would help drive the woman from his head.

He caught up with the first pair of the ground team at the southernmost edge of the firebreak. A quick glance showed that they'd chosen the spot well. A run of stony cliff defined the south edge of the break. The break itself was a wasteland of felled trees a hundred feet wide and running more than a mile to the next ridge. The slope crowned out not far above them. To get by them, the fire would have to burn downhill, which was much tougher going for the flame. In addition, every tree in the area had been toppled away from the fire, burying their crowns and upper branches into the supposed safe zone.

Now he could see the strategy that Henderson and Dobson had been working all morning. The air tankers and helitankers had been flanking the fire with hundreds of thousands of gallons of retardant to herd it toward this break. They'd chosen a tight battle line. If the Santa Ana wind carried a single spark across the break, the fire would be into downtown Santa Barbara before they could stop it.

As he tramped closer, Cal realized that he didn't recognize the ground team. Then he shifted focus: these guys had parachutes on their backs. He hadn't found his hotshot crew; he'd found a team of smokejumpers. They'd looked the same as hotshots when they were tiny dots on the drone's infrared imaging. But these guys were the elite of the firefighting ground forces. Hotshots were known for hiking into impossible places, but these guys jumped into areas where even the hotshots couldn't go. Of course, in a Type I incident you used every asset available, no matter how they got there. So, his team must be farther around to the north.

"Where do I find your boss?" he shouted to a guy running a chain saw to trim the branches off the latest tree he'd felled. Get the fuel to lie down and there was less chance of it catching a spark. A swamper followed behind the sawyer, chucking all of the cutoff as far downslope as possible. Brutal work. They'd trade off every time the saw ran out of gas. Cal tossed some material downslope to help out as he came up to them.

The guy with the chain saw pointed with his blade and shouted, "Find the midget and the giant. You want the midget." Not a guy, a gal. Face obscured under all the smoke smudges and the bright yellow hard hat, but with a high voice. For a woman to make hotshot was common enough now, one in twenty or so. To make smokie? That took a special breed.

Cal shouted his thanks and continued along the firebreak. He admired the handiwork. This team was good. They'd taken every advantage of the terrain, sometimes dropping trees at odd angles so that they'd lever off one another and roll farther down the edge of the break. He wouldn't expect less from a smokejumper, but his trained eye said this was even more than usual.

Back when he was a sawyer, he couldn't have done

better, and he'd been pretty damned good. He could definitely learn things from this lady. There were some good photos here if he were writing a training manual, but he'd never been arrogant enough to think that he was at that level, so he left his cameras tucked away at the moment.

He continued north past three more sticks of smokies, as their basic team unit of two jump partners was called, before he tracked down the crew boss. He really was easy to find. This guy or gal was as powerfully built as any smokie, but also a foot shorter than any other smokejumper around. The guy beside the crew boss, per description, stood a head taller than even Cal. He pulled out his camera and snapped a photo of the odd pair at a moment that emphasized both their differences and their common attention to the task of starting a backburn. He came up in clear view and gave a shout—you didn't want to startle a guy with a flaming torch.

"You the crew boss?" he asked when they'd waved him over.

"Akbar the Great," the little guy said with a bright smile shining through dark smoke smear. "And this is Two-Tall Tim because he's twice my size." The short guy was East Indian with a light singsong quality to his voice but also with the easy, confident tone of a seasoned firefighter. Tim was indeed too tall—a stick-thin Eurasian, mostly Japanese by his look. Tim waved and continued along the upslope edge of the firebreak with a drip torch.

They were lighting the upper edge of the forest above the firebreak to pre-burn the closest fuel. When the main fire front showed up, it would find that much less fodder to work with. He saw similar fires being started all up the line.

"Cal Jackson," he introduced himself. The guy had a steel-hard grip. "Red-carded photographer, hoping I can tag along for a bit." Like any trained firefighter, he always checked in first with the crew boss so that he could add Cal to any emergency head counts if they had to bug out. "Red card" to tell him that Cal wouldn't be a burden.

"Yeah, Henderson warned us about you. More than welcome." Then he gave Cal a frequency for the team and Cal switched his radio over, though he was sad to be losing the connection to Jeannie. No—he was glad to cut that connection. Why didn't it feel as if he was glad?

"Henderson, huh?" Great, Cal apparently had some kind of a reputation already.

Akbar just grinned at him. "Something about saving your cameras before your own ass. Crazy, brother. You get yourself a jump card and you'll fit right in. You've got twenty to thirty minutes before the bitch comes over the horizon and we're fully involved. All hell's gonna break loose. Then we're gonna kick some serious fire butt. After we knock her down and out, you should hit the bar with us. Two-Tall has picked us out a good one, says it has lots of local talent."

Tim's smile and nod as he walked by to light the backfire in the other direction indicated exactly what kind of talent he was talking about—firefighter groupies.

"Excellent! Thanks," Cal responded as he always would have. But for perhaps the first time in his fire-fighting career, it didn't sound so tempting. Unless Jeannie went there—Man, that woman was going to turn him into a stark raving lunatic. Maybe he would go barhopping with these guys just to clear his head.

He fell back and checked the line. He counted six
two-man sticks of smokies, pretty typical to have a full
crew of twelve. Off in the distance he saw another crew.
Maybe they were his hotshots or another full smoke
team. The locals had no way to drive up here with their
trucks and heavy equipment. This was all hand work;
the territory of the wildfire specialist. Everyone was
moving slow and easy. A couple of teams had dropped
their tools and were chowing down on a meal and
hydrating as they prepared for the battle to start. Once
the fire hit, it could be a full day and night nonstop.
Or longer.

Cal spotted the paracargo load of drinking water that
had been dropped, probably by Chutes, the guy he'd met
his first night in camp. He raided it, loading his pack
with as much water as he could fit, then clipped on a
couple sacks of energy bars. The extra sixty pounds or
so of load dragged at him as he set off over downed
tree trunks, kicking aside brush and circling around tall
stumps. He traded full bottles for the crew's empties all
down the line, getting some good shots. It earned him
instant points with the crew and gave him a chance to
meet them all, however briefly.

He also kept his camera out. Partly for the relaxed
shots that he'd pair up with those when they were facing
fire, but also so they'd get his role here. Observer, but
obviously knew what he was doing because he was
working the line without an escort. That way they
wouldn't depend on him in a normal-level crisis, but
they wouldn't feel the need to keep an eye on him.
Of course any trained smokie or hotshot would have
an awareness of Cal anyway just out of habit. It was

ingrained to always know where your entire team was in case trouble came in hard.

Halfway down the line Cal broke down and reset his radio. He'd put down the hard cash for a two-way of as high quality as his cameras. One of its cool features was that he could set two frequencies, but prioritize one of them. He set the smokies' team frequency as the priority so that he could stay informed of when they were on the move. He set the second frequency to the helitankers. In moments, Jeannie's acknowledgment of where to target a flanking load sounded from the radio.

How much better it made him feel almost made him shut her frequency back off. A woman like her wasn't for him, but hell, it didn't hurt a guy to do a little daydreaming.

The top of the ridge above them was now alight with backfire, burning low and slow, just eating up the fuel and lighting up the heavily shadowed afternoon.

Jeannie watched the monster coming. They'd flown continuously since dawn to herd this fire. They'd cut off the south front, forcing it to a standstill where, unable to progress, it burned itself out of fuel and slowly died. So damn slowly.

The growing Santa Anas had actually solved the problem of the northern and western fronts. With the wind driving the fire southeast, it had been turned to reburn the black. Now that the fire had to desperately clutch for fuel rather than gobbling it up as it went, containing its upwind edges was a fairly easy task.

The heart of the black had been a beast. Jeannie had

doused so many flare-ups that she'd lost track. Normally the 212s and the MD500 could handle that, but there'd been too many. Overheated, unburned fuels threatened to reignite whole fronts unless the spark and ember were beaten severely with tons of water.

Jeannie wanted to be flying against the main front because she knew Cal was down there. Though she'd be damned if she knew why he was there rather than aboard her chopper. Maybe he saw something wrong in her that she didn't. The man's vision was unreal. Those photos had delivered gut punch after gut punch. Sometimes knowing what he must have done to take the photo was what really made it powerful.

To see the triumph on a hotshot's face shimmering through the flame meant Cal had stepped around an active fire, probably placing the main body of it at his own back. To capture the anger when a firebreak failed beneath a windstorm of embers meant he'd been right there in the fire and heat, constantly brushing off the embers that stuck and burned on clothes.

The short sequence that had really struck her to the core had been in the folder with the *National Geographic* cover. But she knew that article by heart, and Cal hadn't published the most powerful sequence of photos he had taken.

It was a burnover.

Overrun and unable to escape the flames, a hotshot or smokie crew would pull out their foil emergency shelters. It was a choice of last resort. It meant that many, many things had already gone wrong and the chances of survival were marginal at best.

Jeannie had trained for it, even now had a shelter

pouch tucked in the door-pocket of the chopper just in case she went down hard and couldn't escape the fire in time. The training alone had scared her close enough to death to never want to experience the real thing.

Cal had caught four shots. The moment as everyone pulled out their shelters. A towering wall of flame on the rampage beyond a team of yellow-clad, hard-hatted fire-fighters who looked like they had all chosen the same moment to fly a silver foil kite.

The second had been a row of small silvered mounds all in a neat line, glittering orange with reflected firelight looming just beyond. He must have been the last into his shelter, waiting those few seconds of immense risk to get the shot while the heat and smoke ached in his lungs.

The third, the crew emerging, as if reborn. Their faces red from the heat, the foil shelters still wrapped about them like protective shawls, and the look of wonder on their faces that they'd survived.

The last, the one she couldn't believe, must have been moments later. The crew, still wrapped in their shells except for one man kneeling by the head of a lone shelter still on the ground. The person on his knees was replacing the shell back over the body of their comrade as others around them reacted to the shock of losing someone they'd lived and fought fire with until minutes before.

She hadn't been able to face Cal after looking at that one. She had nothing to hold up to that. When her home had burned, she'd already heard that her parents were out clean and she'd been safe in the sky. Before the fire had taken everything, Mum had always talked about how Da's strong spirit lifted her up. When the fire had burned away their home and their livelihood, it had broken his heart. And just as surely as he'd lifted Mum up, Da had dragged her back down after the fire until Jeannie could barely stand to visit them anymore. They were both fading away so fast. The fire hadn't killed them, though it was taking them nonetheless.

It was as if Cal had shown Jeannie the pictures only to emphasize that he was from another world. A world where lives were on the line every minute of the fight.

And that was the choice she saw him make today. Armed with nothing but a camera, he'd walked away from her and her helicopter to rejoin his team. To go back to where he belonged. And she didn't.

Damn him! Damn him for making her feel small. She'd worked hard to get where she was. Well, it wasn't going to work. How many spot fires did his hotshot buddies not have to deal with because she'd been there today? Hell, for that matter, he'd be one dead little photographer right now if not for her saving his sorry behind.

Feeling a little better, she turned her full attention back to the fire. They'd killed or at least trapped most of it, losing only two small neighborhoods totaling perhaps fifty homes. No fatalities yet.

The heart of the fire was making up for all of the avenues that the firefighters had cut off and throwing its force against the last front. She heard Henderson warn the ground team that they were minutes from contact.

Then instructions began flying fast and furious. First, all of the ground teams were told to go to the uppermost edge of the firebreak.

Steve's drone image showed that every infrared dot of the crew was against the high side of the firebreak.

She and the air tankers laid down massive swaths of retardant on the lower edges of the firebreak. Any sparks that jumped into the slash hopefully wouldn't be allowed to reignite.

Then they flipped to water to try to slow down the fire itself. The heat currents made the flying chaotic in the semidarkness of mid-afternoon glower. They had to climb an extra couple hundred feet just to make sure some microburst didn't slap them into the ground.

They should have drowned the monster with the volume of water they dropped. He just shook them off like a spring sun shower and drove against the firebreak at full roar.

Jeannie flew. The time and flights blurred. Spot fires jumped the lines and were doused. Several times the slash at the lower edge of the firebreak ignited and was beaten back. Twice Henderson had called her in to drop water directly over a ground crew. The warnings had gone out that a thousand gallons were about to fall from the heavens in a single dump. She hoped Cal had time to get his cameras covered and brace himself before she released her load. Wouldn't that tick him off, if she was the one who ruined one of his precious cameras or tumbled him down a slope and broke his leg.

The recall came as a shock. Night was falling somewhere beyond the smoky pall. Only Beale was certified to stay aloft after dark. And she did.

Jeannie dragged her Firehawk back to the helispot and parked her bird. She did the shutdown and patted her bird on the nose for a job well done before collapsing onto the grass.

Too damn tired to move, she lay there and looked

aloft. Night certified. She had to get her ticket. If something happened because she couldn't fly, she'd…she didn't know what. It was like all her worst nightmares were surrounding her, even though she was awake. The fire breaking through and heading for the heart of Santa Barbara. Her childhood home burning in the Outback. All of her memories burned and gone. A photograph of the one lonely foil shelter over the dead body. Except this time she could see the face and it was Cal.

That was the image she couldn't shake. She should have said something to him. Would if she saw him again. But what would she say? Exhaustion took her before she figured it out.

She woke only briefly when Beale's chopper finally came in. Someone draped a blanket over her and she fell back asleep.

Chapter 5

CAL SHUDDERED WITH EXHAUSTION AS HE LOOKED down at Jeannie asleep in the dawn light. He considered kicking her, lightly, just because turnabout was fair play, but his knees didn't hold out long enough and he simply sank to a sitting position.

Somewhere in the long, hot night he'd known that he had to take the risk and talk to her. It had gotten to the point where he'd swear he could tell the difference between the two Firehawks on a drop run. At first by the way they flew, and finally by the way they sounded. Beale's flight was arrow perfect and absolutely steady; her bird didn't wiggle or mistrack for a single second, no matter what crazy turbulence the fire's heat was kicking out. Jeannie's flight swooped and flowed. Beale arrowed to the target; Jeannie snuck up on it. Both appeared to nail it perfectly every time, so same result, just different technique.

When Jeannie was called to return to base at sunset, he'd felt the physical blow. Gods, it must have pissed her off.

Cal smiled as he looked down at her sleeping form. No matter how pissed she was, it hadn't sustained her more than three steps from her chopper. She must have been as exhausted as he now felt.

Maybe he fell asleep sitting up himself. One moment he was staring down dreamily at one of the most beautiful and amazing women he'd ever seen, and the next he was flat on his back and his arms were full of Jeannie.

"You're alive!" She threw her arms around his neck and kissed him.

Any thoughts about some humorous response were washed away by the heat of that kiss. It scorched him right down to his gut.

"I'm getting you dirty," he finally managed to gasp out. That broke the moment as she rolled off him and looked down at herself. The blanket had shielded most of her front. He decided he'd better keep to himself the large sooty palm print on her butt. He didn't exactly recall groping her in that instant she lay against him, but he'd wager she'd felt damn good. Would have been nice if he'd been awake enough to enjoy doing it.

What the hell.

He dragged her back down on top of him and kissed her hard. One hand brushed into her long hair—so damn soft—and, sure enough, the other hand just naturally seemed to wind up on her butt to hold them tight together. And his guess had been right—she felt amazing. She might sit on her backside all day while flying, but it was an exceptionally fine one despite that. Tight with muscle, full with shape that complemented her as nicely below as her chest did above. Not bountiful, no need for it on her frame, but every inch of her exceptional.

She felt so good that he barely resisted pawing more of her. But he was aware of his grubby hands. Jeannie didn't appear to be in any hurry to get away. When she finally propped herself a few inches away and looked down at him, he was again breathing as hard as she was.

"I really like the way you wake up, Helitack."

"Huh. We do seem to have this thing about waking up together."

"Remind me to try it again after I've gotten some sleep."

She blinked at him several times as if she were the one lacking sleep. It gave him the opportunity to admire her forest-dark eyes and again appreciate the liveliness of her face that he'd managed to capture in pictures.

"The fire. The fire!" She tried to jerk up and away, but he kept her pinned comfortably against him with that hand still on her butt.

"We beat it."

She stopped struggling and looked down at him, obviously waiting for more details.

"I found out that Akbar the Great isn't named that just for the fun of it. He and Tim were bloody everywhere at once. I tagged along as well as I could. He finally gave me a break by latching me onto an inch-and-a-half hose for a couple hours, but I guess having to work for a living wasn't much of a surprise under the circumstances. Hell of a fight."

"And you got it all?"

"In living color." He patted the camera case that she'd knocked aside when she tackled him.

This time when she moved aside, he let her go. She sat up and pulled her blanket around her.

He shrugged off the pack he'd been too tired to realize he was wearing and the Nomex jacket; the under layer of long cotton underwear was enough to keep him warm on the balmy morning. He looked up at the sunlight. It was still bloodred from smoke and ash, but the eastern light was able to punch through. There was still plenty of cleanup for the choppers to work on, but they'd probably be able to turn it over to a Type II Incident Management Team sometime this morning. The tedious work of the mop-up crew had probably already started along the south edge. It would take them weeks to first make sure this one was beaten. Then the rehab crews could take over to figure out how to stabilize the burned-over slopes for the winter.

When he looked back down at Jeannie, she remained wrapped in her blanket, her eyes hidden by the shadows of her hair. Made it hard to see what she was thinking.

"I—" they both started simultaneously.

She clamped down hard on her lips. Rather than play the game of who should go first, Cal took that as a signal that it was up to him to speak first.

"I'm trying really hard not to be freaked out by you." He blurted out the truth despite all of his years of avoiding just that. "Though that kiss went a long way toward making me not worry so much." And it was true. She certainly hadn't greeted him like a pariah.

Jeannie hunkered in her wool blanket cocoon and inspected him through narrowed eyes.

He tried to read her thoughts. This wasn't the pissed-off warrior that his chin had met that first night. He also spotted no sign of the lusty lady who'd filled his arms moments before. He couldn't read her at all, which bugged him. He was really skilled at reading women. He could sweep up the bar-challenge babe almost every time, the one a fellow firefighter had picked as too beautiful for anyone to go after. He'd pull it off time and again. A couple of times he'd even managed to escort the lady home despite one of his drinking buddies paying her off ahead of time to turn Cal down.

But Jeannie was something else, like no one he'd ever gone after. Was that what he was doing? Going after her? Felt more like he should follow the old Monty Python line and run away.

"I was going to say something very similar." She spoke at last.

Now it was Cal's turn to inspect Jeannie through narrowed eyes. "Similar to what?"

A slender index finger peeked out of one of the blanket's folds and aimed toward his camera case. "Your pictures, Cal. They're breathtaking."

"What does that have to do with you freaking me out?"

"Why didn't you publish those shots of the burnover?"

"Didn't feel right." He shrugged. He'd told himself that he was saving them for a better venue. Of course, *National Geographic* was about as good as they came. "Truth was, I just didn't want to. Still not sure why. Some pictures are too precious to be sold for money or fame." It hadn't been about not wanting to dishonor the dead; he'd probably have paid more of a tribute if he had sold and published them.

"Who the hell are you, Hotshot?" Jeannie's tone was almost sharp. But he was starting to figure out a tiny bit of how to read her. He frustrated her. That was as good a place to start as any.

"I'm a tired and hungry photographer who just spent a long night pretending to be a smokie, Helitack."

She glared at him for a moment longer, then glanced up at the lightening sky. "I'll probably be aloft in another twenty minutes. Could do with some coffee before then myself." She stood up on those long, lean legs of hers. Her form-hugging soft blue jeans stirred even his weary blood. Though not quite enough to let him stand on his own.

He leveraged himself off the nose of her chopper, having to stand and wobble for a few moments before he stabilized. He slung the camera bag's strap over his head so that it didn't go astray.

Jeannie retrieved his pack and tossed it in the rear of her chopper. An interesting choice; he wondered if it was conscious.

They headed over to the food truck.

On the way he admired the easy, rocking motion of his palm print on her butt.

———— ∽∽∽ ————

Cal had stood there on the outside of her windscreen and watched Jeannie go aloft. He made her so self-conscious that she actually had to think about each action in order to be able to fly: up on collective, forward on cyclic with just a bit of left rudder to compensate. Check the instruments. Don't think about Cal. Think about the instruments: altitude, heading, engine temperature.

She huffed out a breath as a slight roll in the hills masked the helispot behind her. If she could no longer see the helispot, then he could no longer see her. No man had ever so unnerved her; his attention was like a caress on her skin.

But there was a dark side to Calvin Jackson. One that woke fighting. One whose gaze avoided hers when talking about those amazing pictures. She wondered if he'd ever shown those particular pictures to anyone else.

Jeannie actually bobbled the controls as she descended toward her first watering load of the morning.

The answer was *no*. He clearly had never shown them to anyone. She knew that was somehow true. Then why to her?

She dropped the snorkel and started pumping.

Even as she lowered the water in some stranger's swimming pool, there was no question in her mind.

She was already in over her head.

———⁓———

Cal waited until Jeannie was out of sight, then looked around at a bit of a loss. He was too damn tired and dirty to be up on the chopper with her. Besides, keeping his hands off a woman whose kiss felt the way hers did was becoming problematic. Wouldn't be his best idea to mess with the pilot while she was flying a chopper. No, staying on the ground had been the right choice.

He then considered bedding down somewhere, but he'd never been able to sleep during the day except in stolen naps on a fire line.

Was messing with this pilot totally out of the question? Maybe it was now that he'd just turned her down again. All of his standard knee-jerk responses were getting a workout today, but he was too tired to deal with them at the moment.

The other problem was that when Jeannie had taken off to help with the cleanup crew, she took his field pack with her. That included his change of clothes, a razor, a towel, everything. His personal kit was in the back of the hotshots' Box, which was parked who knew where. The truck that was the rolling home of a twenty-person hotshot crew was rarely in one place for more than a few days. And his big pack was at their base camp up near Sacramento, four hundred miles away, not that they were often there either. He'd lost his gear before, one feature of his itinerant lifestyle, but he'd rarely been this scattered.

He snagged some paper towels and a to-go ketchup container's worth of hand soap from the food truck and found a water carrier. After taking a wholly unsatisfactory sponge bath, he pulled his grimy pants back on. He couldn't face the T-shirt or boots. The day was warm enough that he'd just work on his tan until some piece of his gear showed up.

Returning to the food truck, he grabbed an iced tea and, parking himself at a picnic table, pulled out his tablet to finish the story of the MHA chopper rescuing a family and a cop car. Had he gotten a shot of the family? Yes, with their home burning behind them. He captioned the photo. Thankfully, it was the back of their heads so he didn't need releases from them; who knew where they were by this point.

For the pilot shots, he had too many choices. He glared at them. Yes, Jeannie was immensely photogenic, but he had a disproportionate number of images of her: looking over her shoulder from the cargo bay, looking down through the bubble window on her door as her chopper sucked up a fresh load of water, of her curled up asleep under a blanket. He didn't even recall taking that last one. It was embarrassing how many photos he had of her, but even with the blurry ones, he had a debate with himself before deleting. Even after he was done sorting, he'd kept far too many.

He finally included the second shot from the triptych he'd taken at their first meeting. The deadpan shot of her surrounded by her chopper, fire out the window behind her, and the photographer reflected in her sunglasses. She looked so damned powerful in that shot. No fire was going to dare even breathe wrong in such a woman's presence.

Cal got himself a fresh iced tea. It was too warm now for coffee, and he really didn't want to be fighting the caffeine. He reread the story, polishing and tightening. He'd been a decent enough writer in school, when he cared. When he was a hotshot in Alaska, then Idaho, he'd started doing the team's newsletter and updating their website. Now he edited from long practice with little real thought. He'd long since learned that if he thought too much, he destroyed the story. He simply looked for sections that didn't feel right and tinkered with them until they fit. It wasn't efficient, but the method worked for him.

Someone thunked down a tall soda and a burger with fries beside him. He looked up—right into the sun— and couldn't see shit. Henderson dropped down across from him.

"Why aren't you up there?" Cal nodded toward the sky. The sun said it was barely ten a.m.

"You guys kicked it so hard last night that they don't need me anymore. One of the fastest downgrades from Type I Incident Management Team all season. We just handed off to the Type II team. It'll be down to mop-up in a couple days. You came out with the smokies.

Hotshots probably out by end of day. The choppers are still in it for the rest of the day and maybe tomorrow, but Carly and Steve have that wired." Henderson chomped into his burger.

"Where's the kid?"

"Kidnapped."

At Cal's shocked expression, Henderson nodded toward the food truck. "Betsy's had her all morning and won't give her up to me. Claims my daughter needs more gal time." He shrugged his indifference, but Cal noted that rather than sitting straight across from him, Henderson had landed at the table so that he could turn just enough to keep an eye on the truck.

"Should I go steal her back? That burger looks good. I could use one too."

"Five says you can't do it."

"Ten says I can."

Henderson nodded that the bet was on.

Cal went for his burger, a fresh iced tea, and the kid. When he came back to the table alone, Henderson laughed at him.

He held out his hand for money.

Cal shook his head. "Nope, you owe me a fiver."

"Bet was ten."

Betsy came up behind Henderson with the girl in her arms. "You owe me the other five."

"Aw, crap!" Henderson dug out a pair of fives and handed them over.

Betsy made a show of tucking the five in her cleavage and then turned back to the truck, still carrying the little girl.

"Hey! Bring back Tessa," Henderson called.

His daughter cooed at him over Betsy's shoulder and waved bye-bye.

"Women," Cal intoned solemnly. "They sure can be a fickle lot." Then he wished he could bite off his tongue. It was a classic hotshot line when a woman picked up in a bar for a shallow, sex-only fling suddenly wanted a relationship on top of it. It was so inapplicable in a world inhabited by the likes of Beale and Jeannie.

Henderson must have seen Cal's look of chagrin and let it slide by. Instead he grabbed back the five-dollar bill that Cal foolishly hadn't pocketed. "There goes your five."

Cal grinned his indifference in thanks for Henderson not nailing him for the bad line. So he went for a subject change.

"Got something for you to look over before I send it out." Cal swiped his screen to the top of his article and turned it for Henderson's inspection.

Henderson went silent while he read and worked on his burger.

Cal did his best not to be nervous. He wasn't used to watching someone read his work. Usually he just sent it out and was done with it. "Write and release" was how he liked to think of it. But on the chance that he would end up working with these folks... Henderson handed back the tablet.

"Irene, Jimmy, and Kate. Single mom, no phone or radio. Didn't hear the evac order. Cop was an Officer Reynolds and asked me to kiss your feet right after he kissed Jeannie's. Apparently there's a hell-load of paperwork to replace a cop car. Accounting for every round of ammo, the assault weapons, each piece of gear...worse than an IRS audit, at least so he said." Henderson pulled some crumpled paperwork out of his back pocket. "Here are their releases to use their images. Jeannie told me what you did."

"In that case…" Cal made a couple quick edits and inserted the picture he'd left out before and handed it back to Henderson.

"Damn, that's a good shot." It was a two-parter. The long shot of the chopper, cop car dangling below, and a home going up in flames. The inset was their faces. The cop staring down at his car looking terribly pleased with a job well done; the family, horror-struck. You could even see the little girl clutching a small stuffed toy, a white cat, tightly around its middle. It was a real tear-jerker of an image. The MHA logo on the door stood out clearly in the close-up.

"We okay?" He normally wouldn't ask, but MHA figured so prominently in the story that Cal preferred to check in. More than that, he wanted Henderson to like it. And Jeannie.

"Send it."

Cal had already composed the email to a couple newspapers and two of the wire services. He attached the article and images and sent it off along with his standard contract. He shoved the computer aside and turned his attention back to his own food. Cal could feel Henderson watching him.

"What?"

"You got a passport?" Henderson sounded as if it were a perfectly normal question.

"Yeah." In Jeannie's chopper.

"Any criminal record I should know about?"

"Not that I've ever been caught for." Some juvie crap and lying about his age to get on a hotshot crew at sixteen. He'd fixed that record when he jumped from Alaska down to the lower forty-eight and legally changed his name. He'd been nineteen by then and no one cared about his age. All they wanted to know was that he'd already been working three years on a fire crew.

Henderson's totally impassive stare said that wasn't good enough.

"Long in the past, just some stupid kid shit." Show him a foster-care kid who passed through a dozen homes in ten years and didn't jack some booze or steal a few issues of *Playboy*, and Cal would pay them a grand. He'd never escalated to grand-theft auto or groped a girl who wasn't willing, so he figured that rated him dead clean. Hell, with his looks he'd never even had to pay a girl to join him. How clean did a guy have to be?

Henderson eyed him a moment longer, then nodded as if satisfied.

"How do you feel about Australia?"

"Like it fine. Why?" Cal usually went to South America for the off-season. When the northern hemisphere wasn't burning, the southern usually was. The whole Amazon fire-ecology thing was one of those perennial stories he could cash in on each year. He also found the images he saw to be of constant fascination to himself as well as his readers. He'd spent one season embedded with a small tribe as their jungle habitat was systematically burned out from under them. He'd gotten an inside article in *Outdoor* and another in *Condé Nast Traveler* from that summer. He hadn't been Down Under since his last year as a hotshot on those Black Saturday fires.

"MHA has a summer-season gig down there this year. We're number one under a CWN contract. So, we want to be local."

A call-when-needed contract was how most places, including the U.S. Forest Service, kept costs down. Or tried to. CWNs had higher hourly rates than dedicated contracts, but supposedly that was offset by fewer hours of usage. The last five years of fires had run so hot that the Forest Service would have been better off keeping outfits like MHA on permanent retainer, paying them even when they weren't flying. Thankfully all of those decisions were done way above Cal's pay grade, because they just sounded like a goddamn headache to him.

"Number one, huh?" That was sweet for MHA. It probably meant steady work, but it would also mean that they weren't called out for the grunt crap. When called, they'd really be needed.

Henderson wiped the last of the ketchup off his plate with the last french fry. Clearly waiting for Cal to finish his thinking.

"Why me?"

"I have an uncle who is always quoting business books at me." Henderson shrugged his indifference to the subject. "Since in addition to being my uncle he is Marine Corps General Edward Arnson in charge of the President's Marine One helicopter squadron, I do try to listen to what he says at least some of the time. He also treats Emily like his favorite daughter for reasons I still can't find out. Anyway, he's always told me to worry about finding the right people first, then figure out what to do with them. It certainly worked in Special Operations Forces, so I suppose it will work here in MHA as well."

"Special Ops?" Two contracts pinged into his email in-box. He ignored them for the moment. Jeannie had said something about Beale and Henderson being in the Army, hadn't she? Beale was a major or something.

"My Emily and I flew with an outfit called the Night Stalkers."

"Shit!" Cal had heard of them. The Army's 160th Special Operations Aviation Regiment had the best helicopter pilots on the planet. No wonder Jeannie was so impressed by Beale's flying. She really was that good. Even if he didn't have the training to tell the difference, Jeannie did.

The choppers were coming in for their scheduled lunch break. Cal heard the diesel engine on the fuel truck fire up, so they could be refueled and ready to go. Henderson didn't look up, but probably knew exactly who was where just by the sound. Instead, he sat quietly, awaiting Cal's response.

"What are you doing here?" Cal asked. "Why aren't you out…?"

"Keeping America safe?" Henderson completed the thought for him. "We got a little surprise along the way." He nodded toward the food truck where Cal could see Betsy sitting in a chair with a book and the baby snoozing in a swing chair beside her. "Didn't seem right to stay on the front lines after that."

Cal watched the pilots climb down. The tall, blond ex-SOAR pilot Emily Beale, every movement so precise, so practiced. Carly the Fire Witch climbing out the other side. From the second Firehawk, the lithe Jeannie clambered down like she was descending from a great carnival ride. She shed her Nomex gear and turned away to toss it back into the helicopter. It had smeared to an indefinite smudge, but his sooty palm print was still in place.

Right people? Henderson thought he was one of the "right people"? Whatever in the hell that meant. Didn't seem likely to Cal, but he was looking at another reason not to argue. Jeannie shot him a smile as soon as she spotted him and sauntered in their direction in that delightful way of hers. Rather than reaching for a camera, he simply enjoyed the spectacle.

Just before she arrived at their table, he managed to break the hypnotic spell the woman cast and turn to Henderson.

"Australia sounds like a great idea."

———

Jeannie made her decision as she crossed from the chopper.

Cal was sitting there with Henderson, as if hanging out at a helibase with that magnificent chest all out in public was perfectly normal. The man was beautiful! Given a choice, she'd tell him to never put on a shirt again. He might be a photographer, but there was no question he could still pass all of the wildland firefighter fitness tests without even thinking about it.

He was absolutely dazzling, not that she'd ever admit it out loud.

She also liked that she freaked him out. Jeannie couldn't imagine why. She'd spent much of the morning aloft considering just what she had done to cause that, but hadn't come up with a decent answer. She ate lunch at the table with them, Emily, and Tessa. And enjoyed Cal's easy manner. He was fun to flirt with, sharp and funny.

He walked her back to her chopper. She'd never been self-conscious about a bare-chested man walking beside her. Too many firefighters, once clear of the flames, stripped off all the clothes they could as if the fire's heat still burned nearby. But with Cal, she was aware of every breath he took. He wasn't some muscle-bound grunt. Walking beside her, he just looked like a normal, strong guy.

When they reached the chopper, he reached into the back and grabbed his pack from where it dangled on a hook in the cargo bay. It wasn't until then that he turned his back to her—and she saw a hundred thin, white lines crisscrossing his back.

"What the hell, Cal? You get dragged by a camel across the entire Outback?"

He glanced over his shoulder at her, then grimaced at some dark memory. "At least they aren't burns." He dug around in his pack. "I didn't have a clean shirt."

It was a shame to cover such nice skin. She couldn't feel too guilty about taking his only change of clothes aloft with her when she'd so enjoyed looking at him through lunch. She took a deep breath and decided to go with her gut instead of her brain.

"If you put it in the third tent down the row on the left, you'll know where to find it later."

He turned slowly to face her. After what felt like forever, he shook his head no.

"Not the best idea, Helitack."

"Probably not," she admitted. Then she reached deep. "But the offer stands." She turned away quickly to preflight her chopper. It had only been thirty minutes, so she really only needed to do a minimal check, but she'd seen that Beale always did a full preflight on her Firehawk and Jeannie wasn't going to do a single bit less. She also didn't want to face Cal's turndown. The shame was burning her cheeks. And she was the one freaking him out?

He just stood there being all handsome and quiet and interesting while she did the full circuit of her machine: checking air filters, no water polluting the fuel tanks, and inspecting for physical damage. She closed one of the big cargo bay doors to expose the built-in toe and handholds so that she could climb up and inspect the rotor. On her MD500, she'd been able to span the shaft with her two hands. On the Firehawk, the assembly was bigger across than her shoulders; the blades themselves almost eighteen inches wide. She sighted down each one looking for signs of damage or weakening. She popped the engine cover, but saw no signs of blown hydraulic fluid. All pretty damn clean considering the last few days' workout.

Jeannie wanted to get away from him, but he held her door open for her while she climbed aboard. She buckled in and reached for her headset.

A brush of his hand on her cheek made her turn back to face him. He stood there filling her doorway, his pack hanging easily from one shoulder. His light brown eyes were alight with amusement, but his smile was small.

"What's so damned funny?" Her voice was sharper with irritation than her feelings actually justified.

"Me, Jeannie. Just me. Do me a favor?"

"As long as you don't take your hand from my cheek,

I'll do anything." It was true. The simple brush of his thumb was sending shivers of heat up her spine.

"Next time I'm dumb enough to turn down a woman as amazing as you, just kick my ass for me right off rather than leaving me to stew on it. Okay?"

"Sure, Cal. Glad to kick your ass anytime. I just dare you to fall asleep on the ground again."

He leaned in and kissed her so lightly that it was more caress than kiss, then stepped back and closed her door before backing away.

She cycled up the engines, finished her checklist, and headed aloft.

Cal stood just beyond the rotor tips and watched her the whole time. Again the self-consciousness was overwhelming, but this time it steadied her hands on the controls. Her cheek still tingled where they had brushed skin to skin.

His skin had surprised her. That beautiful, muscled male chest and the back so scarred that it really did look as if he'd been dragged across the Outback. A part of her wondered what could possibly have caused such marks. Another part of her wondered at the contrast. The man radiated light as if he were fire himself. The warmth of his smile, the heat of his embrace, and the out-and-out scorch of his kiss.

Maybe that darkness she had noted before was tied into the scarring. What was his past, so carefully hidden? Or was it? They'd barely started to know each other, and here she was worrying about his past as she flew back to the fire.

Jeannie had only meant to offer sex. It had been way too long since she'd taken someone to her bed, and there was no denying the physical attraction between them. But she was intrigued by far more than his body, which was totally unexpected. And what she really hadn't counted on was Cal being so goddamned nice that she might want to keep him around for a while.

She hadn't counted on that at all.

―⁓―

Jeannie didn't see Cal when she landed at the end of the day. Nor was he at dinner. He couldn't have meant he really was turning her down. Not after that kiss. That one had kept her thoughts and her body firing hotter and hotter as the Grindstone Canyon Fire cooled and burned less and less inside the ring of a hundred percent containment.

She was past frustrated and well down the road to peeved when she finally gave up the hunt and headed to her tent.

Jeannie didn't bother with a flashlight as she unzipped the mozzie net and ducked down and through the front flap. Then she face-planted into her double air-mattress when she stumbled over a pack just inside the entrance. Groping around, she found the tent light dangling from the peak and snapped it on.

There, sprawled like a slain man, lay Cal, passed out so deeply that her arrival hadn't disturbed him for a second. He must really be exhausted. Of course, he'd fought the fire straight through last night while she'd slept beneath the stars. He still wore his T-shirt and pants, though he'd managed to remove his shoes before lying down on top of the covers.

Horribly self-conscious, far more than she would be

if he were awake, she shut off the light and turned her back on him while she changed into the long T-shirt and shorts she usually slept in. She even debated keeping on the bra, but it was too uncomfortable for her to be quite that stupid. She slid down under the covers, turned her back on him, and spent a long time listening to his breathing before she managed to find sleep for herself.

—⁓—

The night was pitch-dark when Jeannie woke. Not even the lights from the food truck or the service teams working over the choppers filtered through the thin fabric of the tent. The camp was all shut down for the night.

She went to roll over and discovered she couldn't. In his sleep, Cal had wrapped an arm around her waist, pinning her beneath the covers. Well, it was certainly a comfortable place to be, even if he was unconscious.

Then his arm tightened about her waist and pulled her back against him. In the cool night, the man was cozily warm, even though he lay atop the covers and she beneath them.

Cal nuzzled his face into her hair and breathed in deeply. "You smell wonderful." His voice was still thick and slow, filled with sleep.

She managed to extract an arm from beneath the covers and laid it over his arm around her waist. He slid his other arm so that her head rested on his arm rather than her pillow. He wrapped it around, but rather than landing his hand on her breast, he reached across her body to her shoulder and simply held her against him.

"You feel downright spiffy." She wiggled back tight

until they were spooned together. It was dreamy to simply be held like that.

Jeannie wanted to correct herself, but couldn't. She didn't get dreamy; it wasn't her style. But she was. Probably something to do with it being the middle of the night after an exhausting day. Well, if she was going to change her mind, she'd better do it fast.

The hand that had been around her waist began to travel, stroking down over her hip and thigh and then traveling back up to her waist and rib cage, and back down. To hell with common sense and changing her mind. She was exactly where she wanted to be.

"Cal?"

"Hmm?" he hummed sleepily in her ear.

"Whatever you're doing, don't stop? 'Kay?"

She allowed her hand and arm to ride on his as he stroked up and down her body. She used her fingers resting over the back of his to turn his path, to guide him where she wanted him to go: across her belly, up between her breasts, down her hip. Through the fabric, he traced down the front of her thigh and came up the back of it. When he hesitated at her waist, she coaxed him up to her rib cage and eventually to her breast.

Jeannie moved to brush the sheet aside, the blanket long gone, but he blocked her movement and continued his gentle exploration through the thin material. She may have groaned as he toyed with her. The various tents weren't all that far apart, so she bit her lower lip to keep it to herself, but he felt so good. Made her feel so good.

He brushed his hand down between her legs, but traveled back to her hip before she could open to him.

She managed to huff out a soft, "Good on ya," the next time his sure hand stroked over her.

Jeannie liked to make love the way she flew—in total command. If that didn't scare guys off, eventually it pissed them off. Either way, they were gone. For now she was content to lie in the dark inside Cal's embrace and let him tease her body to life. Let him trace and follow her curves until she burned for more.

Still holding her shoulders tight against his chest, he at last gave her the caress she'd wanted. She had to raise both hands to clamp onto his forearm and just hold on as her body writhed, shuddered, and finally exploded beneath his stroking investigation. It was so intimate, so personal, yet she didn't feel at all exposed. She simply felt wonderful.

When at last the fire's roar inside her had settled back enough for her to think, maybe to thirty percent containment of the blaze that still scorched along her nerves, she finally managed a whisper. "Damn, Hotshot."

"Damn yourself, Magic Lady. You're amazing."

This time when she tried to roll over in his arms to face him, he let her. His hand landed on exactly the same spot on her behind as it had this morning. She'd been able to feel the palm print all day, stunned by the strength that held her so easily in place, but didn't make her feel trapped at all.

She'd never been with a man who was interested in making her feel more splendid than himself. Of course, Cal had never struck her as stupid, except for being caught on a cliff edge. And maybe throwing his camera case aboard before jumping aboard himself. Or walking away from her chopper back into the fire. Or initially turning down her invitation to her tent… Okay, maybe she could make a goodly list of dumb moves even though she'd only known him a couple of days.

But she'd wager that while Cal paying such attention to her was a kindness, it was backed by the knowledge that she was now in a mood to be especially nice to him. And he was right—she was. Her body felt hot and loose. And his body felt hard and wonderful.

She started with such a long, slow kiss, that she completely lost herself. His mouth was like the rest of him: skilled, strong, but holding back as if there were secrets to plumb, a hidden layer just begging to be discovered.

Well, she was the gal to do it. She worked down to that wonderful chest. When she went to work his T-shirt off, he moved to assist her. She wanted to rub herself all over that beautiful chest, but she kept the sheet between their bodies as she researched the terrain laid out before her. Jeannie let her lips do the traverses as she investigated the sloping terrain of his pecs, circling in tighter and tighter orbits until he hissed when she finally took his nipple in her teeth. There was a long valley down from his sternum.

Through the soft sheet and his pants, she studied the shape and hardness of him until he groaned in suspended anguish. His legs were no less well-formed than his butt. Damn, but she'd enjoyed watching every time he'd walked away from her during the last two days—it was amazing. She freed her hand from the covers and ran it up onto his back.

She could feel the long, thin white scars. They were raised, as if…

He went to roll onto his back, but she hooked a hand on his pants pocket and kept him lying on his side facing her. Very slowly, she returned her hand to his back. He didn't want to talk about it, fine. But he wasn't going to shy away from her, not if they were going to be lovers. She snuggled her face back into the center of his chest and ran her hand up and down his back. Her palm and fingers felt cool in contrast to his heated skin. Jeannie continued her gentle, brushing investigation until he calmed and relaxed.

It was enthralling, as if it was in her power to tame the beast. This man who stared down wildfire, hiked easily over brutal hills to rejoin his team, and could take photos that still made her want to weep with their power. He moaned and twitched with each of her touches. He repeatedly resisted then succumbed, as if tortured by her cooling touch until she made him flare up once more.

She removed his pants and spent some time admiring him with her fingers, the tip of her tongue, and doing her damnedest to drive him totally crazy. He began cursing as she let her hair hang down and dragged it slowly along his body like a long, long fall of cooling water, which drove his heat toward blazing until he throbbed in her hand.

Digging out some protection, she sheathed him carefully, not wanting to push him over the edge, not yet. He didn't get to go there before he had filled her so full that she could think of nothing but how they burned together in the night.

And he did. She straddled him, her hair brushing the top of the dark tent. He filled her until she flamed with desire, with desperate need, and finally they both flashed over. Their releases had them shuddering against each other as they fought for breath in the midst of the firestorm.

Chapter 6

CAL WASN'T SURE WHAT HE'D SIGNED UP FOR. SOMETIME in the night, perhaps even as Jeannie was forever altering his definition of incredible sex, Mount Hood Aviation had been released from the Grindstone Canyon Fire. The California Department of Forestry had decided they could handle it from here.

By dawn, MHA was in motion. Breakfast was a hurried affair. Tents were packed; pallets of camping and smokejumper gear were slid into cargo bays. Service trucks were closed up, and the roar of diesel engines filled the field by sunrise as retardant and fuel trucks departed the helibase. Four boxes of gear were moved from Steve's drone control truck into the back of Beale's chopper, and the launcher trailer was hung from a load line beneath. Someone showed up and drove the truck away. With Jeannie's chopper, they picked Denise's loaded service box off the back of the flatbed. It had all of the tools and spares she and her crew were likely to need to field service the choppers.

Cal liked that these guys were geared to be on the move. He'd chosen a no-roots lifestyle at sixteen and hadn't felt the lack of a more stable existence at all. He'd left nothing of real value in the pack in the hotshots' truck, just a couple changes of clothes. At their base, he'd left a pack with winter gear that he certainly wouldn't be needing in Australia during their summer and a small locked suitcase of his past. He'd never quite had the heart to just throw it out, nor had he opened it in years. It wouldn't hurt anyone if it sat in their storage locker for a season.

By the time the five MHA choppers lifted off an hour after sunrise, the farmer's field was once again empty except for compacted squares in the hay stubble that would be eradicated by the winter plowing. No sign remained of the battle fought from here and won on the nearby hills over the last week. No loss of life. The only real injuries were a couple of broken arms and a broken leg when a wildfire engine tumbled down an embankment. They'd been blinded by a sudden cloud of smoke on a narrow curve. Seventy-three homes were the insurance company's problem. When it came down to the wrangling, no one except the firefighters would remember how close that number had come to being seven hundred and thirty.

He and Jeannie gazed east as soon as they'd reached their cruising altitude of five thousand feet. The smoke had thinned to small spot fires. They were high enough to see the black. Eighty thousand acres of park, forest land, and homes gone. But it would be back. One thing Mother Nature always did well was bring back life where you couldn't imagine it. Then they turned and headed west to the coast.

Cal simply enjoyed the ride as they flew high over Santa Barbara, the Pacific Ocean stretching out to fill the horizon as they approached it. Jeannie had left him feeling immensely mellow. He'd never been with anyone who responded to him with such heat, nor offered it right back. And usually heat left him simply greedy for more.

Jeannie doused the fires in him just as effectively as she did with her chopper, as if she'd somehow washed his insides clean as well.

Tell her, you idiot.

"You're an incredible woman, Jeannie Clark of the dark-red hair." He watched her as she checked something on her instrument panel, then adjusted their heading, such a tiny shift that he knew it was a delaying tactic. That was okay, he could wait. There were only the two of them and a breathtaking morning light aboard Jeannie's Firehawk.

"Why?"

Not the response he'd expected. No empty rituals of compliments shared before the subject was dropped— not with this woman.

"Why are you incredible? Let me count the ways."

"No. I—"

He cut her off. "This should be fun. Don't interrupt." He ignored her glare and waited while she acknowledged a direction change from Henderson that had them turning north along the coast. It was just another beautiful early November afternoon a couple thousand feet above the California beaches.

"Let's see. Chronological or order of importance?"

"Crap, Cal."

"Told you to shush. I'm considering serious matters here."

"Give me a break, Hotshot."

"Not a chance, Helitack. I could start by enumerating your womanly curves and just how much I enjoyed them last night."

"And this morning."

"Shush. Though I'll accept the correction. Chronologic, I think. Better yet, reverse chronologic. We've already covered last night."

She sputtered and turned to glare at him.

"Watch your heading, Helitack," he ordered her, though she hadn't wiggled off her flight path in the slightest.

She continued to glare for a long moment before abruptly laughing and turning back forward.

Damn! Why were both of his cameras in the bag? That laugh had lit her up brighter than the morning sun. It was the first time he'd heard it up close rather than across half a camp, and it transformed her from merely incredible to downright magnificent. What in the hell was he doing presuming to even be aboard this woman's chopper? He had no more qualifications to be here than... *Cut it out, Cal. She invited you. That's enough.* Enough for now, anyway. Where had he been before that laugh? And what would he have to do to elicit its return?

"I thought you were busy making lists," Jeannie poked at his silence.

"Uh, right." Could he sound stupider? Probably. "So last night and this morning, we had positively incredible sex that I can't wait to try out again at the soonest opportunity."

"Roger that, Hotshot."

"Don't interrupt. I could easily waste a lot of time on how good you look, feel, smell, taste, but that's all pointless at the moment because it would just make me want to jump you again right now. I'm guessing that isn't my best option while you're trying to fly a helicopter that my life depends on at the moment."

She kept her silence this time, perhaps thinking some of the same thoughts he was. Definitely time for a subject change.

"The way you fly. I didn't really appreciate it at first, don't know much about choppers, but I'm learning. I can now see that Beale is incredible. I wouldn't expect less from SOAR."

"I heard she was one of their best."

"Okay, that's even more humbling. But you're not far behind, Helitack. I've had a lot of time to watch you these last days, from both in the air and on the ground. You really get it done. And what you do with it against fire is something I haven't seen much of in the ten years I've been hotshotting. So, as much as you're humbled by Beale, I'm finding the same thing with you. That's what I meant about you freaking me out."

This time she didn't try to respond, and he was glad of it. He knew he had her up on a totally ridiculous pedestal. The problem was that the more he learned about her, the taller the damn pedestal grew. He was used to women who started with those perfect stars in their eyes and bodies that didn't quit, who looked amazing through a two- or three-beer haze. Often fun, but never sustainable.

He was definitely not used to women who flew twenty-million-dollar machines like they were a second skin and looked at him with a frankness that he couldn't escape, as if she could see right through him. She could do that, yet she hadn't cast him aside. Quite the opposite. And he didn't know what to do with that, either. Continue his list.

"I'm jumping around a bit, but the next two seem to

be equally prominent in my mind. One, that you saved my life. Thank you again."

"No worries." Her voice was little more than a whisper. He'd always liked that Ozzieism. Was that even a word? In Australia, "no worries" was the standard response to any problem, delay, or misstep. And it wasn't just a phrase as he'd first thought. It was infused throughout the culture, making it so much easier going than the American answer to everything less than perfect: "sorry." As if someone being at fault made it better, even when they weren't.

"Well, imminent death worried me, I can tell you."

"Even though you were busy taking pictures when I arrived."

"Even though."

Henderson called in a turn to the east.

"Are we going in circles?" They were now well north of Santa Barbara. Actually, there wasn't a whole lot here. Their flight of five choppers climbed until they were high above the mountains. He had spotted the altimeter among all of the gauges. They were at ten thousand feet. He leaned over and looked out the bubble window—hell of a long way down.

"Not sure where we're going," Jeannie answered after puzzling over the map display on the console for a bit. "Henderson says follow, I follow. So, what's right up there with saving your life? Don't think I did anything else particularly noteworthy."

Cal couldn't help grinning. "I didn't say it was important, just said I couldn't stop thinking about it."

"Okay, Hotshot, I give up."

"The way you walk, Magic Lady. Damn, but you

have a walk of such power and beauty that you stun me past any ability to even photograph it."

"I guess that's high praise from a man who saves his cameras before he saves himself." Again that laugh edged in.

"It is, Helitack. It really, really is. Trust me."

Jeannie tried to digest Cal's startling view of her as she followed in formation behind Emily's Firehawk. The terrain below rapidly shifted from coastal bounty to arid California hills. At this rate, they weren't far from the Mojave Desert.

To distract herself, she tried to mirror Emily's every move. Jeannie could feel herself smooth out when Emily did, but she couldn't do that rigid control for long. The woman was textbook and Jeannie was more seat of the pants. When Jeannie flew that rock steady, she actually lost the feel of the chopper. If she rode the air currents just a little, slalomed back and forth even the tiniest fraction, she became far more aware of what the Firehawk and the air around her were doing.

She was sure aware of Cal Jackson, and not just the latent tingles that still rippled through her body. His compliments hadn't sounded crafted; they'd felt genuine. That they liked each other's bodies so much after a single night together wasn't any big surprise. That was bound to wear off, and she just planned to enjoy it while it lasted.

That he'd complimented her flying next, and not just with empty words, struck her right to the core. Wildfire was the enemy. Yes, she understood the natural cycle, but it had taken her family's home. It had taken friends. It would be the enemy until the day she died, and her ability to fly was the only weapon she had to bring to the fight. That a skilled hotshot, praised by both the hotshot crew boss and by Akbar, had paid her the compliment made it ten times more real.

That MHA, through Emily and Mark, was recruiting Cal added several points in Cal's favor. Of course, she'd already let him into her bed, so maybe she should stop counting points on him. Either way, MHA only went after the best. Steve's drone was so cutting edge that even the U.S. Forest Service didn't have one. Steve's wife, Carly Mercer, was called the "Flame Witch" far and wide, and generally acknowledged as the best fire behavior analyst working in the business today. TJ and Chutes had been in on the founding of the Mount Hood Aviation firefighting team, along with Carly's father. All of which often left Jeannie wondering why she was there, not that she was complaining.

And Cal's final compliment had gone to her head. She wasn't sure if she'd be able to walk when they landed, because she'd be far too self-conscious. What she did know was how good she felt when she was walking toward Cal. And how awful she felt when he was walking away.

"Hey, is that Edwards Air Force Base?"

She glanced to the south. They were high enough to have a good view of the long runway lying about ten miles to the south. It was Edwards.

"Where are we going?"

She shrugged. "Back of Bourke for all I know."

"What was that?"

"Australian saying. Bourke is this town that's way out there into the Outback. Back of Bourke, there's nothing much but the Simpson Desert for close enough to forever."

Cal's low chuckle did things to her. It came so easily for him. She felt as if the laughter had been driven out of her years before. Sure, she enjoyed a good joke, but she always felt like the odd cog out when she merely smiled while others laughed. Cal was appreciative, not judgmental. That allowed her a little room to ease out of her overly self-conscious state.

For now Jeannie would do her best simply to be in the moment and accept what was. Neither were things she was terribly good at.

They started their descent. She didn't recognize where they were, somewhere in the Mojave Desert east of Edwards.

"Cal, you on the air?" Henderson called.

Jeannie lightly tapped the microphone transmit switch on the back of her cyclic control and then nodded to the one in front of him. Rather than just resting his hand there and thumbing the switch, he reached out and tentatively pressed just the button with a fingertip.

"Here." Then he released it as if it might bite him.

"From here on, cameras stay in the bag until I tell you otherwise. We clear?"

Again, the tentative finger pressed the button. "Okay. Sure."

"Thanks. I'll explain later, out."

"Press the button again, and say, 'Out,'" Jeannie instructed him.

Cal did. Was the man really that thoughtful about not wanting to jar her controls or was he…

"You afraid of a little helicopter, Hotshot?"

"Uh, no more than I am of its pilot, Helitack."

Gods, but she could enjoy being around this man. "Rest your hands on the controls and your feet on the pedals."

He spun to face her as if she'd lost her mind.

"Just do it, Cal. You won't send us spinning out of control."

Apparently deciding she was serious, he studied her hand and foot positions intently for several seconds, glanced at the matching controls around his seat, then back at her hands. He reached out, settling his hands in place so smoothly that she barely felt him through her own set of linked controls. It wasn't expected; his hands were large and rough with hard work. But it made sense when she thought about how delicately and delightfully he'd handled her body… which was definitely a thought she shouldn't be having at the moment.

"Okay. Your left hand is on the collective. 'Collective' because it affects the angle of all of the blades at once. You pull up, we go up. You lower down and we descend. On some choppers, if you twist it, you change the engine speed. But the Firehawks have throttles up there." She nodded at the overhead controls on the cockpit's ceiling. "Make sense so far?"

"If I press any of these little buttons by my thumb, do I kill us?"

"Well…" She couldn't resist. "Most of them are safe."

He looked at her in horror and she couldn't help

laughing. "How can you know so much and yet know so little?"

"Lady, prior to working a camera, I spent seven years out in the woods where the most dangerous thing they let me have was a Pulaski fire tool. They didn't even let me have a McLeod rake. They only let me handle a hose and a pump if someone was watching me closely."

She knew the last was a total fabrication. She'd chatted with Akbar last night when she'd been unable to locate Cal. He'd been really impressed at how well Cal used his hose exactly where and when it was needed without wasting a moment of water flow. Said he wanted to get Cal jump-certified just in case he ever needed an extra man. That from a top smokejumper. Smokies were very particular about who they had beside them in a fire.

"Well, the tanks are empty so the dump-and-pump controls aren't going to matter. The searchlight controls won't matter in broad daylight, and the emergency release would be best left alone or we'd dump that big load of all our service gear that's slung below us on the cargo hook. By the way, thanks so much for asking permission before attaching a cop car to my belly." Then she took her hand off the collective, trusting the steadiness of his hold, and flicked off a couple overhead breakers. "There, all shut down. You can press them all you want."

He ran his thumb briefly over the controls, but didn't press any. He clearly didn't realize that he'd had sole control of the collective for several seconds. He also wasn't apologizing for the cop car. He'd been right, and he'd have stopped if she told him to. He hadn't bothered to waste those precious moments by asking; he'd just gotten it done.

"The one in your right hand is called the cyclic because… Well, it just is." It was always easier to show someone the swash plate in action rather than trying to describe it. "It gives you forward and back, and tips you to either side. You're going to fly in the direction you're tipped. The buttons are mainly radios and autopilot." Jeannie glanced out to either side. Emily was left and ahead. The 212s and the MD500 were following in loose formation behind—plenty of maneuvering room. "Try it. Just don't bump the nuclear missile launcher."

"Nice, Helitack. Real nice." He eased the control ever so slightly forward, then back. He was one of the first people she'd ever shown the controls who didn't over-correct. One of the big secrets of flying a chopper was constant small corrections. If you had to do a big cor-rection, something was really wrong, or you were over a really aggressive fire that was trying to slap you around.

"Good. You can do more than that. Don't worry, I'm still pilot-in-command. I still have control."

He wobbled them side to side. "That's how you wave at people."

Cal didn't make it a question. "Got it in one, Hotshot. Now, your feet. They work the tail rotor, changing which way you're facing. So if you shift your direction with the rotor pedals, you set up a new direction for forward flight."

Again the neatly small maneuvers. She barely had to compensate for his actions to keep them in place in the formation.

"So how do I do an autorotate landing?"

She looked at him aghast for a moment, then laughed. She couldn't help herself. He looked so innocent as he said it, like a six-year-old who was just asking to be sent to sit in a corner, and knew it.

"The way you laugh, Helitack. It's almost as good as the way you walk."

Jeannie really tried to stop the change in herself, but she couldn't stop liking him just a little more for that.

———

Cal cursed Henderson's "no camera" mandate as the flight of choppers settled to the ground. A half-dozen choppers were already parked on the tarmac that shimmered with the heat. Three lonely looking buildings were doing their best to pretend they were mirages. The thing about the choppers already parked there was that they looked military, right down to the green paint, white stars, and...machine guns mounted in the forward windows.

A half-dozen men trotted up in formation, with rifles held across their chests, to greet them.

"What the hell?"

Jeannie looked as if she was going to answer, then abruptly changed her mind and shook her head. No help there. Maybe Henderson. A guy with a golden oak leaf on his collar walked up to Henderson and Beale and shot them each a sharp salute, which they returned.

"This happen a lot at MHA?" he asked Jeannie.

"Uh, never in my experience." Yet she was very carefully not paying any particular attention to what was going on beyond the windscreen. Too carefully.

"You've really got to learn to lie better, Jeannie."

She replied with a grimace and stepped out into the heat.

Cal joined her and had to gasp to catch his breath. The air was scorching, so dry that it ached in his throat as he tried to breathe. He reached back in for a water bottle and resisted the urge to guzzle the whole thing. Screw it. He knocked back the rest of the bottle. Any hotshot knew that the best place to store water was in your body. Stay hydrated above all else.

Before he could ask her any more questions, Jeannie handed him a long strap, then climbed up on top of the chopper.

"Loop that over the end of that rotor blade sticking out front and drag it around to about four thirty. Thanks." She began working on something on the head of the rotor.

Cal walked out to the end of the rotor blade and tossed the strap up and over just as if it were a tree limb. Grabbing the two ends of the strap, he began walking in a slow circle dragging the big rotor around after him. It was surprising how easily and smoothly it moved.

"Good, good. Hold it. Right there." Jeannie tugged it into place. "Leave the strap there. In the center of the cargo bay's ceiling, you'll find a handle marked 'Gust Lock.' Pull that down until it latches. That locks the rotor in position."

Cal found the lever and pulled it down. He looked around and saw the other helicopters going through a similar process. The Bell 212s already had their two long blades folded back together over their tails. The MD500 had five blades, all small enough that the guy standing up top could do it by himself. Beale and Steve were working on the other Firehawk, while Mark continued chatting with the oak-leaf guy.

"I'm ready for you to bring the blade the rest of the way," Jeannie called down.

"You are your own mechanic? What can't you do?" He grabbed the strap and began dragging the blade back to her. Jeannie had pulled some pin, and the blade folded around without turning the rotor head this time until it overlapped the tail without turning the other blades with it. It now swung free on a sideways hinge.

"Not even close to being a mechanic. I can do basic maintenance, but Denise and her two-person service crew do all of the more complex stuff. They're off with the smokies, probably at LAX hopping a commercial flight."

"Uh-huh." Cal circled around to throw his strap over the blade on the other side and drag it around. Next he went for the front left blade, which tucked under the other two as neatly as a duck's tail feathers.

"Then what the hell are we doing on a military base?" Cal asked as he headed for the last blade, to the front right, and tossed his strap over the tip.

"Some questions"—Mark Henderson stood close beside him as if he'd been teleported in, causing Cal to jump in surprise—"are better if they aren't asked just yet. We barely know each other, Cal Jackson. We'll fix some of that on the flight."

"Uh, okay." As he walked the blade around, away from Henderson, a big jet roared down to land on the long gravel runway. It was definitely military transport with big wings off the top of the fuselage and four massive jet engines, each as big as the main body of the

Firehawk. It rolled up the runway and turned toward them before doing a neat pivot, the gravel crunching beneath the massive tires. With a final wash of hot jet exhaust that drove dust and sand painfully against Cal's exposed skin, the engines shut down, descending from full roar through high whine to rumble and finally silence.

Then the back of the plane opened, one whole section of it folding upward, and another section dropping down to form a steep ramp. At the head of the ramp, the belly of the plane appeared as a dark, yawning cavity. So fast he could barely follow it, the loadmasters were moving the five choppers up a wide ramp with miniature tractors, just a foot high, dragging the choppers while someone walked beside it with a remote control attached to his forearm.

Jeannie had to slap his hand a couple times as he instinctively reached for his cameras.

Henderson finally came up beside them, staying out of the loadmasters' way. "Australia's a long flight. You play poker?"

"Sure. Do you?" Cal shot the challenge right back.

Henderson just smiled from behind his mirrored shades. "I've been known to." Then he nodded toward the big jet currently swallowing the third chopper. "We were supposed to fly cargo next week out of LAX. We would have had some time to check each other out. However, the Ozzies have a couple hot fires and asked for international aid. The military is giving us a free ride as a part of that aid package."

"Makes sense." Cal was glad something was finally making sense this morning.

"At least that's the official story," Henderson continued.

Cal eyed him carefully, but the guy hadn't changed his stance. He just stood there, arms crossed over his chest, military stiff despite his jeans and T-shirt. He didn't miss a single thing the loadmasters were doing as they loaded his birds.

"I thought you'd be helping them. Some kind of union thing?"

"Uh-uh." Henderson shook his head. "If one of these choppers is out of place by more than a foot or two, it can totally unbalance the plane, which gives it a real tendency to crash on takeoff. You never, ever mess with a loadmaster. I'd screw with a pilot long before I'd get in the way of one of these guys."

"Got it, lesson learned. So, when do I get the unofficial story?"

Henderson pretended he hadn't heard him.

Jeannie's face revealed that she knew at least part of what Henderson was talking about. That meant she wasn't allowed to say.

Military, Australia, two former U.S. Army SOAR majors, and the old rumors about Mount Hood Aviation. MHA had supposedly purchased the CIA's old Air America equipment at the end of the Vietnam War. Further, it was said they'd also purchased the contracts to fly transport for the CIA. Nothing much was said about when that association ended, or if it ever had.

There it was. Now Cal could see the whole picture, or at least a lot more of it. MHA still flew for the CIA, on call just like their summer contract in Australia. Or was that trumped up as well?

"Is there a war on?"

Jeannie looked at them in alarm.

Henderson shrugged.

Christ, what had Cal just stepped into the middle of?

Chapter 7

"ANTE UP," HENDERSON CALLED OUT LOUD ENOUGH for Cal to hear him over the four roaring Pratt & Whitney F117 turbofan engines.

They were on the ground in Hawaii only long enough to fuel up. They were doing the twenty-hour flight straight through, with only two stops en route for fuel and fresh crews.

Once airborne again, they had gathered inside the belly of the roaring C-17 for lunch. The helicopters were crammed in, each twisted slightly so that the tail sections overlapped, strapped down so that they couldn't shift an inch in flight. He'd chatted with the loadmasters. Five helicopters crowded the bay but weighed only about a quarter of what the transport plane could carry. Apparently a C-17 could easily carry an Abrams main battle tank. He didn't know what that meant beyond really big and really heavy.

People were obviously an afterthought. Many of the fold-down seats mounted along the sides of the fuselage were blocked by the tight load. The MHA crew had clustered in a forward corner for poker. They had to be careful not to stand up too quickly because several of them had to sit on crates beneath the tail of a parked Firehawk.

At Henderson's call, the crowd shifted about. Soon, a crate of smokejumper water pumps was set up in the middle as a table in a circle of seats, some on the air-craft's side fold-downs, some made of packs. Two guys had scrounged up a life raft and sat side by side on its hard plastic shell.

Cal sized up the crowd and decided it would be an interesting game. Henderson, ex-Army major, wearing his trademark mirrored sunglasses despite the plane's dim interior, was obviously a serious opponent. His wife kissed him on top of his head, then very deliberately pulled out a paperback and moved over to the other side of the plane to find somewhere to read, her daughter asleep in one of those car seats converted into a car-rier that she took with her. Some story behind that one. Maybe she couldn't bear to watch him play.

Mickey Hamilton, one of the 212 pilots, and Vern Meany, a MD500 pilot, pulled up seats. Bruce Menotti, the other 212 pilot, bowed out.

Steve sat in and Carly sat beside him with an arm over his shoulder. They were an interesting couple themselves. Steve was some kind of drone wizard and a former lead smokejumper who walked with a distinct limp that no one paid any attention to. Carly was like Beale in some ways. Emily Beale looked like the U.S. Army recruiting poster, "Yes, our women really do look this amazing." Carly, with her light-blond hair and softer features, was obviously civilian and belonged in a Hollywood movie as the one woman to anchor some team of handsome guys doing impossible things as if they were easy.

Jeannie dropped down beside Cal. "I'd like to play. So how does this game work?"

He and Henderson shared a groan. At Henderson's

shrug, Steve turned to explain the game: pair, two pair, three of a kind, straight, and so on. He went through it all a couple of times to make sure she had the order right and explained basic play.

"You play nickel to the dollar for the first five hands," Henderson decreed. "Then you're on your own."

Jeannie nodded her willingness.

Early on, they were just getting a feel for each other. Mickey wasn't a threat. Vern was okay. Carly was a better player than Steve, often changing his bets even as he made them. Henderson was impenetrable, no way to read the man. Jeannie was just having a good time. She'd sat close enough to Cal that their legs pressed together from foot to knee and they kept bumping elbows, though they kept their cards to themselves after the second time he reminded her to keep her hand up.

By the end of five hands, Jeannie had turned two dollars into twenty, but at a twenty-to-one exchange rate, playing nickels and winning dollars, it didn't mean much more than beginner's luck. He and Henderson were about even. Carly was also up a few dollars. Vern and Mickey were looking unhappy.

By twenty hands, Vern and Mickey were tapped out. Cal and Henderson were still pretty even, and the Carly-Steve team was struggling to stay afloat. Interestingly Jeannie was still doing okay.

By thirty hands, Jeannie had swept the table.

"What the hell, Jeannie?" Henderson cried out in frustration as she raked in the final pot.

"Older brother in the Oz Air Force. I can't believe you two were dumb enough to buy the helpless woman act. Do both of yourselves a favor; don't try playing poker when you're Down Under. We're an entire nation who are descendants of Britain's worst criminals and dissidents. We gamble as easily as you breathe."

Cal burst out laughing and dragged her into his arms. He was really getting to be totally crazy about this woman filled with a hundred surprises. Despite how much of his money was now in her pockets.

———

Jeannie had one more surprise for Cal.

She waited until after the C-17's refueling stop in American Samoa. After that, people spread out air mattresses and tried to get some sleep. No matter what time they arrived in Oz, it wouldn't be their body time, so a padding of sleep should help the readjustment.

She set her own mattress up in the shadows at the rear of the plane behind her old MD500. Half a very cluttered football field away, she was well out of sight of the others. Then she fetched Cal and guided him to the rear of the plane.

"You a member of the mile-high club, Hotshot?" It was terribly forward compared to anything she'd ever done, but she didn't hesitate. When it was right…

He grinned at her. "Not yet, Helitack."

"We're flying over a mile high, more like five. Wanna join?"

His answer was to gather her in those strong arms of his and pull her so tight against him that she wondered if she'd ever breath normally again. His merest touch sent her pulse flying high. She'd used the gentle rubbing of her leg against Cal's to distract him during the poker game. Had made it subtle enough that Cal hadn't noticed, but so that Mark Henderson had, distracting him in turn by being amused at her antics. It wouldn't work a second time, which was why she'd warned them off—they were both really good. Still, she'd made a quick two hundred, well worth the effort.

But the plan had almost backfired. She'd been thoroughly distracted as well by the electric heat that never stopped between her and Cal at even the simplest contact. It was supposed to be wearing off by this point. Instead it kept finding more and denser fuel and burning hotter and hotter.

He undressed her layer by layer until she stood naked before him. She hoped that the rest of the crew were indeed sacked out. But a part of her didn't care. Even though the shadows here were deep, it was far lighter than the tent in the middle of the night. She could see his appreciation as he inspected her as thoroughly as last night, but with the added sense of sight.

Each time he moved over her body, she stripped another piece of his clothing until they were both naked in the back of the C-17's cargo bay. When he went to lay her down, she refused. Instead, she pushed his back against the MD500. He shivered as his back came in contact with the cool sheet metal.

She kept him pinned there with her body. She'd flown the same model in Australia herding cattle in the Northern Territory, spreading fertilizer in New South Wales, even carting around a marine scientist in a version with floats instead of skids as he spot-checked the health of the Great Barrier Reef. And she'd flown this exact bird for three summers and more than a year full-time with MHA before she graduated to the Firehawk.

She knew every nut and bolt of this machine. It was as close to being hers as any craft on the planet. And now that her parents lived in a small apartment on the coast rather than a sprawling cattle station in the Outback, this chopper was as close to a home as she had.

She'd never before made love to a man against or in a chopper, and there wasn't room to do so inside this one. The MD500 was so small that they flew without doors on the cockpit because there really wasn't room for two men to sit side by side if they had broad shoulders. It also improved the visibility immensely.

At the moment, what it allowed her to do was grab the door frame with one hand and pull herself tight against Cal. With one foot she stepped up onto the landing-strut footrest, then wrapped the other leg around his hips and lowered herself against him. He cupped her behind with both hands, kissing her hard.

She leaned back until only her grip on the door and his grip on her kept her from tumbling over backward. He leaned forward, capturing one of her breasts in his mouth. She felt his suckling draw right down into her insides. She flung her free arm around his shoulders to hang on.

It was too much.

Jeannie wasn't ready to be feeling this for any man. Not Cal, not anyone.

But she couldn't stop him any more than she could keep her emotions from shifting as fast as flame. No one had ever evoked so much from her. She'd always thought of her heart as burned out, but Cal kept finding embers buried deep in the ash. He didn't nurse them to life; he caused them to be reborn at full blaze.

When at last he pulled her into a kiss and plunged into her, he created some circuit of fire that flowed and cycled through her body, out through her breath into his mouth, and back in through his penetration. Even the sheath he'd put on didn't block the runaway cycle.

She tried desperately to find a way to pull herself back together. To haul herself back to her chopper. To hold on to something solid with more than one shuddering hand and a barely maintained foothold.

But she didn't find it. Couldn't do it.

By the time she came, she was long past thinking, long past caring—she was falling. Tumbling free into the sky and falling straight toward Cal Jackson.

The heat roared through her as he held her tight in his embrace.

It burned when he turned and laid her against the 500's metal skin where he'd warmed it with his own body. He finished her and himself off against the helicopter she'd flown alone so many hours into so many fiery battles.

And he had left her on the edge of weeping when he lowered her to the air mattress with an infinite tenderness and kissed her to sleep.

Chapter 8

CAL WAS BARELY CONSCIOUS AS HE WATCHED THEM UNLOAD the choppers. Even the chilly nighttime air had little effect except to make him shrug on a flannel shirt. He hadn't been able to sleep. Courtesy of the International Date Line and way too many time zones, after twenty hours in transit, it was oh-dark-thirty-something two days after they'd left California at ten a.m. It was like Thursday had never existed except in some body-numbing vibration machine. His ears still rang though the C-17's engines had cycled down more than thirty minutes earlier.

Jeannie made a lousy counterpoint to his mood, having slept nine straight. She kept bubbling over with how great it felt to be back on home soil. How much she couldn't wait to try the first Firehawks ever to enter Australia. Thanking him several times for how incredible she felt as she rushed about prepping her craft.

The customs guy who, despite the hour, welcomed them with a cheerful, "G'day, mate. Welcome to ruddy Australia, Calvin Jackson," as he stamped the passport didn't help matters in the slightest.

"I still can't believe that your parents named you for a cartoon character."

With his middle-of-the-night wit running as foul as ever, he kept his mouth shut.

No, the nuns at the orphanage had named him for

stupid St. Francis Bernard who had done nothing of much interest except be nice to a bunch of animals. When he was nineteen, Cal had renamed himself for a feisty, badass cartoon character. But he could find no way to explain his rootless past and more rootless present to this woman who spewed family with every other sentence.

She was beloved and knew it.

He was unwanted. And knew that truth just as assuredly as she knew hers. Cal was spared making any explanations when she rushed off to check in with the refueling team.

Cal moved to stand outside the circle of lights surrounding the unloading zone. The moon was low in the sky. And that was north, not south. He was in two different hemispheres than the last time he'd slept. He'd traded north for south and west for east. He didn't know which way to turn any more than he had last night.

On the flight, as Jeannie sighed happily in her sleep, Cal had dressed and watched her. There was something going on that he couldn't place. Couldn't figure out. Something that was going to make him into a stark raving lunatic if he didn't solve it soon. He wanted to lie down beside Jeannie. He wanted to wake up with her. He wanted to do that over and over again.

And it scared the shit out of him!

Cal was homeless, even more so than the bum on the street. The bum at least had a past and a place to go, even if it was a cardboard shelter. While Cal wouldn't trade his comfortable itinerant lifestyle with the street homeless for a moment, neither did he have a home, a city, or even a state to call his own. American, that was the closest label he could come up with. Mostly out West because that's where the fires were.

Cal had made that homelessness into a lifestyle since he was sixteen. He didn't need this beautiful, kind, sensual woman messing with that.

"You didn't sleep at all, did you?"

He twitched as Jeannie slid a hand around his waist.

"Not much." He almost said he didn't sleep well on planes, but it would be a lie as he always had before. And while he might not be willing to tell her the truth, he wasn't going to lie to her.

They stood a long time in companionable silence, just watching the night beyond the end of the Australian airfield. It smelled different. Dry, arid, but not with the oak and scrub grass of southern California. The air here smelled as if this was where it was born to begin with. Like standing on the ocean, but without even the salt and algae smell. Pure. Clean. And, except for some continuing service sounds back at the choppers, so quiet that his ears were ringing.

"Did I do something wrong?" Jeannie's question was as soft as the night.

"Other than being amazingly incredible, not a thing." Also truth.

"And is that such a crime?" This time he heard the pain in her voice and it nearly broke him. The last thing he wanted was to hurt this woman. Normally he didn't care all that much. If women became too clingy, then they were just asking for what they got. If they tried to trap him, well, he knew how to work his way out of those places too. Usually by leaving.

Jeannie was killing him with kindness. With an open

and generous heart. He was going to hurt both of them; that was becoming inevitable. He wished to God he could figure out how to avoid doing that.

Cal wrapped her in his arms, enjoying the way they fit together as she rested her head on his shoulder and snuggled. He breathed her in, as unique and rare as a spring bloom in the middle of the Outback.

He'd seen that once. Hundreds of miles of sandy soil covered with the occasional patchy scrub grass or rare tree. He'd been halfway "down the Alice." Somewhere between Darwin and Alice Springs over a small rise on the Stuart Highway, an acre, maybe two, had decided it was springtime. A localized rain shower, a brief rise in the water table, a bit of whimsy by Mother Nature…no idea what caused it. All he knew was that in a land of endless beige and brown beneath a shockingly blue sky, he happened upon a thousand colors of flowers blooming as if there was no tomorrow.

And there wouldn't be here. Such blooms are very short lived in the Outback—take advantage of the water, duck back under the soil. He'd stopped his rented motorcycle and just watched it for hours. Oddly, when he checked later, he hadn't taken a single photograph of the spectacle.

Yet now it revisited him years later. It came back as a woman who bloomed in his arms. At least in this moment, in this place, she belonged there. Maybe if he simply accepted that it wouldn't last, he could enjoy what it was now.

And if it did last?

He stared out at the fathomless dark lit by a hundred thousand stars and the moon on the wrong side of the sky.

He'd always been so comfortable with the unknown, the only common thread that traced through his whole life. This time, the discomfort made him shiver despite the balmy night and the warm woman in his arms.

Chapter 9

"WHERE THE HELL ARE WE, ANYWAY?" CAL ASKED WHEN Henderson strolled up beside him.

Jeannie had gone off with Beale somewhere. Probably some pilots' meeting. The 212 guys and Vern were missing as well.

"Australia. Exactly per plan. I need a plane. You coming or not?"

Cal looked around. Just the two of them left. Not even the C-17 crew. After unloading, they'd fired up their plane and roared off into the night. The airstrip itself was dead quiet.

"What the hell?" He kicked at the soil. There was something familiar about it. He pulled his tablet out of his camera bag, tapped it awake, and turned it around to shine on the dirt. Red. Dry. Almost dusty.

"Your prognosis, doctor?" Henderson was still waiting for him.

"Nothing better to do; I'll go with you." He'd only seen this kind of dirt in one part of Australia. They were in the Red Centre, the geographical center of the country and the heart of the Outback. The only airports big enough for a C-17 in the Red Centre were Alice Springs or the big tourist strip out at Uluru Rock. Both were commercial airports with plenty of traffic. Well, he was good and stuck for now, but in the morning—whenever that was—he could catch a flight out and be gone.

After all, he wasn't stupid. He could see where this whole thing with Jeannie was heading. He hadn't ever been this far down Relationship Road, but neither was he ever stupid about women. While Calvin Jackson was old enough and hormone-laden enough to no longer think that girls had cooties, he certainly knew they had talons. And who the hell was he kidding with a woman like Jeannie Clark? If he ended up with someone, it would probably be an undereducated tough bitch to match his own undereducated tough bastard.

He checked his watch. Ten a.m. In Santa Barbara. Okay, that was a useless piece of information. Midnight here? Maybe? Long time until any flight out was all that meant. His brain just wasn't working. He'd been awake a day and a night, felt like two.

"Where are you going to find a plane at this hour?"

"Where's your faith, Cal Jackson?" Henderson headed toward a dark hangar area.

"What, the good Lord will provide?" Cal fell in beside him for lack of anything better to do until the sun rose and the airport started back up.

"If the good Lord starts dispensing aircraft, I'll climb back aboard a DAP Hawk."

"DAP?" Cal hadn't heard of that one.

"Direct Action Penetrator. It started out as a Black Hawk, before we started messing with it. Nastiest helicopter ever launched into the night sky by any army."

"You miss SOAR?"

"How about I take away your cameras, then tell me how you'll feel after a year?" Henderson's easy tone had suddenly turned into a snarl. For all his easy manners and pleasant attitude, the man did have a sore spot. Cal wondered if anyone else knew about it. Even his wife.

"Then why?" They crossed the airfield's centerline, no runway lights at this hour. Not even a need to glance for incoming traffic. Just the moon glowing off the center stripe for a long way in either direction.

"Little girl comes along, it changes your world. You'll see someday."

"Not a snowball's chance in—"

"—the Outback?" Henderson cut him off.

"Yeah. That's about right."

They made it to the hangars in silence. Henderson approached a small twin-engine aircraft parked out on the apron. An envelope with Henderson's name on it had been taped to the pilot's window. He peeled it, pulled out a key, and unlocked the small plane. Security wasn't much of an issue when there was no one around. With a flashlight he circled the airplane to inspect it, signaled for Cal to climb aboard, and started the engines.

Cal let himself drift, floating along. No doubt the lack of sleep explained his lack of willpower. No questions. No real thoughts. Just along for the ride. He tried, but he really couldn't picture himself with a kid or giving up everything he wanted to keep that boy or girl safe. What about his life? Definitely not a snowball's chance.

As the plane rotated up into flight off the dark runway, Henderson spoke quietly, so softly that Cal didn't know if he was supposed to respond or even hear it.

"I thought the same thing just a few years back."

Cal knew his life was changing faster than it had since he'd run away to fight fire and changed his name, but some things weren't going to change anytime soon.

He'd definitely catch the next flight out in the morning, didn't matter where it was going as long as it was away.

Henderson climbed and turned west.

Or was that east because they were south of the equator? No, that was stupid. Cal must be even more tired than he thought. If he dozed, he wasn't aware of it. After some indeterminate amount of time, Henderson pointed.

"Your analysis, Mr. Jackson."

A broad vista before the plane was filled with the blood-orange of a fire at night. From their altitude he could see the extent of the fire. At least some of the extent; it stretched out of sight to both the right and left despite their altitude.

Australian Outback bushfires were different from American fires, the fuels more spread out. Even the big savannah fires didn't act this way. There were some dense forests that existed to the south and the tropical jungle in Queensland along the coast, but here it was primarily grassland with a few trees. That meant a very thin front from the leading to the trailing edge of the burn. It looked as if some drunk had drawn a wandering line of orange flame across the black night. The front wasn't deep, but it had sprawled very wide.

"What are our assets?"

"Six local engine crews, five helicopters, and Akbar's team, which should be arriving in another couple hours."

"That's a laugh." The local crews might total fifty or a hundred guys, mostly trained in structure fires. Akbar the Great and his dozen smokies, and the five choppers. "Anything else?"

"There's a broken-down road grader for cutting firebreaks, but no one's been able to get it started. We'll let Denise's team loose on it tomorrow. Even if they can fix it, we're still miles from the nearest track. Attack begins in three hours."

Henderson turned to fly up the line. As he did so, Cal could see that the fire was moving.

"Is getting the hell out of its way an option?"

"Alice Springs is about a two-day burn away at the current rate of damage. Most of the Aussies' assets are tied up in trying to save Canberra and someplace called Ferntree Gully."

"That'll definitely keep them busy. National capital and a suburb of Melbourne."

"How did you know that last one?"

Cal smiled at the memory. "A nice blond Sheila took me home for a while at the end of the fire season a half-dozen years back. She lived up there in the hills, but there's a lot of population around about. It'll be as ugly as what we were just doing in Santa Barbara." That wiped away any smile he'd been feeling. Susy had been fun. She'd been disappointed when he left, but her emails hadn't followed him for long. Some homegrown boy swept her up. No real surprise—she'd been cute, sweet, and cuddly.

Which left him thinking of Jeannie. Was that how he'd describe her years from now? Not a chance. Splendid, challenging, stunning—much better descriptors for her. He wished he didn't feel the twinge when he thought about her in the past tense. Well, he'd worry about that after he flew out tomorrow. Or later today?

The fire line continued to snake ahead for a long way. At least there wasn't much out here. Not even many cattle stations, as they called their ranches. There might be three or four in fifty miles. Fodder was thin out here in the Red Centre, so their cattle would roam far and wide, some of them birthing, living, and dying without ever seeing a human. But the fire wouldn't let them go.

"Cut the fire into three or four parts," Cal decided. "Assign a pair of choppers to each of the outer ones until we kill them."

"But then we're fighting three fires," Henderson protested.

"If the winds kick in, these can move at fifty klicks, thirty miles per hour. We need to cut them up, narrow each side part out of existence. Then, if we have to, we can steer the narrower damage path of the central fire away from people. Aim them into dry arroyos or cliff faces if we can line any up."

Henderson flew for a while, barely resting a fingertip on the wheel to keep them straight and level over the fire. How different from his attack helicopter or even Jeannie's far simpler Firehawk?

Behind the blaze, the black stretched away as dark as charcoal except in a few spots where scattered trees still burned. Mulga trees, some part of Cal's brain recalled. They weren't just burning, they were being turned into ash as well. This wasn't your average bushfire; it was burning too hot. Normally a tree would catch fire, but it wasn't an intense heat, at least not for the tree. The fire would scorch off dead limbs, old leaves, and some bark and the tree would be back next year. These fires were burning so hot that there'd be nothing left of the trees when the bushfire was done.

"Go lower," Cal instructed Henderson. "Hit your landing light and fly in front of the fire line."

Henderson swung down until they were close enough for the bright light under the wing to light the ground. Thick clumps of brown grass came into view. It was tight, closer together than over much of the Outback that he'd crossed. He had enough pictures of this type of vegetation from his last trip to Australia. He felt a shiver of cold up his spine. He remembered the Black Saturday bushfires and really wished he didn't.

Then he thought of Jeannie. This was going to be a tough fire for her. She'd lost something in that fire. A house, maybe even a friend? The similarities would get to her.

He cursed, then signaled to Henderson to take them back.

Cal wouldn't be flying out to anywhere in the morning. He couldn't leave the woman who'd saved his life to face this alone.

***

"Buffelgrass." Cal purposely hadn't looked directly at Jeannie when he said it, but he was absolutely right. She flinched as surely as if he'd kicked her feet out from under her again.

"What's that?" Akbar asked. The rest of their crew and gear had arrived just before sunrise on the first commercial flight into Alice Springs.

Denise had her team going over the choppers to make sure that the fliers hadn't screwed them up without her there to oversee them. She'd already been en route to LAX when the plans had changed sending the choppers into the Mojave Desert to get transport to the Australian desert. Apparently that had made her very nervous. She'd muttered something about never trusting a pilot with anything more complex than a joystick and headed off.

The rest of the teams had assembled for an immediate briefing right out on the tarmac. They sat in a circle amid the helicopters, some of the team sitting on gear, others on the ground, a few standing. Jeannie had been in a low squat that looked as uncomfortable as could be, except she looked very relaxed in that position, feet spread wide and flat on the ground, her butt a few inches in the air.

At his mention of what was fueling the fire, she sat down hard.

Cal kept his silence, knowing that if Jeannie had to explain the significance of buffelgrass to the group, that would help her not dwell on whatever memories were fighting for her attention. Others noticed where his focus was, and several turned to face her. When she finally caught on that others were waiting on her, a brief flicker of annoyance crossed her features. But then she offered Cal a nod of deep chagrin and stood. A quick scan, and she pointed at a waist-high patch of dead grass growing off the edge of the paved parking area they'd taken over.

"That's buffelgrass. Doesn't look like much, does it? They seeded much of central Australia with it decades ago. It does well in arid environments and is an excellent dust suppressant as it grows densely and remains in place even after seasonal plants die off. Normally it wouldn't be so bad, but Oz had unusually heavy rains last year and the grass really grew, making for much more fuel per hectare than typical. It also burns far hotter than native species, especially because of the denser growth. So, a buffelgrass fire kills everything in its path: trees, cattle…homes."

Cal spotted the brief pinch across her features. He doubted anyone else would see it, but he already knew her expressions so well that they were like a storybook for him. She'd lost her home? Seemed likely. More than four thousand buildings had gone up, along with a million acres of grasslands, as four hundred separate fires burned on that dark February day.

"It will behave like a denser American forest. We can't just slow it down so that it loses momentum and peters out like most bushfires this deep in the Outback. Instead we'll have to really kill it dead. And anything that gets ahead of us will start fanning back out. The material is dense enough to reach sideways to start new fires as well as expanding downwind."

"Any suggestions on how we do that?" one of the other pilots asked.

Cal looked at Akbar, who shrugged. They'd had a moment where Cal had described the fire to the lead smokie and to Carly. Steve had launched his drone after the mandatory sleep period that Beale had set for all active crew. Cal figured that made him chopped meat, because he'd gone off flying around with Henderson instead of sleeping. But the best fire behavior analyst in the business and a lead smokejumper had come up with no better plan than Cal's. Which told him they were really screwed. So they were leaving it to him to explain and be the bearer of bad news.

"We're dealing with a five-mile-wide front right now. So—"

"Eight kilometers, mate," one of the smokies called out. "We're Down Under after all."

"Chas, you're from Poughkeepsie, New York. Shut up," one of his team razzed him.

"So," Cal continued, "we're going to chop it into three chunks, a *kilometer* on either side, and let the center keep burning. Vern in the MD500 will keep hitting the sides of the central head. Don't try to stop it. Just don't let it get any wider. We'll put a Firehawk and a 212 on either side-head along with three engine crews each. Akbar, your team will embed a two-man stick with each local engine. The goal is to choke the two side-heads off. Then, we leave a mop-up engine on either head and cut off the next two kilometer-wide chunks. We keep chasing it inward from the sides."

"Here's the kicker," Henderson stepped in. "We have to kill two kilometer-wide fires every four hours, because if it takes longer, the central head will overrun downtown Alice Springs and we'll have twenty thousand people living in the desert and a bunch of smoke eaters looking to dodge a lynch mob. We clear?"

Bruce from one of the Huey 212s raised a hand. "Where are you setting up the retardant mixer?"

"You're Down Under. The United States is still pretty much the only country to use retardant. So, we use water. We've at least got foam, but no retardant."

"Water? Where do we get that? This place is so dry, it hurts to breathe. Is there a river we can dip?"

Jeannie snorted out a laugh.

"You wanna break the bad news, Jeannie?" Cal asked her.

"Sure. The Todd River cuts right along the eastern

edge of town. Its tributaries are up in the hills to the north and south. You missed the annual Henley-on-Todd Regatta by a few months. It's held on the riverbed itself and is the world's only dry regatta. The boat race has been canceled just once in the last fifty years."

Many of the crew were looking at her like she was nuts. Someone fell for the trap and asked, "Why'd they cancel it?"

"Flooding. There was actually water in the Todd River and they had to cancel. Of course, the race is held in August in the middle of the Dry, that's the arid winter season, and people wear their boats rather than ride in them. They run down the coarse sand. There are also sand skiing, mini- and maxi-yacht races, the "Tour de Todd" race in human-sized hamster wheels, and even a battleship war—quite majestic. Whole ships built on four-wheel drives complete with fireworks cannons. As this is Oz, they're often blind drunk while doing this. It's a great party."

She had them laughing and joking about entering a papier-mâché helicopter next year to show those yachties how it was done. Cal watched as she let them joke but not run it into the ground before she cut them off. She was good with groups, yet another professional skill she had hidden up her sleeve.

"This is November and the Wet is now here. They typically get as much as thirty millimeters, just over an inch, of rainfall…total for the month. Don't be fooled, though. It will come as a single dump and create flash floods that will kill more than their fair share of tourists who think it's funny to go wading in the river as it actually fills in."

Cal and Henderson had scoped it out from the air on

their way back from the fire and then talked to the local fire crews, so Cal had already heard the background. He took back over.

"You scrounge from swimming pools, just like in Santa Barbara, or you head out to the big pond in the middle of the golf course to the east of town. It's pretty shallow, but they've promised to keep their well pumps running. We're trying to put together some water trucks, but the tracks out to the fire are mostly deep sand and need special vehicles to navigate them. In Oz there aren't sealed roads once you're off the Stuart Highway. There are just tracks across the Outback."

Henderson slapped his hands together. "Sun's up in five, in the air in ten."

"What about the half-hour hold?" Vern called out, already turning for his small chopper.

"One, that's U.S. Forestry rules. Two, we're in the desert—sunrise to full light is about a three-minute transition. Stay hydrated, people. Let's show them what MHA can do!" And Henderson had them all on the run.

"You get any sleep yet, Cal?" Jeannie settled into the chopper, glad to have Cal climbing aboard beside her. She hadn't slept much after they landed. Partly because she'd slept so well on the flight, but also because each time she'd cracked open an eye, Cal hadn't been sitting there watching her. It had been weird at first on the flight, but she'd come to like the idea of him watching over her. As unlikely a guardian angel as he might be, she wouldn't be lodging any complaints with whatever forces had made their paths cross.

And she so loved being back in the Outback. Her family home and cattle station had been down in New South Wales, which smelled more of eucalyptus. They'd frequently traveled to the Red Centre, which smelled of its rusty-red, iron-rich soil, and she'd also worked for several more years as a flying taxi out of the Top End of the Northern Territories, where the ocean smell pervaded for hundreds of kilometers inland. When she was here, a part of her that she'd never felt tense up simply relaxed. The way Cal had held her as they'd watched the night had been such a sharing of that feeling. No other man she'd been with had understood so easily.

"Cal?" He still hadn't responded.

"Huh, oh. No. Last sleep I had was at the Santa Barbara helibase."

She aimed a smile at him. "Not sure I let you sleep all that much, then."

Again no response, which hurt. Well, if she'd been awake for two days, she'd be out of it too. She'd just give the guy some slack.

One of the things she found interesting was that they'd had some very skilled firefighters in this morning's meeting, so why had Cal done the briefing? And the plan had apparently been his. Sure, he'd seen the fire, and neither Akbar nor Carly had. But they'd listened to him. And the more she listened, the more impressed she became. He'd understood the interplay of the fire and the unique environment of this section of the Australian Outback. He also understood how to communicate that to firefighters in a way that made them feel secure in understanding what they were about to face.

"Do you have any idea how good you are?" She tried to tease a response out of him, but it was no less the truth for her doing so.

"That's the sex talking, and thanks, it was fun."

Fun? She wanted to smack the man again. If her hand wasn't busy on the collective, she might just have gone for the satisfaction of another left to the jaw. Their love-making had been way more than fun. And he'd missed the point.

"No. I was talking about your fire assessment."

"You haven't even seen it yet."

"Cal! You're avoiding the goddamn issue here. MHA has all of these amazing resources, and you were the one they were listening to."

He shook his head like a bull coming awake. He studied her silently for several minutes while his mind churned at something.

Finally he made a grunt and faced forward again.

Next time they were on the ground, she'd have to beat a response out of him.

They'd taken off with a full load from the airport's pumps. They weren't going to provide anywhere near the turnaround time they'd need, almost three minutes a load. Even with a fifteen-minute round-trip, they'd lose a load an hour to such slow pumping to fill the chopper's belly tanks. They were going to be dipping water all day at forty seconds a load.

"This is the vasty nothingness," she observed as they flew over the rolling hills along the bed of the dry Todd River.

Cal still didn't respond. Must not be a *Firefly* fan, yet. She'd have to take care of that soon. Another newbie to abduct into the browncoat fandom — she could hardly wait. How easy it was to picture being curled up beside him, sharing a pizza and DVD. Almost too easy, as if they'd been together for months rather than days. Strange, that wasn't like her at all, not that she was complaining.

For now, she'd focus on the task at hand and make sure to keep her temper until the man had some sleep.

They definitely needed dip tanks. As she followed Henderson's directions to the northeast, she could see that no one would be setting a tank out here any time soon. The nearest track lay well north of the riverbed, and she couldn't spot anything to the south.

No question about where they were headed, though. The line of black and gray smoke rose like a vertical wall to the east. A line of flame dozens of feet high rose from the soil like a shield wall around an ancient city. Except this one was on the move and killing everything in its path.

She was assigned the southern edge of the fire, and she hit it and hit it hard. Bruce in his Huey came in tight behind her. She spun to face the fire and see what they'd done. They'd punched a twenty-meter hole in the fire line to cut it off from the centerline, which started closing even as she watched.

"Damn!" Cal's soft curse echoed her own feelings.

It was going to be a really long day.

After the first run, TJ, Chutes, and Akbar had the smokies organized and had put together a ground plan. The engines were already headed out toward the fire, but with no roads, it would take them hours to arrive. So, she and Emily loaded up six smokies each, along with all of their gear. Almost all. They wouldn't need their parachutes, and there was nowhere for them to dip water with their portable pumps and inch-and-a-half hoses.

Akbar and Two-Tall Tim looked distinctly unhappy about that last, but no one had a better answer. She flew out and, after giving them a visual of the blaze, dropped them about three klicks ahead of the fire where a ridge climbed across the path of the southern head. Akbar had wanted to go for a nearer drop site, but Cal had warned him off. The fire would be moving too fast to create a firebreak any closer to the blaze.

Before she was even back aloft, they had the chain saws running. By the time Jeannie and Cal were back with the first load of water, she could already see a line of felled trees along the back of the ridge. She left them to it and returned her attention to the fire itself. Their job was to make a break that the fire couldn't cross. Her and Bruce's job was to punch it down hard enough that the sucker would actually die against the smokies' firebreak.

The fire knew someone was after it, and it fought back. When they punched a gap, a falling mulga tree would reignite the black and start a new expansion of the front. She'd lay down a thousand gallons of water with foam along the top edge of a wide gully, and the fire would leap straight over to the opposite bank as if the twenty-meter gully wasn't even there. She'd had to go back to the airport to refuel after three hours before they even broke the back of their one head. It was small comfort that Emily and Mickey Hamilton were having little better luck on their own battle to the north.

By the time she made it back to the blaze, it was hard against the ridge. The three engine crews for their side of the fire had arrived to reinforce the smokies, but they wisely had all of their engines turned around and aimed west just in case this didn't work out and they had to run for it. They each had a half-dozen hose lines out.

"Steve must be sending down his drone images to them as well." Cal pointed down at the defensive positions.

"How can you tell?"

"Look at how they're arranged. Just about perfectly for what's coming at them."

Jeannie looked again, but obviously Cal was seeing something that she couldn't. Of course, a decade as a hotshot versus her half-dozen seasons flying helitanker gave them different views of what was happening.

"Just don't let that north edge get around the ridge."

"That would be bad?"

"That," Cal acknowledged, "would be really bad."

Jeannie punched it down with a thousand gallons of water and foam, and headed back for another load.

Impossibly, Cal had felt himself come awake as they continued to fly, due to the challenge of the fire, the adrenaline that surged as he tried to second-guess what was happening.

Henderson was good. His advice from seven thousand feet above in the twin-engine Incident Commander Air position was solid. Cal could start to see where his tactics were rooted. Henderson was sneaky, sliding his helitanker assets sideways, as if to catch the fire unaware. He'd often hit the hottest spots first.

That worked some of the time. But unlike an entrenched enemy, if you killed off the stronghold of the fire, it still had plenty of life out in its limbs and it could rebuild the central stronghold quickly.

Cal began calling advice up to Henderson about how to pinch the fire, squeeze it hard. The center didn't burn hotter; it couldn't. There was only so hot a flame could burn, and there was only so much fuel available to feed the fire at any one place. By flanking it from the sides, they forced the fire to slowly cave inward.

Over the next couple hours, Henderson's tactics shifted. He began incorporating Cal's plans as often as not in his initial instructions. Damn, but the man learned quickly. He must have been a hell of an amazing commander when he was flying military.

In the end it took seven hours, but they killed off the first two heads. The main fire was still on the move, still driving toward Alice Springs. Perhaps unaware that it was a quarter narrower than it had been.

"I bet the fire engines on the ground are getting low on water."

Jeannie made a quick call on the ground frequency and verified they were.

"How the hell did you know that, Hotshot?" She turned the Firehawk back for a refill.

"Drove an engine for part of a couple of seasons."

"Thought you couldn't drive a car."

"Highways scare me to death. People are crazy. But I'm pretty good at getting a wilderness engine where it needs to go."

Jeannie looked at him as if he'd lost his mind.

"What?"

She shook her head and focused on the run back for water. This time, rather than dumping on the fire, she moved to each engine. While she hovered, they hooked up a hose and filled their fifteen-hundred-liter onboard tanks. One chopper load just about equaled three wildfire engines. A quick call to Emily, and the senior pilot set off to do the same for her ground crews.

As they returned once more to the golf course pond, he asked again, "What were you going to say earlier?"

She brought them down low over the water, lowering her snorkel before replying with a shrug.

"I'm still trying to find something you aren't good at, Hotshot."

Cal watched the gauge as the tank filled. No one ever saw him as competent before. A good man on a fire crew, sure. But not as broadly skilled as Jeannie appeared to believe he was. He tried to figure out how to tell her he wasn't even clos—a loud *thunk!* reverberated through the chopper.

"Damn it!" Jeannie swore.

"What the hell was that? Are we going down?" Cal studied the console, but didn't see any flashing red lights or hear any alarms or whatever helicopters did before they fell out of the sky.

"Golfers!"

Another loud bang elicited another curse from Jeannie.

"They're drunk enough to think that pinging a chopper is fun. They're going to dent my nice finish. That'll piss off me, Henderson, and Denise in that order. No damned way we'll ever pin down these assholes, either."

Cal stared aghast straight ahead where Jeannie indicated a foursome with a nod of her head. Four guys were lined up at a nearby tee with the clubs out. They all cocked their clubs ready to strike the balls.

"Move, Jeannie! Now!" He flipped open the window and snapped a shot with his long lens.

She flipped off the pump and drove forward and up.

Cal glanced down as all four balls passed low or to the side. Barely. The chopper had little speed yet, especially with a full load of water in her belly. He thought for a second, waited three more, then hit the dump switch on his own cyclic, careful not to jar the controls.

"What the hell, Cal?"

"Oops. Let's turn and look." He flipped over to video mode and concentrated on his viewfinder.

Jeannie spun them around. Cal sighted and caught the video as the last of the water was still pounding down upon the golfers. In this mode he also captured a high-res image every second on top of the video. The tee was drenched and wouldn't be usable for hours. The two golf carts had tumbled down into a sand trap. They'd be there for a while.

"Gee. I sure hope they signed the extra insurance clause for those." He flipped off the video and kept snapping stills.

Golf bags and clubs were scattered everywhere. The golfers themselves huddled on the ground, their heads still covered in case more retribution was going to fall from the skies. With the telephoto he even caught their drowned-fish looks.

"Uh…" Jeannie apparently didn't know what to say.

"I guess I must have hit something with my camera.

I'm so clumsy sometimes. You'll have to reload. I'm really sorry about that."

Then Jeannie unleashed one of those radiant smiles at him that made him glad to be alive and in her presence. Far better than any fire-based adrenaline response. She made him feel good and worthy until his body was humming with it.

"Right. Watch yourself next time," she offered drily as they circled back to the pond for another load of water. No golf balls were pinged at them this time.

Cal pulled out his tablet computer and started working.

"What's up?" Jeannie got her snorkel back into the pond, kicked on the pumps, and began refilling the belly tank.

"I'll show you at lunch."

Some days, Cal admitted to himself, were good days. And others, like today, were really good days.

Chapter 10

THEY SETTLED BACK AT ALICE SPRINGS AIRPORT FOR their second load of fuel for the Firehawk and their first load of food for the fliers. They'd killed the first head and they had an attack plan for the next kilometer-wide chunk.

Jeannie had once again airlifted Akbar's crew well ahead of the fire to their next planned firebreak. Two of the engines would follow as fast as the terrain allowed. One remained behind to explore the black, where the fire had burned, and kill off any hot spots. Already Steve was calling in sightings of flare-ups and hidden coals for them to douse. His drone's infrared camera uncovered areas of high heat, even those hiding beneath the surface debris. It was brutal work, much of it done by individual firefighters walking the tortured land with a Pulaski and a five-gallon water tank on their backs, breathing in the black charcoal dust as they hunted down the last of the fire in the brutal summer heat.

Back at camp, Cal was fooling with his tablet some more, just as he had been for the last several flights back and forth. She'd kept glancing over as they flew. The man was practically chortling at whatever he was doing, but refused to explain when she asked again. She wasn't even sure he heard her.

On the ground, the temperature had soared into the mid-thirties, about a hundred Fahrenheit. The air was so dry that no matter how much water she drank, she was still thirsty. Over the last year in America, her body had adapted to the much moister American air, especially at MHA's home base in Oregon.

Several of the crew started for the air-conditioned terminal, but she warned them off. It was a sure way to get a chill and the shakes when you returned to the heat. They kept it cold for the tourists. Any self-respecting Aussie stayed put in the Alice. If you had to leave, you took the bus, because no one should be in such a damned hurry all the time that you had to pay the serious tariff to fly to the Red Centre.

So, the crews all ended up in the back of a hangar where the cool concrete made the air tolerable and cut the sweat down to merely irritating. Denise's service team hit the choppers. The three of them could do more in thirty minutes than most could do in an afternoon. Once again she was struck by the exceptional people MHA attracted.

Speaking of which, Jeannie glanced over to see Cal send something on his email before he tossed his tablet down in front of her roast beef and Vegemite sandwich. So good to be back with the tastes of home.

It was an article.

"Just sent it off to the *Alice Springs News*."

Jeannie looked down at the title.

"Subpar golfers need nappies changed!" And subtitle, "Dumbest golfers on planet attack firefighters! Would you date these wankers?" She could think of several other things to call them, but most of them wouldn't be publishable, and the play between the Ozzie slang for dickhead, "wanker," and golfing was really good.

The first photo was an MHA chopper looking min-
iscule before a towering flame, representing the valiant
flight into the fray against the monstrous foe. The cap-
tion noted it was from a recent fire in California before
they had rushed halfway around the globe to aid in
saving Alice Springs. In the next photo, all of the golfers were lined up, finishing their backswings in unison,
their faces clear as day. Then a brilliant shot of the havoc
wreaked by the deluge Cal had dropped on their heads.
The final was a shot of four of the five MHA choppers
rising in unison into the dawn light that was unmistak-
ably in the Red Centre to anyone who knew it. He must
have taken the shot this morning.

Jeannie started reading the article and almost snorted
her sandwich. Good thing she hadn't been drinking a
soda or something. Cal had written a straight-toned
article attempting to assess the intellectual capabilities
of each golfer based on his desire to foment an international crisis by a direct ballistic assault against civilians
trying to save the Alice Springs from burning to a crisp.
The extravagant, even inflammatory wording contrasted
hilariously with the dry tone.

Cal went on at length discussing the golfers' lack of
skill, deeply critiquing each of their forms based on the
photo and obviously questioning their manhood without
quite saying so, making it all the worse. He'd made it
completely clear that golf and "wanking" were the only
two satisfactions these blokes would ever find. He didn't
quite say "wanking themselves off in a dark closet," but
he cleverly implied it.

"I also sent it to all of the pubs who list their email
addresses in Alice Springs. Might have accidentally cc'd

a buddy at Reuters International News while I was at it. Maybe I posted a bit of video on YouTube, Vimeo, and a few others. I don't really remember."

They'd be laughingstocks. Cal couldn't have written it more perfectly to make every Ozzie love it. These men would never live down having their faces plastered on every bar mirror in the Red Centre. There wasn't a bar in the area that would ever serve them. She knew the people of Oz. The men would have to leave the country to find a beer. This story would definitely go viral.

"Do you think it's too much?" Cal looked all innocent as he stole some of her chips.

"It's bloody brilliant. Good onya!"

Cal simply smiled and reached for another chip, changing his mind when she stabbed a fork hard enough into the wooden table to stick not two inches from his fingertips.

After lunch, the day began to drag. The heat was brutal, the fire tenacious. The distances from water supply to fire line were shrinking at an alarming rate. They cut off two more segments, leaving a single engine to clean up each one. The rearmost engine moved forward to bolster the flagging energy of the team at the fire's leading edge.

To help keep her focus and her edge, Jeannie started teaching Cal how to fly. Showing him which instruments to watch and which to ignore. Even configuring one of his screens so that it only showed the few primary elements he'd need: artificial horizon, heading, altitude, and the engine's health and usage monitoring system. He laughed that wonderful laugh of his when she explained it was abbreviated as HUMS. To help pass the time, he began composing a HUMS song that sounded suspiciously like a hummed Beatles' tune. Once he had some idea of those instruments, she added fuel usage rate and tanking controls.

The ease with which he picked it up told her that in addition to being a natural, he must be even smarter than she'd thought. She rarely had to repeat an explanation, and his touch had remained just as gentle as the first time he'd gingerly tried the controls. By mid-afternoon, he could handle straight-and-level flight and simple turns. As end of day approached, she let him do one of the dump runs. Not that he wasn't following every word and instruction she fed to him, but there was still something about how a chopper felt when you were doing it yourself.

They killed the second head right before sunset.

"We have to move better and faster tomorrow, or by end of day we're going to start losing parts of the town." Jeannie looked in exasperation at the wide fire front still traveling westward.

—⁓—

Cal stared out at the fire and the sun almost kissing the western horizon. They couldn't see Alice Springs yet, but it wasn't far enough over the horizon to be safe. Their successive runs for water had been growing shorter and shorter with each passing hour.

"One more run, then I'm grounded," Jeannie practically wailed.

Her voice tore at him. She'd kept it inside all day. He could tell that by how much more aggressively she flew this fire than Santa Barbara. Not faster or more efficiently; he wasn't sure that was even possible, she was so damned good. No, she flew this fire angrier. Her dumps were tightly done, not a single second wasted.

Was she even aware of the emotions radiating from her body? He'd bet not. She'd think she was simply flying at the fire: calm, professional, cool. The truth was: outwardly calm, absolutely professional, and no hint of cool anywhere in sight. She burned with the need to kill this thing. It was so deeply personal that she didn't even see it.

The odd thing that struck Cal was that she cared so deeply about the loss. Yet another vast difference between them. She had a past to lose, and its loss had eaten at her. He'd never had a past worth keeping—and what had that done to him? How was he revealing that without being aware?

The loss of a single home would wound her here, far more than a dozen losses had in Santa Barbara. If it was in his capacity to avoid that, he'd find it.

On the last run out, after she'd dumped her load of water and foam, he had her set the chopper down near Akbar's crew. He grabbed his personal radio, his hard hat, and a Pulaski. Then, after a moment's consideration, he clipped his camera bag on the seat that had become his, right in plain view beside Jeannie.

"Go."

"Cal, no!"

"Go!" he shouted at her.

When she still didn't move, he did about the stupidest thing he could think of for a man who was supposed to be on an outbound flight a dozen hours ago. He stalked around the nose of the chopper, wrenched open her door, grabbed her head with both hands, and kissed her hard and long. If he was going to be supremely stupid tonight, if this was going to be his last act on earth, he wanted the taste of Jeannie Clark on his lips.

The woman was like a dose of supercharger on a racing engine. When she moaned, he was half tempted to drag her from the chopper and see just what they could both do, the fire be damned. Instead, he brushed his thumb down her cheek and whispered softly, "Trust me, Helitack. Now go."

He latched her door.

She went.

Cal watched her aloft until she caught the light of the setting sun a hundred meters up, making her Firehawk glow. Rather than watching her fly off into the distance like some lovelorn mooncalf, he dialed Henderson's direct frequency.

"Henderson, Cal here. I've got a stupid idea. You want to do some night flying in a chopper?"

"I'm not certified for night drops, and Emily has to get some rest. All our helitacks need the legally mandated rest. They're totally jet-lagged."

"Just need you to fly, not drop."

There was an eagerness in the man's voice when he continued, "Keep talking."

Six wildfire engines, twelve smokies, one helicopter, and a dumb-ass, sleep-deprived, overzealous, ex-hotshot photographer too stupid to keep his mouth shut. And he'd hung up his cameras. In a woman's chopper! He wasn't just losing it; he'd gone and totally screwed himself up over a woman. Some form of insanity had overcome him, one he certainly didn't recognize. That had been Cal's assessment of their situation when he'd climbed off Jeannie's Firehawk, and that was his assessment now as the first hint of pink sunrise graced the horizon.

But through the night, they'd pulled off a friggin' miracle. Henderson had taken his wife's helicopter aloft. The entire force had positioned itself on the south side of the fire. Foot by foot they fought the battle, letting the flames burn north or west, but never south.

Slowly, they gained on the fire by cutting down trees. Henderson spent part of the night circling back to keep the wildfire engines charged with water. But most of the time, he was dangling a long lead line, which they used to haul the cut trees outside of the fire's damage path, slowly robbing it of fresh fuel.

They'd spooked several mobs of 'roos that exploded abruptly out of the night in giant bounds, then disappeared westward. Panicked cattle trotted by and, every now and then, the sharp smell of burning meat filled the night air. They'd take a quick head count to make sure every person in the ground crew was still accounted for. They were. The smell was some poor critter who didn't make it out ahead of the flame.

When at last they found a particularly long and stout tree trunk, Cal hooked a double line to either end and had Henderson drag it across the ground, tearing up great tufts of the dead grass, which were hastily dragged aside.

Akbar flogged his team, as did the local fire chief.

As the night deepened and they drew nearer to Alice

Springs, local residents in their SUVs started showing up. They brought food, water, and good cheer. They were quickly recruited to drag off the smaller trees.

The teams' south line pinched the main blaze. Trapped it and forced it to turn north. Steve kept the drone aloft and fed Cal information throughout the night. It was going to be close, so damned close.

Cal's face was sore from the heat baking his skin dry. His back and shoulders hadn't stung like this in ages, zinging with lactic acid buildup from cutting apart grass clumps with his Pulaski, breaking the root ball into manageable pieces, and dragging it outside the fire's path.

The engine crews soaked the fire's flank, driving it ever northward.

As day broke, they could see the houses of Alice Springs. The teams were practically in the backyards. They had walked five miles in the night, fighting every single step of the way.

The farthest north cattle station—a half-finished geodesic dome, a large barn and main building, and a whole jumble of old cars in varying states of decay—lay right in the fire's eye when Jeannie roared back into the sky.

Like an avenging demon of war, she hammered the fire away from the house and the barn. The other four choppers rode hard in her wake and pounded away at it as well, but she was magnificent to watch.

Thirty meters. The blaze itself missed the cattle station by thirty meters. But it missed.

The fire front was still more than three kilometers wide; they hadn't beaten it. But they had chased it past the farthest-northern residence along the Stuart Highway.

Then the flames hit the highway.

There was no time to prepare. No time to set up fire-breaks, not even time to drop a single load to wet the road. They just had to let it run. Jeannie remained in the lead, driving harder and faster than the others. The cattle station had a small swimming pool. Jeannie was so in the groove that the other choppers simply left it to her and went for other water sources. She was picking up and dumping a thousand gallons every five minutes. At that rate, it took her barely two hours to empty the pool.

With the heat of the fire, the highway melted and buckled, cutting off the Alice, as the highway to Alice Springs was commonly known. It was one of only two roads that connected the Alice, as the town was also known, to the outside world.

The highway had two lanes, with shoulders and sandy verges. The shoulders were mowed, plowed, or hit with herbicide to keep the growth back from the edges and the kangaroos from feeding too close to the sealed road. Typically, the night dew built up on the road's surface and trickled off to either side. This made for lush growth on the shoulders that attracted the 'roos—from the little wallabies to the big reds at two meters tall and a hundred kilos. Their feeding habits made it so dangerous to drive at night that only the buses and the crazy tourists ventured to do an Outback crossing in the dark. The buses had massive "'roo bars" on the front, which at least kept the bus from being destroyed if they clipped a big red. The tourists who ventured out and clipped a red usually just ended up dead.

Using the highway as a firebreak—it was a better one than they'd had at any point during the night—they narrowed the head to under a kilometer wide before it crossed the road. Akbar led the teams to create one last firebreak well to the west of the highway. And there the bushfire finally died.

Cal vaguely remembered climbing aboard a chopper, but he wasn't even sure which one. Someone had guided him back off. He woke up in a bed. It was dark. Just a little light through the edges of a curtain, but it looked artificial. Nighttime.

He considered what he'd done. Rather than following his common sense and getting on a flight to anywhere, he'd actually walked back into the fire. And for the first time, he hadn't done it for the fire and the adrenaline rush, or his never-ending quest for the perfect photograph.

No. He'd done it for a woman. And not even to impress her. Just to keep her from hurting so badly. As if he could fight her internal battles for her. And the craziest part of all was that it had worked. They'd saved the town and he'd saved Jeannie from the reminder of her loss.

Now that he was waking up, he could feel the clean sheets, could tell that his face wasn't caked with salt sweat, ash, and grime. He could vaguely recall the feel of the cool washcloth as Jeannie cleaned him up and put him to bed. He was alone now, but the pillow beside him was dented, the covers disarrayed.

He really had to get out of here. Clean up and go. That was the only answer for him.

His camera case lay close beside the bed, so close he had to step over it as he dragged himself into the bathroom. Damn the woman for being so considerate.

Of course she'd know that would be one of his first questions. The cameras really were his only possessions of any importance. The bathroom was clean and spacious with everything neatly prepackaged. Hotel. An okay one, certainly way better than his last time here in a backpacker hostel. This place had privacy, little bars of soap, shampoo, and fluffy white towels way bigger than a napkin.

Into shower stall. Water, hot. Immerse head in spray. Close eyes and lean against the wall as every muscle bitched about the unaccustomed workout of the last twenty-four hours.

Lean there and soak until he could imagine a cool hand tracing the scars on his back. Until—

"Shit!" He jerked forward, but there was nowhere to go and he impaled his sternum on the faucet, then stood up straight and rapped his head on the shower nozzle. He spun around, catching the temperature control with his elbow, and suddenly the water was full cold.

"Jeannie! What? Crap! That's freezing!" He turned back to adjust the temperature, which went blazing hot. Then, despite his hands still shaking from the surprise, he managed to set it at something tolerable. He turned back cautiously to face her.

He'd never seen her naked in full light. Where the dim lights at the back of the C-17 had suggested, the bathroom light revealed. Every single thing about her body lived up to the promise made in lesser light. Immensely fit—he could identify the running in her musculature. Incredibly shaped—despite his best intentions, his hands had already slid about her waist, where his palms so perfectly fit the gentle curves of those womanly hips.

A feast for the eyes—if he'd seen a nicer set of breasts he most certainly couldn't recall. Not with those soft brown eyes inspecting his from so close.

Her taste—he hadn't meant to kiss her—was exactly as he'd remembered: warm winter fires and moonlit nights. She flowed against him as the water washed over them. Wrapped her arms around his neck and pulled him in until he couldn't get away if he wanted to.

He managed a passing thought of large jets flying to faraway places, but it didn't take root anywhere of interest. Instead, Jeannie Clark washed into him. Firing him up until he slid one hand into her long, wet hair and the other down onto that fine, fine behind of hers. She slid a leg up around his waist and he pushed her back against the shower wall. They had no protection in the shower, which limited his options in only the slightest way. He also had soap and shampoo, which vastly expanded the possibilities.

He started with the top of her head, and he made it a quest. If this woman was going to throw herself at him, and he wasn't going to be smart enough to run in the other direction, he would learn every shape, every curve, every spot that made her catch her breath or tremble. And he did.

There wasn't much room to maneuver in the shower stall, but there was enough. *Front or back first?* he debated. *Both. Definitely.* He turned her to face the wall, dumped some shampoo on her hair, and began massaging it in. She stopped protesting and braced herself in place with both hands. He worked at it, massaging her scalp, appreciating her slender neck, how dark the red streak became when wet, how her thick hair reached down past the lower tips of delicate but well-defined shoulder blades.

Shifting to soap, he appreciated her strong shoulders, tapered waist, swelling hips, and firm buttocks. Reaching around, he discovered a flat stomach and full breasts that made her groan as he caressed them. Then he rinsed off one hand and, without warning, cupped her to drag her back against him.

This time Jeannie's moan came from deeper, much deeper. He drove her up and up, enjoying the feel of her shifting muscles as she writhed back against him. When she tipped over the edge, she was so far gone that she actually thrashed, throwing herself against his hands until he felt her whole body suddenly go rigid then release in cascading waves that rippled through her flesh, ultimately leaving them both gasping as she sagged in his arms.

When at last her pulse seemed to stabilize enough that she could stand on her own feet, she turned to face him. Her smile wasn't happily sated, calmly dreamy, or any of the other expressions he might have expected. Her smile was wicked.

She twirled her finger like a command to lower a hoist, indicating he should turn around.

No way.

She quirked an eyebrow at him, informing him that she was far from done and was more than happy to wait until he turned his back.

When at last he did, she again did the unexpected: she kissed him right between the shoulder blades. Right where his seventh or eighth foster father had nearly beaten him to death with a thorny switch. He'd bear those scars for the rest of his life, but the man, if he still lived, would never walk again. Cal had made sure of that even as he bled.

Yet Jeannie, without question, without judgment, had just made it clear that the scars didn't repulse her or drive her away. He glanced over his shoulder at her and she repeated her twirling motion, so that he had to face the wall just as he'd had her do moments before.

But he'd had to check. There was no sign of repulsion, but neither was there any sign of what he'd feared even more, pity. He'd made himself who he was and how strong he was. He didn't want pity, wouldn't accept it.

Jeannie didn't offer it. She offered simple acceptance. He braced his forearms against the plastic, resting his forehead against his clasped hands, and braced himself.

Ever so slowly, Jeannie slid her arms around his waist and simply lay against him. He could feel the pressure of her against him—cheek, breasts, hips. She lay there until he relaxed. She lay there until it was the most natural thing on the planet to be held by her. And finally, until he couldn't imagine being anywhere else.

Then she began to do exactly as he had done, explore his body with soap and fingers. She also used breasts and hair and nose and every possible way they could come in contact—except one.

He grew harder and harder in anticipation, but she never explored right where most women started off. Right where he started off wanting to be explored.

No, Jeannie slid arms around to soap his pecs, found a twitchy spot above his left knee, even scraped short nails along his instep. She kept at it until he was biting his lower lip against the throbbing between his legs.

When he was on the verge of breaking down and begging, she drove her well-soaped hands up between his spread legs from behind. The unexpected attack roared through him hotter than the fire they'd fought and beaten. His pulse pounded in the same wild rhythm as her stroking palms and exploring fingers. She teased and toyed with him until he released harder than he ever had before.

And when he did, she simply held him. Lay against his back and held him as his body shuddered and shook in a way no one had ever caused before.

She held him until he finished, until he relaxed, until he slid down to his knees and finally sat on the floor of the shower stall.

In a deliciously limber move, she too slid down to sit in his lap and lay her head on his shoulder.

They sat there together for a long time under the warm spray. She apparently at peace, and Cal knowing that his opportunity to simply walk away from this woman by catching the next plane out had now passed him by.

Chapter 11

CAL HAD BEEN STRANGELY WITHDRAWN WHILE THEY'D eaten breakfast together before returning to the airport. Once again, Jeannie found herself making excuses for him; he'd been awake for three days and then slept a dozen hours like the dead. Maybe that was it.

But what if it wasn't? Was it about the sex? About their growing relationship? Was it…

They were the last to arrive at the Alice Springs airport, even though it was still before dawn. Everyone was gathered around the back of the hangar.

Jeannie attempted to apologize for being late, though she didn't recall any meeting being called. Henderson waved her off, signaling that everything was okay.

Cal simply grabbed a coffee and dropped into a chair.

Henderson stood and any morning chatter faded away.

"We've actually been asked to work two separate fires." He pulled a slip of paper from his pocket and handed it to Vern. "The 212s and the MD500 need to report to this chap in Hamilton, Victoria. You'll take the smokies and Denise's crew with you. Sorry for the long flight. Go get ready, but don't leave until I check in with you. The Firehawks will be there as soon as we can deal with this other fire."

The three pilots shrugged and headed back out to the pad to get ready. Denise eyed them strangely, then departed as well. Clearly she wasn't happy about being separated from her two most important helicopters. Entrusting them once again to mere pilots was not making her happy at all.

Jeannie looked around, and that was when the nerves really overtook her. Now she understood what was going on. She'd sat with a group like this just six months before. That time they'd been crouched together in the middle of the night around a small picnic table in western Oregon as they fought the New Tillamook Burn. It was an immensely uncomfortable moment that had changed her naive view of the world. She actually felt sorry for Cal. He could have no idea what was about to happen.

Henderson and Beale sat at one end of the table, Tessa content with her milk bottle. Carly and Steve sat there looking as grim as Jeannie felt. And then there was Cal.

Cal glanced around the table, then nodded to Henderson. "So, you ready to reveal your cards?"

Jeannie blinked. She kept forgetting how smart Cal was. Smarter than Jeannie had been. She hadn't seen it coming, but it sounded as if Cal not only expected it, but knew ahead of time what was going on.

Henderson nodded an easy acknowledgment. "We've done some checking on you, Calvin Hobbes Jackson."

Jeannie tried not to snort. He really had been named for the cartoon characters and it fit him. Both the wildly independent man and the thoughtful, quiet tiger. The light and dark twins she'd guessed at when they first met were the same man. His name fit him perfectly—even more perfectly than she'd thought.

Cal, however, had a very different reaction. He tensed and balled his fists, as if a real tiger was about to come into play.

"By what right—"

"By the right of what I'm about to ask," Henderson cut him off. His voice was suddenly rough and brooked no argument. That must be how he'd sounded when he was a major in the Army.

Jeannie wondered just what Henderson had found out about Cal. She'd very much like to know. It was the first time she realized how little she knew about her lover's past. Prior to fighting fire, he didn't exist. Actually, other than that he fought and photographed fire, she knew absolutely nothing about him. She'd told him all about her family, the effect of their losses during the Black Saturday bushfires, her brother's career…yet Cal was a cipher. She didn't even know where he lived. Just who was sharing her bed anyway?

After considering, Cal nodded tightly for Henderson to proceed.

Jeannie had seen many aspects of Cal Jackson, but she'd never before seen anger. She hadn't even known he was capable of it. The man looked positively dangerous. Did she know him at all?

"Mount Hood Aviation occasionally—"

"—flies for the CIA. I figured that out on my lonesome. What does that have to do with me?"

Henderson appeared unfazed. "What it has to do with you is that we're on hold for a possible assignment. My question is: Do you want in, or do you want to climb onto one of the 212s and go take photographs of bushfires? If your answer is the former, then I somehow need to truly know I can trust you all the way."

The silence stretched out. Emily sat quietly, as unreadable as ever. Carly and Steve were holding hands tightly, seeking mutual comfort. Jeannie had no one. She was the odd woman out, always had been. Never fitting in, even when she was welcome. MHA was the first place other than her family that she'd ever really belonged.

"I get nothing else to go by?" Cal asked.

"We aren't military, at least not anymore." Henderson shared a wry grin with Emily. "We are never asked to do anything more dangerous than fight fire. But we are asked to go places where firefighters are welcome and others aren't, in order to see what we can see. The other rule is that except for the people in this room, you can't discuss anything we do on those special assignments, ever. Not with the military, not with the law, definitely not the press or media, and not even anyone else in MHA. This group is as big as the circle has ever gotten."

Cal turned to Jeannie and finally offered a nod acknowledging her tongue-tied moments. But she couldn't read what he was thinking beyond that. She wanted to reach for him. To beg him to join them so she wouldn't feel so alone. But she didn't, couldn't. He again studied Henderson at length.

"Why me?"

"Trained observer. You see things even I don't. Carly sees pattern and flow like no one I've ever met. You see detail and connection at a similar level. I've talked to every crew boss you've ever worked with, including Alaska. Found him despite your name change."

Name change? Jeannie didn't even know the real name of the man sharing her bed? He really had tried to leave his past behind. Maybe she now understood his reactions a bit better each time she touched his back,

his poor, scarred back. The damage looked old enough
to have happened to a child. Maybe she did know his
real name: Calvin Hobbes Jackson. That was the man
who mattered.

"Every single one said the same thing," Henderson
continued. "That you were good, better than most, but
not the best. Except for one thing. Every single one
remarked that you always saw the details long before
anyone else and that they were sorry every single time
they didn't listen to you. In these kinds of situations, I
need to be a step ahead and I'm gambling that you can
help me get there."

Cal brooded. Jeannie could see him getting ready to
refuse, to walk out. She didn't know why; what could
possibly be driving him away? MHA had welcomed her,
given her a home and a purpose, a gift of immense price.
And yet Cal was preparing to walk away from it all.

From her...

Could that be it? Was she somehow the one driving
him away? She wasn't ready for that. Dammit, her heart
wasn't ready for that. As much as she wanted to deny
it, her heart was fully involved. She had to stop him,
but how?

"Cal."

"What?" He practically snarled at her, but she didn't
take offense. She could see that something was hurting
him, no matter how hard he was trying to hide it.

"Show them the pictures."

That stopped him, but it didn't quite alter his course.
He was still on the verge of telling them all to go to hell.
For invading his carefully protected past? She'd made
up a hundred theories of how his back had been scarred,

but somehow knew that not a one of them was even close. And the scars inside were clearly worse.

"Please?"

It cost him, but he finally reached into his camera bag for his computer. She just hoped it wouldn't cost the two of them what they already had. It was so new, so precious, so fragile. If only she knew why he was fighting against it so hard.

For her, answering the call to join had been easy. They were the best people she'd ever flown with. If Emily Beale asked her to fly to the moon, she'd sure try. And it had been an acknowledgment of her own value as well. She knew she flew well. MHA's welcoming her to the inner circle said that she actually was of value in someone else's opinion as well.

Cal set up the picture viewer on the *National Geographic* folder and then tossed it down on the table in front of Mark hard enough for several of them to wince.

Beale leaned forward from one side, Carly from the other. Steve rose to look over Mark's shoulders.

Cal sat back and crossed his arms tightly over his chest as if trying to hold himself together. He didn't look at her. Twice she raised a hand to comfort him, and twice she pulled it back before she touched him.

"Hey"—Carly pointed at the tablet—"that wasn't in the article."

Jeannie watched as Henderson slowly swiped through the four pictures of the waiting silver shelters, the burn-over, and the tragic aftermath. Especially the aftermath. After the last, Carly hid her eyes in Steve's shoulder and cried quietly. Right, Jeannie kept forgetting that Carly had lost her father and her first fiancé to burnovers. Steve looked grim and held his wife. Emily faced the images unblinking, though a single tear ran unnoticed down her cheek as well. She reached out to rest a hand on her daughter's head.

Henderson gently set the computer back in front of Cal. "Okay, I trust you. Are you willing to trust us?"

One last time, the steady gaze of the angry tiger.

Jeannie could feel the anguish clogging her throat. What had been easy for her was a cliff edge for Cal Jackson. She wanted to beg him to cross over for his own sake, if not for hers. It was her first clue that there was something broken in him. He was as twitchy as…as when she'd touched his back. There was a connection, but she didn't have enough of the pieces to find it.

He started to turn in her direction, but then didn't. Finally, staring at Henderson, he simply said, "Anything else you want me to tell the other pilots?"

Henderson shook his head.

Cal tucked the tablet back into his camera bag and walked out.

Jeannie was devastated. They had already come so far together—too fast, but so far. And now he was gone. How could he just walk away from—

Emily shook her arm and said one word: "Go."

Jeannie sat for three heartbeats trying to absorb that it wasn't all decided, then leaped to her feet and ran. She sprinted through the unending hangar, through the narrow gap left between the massive doors, and broke out into the deceptive cool of morning in the Red Centre of the Australian Outback. A low fog danced along the ground, though it would be gone by sunrise.

She spotted Cal standing with the other chopper pilots farther down the apron. His glance back at her brought her to a stumbling halt. For a long moment he looked at her before nodding to himself and turning away. He moved forward, shaking hands all around, then he stepped back and crossed his arms. He watched unmoving as everyone else loaded aboard and they started the engines. They took off, turning southeast. Still he didn't move.

Jeannie forced her legs into motion until she stood beside him. Together they watched the flight of choppers until it was out of sight and the sun had actually moved across the eastern sky.

When he turned and pulled her into his arms, it was one of the best moments of her life. Fearing that she'd never see him again one instant and discovering her role as his anchor the next, she breathed him in and wept out her fears.

Cal kissed her atop her hair and simply let her weep.

Her emotions were a train wreck, a disaster of conflicting needs and wishes. But for now she'd just be glad that Cal was still with her. All she could do was take it one day at a time, one moment at a time.

Long after they'd stilled and simply held each other in the perfect silence that reigned during an Outback sunrise…long after her heart had returned to its normal pace in her chest…

She heard Cal whisper to himself, "What the hell have you done this time, Hotshot?"

Jeannie knew her own answer to that question. Yesterday and last night, watching Cal sleep, she understood what he'd done. He'd left his cameras with her, his most precious possessions, and walked into the fire for her. He had risked everything so that she wouldn't have to face another bushfire destroying another family.

And Jeannie knew exactly what she had done last night. Something she'd avoided so successfully her whole life.

Between one heartbeat and the next, she'd fallen in love.

Chapter 12

"WE NEED TO MOVE NORTH, WELL NORTH, BUT NOT STAYING at some airport. We need to get lost for a little bit." Henderson and the others had come out to stand with them as the barely risen sun sent heat shimmers across the still morning. "Anyone have a suggestion?"

Jeannie nodded against Cal's chest where her head still nestled on his shoulder.

"Apparently, yes," Cal translated for her as she didn't appear to be able to speak yet.

The others moved off to pack up Steve's drones and collapse the launcher to prepare it for transport. Cal wasn't quite ready to let go of Jeannie yet. He might not have wept as she had, but it had been close. Too damned close to his anger driving him away.

Something had shifted in Cal, several things, and he didn't know which was the biggest. He'd put together most of what Henderson had said before he'd been told. It should have seemed like a great opportunity, and certainly it wouldn't be dull. Then why had it felt like a trap closing over his head? Each word Henderson spoke had backed him further and further into a corner with walls Cal couldn't see.

He'd been dependent on no one since he was sixteen, and he'd learned long before that independence was his best path to long-term survival. Now he'd be bound to these people not by choice, as in his choice of what to publish and what not to. No, now he'd be bound by secrets, real secrets. That was a tie he wasn't ready for.

Damn Henderson for understanding why he hadn't released the photos of the fallen firefighter. Damn the man for seeing into his soul and understanding that while the reason might not make sense, it didn't need to. What it had revealed to Henderson was that Cal would follow his own unique code of conduct, and that he would adhere to it against all comers. Cal would rather die broke than release the photos of one of his best friends' death. Perhaps Jacob had been his only true friend over the dozen or more crews he'd worked with.

One thing was for damn sure: Cal would never again go back under a foil shelter and wait to see if he survived. It was the hardest thing he'd ever done in his life. He shoved the memory aside before it could overwhelm him and returned his consideration to the woman nestled in his arms.

Worse—or was it better?—he had ties to her now too. More than to anyone ever in his life. Even as a naive boy, so wanting to belong somewhere, anywhere, he'd never let himself become so attached. And it wasn't as if he was willing to release her, either.

The gods alone knew, but he'd never had such a lover. That shouldn't be enough to do more than provide a happy distraction. But it did, much more. She too was winding invisible snares that wrapped around him. With the best of intentions, she had made it so that he didn't want to walk away from her. She'd already sunk those hooks so deep into his soul that he knew it would hurt them both like hell when he finally had to tear them out. So he could walk away.

And he would.

He knew himself well enough to know that too was a truth. So, why hadn't he been able to cut both of their losses and climb aboard the damn 212 with Bruce?

The answer to that question slowly pulled his head down, and she offered a kiss of such gentle need that he let the next barb sink into his flesh while he relished the taste of Jeannie Clark's mouth like dawn on a still summer morning.

Jeannie took the lead of the flight. They fueled up at Tennant Creek, a sleepy little airport with a single rusting bowser, the sole pump for hundreds of kilometers that dispensed Jet A fuel. In Katherine, they landed on the civilian side of RAAF Base Tindal. Her brother had been stationed here for a while, but was now in Perth, or… They moved him around so often that Jeannie had trouble keeping track. Her family had scattered in so many ways.

Cal sat close beside her in the cockpit of her Firehawk as she turned into Nitmiluk National Park. That was what she cared about. Their flight up had been comfortable, companionable, even if they'd barely spoken. Cal's morning grouchiness had burned off with the morning mist and whatever decision he had reached. Instead, they'd continued his flight instruction.

Beale and Henderson flew behind her with Carly, Steve, and Tessa riding passenger.

Jeannie radioed Dale, the park manager of the Jawoyn aboriginal tribe, as they lifted out of Tindal.

"Jeannie, luv. You been too far away for too long."

"Missing you too, Dale. Wonder if you'd mind if I led a flight up the gorge?"

"No worries, luv. We don't have another tourist flight booked for couple a hours. River she be all yours."

"We need to squat a bit too."

"Trouble, luv?"

"No. Just need some quiet."

"You know the spot."

Jeannie did.

"No be snitching fish in the national park up there. Ranger might catch you."

"You scaring me, Dale."

"Worse, his wife might catch you."

"Looking forward to seeing both of you."

"Fly safe, luv."

Jeannie led them northeast. She went low and circled to avoid the parking area at the park entrance. It would mean missing the first gorge of the Katherine Gorge complex, but it was also the least dramatic of the thirteen, really just a long lake between steep banks and tall trees.

"Where was all this water when we needed it?" Cal glared down.

"Notice how deep the gorges are?" The Katherine River had carved a deep series of gorges down into the sandstone. "This is nothing. You know the Top End has the two seasons, the Dry and the Wet. During the Wet, November to April, the Katherine will rise a dozen meters or more, connecting the various gorges enough for flat-bottomed boats to carry tourists through at least the first five. During the Dry, a few hardy souls rent little plastic boats to paddle the gorges."

She'd done that once. Having to haul the boats over the exposed boulders separating the gorges during the Dry was hard work. Right at this time of year. November marked the very end of the Dry, so there would only be the few most hardy souls past the second or third gorge.

She slowed and slid down into the second gorge. The river was mostly a hundred feet wide, sometimes more. The canyon walls were always two rotors wide, though rarely three. This was what helicopters were made for, swooping slowly along narrow canyons. It was dramatic and beautiful, and another part of her soul belonged here. The layered sandstone snaked in long, sharp curves of red cliff walls.

A quick glance, all she could spare in the narrow space, showed that Cal was relaxing and staring out the forward windscreen in wonder. In moments, his camera was out. The first time since the golf course. It was as if he was slowly coming back to life.

It was one of the most beautiful places she'd ever been. The wonder of nature's handiwork carving deep canyons through the colorful stone, the unexpected bounty of water even during the Dry. It was like a salve on her soul.

Unexpectedly, Cal laughed. A deep, rumbling laugh that broke from him like a shot of flame that filled the cockpit and her heart. He leaned over and kissed her on the shoulder. With that simple gesture, she knew she'd done it right. That he too could appreciate where they were, what Mother Nature had done here.

She kicked the rudder left and tipped the cyclic so that they were flying somewhat sideways down the gorge, giving him a clear shot straight ahead out the photographer's window she'd had installed on his door.

The man chortled. He actually chortled with glee.

The gorge walls soared above them, often vertically for thirty or more meters. Kayakers twisted and turned to spot the source as the pounding of their rotors echoed up the canyon. When they waved, she rocked the rotors to wave back.

As they proceeded from one gorge to the next, the character changed. Even in a dozen kilometers, the more lush lower reaches by the park entrance gave way to the starker land of the interior. And they passed over fewer and fewer kayakers. The waterfall at the head of the fifth gorge stopped most. Also, as they traveled inland, fewer of the women bothered wearing the tops of their bathing suits. The feeling of privacy and freedom this far off the beaten track was immense.

They saw the last kayaker in the sprawling ninth gorge. The portage to the tenth stopped even the hardiest of souls. That was how she'd met Dale and his wife. She'd struggled on until she reached the uppermost thirteenth gorge where she'd thought to find herself all alone. She had planned to sit there and lick her wounds after Jeoffrey. Just sit there and see if she had some chance of finding herself again. He'd been insidious, slowly convincing her that she wasn't pretty and was lucky he wanted to be with her. That she wasn't competent and she was lucky that he was there to take care of her. She'd bought into that for far too long.

When she came to her senses, she'd plunged into Katherine Gorge with little more than a couple days of food and water and a plastic kayak. By the third gorge, she'd stripped off her T-shirt. By the sixth, her bikini top had followed it. The attention that had garnered her from the few men who'd made it that far had further convinced her that Jeoffrey was a manipulative asshole, which only spurred her on until she'd left even the hardiest pursuer behind.

She'd been all alone in the last gorge when Dale and Kalinda had found her. Rather than weeping alone in the wilderness, she'd made friends she knew would last forever. She'd spent a week with them, fishing and living off the bush before they'd all reluctantly returned to civilization. She'd also rediscovered something of herself in those vast canyons. Perhaps Cal could do the same.

As they progressed from gorge to gorge, she allowed herself to become lost in the easy rhythm of the flight, the languid flow of the river at the tail end of the Dry, and the joy that she felt in returning to one of the hearts of the Outback. Her home had been burned past recognition. But here, it was the land that called her back time and again.

Past the last gorge, the Katherine River wound through the landscape toward Arnhem Land. Past where anyone except the aborigines ever traveled. Emu Creek joined the Katherine and created a wide, sandy island big enough for both choppers to land comfortably. She shut down the electronics and engines. The heavy rotor slowly thudded to a stop until all that remained was an ear-ringing silence. She knew that soon the seemingly lifeless Outback would come back to life in its own voice of bird and wind. Clusters of low trees offered refuge from the sun. And the meeting of the waters made for good fishing and hunting. An ideal place to simply stop.

Thirty minutes from Katherine, their chances of being found by another white soul was very close to zero.

She climbed down and stripped off her flight gear. Mid-morning and it was already in the high eighties Fahrenheit. It would be twenty degrees higher in a few hours. Reaching in through the open cargo-bay door, she pulled out her pack and dropped it on the pilot's seat. She dropped her pants and dragged on shorts. She fished out an oversized, white button-down blouse to protect herself from the sun and shed everything else before putting it on.

She heard a tiny sound as she was changing. She glanced up to see Cal standing across the cockpit, outside the open copilot's door, a camera raised to his eye.

"You son of a—"

"I promise to cherish that shot."

"I promise to rip your throat out if you don't delete it right now, Cal." Jeannie buttoned her shirt up quickly.

"But you're so damned beautiful, Helitack. It would be a true waste."

"Do it!"

He made a show of pouting, but fooled with the controls.

"So damned beautiful." She knew she was pretty enough, but no one had ever called her that. She was almost sorry she'd made him delete the photo. Almost.

―――⁓―――

Cal made a show of putting a password on the image and hitting Save. There was no way on earth he was going to delete that photo. Framed by the complexities of the machine that she flew like a dream, the sun shining from her left had lit her bare body until she glowed. Every curve a perfect testament to womanhood. The freedom and power, the woman and the top-notch pilot in such perfect juxtapositions. Beyond her, past the promise of sunglass-covered eyes, the river wound lazily past high banks of rust-red soil. Nothing like the gorge itself, but only adding to the overall image. Here they were out in the nothing, and she was the sole icon of power in view.

Just looking at her roused his desires all over again. And not only the desire to drag her down under the nearest paperbark tree and once more give himself in thrall to her incredible, creative lovemaking. He also felt an inexplicable need to be with her, as if the world were a better place when she was beside him. Down that path lay a madness he wasn't ready to face. So, instead, he took his camera and went exploring.

He found a good angle on the choppers, two firefighting machines perched on a sandy embankment. He liked the downtime shots almost as much as the fire shots. It humanized the men and women who heard the call to fire. Though he did shy the camera away from Henderson and Beale's embrace, offering them a little privacy. Then he spotted Steve and Carly, doing a bit more than embracing.

Two couples. He and Jeannie made three. Shit! Yet another thing he hadn't signed up for had slid by him unnoticed until it was too late. He wasn't going to think about it right now. What he was going to think about was—

"Fishing?" Henderson's cry of joy resounded above the gentle rustle of the slow river moving over the rocks.

"Sure." Jeannie was sounding terribly pleased with

herself. "You didn't think we were going to be eating MREs when there's so much food out here?"

Cal had heard about people who could do that, live off the Outback. Aborigines. Not beautiful white chicks who flew massive helicopters.

"Best eating fish on the planet is barramundi. They like to congregate over there." She pointed toward the northern spit of the island they'd landed on, just a few hundred feet away.

Henderson literally fell to his knees and kissed her feet. Carly was doing a happy dance. Two rabid fisherfolk. In mere minutes they'd grabbed their poles tucked aboard the Firehawk in fancy carrying cases, and then they were gone.

"Last we'll see of them for a while," Emily remarked, her tone as dry as the Outback. She and Steve began setting up a small camp under one of the gum trees.

"Especially"—Jeannie laughed that wonderful laugh of hers—"because they won't get a bite until toward sundown, which is a good seven hours away."

Cal noticed that she wasn't checking her watch, but had instead glanced up at the position of the sun in the sky. Who the hell was she?

Emily smiled in return. "They won't care."

Jeannie pointed to the tall trees along the western edge of the island. "The outer layers of the paperbark tree will make great kindling for tonight's fire. Never camp under a paperbark tree—you're likely as not to catch it on fire. See if you can find a dead beech or gum for the main wood. It will give the fish a better flavor. Come on, Hotshot."

"Where are we going?"

"Bush tucker, mate." She waved a small sack at him that she'd use for a collecting bag. "The season's a little off for some of the really good stuff, but maybe we can score some pencil yams or figs. There's bound to be some bush tomato or conkerberry. Leave the cameras. There's a stretch we have to swim a bit."

"I've got a waterproof housing for one of them."

"Leave the cameras."

She wasn't making it a request. Cal wasn't very happy about it, but he'd already put her through enough today with his crappy mood. He packed the cameras away and slid the bag into the back of the Firehawk where the sun wouldn't try to cook them. He found an MHA-logoed hat and pulled it on for sun protection.

Jeannie handed him a white square of cloth. Before he could ask what to do with it, she picked up a hat of her own, flipped one edge of the cloth into it and then pulled it on. The cloth hung down all around the hat. It hid her hair except for the last few inches in the middle of her back. It shaded the sides of her neck, her ears, and even part of her cheeks. He did the same, though a lot less smoothly.

She led off. "I've lost my Outback tan, so I have to be careful. You'd have liked it, Hotshot. Not a whole lot of tan lines in the Outback."

He'd have to agree with her. The image of Jeannie striding across the Outback in nothing but a bit of cloth slung around her hips was something he would definitely like to see. Tanned all golden would be even better. He followed her for a way simply admiring the view, even with her fully clothed. For what he was sure would be just the first of so many times today, he cursed not having his camera. Gods, but the woman could walk.

"This is where you make sense, Helitack." He said it without thinking, but it was true.

"What do you mean?"

"I always thought you walked like a sexy lioness." She did. "But I'm thinking that was pretty lame now that I see you here. You're definitely goddess status—sexy goddess. Ooo! Wow! Pant! Pant! And all that." The thing about it was, she really looked that amazing. And she was leading him willingly toward his own doom.

"Uh." She actually stumbled as she looked back at him in surprise, though it didn't break the image.

"Okay, kinda crass, I know. It's that you walk as if you belong on the earth, belong right here striding across this arid soil that you see as a land of bounty."

"Wow, Hotshot. If you is trying to turn this girl's head, you is right on the track."

"Wasn't the point I was—"

"No, I get that. Just letting you know that anytime you want to remind me that I actually belong anywhere on this screwy planet, feel free to let me know."

Jeannie had continued another fifty feet before she realized that Cal was no longer behind her. That an American man was almost as silent-footed as a bushman had made her lose track of him. He walked as if he wanted no one to hear his passage. A useful skill, one she'd worked hard to learn from Dale and Kalinda. Only now did she have a bad thought about how it may have been the boy who had learned the skill, rather than the man.

She circled back around a scrub palm to stand in front of him. His face wasn't twisted with anger as it had been this morning, which was a relief. His emotions were so powerful that they battered her at times. Instead, he simply looked confused.

"What?"

He shook his head slowly like a water buffalo waking from a nap.

"Come on, Cal. For once, tell me what you're actually thinking."

"I'm..." His voice was low. "Thinking you are absolutely completely and totally whacked out."

"Huh. Not quite up there with sexy goddess, is it?"

Cal cracked the amazing smile of his. "No. But it's just as true."

"Why am I whacked?"

"Because you're grounded to 'this planet' in so many ways that they're beyond counting. I mean, just, just look at you!" He held out those nice hands of his in a totally helpless gesture. "You're connected to your family, your brother, Mount Hood Aviation, and now the goddamn Outback. You're one of those people who could cross it on foot, aren't you? How many white people can do that? For that matter, how many aborigines still have those skills? You're connected in so many ways and you don't see it. What's up with that?"

Okay, Jeannie could see that she wasn't in love with him. She was only in love with the parts she already knew. There were so many other parts of him for her to get to know. He just blew her away. But if she came at him head-on, he'd just balk again. And that wasn't going to get her anywhere. Time for a different tack.

"So, you're angry at me on my own behalf for not seeing what I have?"

He brushed a hand through his hair, knocking his hat and sun scarf off. They fell to the sand despite several fumbling attempts to catch them. By the time he had them straightened out and back on, he seemed to have calmed a little.

"Well, I admit"—he seated the hat more firmly—"it does sound pretty damn stupid when you put it that way."

She'd go with charming. Cal Jackson was more protective of her than she was of herself, and probably more than he was of himself.

"Damn, you're cute, Hotshot." She let it drop there, for now. She led them to the south tip of the island and walked into the bath-warm water. "It's just a short swim. If you see a freshie, don't worry. They're harmless as long as you don't tick them off."

"A freshie?" He'd paused where the water was just ankle deep.

When it was up to her waist, she began swimming; this small branch of the river wasn't more than a dozen strokes across and had no real current to speak of.

"It's the salties that will eat you for the fun of it. We're fine. They don't get this far upriver during the Dry."

"Salties?"

"Crocs." Jeannie tested and was able to set her foot down, about waist deep again. She remained with just her head out of the water and made treading motions with her arms as if still in deep water, then turned around to wait and watch the show.

"Crocs?" Cal croaked out.

"Saltwater crocodiles."

He looked down at the water swirling around his ankles in panic.

"How big?"

Oh, this was just too much fun. "Four or five meters is pretty common. Dale spiked a six once. Weighed in at two metric tons, give or take a bush hog."

"Two metric tons?" He still hadn't moved and his voice was even more strained.

"Yep, that's forty-four hundred pounds to you Yanks."

"You're shitting me?"

Actually she wasn't, but that didn't stop her from making it sound like a whopper. "He'd be glad to show you, if you'd like. He had it stuffed and it's mounted at the entrance to the park to sort of wake people up before they get all stupid."

"Like hell I'm getting in that river."

"You sure, Hotshot?"

"I'm not just sure. I'm damned sure."

"Pity." Jeannie planted her feet on the river bottom and stood up slowly. Her soaking wet blouse would be near enough transparent. When she was standing, she continued backing slowly toward the far bank. "You really sure, Hotshot?"

She'd actually struck him speechless. She'd always thought that only happened in movies, but while he was obviously trying to speak, no sounds were emerging. She turned her back on him and continued toward the bank, letting her hips swing loose. She even twisted her head sharply to flip her wet hair over her shoulder as she glanced back over her shoulder. Jeannie considered batting her eyelashes at him, but that was too ridiculous.

With a roar like a wounded beast, Cal plunged into river, hit the midstream with a racing dive and was coming up fast. She sprinted for the bank, but didn't make it. He tackled her in the shallows, bringing her to her knees in the soft mud.

When she tried to rise, he dragged her back. He pulled her so hard against his chest that he knocked the air out of her lungs. His hands were everywhere, and his mouth was locked on hers. She wrapped her arms around the back of his head and simply did her best to hang on. At some point her blouse and shorts hit the beach with a wet splat.

He took her with his mouth and drove her up until she cried out at the midday sun. When he was done, the feeling of floating pervaded from the shallow water outside her body right down into the deepest center within. She wasn't sure where she belonged, other than with this man.

———

"You're a drug," Cal said as they headed back toward camp in the late afternoon. He counted three times, or was it four, that one of them had jumped the other in the last couple hours. That they'd collected any food at all was a miracle. That they had no protection with them just meant they were finding some creative ways to have sex. Really creative, though the time against the ghost gum, its eerily white bark a sharp contrast to her lovely pinking skin, had to be the best for sheer visual imagery.

In between bouts, she showed him the elusive bounty of the Outback. "This isn't deep Outback. That can be hard. Pickings are pretty easy here in the grasslands. Go out beyond the Red Centre into the Simpson or the Great Victoria Desert…those are harsh. And ten to twenty degrees hotter than this."

They napped through the peak heat of the day. Too hot to do more than hold hands, they'd waited it out in the scattered shade of a gum tree just as any sensible Australian would.

"Am I an addictive drug?" Jeannie teased him as they came back toward camp.

"You have no idea, Helitack." She was the most damn addictive drug he'd ever tried. He was hooked, lined, and sunk. "What is it about you?"

"It's a secret."

"You're a lousy liar, Helitack. Give."

"Trade."

"Trade what?" He leered at her and hoped that was what she was talking about.

She stopped at the bank edge and faced him. Resting a hand on his chest, she looked up into his face. He could see that she was suddenly serious.

"If this is going to work, then we have to trade. I tell you about me, you tell me about you."

He could feel the walls coming up. Could feel a need to turn and run. He dug in, planted his heels in the sand, and managed to stay in place and face her.

She searched his face, looking for something. Seeing something that abruptly made her look infinitely sad.

At least she didn't slap him. He wasn't sure if he could take that from her.

"I'll try, Jeannie. I really will. So ask." Cal braced himself.

She opened her mouth, then thought better of it. Going up on her toes, she leaned in and kissed him lightly.

"Ask, already!" Cal's fingernails dug into his palms painfully as he tried to prepare himself.

Jeannie shook her head. "No. For tonight, let it be enough that you're willing to try."

Then she took his hand and led him into the clear, cool water of the gently flowing river.

———

"What is it with you?" Henderson sounded furious. Carly's barramundi was six inches longer and several pounds heavier than Mark's.

"Women rule," was Carly's response.

Emily laughed at her husband, which elicited a matching laugh from the baby.

"C'mon, guys," Henderson begged. "Give me a hand here."

Steve shook his head.

Cal raised his hands, begging off. "Way outta my league, boss. Woman outfishes you, you're on your own."

"Crap!" Henderson knocked back a swallow of beer and glared down at the fish as if it was the barra's fault.

Cal just sat back to enjoy the show. Jeannie had wrapped one cleaned fish in some soaked palm fronds. She'd dressed it with salt, pepper, and eucalyptus, then stuffed it into the fire's coals as the sun set. The other one she laid on a rock she'd kept covered in coals for the previous half hour. That one was dressed with some tiny bush tomatoes just an inch across, pink, yellow, and green and shaped more like warped jelly beans than tomatoes. They'd found no yams, but she'd also tucked some large pigweed in with the fish that she swore tasted like potatoes, as well as steamed parakeelya that she said went better with a salad dressing. Looked nasty to him, kinda like psychotic asparagus.

Jeannie squatted back on her heels, her elbows resting on her knees and her butt about an inch off the ground. She looked completely comfortable, but every time Cal tried it, either he fell over or his knees started hurting after just seconds.

"You gotta loosen up, Hotshot. You're way too tight."

Jeannie didn't say "uptight" or even imply it. She'd even flexed one leg out and back, while balancing on the other in her squat, to make her point. While he admired the long length of golden skin in the firelight, he heard her words the wrong way anyway. That she was right didn't make it any easier. He'd always thought of himself as pretty mellow and easygoing. Before Jeannie, it was easy to brush off his past. But she came straight in like a helicopter strike. Dodging around a little looking for the best approach, but nailing the target nonetheless.

He'd appreciated her letting him off the hook this afternoon, but that meant soon he'd have to begin answering her questions. Or she'd start drifting away, and while he didn't know what he wanted, he knew he didn't want that. He couldn't stand distance between them. Hell, the six inches between them at the moment was almost too much. He nudged her shoulder with a fingertip, trying to ruin her balance, but she was too well planted so he turned it into a caress down her back that almost did unbalance her.

Henderson poked a stick at the fire. "I remember the
first time I tasted barra. I was—" He cut himself off,
then looked over his shoulder into the darkness. "I was
flying somewhere unmentionable north of here. We'd
just inserted a team way deep, carrying more fuel than
ammo because there was no way to get a refuel in there.
Squatting by a river for three days, the choppers buried
in tree branches, hoping to God no native fisherman
would be out that time of year. Dangled a line because
we didn't have anything better to do. I caught a barra.
He was—"

"How big?" Carly cut off his story.

Henderson groaned. "Not as big your damned fish.
You happy?"

"Totally!" Carly leaned back against Steve and
waved for Henderson to continue his tale like a queen
commanding her court.

"Problem was we didn't dare light a fire, and all we
had were a tiny, white gas camping stove and a fry pan
about as big as Tessa's face. We sat there all night cooking these tiny fillets. Damn good eating, though."

"And the point of your story?" the reigning
queen asked.

"The point is, if that fish isn't ready soon, I'm going
to eat it raw."

Jeannie poked the one on the rock with a practiced
finger. "Almost there."

"You have permit for dat fish, cobber?" a deep voice
asked from the darkness.

Henderson spun to face the intruder, slapping his hip
as he reached for a gun that wasn't there.

"Dale!" Jeannie leaped to her feet straight from her

squat in a motion that made Cal's knees hurt in empathy. A moment later she was wrapped around a tall, spare black man with shots of gray in his hair catching the firelight. "Kalinda!" Jeannie squealed. She actually squealed like a little girl as she threw herself into an even darker woman's arms.

The man and woman who stepped into the firelight were spare without being gaunt. They could be in their forties as easily as their sixties. Cal had no way to judge. They both had the wide features of their Aboriginal heritage.

Introductions went around.

Cal kept expecting some mystic, insightful statement, but they just smiled, shook hands, squatted beside Jeannie, and talked about the beautiful hike up from the national park. It was twenty or so miles over rough country, but they didn't appear tired.

Dale poked a long finger at the fish. "You watch that, skygirl."

"I was watching it before you distracted me. And there's another in the coals."

They worked in easy harmony, shifting the dinner from cooking to serving.

Dale and Kalinda refused beers. "Black man's blood is no good with alcohol. We live in a dry community."

The love they had for "skygirl" was obvious. The ease with which they chatted and touched and smiled, this was her Outback family. Cal wanted to ask questions. How long had they known each other? Were they the ones who had taught Jeannie so much about survival out here?

But if he asked questions, he'd have to "trade." That

meant answering questions that he'd never answered for
anyone. Not for foster parents, not for child services, not
for that doctor who had patched him up that one time
with a grim look on her face before he was moved to yet
another home.

Instead he waited and simply enjoyed the company.
Dale and Kalinda had intimate knowledge of the land
for an area ranging hundreds of kilometers around. And
they had amazing "dumb tourist" stories that made his
sides sore from laughing.

Jeannie was yet another woman when she was with
them. She was even more herself. Not self-conscious,
she held his hand as the conversations went late into the
night. Dale and Kalinda didn't comment, but there was
no doubt that they noticed.

A dozen hours sleep had barely dented the deficit of
three days awake. By the time the party wound down,
Cal's eyes were crossing. The fire was suppressed as
only a firefighter could—doused, dug over, repeat twice
more, then check it ten minutes later and douse it again
just to be sure.

He followed Jeannie back to the Firehawk and helped
her pull an air mattress to the ground. The last thing she
said to him was a whispered comment: "Remember to
check your shoes in the morning before you put them
on. Scorpions like the warmth and will curl up in there."
Cal assumed she was joking, but decided he'd check
just to be sure.

Too tired to sleep, having crossed over that point
hours ago, he lay for a long time and watched the
Milky Way turn across the sky—so much brighter
from the southern hemisphere that it was like a streak

across the heavens. By its light he could see both choppers, spot the other sleeping couples, and watch the gentle smile on Jeannie's lips as she slept curled against him.

Chapter 13

JEANNIE DIDN'T WAKE ALONE. SHE'D HALF EXPECTED TO. Half expected Cal to be walking down the river, hiking out to avoid her questions. But he lay there dead to the world as the last stars faded with the beginning of the day. She tried exploring her own feelings with little luck. They were still a jumble.

She'd never been the sort to make lists; they never seemed to help. Best lover ever? Check. Thoroughly decent? Check. Insane amounts of integrity? Check. A total and complete mystery in almost every way? Check. She was a hundred percent desperate for something he might never be able to give? Check! That was why she hated lists. Once you got through the easy questions, you always arrived at the really hard crap.

"What are you thinking about, skygirl? Thinking hard on such a pretty morning." Dale crossed over and squatted close beside the mattress, across Cal's chest from her. He could speak so quietly that a kangaroo wouldn't blink or a chameleon run.

She wasn't that good, but Cal was dead to the world. Keeping her voice low should be sufficient. Hell, she could probably shout without fear of waking him. "I'm thinking that I have stepped into an unknown world. He sees me in ways I've never seen myself."

"Ah." Dale nodded. "He sees you as you truly are, rather than the limited way you see yourself."

Okay, she wasn't ready to believe that one. She knew from experience that in the long run Dale was almost always right, but it often took her a long and winding journey to arrive in the same place he started.

"He is very observant."

"That was easy to see last night, luv. You can't even breathe without him observing you."

"He's having the same effect on me."

"No. You offer him so much more."

"I do?" She sat up and did her best not to jar Cal, even if he was past caring.

"It's not that you see him as he is, skygirl. It's that you accept him as he is."

She was quiet for a long time, considering that. Dale left her the space to think until the sun had cracked the horizon and then passed it by and reached into the sky.

"I suppose I do. But it's hard, Dale."

"If it were easy, everyone would do it."

Crap! She hated it when he was right. "How do you know when it's too hard?"

"You'll know, skygirl. That is a long way off from where you now tread. Patience."

"Yes, Dale." She always felt like a little child taking her first steps when she spoke with him, but his patience with her was infinite. Perhaps that was the next lesson she had to learn.

"Come, luv. Walk with an old man partway down the trail. The park does not manage herself when I am away."

"Must you go? Don't you want to talk with Cal?" Was she so desperate that she wanted Dale to break down the barriers that she'd only begun to see and couldn't begin to get around? Yes, she was that desperate.

"Oh, I've already said everything he's willing to hear. Come, girl."

———————

Cal felt the mattress shift as Jeannie slipped off and followed Dale. He'd lain there in a dreamy state while they spoke about him. Normally he simply woke up and got up. Maybe it was because he'd been so sleep-deprived the night before, but he'd simply lain there and listened. At first he'd thought it was a dream, but it was so concrete. So real that he'd finally decided he was awake. But still he hadn't spoken or reacted.

And Jeannie had treated him as if he still slept.

Was he somehow drugged? No. His fingers flexed, his eyes opened and saw blue sky. He heard the others going about the business of starting the fire for breakfast. He joined them quietly. None of them had apparently seen Dale, Kalinda, and Jeannie leave camp.

How far was "partway down the trail"? He didn't know what he wanted to say, but he knew it was there. Something that needed saying. But he couldn't do it if Jeannie wasn't around to say it to.

They were past breakfast and well on their way to lunchtime when she finally came back into camp. He did his best to not rush to greet her, but expected that he didn't cover it very well.

"You okay, Helitack?"

She kissed him lightly and accepted his hug, but there was a distance. Not as if she were angry, but rather distracted. He was going to ask what had happened and do his level best to trade back, but Emily Beale chose that moment to walk up.

"How are you feeling?" It wasn't some friendly greeting. Beale was asking her number two pilot for an assessment of her condition.

"Hot, tired, need to just stop for a bit."

"Perfect. Come with me." And just that fast they were moving away from him. He scrambled to follow.

Beale shooed Jeannie into her helicopter in the pilot's seat, then circled the bird and climbed aboard in the seat Cal normally occupied. They didn't preflight the bird or close the doors, so Cal moved up beside Jeannie's still open door to see what was going on.

Beale's glare was sufficient to warn him not to distract Jeannie. He climbed into the cargo bay and sat cross-legged on the deck right behind the end of the central console for the best view. Here he was out of Jeannie's range of vision unless she deliberately turned and looked.

"Okay, you're tired, out of sorts, and probably low on blood sugar," Beale started out.

"About right," Jeannie agreed.

"Perfect. Imagine that you've flown fire for a full day, the sun has set, but the fire has not. This is how you will feel, only worse. I have loaded a night-flying scenario into the onboard systems. Let's power up everything, except the engines, and get some practice."

She reached for the checklist and Beale pulled it out of her nerveless fingers.

"Do you know how many steps there are in a full startup?"

"Yes."

"Good. Count them aloud as you go. Check your totals by group."

Jeannie nodded to herself as if getting her brain organized. "If preflight is complete, the next group is 'before starting engines.' Number one, 'Copilot's collective— extended and locked.' Number two, 'shoulder harness locks.'" Soon she was off into subparts: a, b, c…

He watched the transformation as Jeannie worked her way through the procedures. She grew sharper with each step, more focused until she appeared to meld into the machine.

Beale looked back at him as if to say, "Do you see the miracle she does?"

He did, and it was absolutely fascinating. It was beyond what he could capture with his camera. Images rarely allowed him to show transformation; instead, they immortalized the moment. Jeannie was evolutionary, growing, changing.

By the time she was done here, she would be different. Not some gross transformation, but incrementally more than she'd been this morning while speaking to Dale when she thought Cal slept. Cal saw her as she was, absolutely magnificent. What possible reason could he have for not accepting her as she was?

While she prepared and finally, based solely on instrument readouts, flew a night flight in her mind's eye, he slipped out of the rear of the chopper. He found a spot of shade beneath a paperbark tree and sat to watch the Katherine River wander southwest as it drained toward wherever it was going.

~~~

It was late afternoon before Emily let her stop. Jeannie had logged three hours of simulator time and was ragged beyond any mere energy bar or flask of water's ability to fix. At the same time she felt exhilarated. Emily had declared her progress as "sufficient," which ranked as high praise from MHA's chief helicopter pilot. Jeannie was already night-certified in the Huey and the MD500. The next step would be night-certified-in-type for the Firehawk. Then the last step, night-fire-certified for drops on a fire, was so close that Jeannie could taste it.

But all she could feel at the moment was the utter drain of the three hard hours of simulator flying in the sun-heated chopper. Emily constantly giving her small corrections, often without words, rather through the flight controls or by altering a screen view. Then repeating and repeating until Jeannie's body did it automatically without Emily's intervention. That then freed her up to think about the next obstacle Emily placed in her way.

She considered collapsing where she stood, but instead dug a can of soda and a sandwich out of a cooler and went searching for some shade by the river.

That was where she spotted Cal. He sat in the shade of a paperbark tree, close beside the Katherine River, his back turned toward her. He looked so good in just shorts and a tight T-shirt, but that wasn't reason enough to go to him, not anymore. She hesitated as she struggled to understand and didn't like that reaction much, either. She didn't want to feel hesitant about "them."

This morning she had walked much farther with Dale and Kalinda than she had intended on their return journey back down to Katherine Gorge. If she had been hoping for more guidance in terms of Cal, it had not been forthcoming. Kalinda had talked of her children, one in university, the other already graduated and married with a child of her own. Dale had spoken, as he sometimes did, with his silence. Today he had silently spoken of listening to the world around her until she found the correct path to walk.

She had accompanied them downstream to the head of the closest gorge where the old sneak had landed the park's search-and-rescue plane. It was the closest place they could land a fixed-wing aircraft. No final word of advice except a hug.

On the long, hot hike back, she'd had a lot of time to think. And she'd done her best to listen for the right path, but it was no clearer than it had been. She only saw two options. One was to drop Cal Jackson stone-cold and be done with him, which she didn't want to do on so many levels. The only other path led her inexorably back to Cal.

Following the only path she was willing to walk, she took her mid-afternoon breakfast to the shade of the paperbark tree and sat beside him.

For a long time they sat in silence and simply watched the river flow. When at last he spoke, she almost didn't hear him. His voice was as in tune with the Outback's sounds as Dale's.

"The name 'Calvin Hobbes Jackson' was created as a joke on an Alaskan fire line when I was sixteen. I made up a name for myself from my favorite comic strip. I have no master's in fire science like you. I have no University of Sydney bachelor's in environmental studies. I have no pilot's license with who knows how many dozens of certifications. I can barely drive a car, and I've never owned one. I never finished high school. At sixteen I ran away from my twelfth foster home in ten years, forged my birth certificate to become two years older, and went to fight fire. I'm not brilliant like you."

Jeannie looked at him, wondering what had changed that he now spoke. Nothing. He still looked exactly the same to her.

"I've only ever done two things well: fought fire and taken pictures of it. It's all I know how to do. You scare the hell out of me, Jeannie Clark. I see a woman who is constantly transforming herself into a better version of who she is. I can't keep up with that. I've dug my niche, and it's a damned comfortable one. It's one I know I can pull off day in and day out. I have no home. I just follow fire, season to season. Other than a second back-pack sitting in some hotshot barracks in California, my worldly possessions are sitting in the back of your chop-per. I think that I want to follow where you're leading, Jeannie. I can't believe I'm saying this, but it sounds right. I just don't know how. Or if I can."

He didn't turn to look at her. He didn't weep. His voice was nearly a monotone. No more emotion showed than if he was reading aloud her preflight checklist. Not a single shred of evidence that he had just bared his soul to her. Again he didn't see his immense strength and how it could hold the world at bay, even when it was the interior world of his own emotions.

"But that's not who you are at all." Her voice was rough with exhaustion, even to her own ears.

"It's what I see."

She wanted to cry for him, but he didn't need her

tears. And the way he saw her. That too was…wrong. They sat again in a long silence as the feelings built inside her. Like the river flowing just beyond their feet, neither of them was any more than they appeared to be. Human, flawed. His perception was wrong. It wasn't who he was or who she was that was out of sync. It was how they saw each other that was in the way. Both of them were wrong.

Jeannie had seen Cal as her shining knight. In Alice Springs he had plunged his sword, or at least his fire ax, into the heart of the beast on her behalf. She wasn't some goddamn princess in an ivory tower. She could fight her own battles. But that he'd faced the fire on her behalf spoke of his own deep reasons, even if he couldn't see them. And those reasons made her appreciate him so much.

"This is all wrong."

"What?" He leaned in as if to hear her better.

"I said, this is all wrong."

He stared at her in shock for several seconds, then jerked to his feet.

She was so tired that it took her a moment to run after and follow him down to the water's edge.

He pulled away from her hand when she rested it on his arm.

"Wait. Listen to me."

He pulled away again.

So she took him out at the back of his knees with a sweep kick that big brother Randall had taught her. Cal actually fell into the river. When he tried to scramble away, she shoved hard against his hip, knocking him farther in.

With a scream of rage, he charged her, grabbed her around the waist, and heaved her up and out over the river. He was so damn strong that she actually had time to experience free fall before she belly flopped into the river.

She surfaced in waist-deep water, her shorts soaked and her blouse clinging once again. She didn't feel like some goddess rising from the river's water. She felt pissed.

In a similar mood, he glared at her from knee-deep in, his fists on his hips.

"You're going to listen to me, Calvin Hobbes Jackson, if I have to beat the shit out of you. And if that doesn't work, I'll get Mark, or worse, Emily, to pin you down until I'm done. So, I'd advise that you just goddamn well listen to me."

"You already said, 'We're all wrong.' That's all I need to know." He practically spit the words at her.

"That's not what I said. You're an idiot, Hotshot! But you're not stupid, so use your goddamn amazing brain."

He might be glaring, but at least he also appeared to hesitate.

"I was saying, no, I'm not some goddess. I love that you see me that way, but it's not who I am. I'm just as lost, confused, and fucked up as the next person. I'm about half as smart as you are. I worked hard, so damn hard to get what I have. Somehow you just reach out and there it is in your hand. I wish I had a tenth of your creativity. I want to someday earn the reputation of integrity that you swept up off that table in the Alice Springs hangar along with the morning coffee. God, Cal, I want so much. I want to fly like Emily. I want to command one tenth of the respect she has in her little finger. And the one I can't get around, Cal, is how much I want you. I love you."

His eyes flashed wide.

Shit! She'd gone one too far. She hadn't meant to say it out loud. "I barely know what it means, but that doesn't make it any less true."

He dropped to sit in the water that now lapped around his chest, his kneecaps just breaking the surface.

She trudged through the water until she stood in front of him. "Look, I know it's too much. I know I shouldn't have said it. I know that it makes absolutely not one iota of sense, but it's truth. The best I know how to speak it. It is bald truth. That's all I have to offer you, Cal. Truth, every time I speak. I'll never lie to you. Not about how I'm feeling, not about what I want, or what I've done. Because I think that's what love is. At least partly. The part I can see anyway."

He looked up at her. Not at her body. Not at her chest wrapped once again in a blouse gone sheer with another soaking. No, he looked her right in the eyes.

She loved his eyes. It was the one place his mood was always revealed. There was a glint of humor lurking around the edges.

"You done, Helitack?"

Done. Done in. Done for. "Way done," she told him.

"Good." He snagged one of her legs and leveraged it to land her in the water beside him.

She emerged spluttering and had to wipe her dripping hair off her face before she could see him.

"Because there's one thing I have to tell you."

Jeannie braced herself on the river bottom. This was

going to be bad. He was married or had a child or a criminal record or—

"You're the first person in my entire life to tell me that they loved me. I'm not sure I heard anything else you said after that. Maybe there's some water in my ear." He tipped his head one way and then the other as if draining them, then shrugged indifferently. "I don't know what to do with it yet. I don't know if I will ever say it back to you. Because if I do, it will be just as you said, absolute truth. But I can tell you this much. I've never wanted to be with someone even a tiny percentage as much as I want to be with you. And if you don't think that's scaring the crap out of me, you need to turn in those college degrees and ask for a refund."

"I'm the first?"

"If you discount a couple of stray comments at the height of, well, you know, by women who wouldn't know love if it were named Fido and bit them on the ass, then yes."

"That really sucks, Cal." How many hundreds or even thousands of times had she been told that growing up? Even her dad, who wasn't the most communicative guy, had told her that. Even her turd head of a brother now said it almost every time they talked.

"Hadn't really missed it until just now."

Jeannie looked at this wonderful, troublesome, talented man. She sloshed around until she was straddling his lap and her arms rested on his shoulders. Their faces were just inches apart. She brushed aside stray water drops, enjoying the intimacy of the gesture. Leaning in she kissed him long and slow.

"That was a damn nice kiss, Helitack."

She sighed as she felt so much of the burden she'd been carrying these last days sloughing off her to drift downriver. "It was." She sounded all female and fluttery even to her own ears. Ridiculous, but she couldn't stop feeling it.

"So, what are you thinking, smart lady?" His smile grew. "Truth now."

"Truth?" She wanted to laugh. "I think that we're both such messes that we'd make a pretty good sideshow at a carnival. Also, I think that if we decide to work at this together, maybe between your smart brain and my overeducated one we have at least a snowball's chance of figuring this out. What do you say, want to give it a try, mate?"

"Together?" His smile was blooming.

"Together." She could feel her own smile following suit.

"Worth a shot, I guess. It's a beginning, at least. And, hey, with two brains like ours, nothing much can go wrong, can it?"

"Not a thing." She leaned and kissed him, pulling them together until her lips hurt. His hands cupped her behind so hard and her head so gently that she'd gladly never move again.

"Hey, you two."

Jeannie looked up to see Mark standing on the bank looking down at them.

"Are you going to be done anytime soon?"

"Not for a really long time," Cal mumbled into her neck. It tickled.

Jeannie threw her head back and laughed. "The answer is no. We'd like you to go away, Mr. Henderson."

"Tough." He sounded calm and jovial, and as if he didn't give a damn what they thought or said. "We're going to fly a mission, and absence isn't an option. Briefing is in five minutes, airborne in thirty."

"A mission? Like we're supposed to care."

Henderson just smiled at her, then turned a fraction of an inch to indicate to her that he was now talking to Cal, even though Cal was still occupied ever so nicely with her collar.

"A fire. Big one."

All of Cal's hotshot instincts were called to action, his body hardening abruptly, just not in the way she'd been looking forward to.

Chapter 14

"FROM THIS MOMENT, WE DON'T EXIST. AM I CLEAR?"

They all squatted in the shade of some kind of scrub palm. Jeannie could probably tell Cal what it was and which parts you could eat and which parts you could use to build an emergency satellite radio with full GPS tracking. Damn, but that woman never stopped astonishing him. She was last to arrive, having pulled on a dry T-shirt and jeans. He figured he'd air-dry fast enough and hadn't bothered. But he was glad she had. The woman was too damned distracting when wet. Hell, she was pretty distracting when dry too.

Focus, Jackson. The three couples sat in a misshapen circle dictated by the available shade. The mid-afternoon temperature was easily a hundred degrees.

Henderson took the time to study each face around the circle of six. When he looked at Cal, Cal could feel his blood run cold. Despite the sunlight still scorching across their little camp, Henderson had removed his mirrored sunglasses for perhaps the first time since they'd met. His steel-gray eyes bored into Cal.

Well, to hell with him. Cal could match that right back. Before the whole thing could decay into some alpha-male titanic struggle, Henderson merely nodded slightly and moved on to Jeannie. He must have seen what he was looking for, though Cal had no clue what that was. He had to keep reminding himself that this guy

wasn't a firefighter first, he was military first. Henderson
had no need to prove he was in charge; he already knew
he was. It was a slick solution to the problem of command on a team.

When Henderson completed his inspection and
decided he was satisfied, he slid his glasses back on. Cal
was a bit pissed, but the rest of them had gone unexpectedly somber. Beale was as unreadable as ever behind
her own mirrored shades, and the baby was asleep. He'd
missed something. Something way bigger than a fire.
And if he was looking for clues from a sleeping baby,
he really was losing his mind.

"East Timor has a fire, and we've been asked to
assist. Any questions?"

No one else spoke.

Well, Cal wasn't about to be cowed by Henderson or
any other man.

"Yeah, about a hundred of them."

"Good. Ask those once we get there." As if he knew
exactly what Cal would ask.

Cal looked around the circle. Not finding any assistance, not even from Jeannie, he shut his mouth, but
he was becoming less happy by the second. Maybe he
should have flown south with the other pilots… Oh! He
finally understood what was happening. There was a
fire, but there was something else going on. Something
big. Fire and East Timor weren't a whole lot of clues.
And since Henderson wasn't ready to be handing out
any more at the moment, Cal would just have to wait.

He hated waiting.

Henderson nodded ever so pleasantly when he saw
Cal's change of attitude.

Cal snarled at him as pleasantly as he could.

Now assured of his audience, Henderson continued, "We're flying to an offshore base with both Firehawks. We should have additional information by the time we arrive. Other questions?"

Jeannie looked up at the sun.

Cal checked his watch before realizing that was exactly what she was doing. He gazed up at the sun as well, but all it told him was to look away quickly, and that he was still disoriented about which direction was north and which south due to crossing the equator.

"Refuel in Darwin." Jeannie was calculating pay-loads, distances, and fuel burn in her head as easily as he adjusted exposures. "We can just make the crossing over the Timor Sea without auxiliary tanks. But it will be at night. I'm neither night-certified in this craft nor long-water-crossing certified."

"Emily will fly with you as instructor. Cal in back. I'll fly Em's chopper with Carly and Steve. Have to impose on you two as babysitters for the duration of the flight."

As Carly was already holding Tessa and looking damn cute about it, that didn't appear to be a problem.

"At the far end, I'll be running fire command from a ground station, so Steve's drone and you people will be my eyes but I'll still coordinate. Jeannie, you'll be hauling our spares kit and gear. We'll be hauling Steve's drones and launcher. Anyone else?"

Damn, but the man had it wired. Cal glanced at the others. Nothing. He shrugged. He was still a crappy fifth wheel in this outfit, but it was far more interesting than anything he'd planned to be doing. Far deeper into...

"Yeah, I've got a question." Hopefully Henderson would answer this one. If not, Cal might see just what it took to hike out of the Outback here and now.

Henderson didn't even wait to let him ask it first before answering. Like he had mind-reading radar installed in those mirrored sunglasses.

"I took the liberty of requesting a full background check on you, and MHA's security division has already signed off on you. All I need from you is to sign a nondisclosure agreement. We'll work out getting you on the MHA payroll at a later time."

"No, wait! I don't work for anybody. I work alone and that's the way I like it."

"Freelance. Nonexclusive use of your skills and right of first offer on any non-security-related images. You'll like our pay scale and distribution channels."

Cal opened his mouth, looked at Jeannie, then closed it. She shrugged. Now he understood something else—how MHA had actually snared people of such quality as the ones now sitting with him under this palm.

In addition to being one of the very best wildfire behavior analysts in the business, Carly was MHA bloodline—her father had been part of their first smoke-jumper team forty years before.

Steve was a former lead smokejumper turned drone expert after an injury.

Emily and Mark were ex-Night Stalker majors.

And they'd enticed Jeannie away from her homeland of Australia that she loved so much. They'd seen something in her and come up with an offer she couldn't refuse. Which meant that she was probably better at her job than even he thought she was.

He had to admit, Henderson had just offered him the freelancer's dream: security without exclusive commitment. What they saw in him, he didn't know. As he'd told Jeannie, he was a bad bet in anyone's business. And he knew a trap when he saw one, all the promise of adventure and oh so tempting. He guessed that if they were dumb enough to offer it, he was dumb enough to walk into this one. For now.

———

Jeannie enjoyed the back-and-forth flow with Emily as they flew. Every move Jeannie made was corrected—no, enhanced. She wasn't doing anything wrong, but Emily's few words and frequent nudges through their shared controls elevated her thinking to whole new levels.

Flying at night was little different from flying through a cloud, except you never flew out the other side. Just like any other instrument flying, you flew high enough to be above any man-made obstacles, as much as you could, and you trusted to your readouts rather than your instincts. The artificial horizon said you were going straight and level, but your inner ear said "Rolling dive!" You had to trust the stupid little readout.

Jeannie was most used to flying by visual rules—stay out of the smoke and trust your eyes. But she had flown plenty with instruments so that she could get through a smoke column or make a simple nighttime transit.

She'd even used the heads-up display a few times. The HUD projected the most important instruments on the windscreen in front of her so that she could keep an eye out the window and didn't have to look down very often. She often lost the HUD when she moved

her head out of the eyebox, the small area from which
the HUD could be viewed. If she leaned over too far to
stretch or look out the side window, the display wasn't
visible. Frankly, using the thing gave her a crick in
the neck.

The Thales TopOwl helmet was something she really
wasn't ready for. It offered night vision, which was useless once they crossed over Bathurst Island off Darwin
and headed out over the open Timor Sea. But it also
offered her the essential readouts of the chopper's attitude in the sky—altitude, speed, and heading. It even
drew the artificial horizon as a line across most of her
view to help her brain stay oriented despite there being
nothing to see.

The clear visor came down to the end of her nose.
She could focus on the images that were projected on the
inside of it, or she could glance through them to double-
check any cockpit controls. She'd done training with the
TopOwl in simulators, but this was her first time really
playing with it in flight and it was awesome.

"Where have you been all my life, baby?" she crowed
after she'd finally gotten used to the helmet's display.

"Hiding in the back of your helicopter." Cal laughed
over the intercom.

"Feh! You're just a guy. These are a work of beauty."

Emily didn't laugh, but when Jeannie glanced over,
she did appear to be smiling.

"They make you both look like bobblehead dolls or
maybe psychotic alien robots."

Jeannie could get down with that if it gave her this
kind of control and visibility. MHA spent the money to
have the very best toys.

Then Emily hit a circuit breaker and all of the cockpit instrument panel lights went out.

Cal's curse of "What the hell!" matched her sentiments exactly. The cockpit was now wholly dark except for the readout on the helmet.

She suddenly had about a tenth of the information she was used to having. *Trust your instruments!* She kept her focus on what data she had. Every few seconds she'd flick the finger switch on the collective to cycle through the various data views: engine conditions, flight instruments, local radar traffic—just the one other chopper flying nearby. As she continued to fly without the main panel, she became more and more aware of what else was going on in her Firehawk.

The engines were still running clean, at exactly the sound levels she'd expect. Lack of stray vibrations told her that the rotors were still intact. The responsiveness of the anti-torque pedals told her there were no problems with the drive train or the rear rotor. There was a sound and a feel to a clean-running machine. Twenty minutes on, Beale gave her back the full cockpit displays and it was almost an affront. She'd just jumped from the dark Outback to the city lights, and it was a dizzying change. But keeping her eye on the horizon marker, she kept her flight smooth and steady.

And she was looking down about a tenth as often as she'd been before. Without a word, Emily had drilled home the lesson to keep your head up and use all your senses. Damn, but the woman was an amazing instructor. Jeannie filed that away as something she'd use when she was the one doing the training.

"Two main hazards of water crossing?" Emily asked.

"Disorientation, boredom, and being stupid enough to do it alone in case you go down."

"You're the highest point. You've just been hit by lightning."

"Engines may run out of control. Rebalance RPMs by sound using engine power control levers. Reduce speed to eighty knots. Land real damn soon."

And so the drill went, mile after mile for the whole flight. Jeannie would be in the middle of reciting some complex procedure, and Emily would be ever so slowly misdirecting the chopper with her controls. Jeannie would get that corrected, but then the flight trim would inexplicably be set wrong.

It was when Emily started in on aircraft-carrier landing protocols that Jeannie kind of freaked out.

"Well, Mark did mention that we'd be landing at an offshore base."

"But a carrier? There's no way I'm qualified for that."

"Actually, you are. Except for the actual number of landings required to make you fully qualified."

"I am?" No she wasn't. She'd never been near a helo pad. Except...

"Remember the flight trainer I sent you to when you switched from the MD500 to the Firehawk?"

"Yeah, I do. The bastard had this obsessive thing about me placing all three wheels each in its own two-foot square box every time I landed. He had a real bugaboo about precision even after he'd cut off one of my turbines."

"Welcome to carrier landing. The flight control officer will guide you down to the deck, and you'd better be exactly where he tells you. If not, your blades could catch in those of a parked chopper on one side or a radio mast on the other. There is no room for error."

"And when the deck is moving? Come on, Emily. No way I'm ready for this." Jeannie could feel the sweat forming on the inside of her palms just thinking about it.

"You set down exactly when and where the flight officer says. If he signals you down fast the last ten feet, you plummet and let the shocks take the abuse. He's timing your rate of descent with the rolling of the deck to give you the flattest landing site he can. The instant you contact the deck, you stand on the brakes and reverse the rotor pitch to pin you in place. Don't worry. The deck crew on a Navy ship knows to keep low in case a blade sucks down while you're doing that."

"You're not actually expecting me to do that, are you?"

"I bet you could, Jeannie," Cal called from the back.

"Thanks, but you wouldn't be the sucker at the controls."

"For all his blind confidence," Emily commented as she tried sneaking the pedals to turn the chopper sideways but Jeannie didn't let her, "Cal is correct. And, no, we won't be forcing you down in a storm."

"Thank God."

"At least not yet."

Jeannie groaned.

"In the meantime, you can land us…there." Emily pointed. "You have command." Then she removed her hands and feet from the controls.

Jeannie did her best not to panic despite the pulse pounding in her ears.

Down below, looking comically tiny in the middle

of a midnight-black sea, was a ship. She could see it in her night vision.

"That's not an aircraft carrier, Emily. You lied. It's teeny."

Emily leaned forward to peer out the windscreen. "How odd. Well, that's where you're landing, so you'd better start talking to the comm officer before they decide to shoot you down as an unknown incoming." Then she read off a frequency.

The next few minutes were a blur. From the moment Jeannie called, "Mount Hood Aviation civilian Firehawk Oh-two requests permission to land," until the moment her wheels smacked down on the deck couldn't have been more than five minutes. But about five hours of new experiences, knowledge, intuition, and impressions had occurred in that time span. She would need some quiet time to process it all—and a lot of practice before she'd be comfortable with it.

"You'll never be comfortable with it." Emily appeared to be reading her mind as they fully settled onto the deck. "That's how you know you're doing it right. Even on the big carriers, it's that bad." The deck crew rolled her chopper as far forward as possible to allow Henderson to land behind her. The "teeny" ship had turned out to be four hundred feet long, and almost a third of it was a helipad. Which meant that the deck just barely had room for two of the big Firehawks at the same time without having to fold their rotors.

Henderson set down Steve's drone launch trailer to one side of his landing zone, then shifted Firehawk Oh-one over and settled down gently.

Jeannie watched him critically, but he made it look

so smooth and practiced that she couldn't see any of the details of what he did. She felt like a beginning pilot all over again, too overwhelmed with not crashing to understand how someone could even fly straight.

—∿∿—

Cal climbed down to stretch his legs after the long flight. It was still well before midnight and the deck was fairly steady. Of course, it took a good-sized wave to shuffle around a four-hundred-foot-long warship.

He almost stepped on a guy bent down to anchor the chopper to the deck with straps wider than Cal's palms—thick enough to survive a hurricane. A step later he was almost trampled by a guy and a gal in crash helmets and purple vests dragging a fat hose that smelled ever so slightly of jet fuel.

He finally found a safe spot near the nose of the chopper where he appeared to be out of the immediate damage path but could observe the controlled mayhem of the busy flight deck. Once again his cameras were forbidden. When in hell was he going to get to use them anyway? The deck lights cast sufficient light, but photos of operations were "not allowed." It was starting to piss him off.

As he watched, he began to see the order behind the chaos. While he appeared to be in everyone's way, they were never in each other's. A cargo team pulled the spares kit off Jeannie's chopper and trundled it forward for storage. Another group was helping Steve set up his drone launcher.

He recognized the service team because they moved the way Denise did. Well, not the way she did, which he had certainly enjoyed watching, but they came up with checklists and began opening covers and making detailed inspections. That was why Henderson hadn't brought Denise along. The U.S. Navy was providing the service crew for their civilian Firehawks. That elevated the whole situation at least another level or two, maybe ten or twelve.

"Where the hell are we anyway?"

"We"—Henderson strode up beside him, walking as smoothly through the mayhem as Jeannie had across the Outback—"are on the littoral combat ship USS *Freedom*. It's one of the Navy's newest ship designs. This is number one and was deployed to Southeast Asia in 2013. It's been so useful, they haven't reassigned her yet."

"And since when does the Navy support civilian firefighters?"

"That is a different question. Let's go below."

Cal observed what he could in the dark, which wasn't much. Beyond the circle of the landing lights was nothing but dark ocean. The rear of the craft was a big, flat helipad with a giant, white target circle in the center and a number of other lines that made sense to someone, but not him. He looked at where Henderson's chopper had landed, all three wheels resting on crossed white lines a foot wide. The deck crew didn't have to move it an inch. They just tied it down right where it was.

Forward from the flight deck, a pair of large doors revealed an empty hangar, just big enough for the two choppers if they had their rotors refolded as they'd been for the C-17. Somewhere ahead of that, visible as no more than a silhouette, rose another level of deck and the radar and radio masts. One glimpse as they circled in to land had told him that the ship had a narrow bow with a lump in the middle of the foredeck that he guessed was a fairly good-sized gun.

Henderson rounded up the others and they headed in through the hangar space. The MHA spares had been shoved to one side and strapped down, clearly not needed in this amazing space. Racks of gear, gleaming chests of service tools—the Navy could obviously deal with anything that came up just as well as Denise could.

They trooped down a narrow flight of steep steel stairs. After a couple of turns along a narrow gray hallway, only wide enough for two people to pass if one put their back to the wall, Cal figured they were now directly beneath the helo deck.

"Our mission module is second on the left as you head aft. Do not, I repeat, not try to open any of the other doors except the one marked toilet." Henderson opened the door that appeared to have neither key nor lock. Right, no security of that kind needed on this vessel. Most civilians would never step aboard a ship like this, never mind wander around unescorted. Anything really important probably had an armed guard standing there.

Inside the room was a line of three computer workstations with narrow bench seats, three chairs that might almost be called comfortable, and a conference table that dominated the center of the space.

Henderson appeared to be in no hurry to start, and Cal would go berserk if he spent much longer contemplating the steel-gray walls. Jeannie was in some intense whispered conversation with Beale. So Cal wandered over to one of the computer stations. When he tapped the screen

awake, he was asked for password and thumbprint. Not
so much. He pulled out his tablet. It showed instant con-
nectivity under guest account access, a relief after his
disconnection in the Outback. He wasn't used to being
unplugged so long except when he was on a fire. Not
even then very often.

The *LA Times* had front-paged his article about the
flying cop car and resold the rights into six additional
channels—a nice spot of change in both of their pockets.
The cop had been labeled a hero and said some nice
things about Cal and MHA that actually made it into
the paper. He'd sent Cal an email of thanks as well.
Sounded like a decent guy. Cal answered with a promise
to look him up for a beer next time he was in town. That
was one thing a hotshot never lacked, even one turned
photographer—a drinking buddy in every town even
close to where wildfires had ruled.

The video about the golfers had indeed gone viral.
There were already spin-offs and parodies, most featur-
ing the faces of the four jerks. Very satisfying. Normally
he wouldn't wreak such vengeance on someone's head
for doing something stupid. Lord knew some of his
own hotshot pranks hadn't been all that much more
admirable. But he still felt the anger in the pit of his
stomach that someone had attacked Jeannie's helicopter, put her in danger if they'd hit something critical.
Making them planetary laughingstocks was too kind, but
it was sufficient.

A woman of about Jeannie's height walked into
the room without saying a word. She wore an Army
uniform and boots, but had flowing brown hair that
scattered down past her shoulders. He didn't think the

Army allowed stuff like that. The only group he knew
that could get away with that was Special Ops guys. And
she looked like the dream girl from next door, not a dangerous warrior of the highest caliber. Though with the
nasty-looking gun in her holster and long knife strapped
to her thigh, he'd give her the benefit of the doubt.

When she spotted Beale, she snapped a salute so sharp
Cal just knew it was textbook perfect. Beale returned the
gesture easily. "Greetings, Sergeant First Class Davis.
Congratulations on the promotion."

"Thank you, Major." Then she did a turn and offered
Henderson an equally sharp salute that he returned just
as neatly.

"No longer in the service, Connie."

"Sir, no, sir."

They shared a smile over that, just a bit sad on both
of them if Cal read it right. She used to fly with them,
which meant she too was from the Night Stalkers. So,
here was another woman who'd be insanely competent
at whatever she did. He looked about the room: Beale,
Carly, Connie, and Jeannie…

"We're outnumbered and outgunned here, guys."
Steve laughed, and Henderson acknowledged that with
a nod before clearing his throat.

"Not to sound rude, Connie, but what the hell are you
doing here?"

Cal wondered that Henderson didn't know. That
meant something even more unusual than civilian firefighters landing on a military ship was going on.

"I'm your mission specialist, sir."

Henderson was considering the implications and
looking perplexed.

"Specialist, liaison, and sole point of contact."

Henderson's attention snapped to her face at the last. He froze for a long moment before he nodded in acknowledgment.

Cal had to puzzle at that one a moment before he got it. Henderson, formerly Major Mark Henderson, had just been told that the only person he was allowed to talk to on the whole ship was a sergeant who used to work for him. Okay, that one had to sting.

"You and your crew have quarters farther aft on this corridor. Meals will be provided in this room. Also—"

"But why you?" Henderson cut her off.

"Need to know, sir. You don't currently need to know."

"Shit!" Henderson looked away toward the bank of computers.

"Sorry, sir."

"Not your doing, Connie."

The whole room had gone dead still, as Henderson continued to inspect the hardware.

When Emily took a step toward him, he flashed some hand signal and she stopped.

A few seconds later he turned back to the room. "Okay. Let's do this." He sounded calm and in control.

Only Cal had been positioned to see the torture on his face. How much had Henderson sacrificed when he left the Night Stalkers and went over to MHA? Things that he was only now finding out about?

It definitely took the shine off the "perfect gig" that Henderson had offered him. How much was Cal being asked to sacrifice that he didn't understand yet?

Chapter 15

JEANNIE LIKED SERGEANT DAVIS ALREADY. ANYONE WHO would salute Emily Beale so seriously was all right in Jeannie's book.

The sergeant went to the computer Cal had poked at earlier. Was he being distant? No. They just hadn't had a moment alone since the river. Not even a little one.

Davis typed in a password, pressed a thumb on a reader, and the screen cleared. Then she went to open some file. A big, red warning flashed on the screen. Connie leaned in close, as if putting one eye in line with the tiny camera at the center of the screen.

"Thumbprint on the machine and retinal scan on the file," Cal whispered from just over her shoulder. "Hell, I use a six-digit password."

"Your birthday?" she whispered back.

"Actually Calvin Hobbes Jackson's birthday."

She didn't even know his real name. Having had a tiny glimpse of his past only told her how little she knew about him. "You and I need to—"

"If you'll all look at the screen."

Jeannie spun around to see that a projector mounted on the center of the ceiling was now lighting the opposite wall. Someone dimmed the lights.

"This is the island of Timor." A long, thin bit of land with nothing else even close. "The west half of it belongs to Indonesia. The other half is the Democratic

Republic of Timor-Leste, also known as East Timor."
With a laser pointer, Connie traced the wavering line
of the border as it cut oddly along rivers, doubled
back on itself in a wide curve over mountains, and
then found another river to follow to the other coast.
It curved like a snake across the narrowest part of the
island. The country was about forty miles wide and two
hundred long.

"There's another little piece of East Timor here as an
exclave about forty miles away." She indicated a small
misshapen lump along the north side of the island. "But
they have no fires there at the moment. Nor are there
any in the Indonesian half of the island so we have no
worries there."

"What's the terrain like?" Leave it to a hotshot to care
about the terrain. Clearly he hadn't switched his brain
over to the idea that they could fly above it.

"Rugged, some of it very rugged. This central mountain range tops out at near three thousand meters, over
nine thousand feet."

"Damn! Let's hope that the firefight doesn't go up
there." Jeannie did some quick calculations of high-
hot limitations on load capacity. Then realized she
was running the numbers for her old MD500. At ten
thousand feet and within ten degrees of the equator,
the Firehawk—her beautiful, big Firehawk—would
have twenty-five percent less power. And since half
of her weight was structural and half of it was a water
payload, that meant losing half of the payload. Plus a
safety margin…

"Crap! We can't even lift five hundred gallons to the
top of that mountain."

"I make it about four-ninety," Connie confirmed, offering a brief smile as if Jeannie had just done something really right.

Cal looked at her with…shock on his features. It wasn't rocket science. It was just…helicopter science. And she'd always been able to do that. Emily nodded to herself as if thoroughly pleased with something. With the fact that her and Connie's numbers had matched? That Jeannie had been able to do the simple calculation that had so gobsmacked Cal?

Connie picked up her narration of facts. "In 1975, East Timor declared its independence from Portugal. A couple months later, Indonesia took over the country and claimed it as theirs for the next twenty-two years. They had—"

"Man, that had to suck." Cal broke the stream of information.

Connie Davis might have been speed-reading from an encyclopedia, yet she wasn't referring to any notes. Even while talking to Henderson, she'd been very cool, but the Majors had both been very pleased to see her. Cool or just steady? She had looked very pleased to see Emily in that half moment before snapping the textbook salute. A woman with hidden layers, Jeannie decided.

"It gets worse. Free in 1999, they had an elected government by 2002. By 2007, presidential candidates had become shooting targets and then their military completely collapsed after half of them were fired. The UN had to occupy until the end of 2012 to maintain order. This is when it starts getting interesting."

Jeannie placed her palm on her heart. It really hurt for those poor people. Cal looked grim.

"In 2011, Indonesia supported East Timor's application to join ASEAN, the Association of Southeast Asian Nations. The military has been rebuilt to thirteen hundred men and women. Most of them have rifles, some of them have handguns. They have four patrol boats around the forty-meter class, but they're grossly undermanned due to lack of trained personnel. No jets, no choppers. They barely have uniforms. That's the political background you're entering into." Davis stopped as if a switch had been turned off. The exact amount of information she'd been cleared to impart had been communicated. But none of it was anything you couldn't find on Wikipedia.

Jeannie looked at Cal to see if he was feeling the same itch. There had to be something else going on. There were too many odd pieces, including Sergeant Davis herself.

Cal looked around the room as if he'd just been woken from a sound sleep and was checking to see who was in the room with him.

Jeannie tried to figure out what he was thinking. He must be wondering why they were here. Why were they here? This was Mount Hood Aviation. They were a firefighting outfit. Oh...

"There's a fire," Cal said before she could.

"Big one," Jeannie agreed and dropped into one of the chairs at the table. "If they can justify us coming in, it's got to be a big one."

Connie Davis nodded and waited for one of them to continue. It was easier to think of her as Connie. Jeannie wasn't military enough to be comfortable with someone's rank becoming their first name. Calling her brother Pilot Officer Clark only worked for her when she was trying to irritate him.

Cal shrugged at her and sat in the chair beside her.

"Where do you start?" she asked him.

"Wait, that's it. Jeannie said it was the wrong season for big fires in this region. Not unheard of, but not normal. That means you suspect something weird is going on, but aren't sure. You want us to prove or disprove that."

Connie nodded definitively, the lesson complete. She pulled up another image. A series of four big fires were marked by distinct plumes of smoke in the satellite photograph.

"Damn!" Cal whispered under his breath and Jeannie couldn't agree more. These were big fires. All in the west end of East Timor, near the border with Indonesia.

"What's the population like?" She could almost picture the homes going up in smoke.

Connie pulled up another image. "There are only two real border crossings. They're right along the coast, north and south. No real towns associated with them. All of the towns are in-country. The biggest is Suai to the south at twenty thousand people, Maliana same size to the north, and Bobonaro up in the central highlands with about six thousand. The main city of Dili is halfway across the country. About two hundred thousand, a fifth of the country's population, lives there—well out of harm's way."

Jeannie cringed. That was still a lot of people and a lot of homes, and two towns, each almost as big as Alice Springs.

"So you want us to fight the fires and scope out what's going on with them?"

"Yes, you'll be doing firefighting but you'll also be acting as on-site observers. Unless there is serious justi-fication, the UN can't send even fire-support forces back in. Because they withdrew the peacekeeping forces so recently, it would send a bad message. It could desta-bilize what little foothold the current East Timorese government has carved out. So, MHA is presently on loan to East Timor as firefighters and to the UN Security Council as observers."

"The who-what?" most of them stumbled out simultaneously.

All except Mark and Emily. If they were surprised, he and Emily were the only ones in the room not to show it.

"Which"—Mark planted his fists on the head of the table and leaned toward them, scanning the group— "none of you can mention to anyone, ever. Inside SOAR, we called this a black-in-black operation. I don't care if the goddamn UN Security Council itself comes calling, outside of this room all any of you ever saw was fire. Is that absolutely understood?"

—⁓—

And it was all they did see.

Whether man-made or from natural causes, this fire didn't care. Cal had rarely seen its like. Three of the four fires had merged. Anywhere in the United States, other than perhaps Alaska, this would have been termed a Type I. A thousand or more trained professionals would have been on-site along with air tankers, heli-tack, smokejumpers…

They had two helicopters. The Aussies had their own bushfires to deal with, so they'd sent just a pair of

Bombardier water-scooping planes. At least they were the bigger CL-415s that could hold half again what the choppers could carry. On lake, river, or ocean, they could refill fifteen hundred gallons in twelve seconds as they skimmed over the surface of the water. Even the high-speed pumps on the choppers took forty seconds to fill a thousand gallons. Which felt like forever when you were just hovering there while the fire was eating the hills.

Their first day had been all about trying to avert disaster rather than fighting fire. The hills climbed steeply from river valley to ridge and back down. The terrain was chopped up by a thousand tributaries that would have made groundwork nearly impossible even if they had the crews.

Like in Australia, most of the rivers were dry at the moment, though not as bad as in the Red Centre. At the tail end of the Dry and with the monsoon running late, the forest and grasslands were parched. They burned so fast that they were practically wicking up the flame in their urgent need to burn.

Citizens, with little to no warning in the outlying areas where neither phone nor electricity reached, didn't know to evacuate until smoke crested the ridge announcing fire was not far behind. Often, the only access road was toward the fire and they were sent racing onto the forest trails to escape the blaze. The devastation was horrific. Whole villages of thatch housing disappeared in a single flash of fire. There wasn't even time to try and save the villages; the crews were just trying to slow the fire enough to give people time to escape.

After the long nighttime flight and this even longer

day of fighting fire, they'd all just crashed into their racks, too spent to move, breathe, or discuss anything.

Cal knew it was making Jeannie twitchy as he lay there on the single-wide military bunk with her asleep on his arm. Once the sunset had chased them from the sky, he'd made sure that she ate and hydrated before her body collapsed into sleep. They hadn't even had sex.

It wouldn't hurt anything if they didn't talk until after this fire was beat. Really, it wouldn't change anything. Some part of him, some smart little voice deep inside, told him that he was being stupid, that Jeannie was already fuming. Tomorrow. Maybe they'd find a chance to talk tomorrow.

But tomorrow arrived too early with a harsh alarm clock, a hasty briefing, and a major crisis.

Steve and Henderson had set up a command center aboard the USS *Freedom*. It wasn't much to look at, but Connie had made sure they got what they needed. Steve's drone was serving about four purposes at once. Watching the existing fire and working with the few East Timorese resources in the western part of the country to evacuate the villages in a timely manner. Watching for new flare-ups. Circling wherever Carly needed a view to analyze the fire's behavior to modify her attack plan. It was a long list that gave Cal a headache over his waffles just thinking about it.

"The Suai Airport is a key element in our plan." Henderson tapped a map that Connie had projected on the wall for him.

"We have a plan?" Cal tried to keep it light, perking up in pleased surprise. It was needed because the energy in the room was fast sliding toward doom and gloom.

"A plan, such as it is," Henderson acknowledged and offered him a nod of thanks. "It's the only airport in this whole end of the country big enough to accommodate the Bombardier scooper planes for refueling."

Even though the Suai Airport was nearby, it had three major disadvantages as a staging area for the big planes. The untended runway was barely long enough for a takeoff in normal weather, and it was bloody hot, which decreased lift. The second problem was that it would take two days to get a fuel truck there overland with the needed capacity. They only had enough fuel on-site for one more day.

Apparently now there was a third problem.

"A new fire, born out of nowhere, is sweeping down-wind toward the Suai Airport."

Steve put up the latest images from his drone. They didn't show much because the sun hadn't risen yet. Then he flipped to infrared. A raging area of intense light was already sprawling over the squared-off areas of farmers' fields and headed toward the airport and town.

Cal's whispered oath elicited nods from several of the people around him. He could feel a deep-rooted need to beat the crap out of the fire. It was a feeling that didn't diminish, no matter how long it had been since he'd actually fought fire for a living.

"If it's destroyed," Henderson continued, "it would be devastating for the Bombardiers. Without the Suai Airport, every three hours the planes would have to make an hour round-trip flight to the airport in the capital city of Dili. It's sixty miles farther from the fire, which equals an additional round-trip time of forty minutes. Their fuel pumps are just as old and slow at that airport as the ones at Suai. The choppers, too, would have to waste about half an hour of every three getting back to the *Freedom* because we're stationed well offshore in international waters."

Henderson scowled in Connie's direction before continuing. "For reasons I don't know—sorry, Sergeant, you didn't deserve that"—he took a deep breath before continuing—"the Navy has deemed that there are valid reasons for not entering Timorese waters at this time. Let that be enough said on that topic."

They clambered up on deck, where the Navy had seen to their birds so that they practically shone. Full tanks, both water and fuel. They'd even restocked the pilots' water and energy bars. They launched into the morning sky to see what they could do about saving the airport and the town of Suai. The airport was east, which meant the only route of escape for the locals was west toward the bigger fires near the border, or up into the hills where the fire would be headed if they failed to stop it.

"Nothing in this country seems to be working." Cal scowled down at the fire and tried not to notice that it looked even worse than it had on Steve's images. Jeannie lined up her tenth, or maybe it was her fifteenth, load of the day to attack it.

"*We're* working," Jeannie reminded him. And she was working hard. Everyone was. Carly was trying to create the best attack plan, while keeping an eye on the existing fires so that they'd know when they had to break off to go help a village. Steve had his drone spinning in mad circles. Henderson seemed to be everywhere at once, though he sat aboard the LCS ship with Steve and

Tessa, coordinating helicopters and fixed-wing tankers as well as whatever limited ground forces could be gathered. Beale and Jeannie were flying their asses off. If there was a wasted second in their motions, Cal sure couldn't see it.

"You're working," Cal bit back against the sharp taste of impatience yet again. "I'm just a goddamn fifth wheel."

"So, stop whining and do your job." Jeannie sounded pretty exasperated.

"Hunh." He'd thought her patience was boundless, but apparently he'd crossed over some line. He reconsidered. Had he been whining? Cal grimaced. It sure sounded like he had. Even to him. Yeah, irritating.

"I remember a first-year rook who did that to me on the Basin and Indians Fires. Just wouldn't stop going on about how nothing was ever the way it *should* be."

"What did you do to him?"

"Well, he sure didn't stick around to see if we'd hire him back for the second year. Not sure he even finished the first."

"Lesson learned?" Jeannie asked, suddenly all sweetness and light, and obviously talking about him.

"Yep, always abuse the rookie. For a bonus, it's fun too."

That got him a laugh. A tired one. Right, he checked his watch, barely two hours aloft and already the strain was taking its toll. That was the second part of the message he hadn't been hearing. She'd been working her pretty butt off. He, on the other hand, hadn't been doing squat, so why was he the one complaining?

"Sorry. I get stupid sometimes. Thanks, Helitack."

She ducked back to the coast and picked up another tank of seawater before spinning back to Suai. The airport hadn't burned yet, but neither was it safe. The fire here was also the smallest and newest fire. Maybe they could stop it before it joined the others and made an even more complex situation.

"So, any suggestions on what I'm doing here that Steve's drone can't do better?"

"You tell me, Cal. I don't know half of what you can do."

"Swing an ax and take pictures."

Jeannie spared a moment to glare at him before dumping her latest load right on top of a row of burning huts at the very edge of the field. He turned back in time to see a Bombardier scooper dump a long line of water right alongside Jeannie's drop. The waterfall kept going and going. At least three seconds, maybe four of continuous flow. Right, it had half the capacity of the Firehawk.

For lack of anything more inspired to do, he took a photo of the end of its drop. It was a great backdrop. The flame behind was smoky dead, subdued under the middle of the drop, and at the leading edge making one last valiant effort to burn even as its death fell from the belly of the brightly yellow-and-red aircraft.

He watched it as they both circled back over the nearby beach to reload.

Jeannie dipped her tanking snorkel just past the line of low breakers running up toward the white sand beach near the narrow outlet of a slow-moving river. The river itself was technically deep enough for the Firehawk's snorkel, over a meter in places, but she said it wasn't worth the effort of making sure she was over such a spot when the beach was so close.

As she hovered, he nudged the anti-torque pedals with his feet and she let him. He slowly spun the chopper until he was lined up to see the run of the Bombardier. There was so little surf that they had to go out only a little farther than Jeannie did. They needed just two meters of depth for their sixty-five-foot plane to scoop up fifteen hundred gallons. He snapped some photos as he kept the pressure on the pedal to let him sweep the entire seaboard.

First, the initial rooster tail as the plane's hull kissed the water at around a hundred miles per hour. Then the long, twelve-second run marked by the belly of the plane being ducked down into the wave. The "full" indicator as excess scooped water was blown out the side of the aircraft by funnels at the tops of the tanks, and then the slow lift as she climbed aloft seven tons heavier than moments before.

Jeannie pulled them aloft and circled back only moments after the Bombardier did. It really was a beautiful ballet that these pilots did. Was catching it on camera sufficient? He'd enjoyed the moments he'd spent holding the Santa Barbara fire line; liked walking the ground with the engine crews of Alice Springs and Akbar's smokies. The two experiences made him wonder about getting back out in the field.

He'd gotten into photography in the first place to share the experiences of the firefighters—the joy and the passion—with civilians. Had he lost too much when he'd stopped actually fighting the fire? Just like the price Henderson had paid when he left the military.

The next thought bugged him as he watched through

another round of drop and return to the ocean. It wasn't so much the thought; it was the question.

Would Jeannie think any better of him if he returned to hotshotting? Or even took Akbar up on his offer to jump smoke?

He watched her profile for probably a quarter hour, through several circuit flights. For some reason, it became a question of great importance.

Cal just didn't dare ask it.

—◦◦◦—

Jeannie knew Cal was studying her, busy doing his "I'm a guy so I don't speak" thing. Did he have to process every goddamn thing internally?

Well, she was too busy to get into it. She also knew herself well enough to not start—she was too angry. Sure, yesterday had been panic-level flying to try and get some control of the fire and this morning had started off even worse, but he was sitting all of one foot away the whole time. You think he could at least—

"Hey!" Cal leaned forward, his seat harness unspooling behind him enough to let him look down and out over the console. "Circle back."

"We don't have time for this."

"Circle back, Jeannie." His voice had changed, just the way it had when he was explaining his plan to fight the Alice Springs fire. It took on depth, power, and certainty. She kicked the pedals harder than she should have, dropping twenty feet in the maneuver.

"There!" He shot out a hand to point. "Do you see it?"

"See what?" All she saw were the bare foundations of burned homes. Made of little more than sticks and thatch, they had burned almost completely to leave cleared spaces, distinctly square, covered in ash.

"Take us down."

"Cal…"

"Just take us down, Jeannie. I need to check this out. Land us over there. I don't want the chopper's down-draft messing this up."

He was out of the Firehawk before the wheels were even on the ground. She'd placed the wheels between two houses. Well, the houses were no longer there, but she felt bad enough for the families without showing them that a pilot didn't care about what had once been their home. She flattened the lift on the blades as quickly as she could to avoid kicking up even more ash than she already had.

Cal sprinted away to where the black met the unburned street beyond. Where it met the unburned *streets*. The black formed a distinct vee here. As if the fire were only just beginning when it had burned this over.

Jeannie dropped the collective, slid the throttles down to idle, and sprinted after Cal.

"Point of origin. Be careful," he said as she came up behind him. He had his camera out.

"Someone's cooking fire got out of control?"

"Someone set a firebomb. Molotov cocktail, only bigger." He pointed. "See the scorch marks on those two unburned buildings outside the black? Ignited fuel spattered against them, but they didn't burn. And the mud-brick building just inside the black that's almost charred past recognition?" He took shots of each as he spoke. "This fire didn't build. It started out instantly hot. That takes an accelerant of some kind. This was deliberate."

"Who would want to burn Suai, East Timor?"

Cal stopped taking pictures and slowly turned, scanning the area. "No. The question is: Who would want to burn the Suai *Airport*? Ocean's that way. Sea breeze in the night heading offshore. That's why the fire was set inland of the airport."

She could see it. Nature's gentle breeze sweeping from the cooling land toward the still warm ocean, little knowing that with its progress, it was carrying lethal fire downwind.

"C'mon." He grabbed her arm and began dragging her back toward the chopper.

"What?"

He practically threw her through her own door before latching it and racing around to his own. "Land breeze coming up!" he shouted as he jumped in beside her.

Jeannie sat there feeling stupid even as her hands made sure everything was ready and cycled the engine RPMs back up.

"Land breeze!" She got it. All they had to do was keep the flames at a standstill along the airport's verge until the land breeze came up in mid-morning. If they could, the flames would double back on themselves. And when they did, the team could kill the fire as it ran out of fuel over the black.

When she went to report it in, Cal cut her off.

"Nothing about what we found. Only how to kill it."

"What? Why?"

"We don't know who's listening. It'll be easier to find the goddamn arsonists if we don't alert them that we're on their track."

It was a long morning and a close call, but they held

the fire at bay. With the heat of the day, and no other weather systems in the area, the breeze stilled, then turned. The fire turned with it, but found no fresh fuel. It attempted to break sideways several times. They beat it down with a hundred thousand gallons of seawater. By mid-afternoon, the Suai fire was done.

Cal insisted that they not refuel at the airport but rather return to the *Freedom*.

—⁓—

"What the hell are you doing back here? There are three more fires out there!" Henderson looked pissed when Cal breezed into the conference unannounced. "Why do you think we went to all the trouble of saving that lame excuse for an airport if you aren't going to refuel at it?"

"Trust me, Mark. Connie, I need to link my tablet to your screen." He handed it to her and wished to God he was wrong. But he wasn't. Jeannie had seen it as well.

He explained the images as he went, pointing out the details. Connie zoomed in on a couple details he hadn't noticed. Boot prints. Not sandals, not bare feet, not even sneakers. That was all a local would have had. No, these were heavy-duty soles.

"Army boots." It was the only thing that made sense to Cal. "Sorry, wish I'd gotten a better shot, but I didn't notice them at the time."

"It's sufficient"—Connie tweaked the image a bit— "to tell that it is a universal brand, probably in use in dozens of countries including East Timor. Maybe tourist hikers, but when combined with the high accelerant, I think your first instinct is right. Look at this hand scythe on the ground."

Cal looked and wondered how the sergeant had possibly determined what it was.

"Melted almost past recognition. And the knockdown of these tools over a dozen feet back in the unburned zone. That's probably a fuse cord igniter and a thermite accelerant. This line here in the dirt might have been safety fuse cord. So the profile fits."

"Not stuff you find on a shelf at Walmart?" Jeannie sank into a chair, and Cal came up behind her and rubbed her shoulders. It had to be her worst nightmare, someone intentionally destroying homes.

"Definitely not. This is a professional job. Again, pointing to military action."

"Whose?" Henderson demanded.

"No way to tell."

Henderson paced off to the far side of the room. Through the whole thing, Steve had sat quietly at his drone control terminal watching the goings-on.

"Steve. Buddy. Pal." Cal walked over to stand behind Steve's triple screens. To the far left were a whole lot of flight instrument readouts, only some of which he recognized from Jeannie's Firehawk. The other two screens showed visual and infrared images broadcast from the drone.

"Cal. Dude." Steve grinned back at him.

"Have you found points of origin on the other four fires?"

"Carly identified three of them." He spun some controls, bringing a map view onto the center screen. Three red *X*s showed up not far from the country's western border. "She thinks the fourth one was burned over by one of the other fires."

"Can you drop those onto Jeannie's chopper display?"

Steve rattled a few keys on his keyboard. "Done."

"Good man." Cal really had to find some time to check out what other cool things Steve could make his drones do. He could see how Steve and Carly made such a tight team; he gathered the information and she made sense of it.

Did Cal and Jeannie make a tight team? What about Mark and Emily? They looked tight, acting in a unison that could only come from years of serving together and more of marriage. But did Emily know that Mark was chafing at the reins?

Time. He needed time to get to know Mark, to learn from Steve and Carly, and most of all to figure out what the hell was going on between himself and Jeannie. Well, whenever that was, it wasn't now.

"You ready to go back aloft, Helitack?"

"Ready when you are, Hotshot." As they turned for the door, Connie called out after them.

"Go ahead and get prepped, but wait for a couple minutes. I'll let you know when."

Cal did his best not to be irritated at not being privy to what Connie and Henderson were about to discuss.

Halfway down the corridor leading back to the heli-deck, a narrow, windowless space with a single light every twenty feet, Jeannie shoved him against the wall.

Before he could figure out what was wrong or how to protect himself, she filled his arms and was driving him back against the bulkhead with a kiss that practically seared his flesh with its heat. Once he understood what was happening, he didn't waste any time with dumb questions.

Despite the heavy flight gear they both still wore, he found groping her a very satisfying use for his hands. And, damn, but the woman could kiss. Then as abruptly as she'd slammed into him, she was gone.

"Come on, Hotshot."

He lay against the bulkhead a moment longer and watched her do her lioness walk down the corridor away from him. That was a sight he would never tire of. Never. Never? It was a strange word for him to use about anything, especially a woman. But with Jeannie, it was definitely true. That was food for later thought. He shoved himself into motion, a harder task than it sounded.

"What was that for, Helitack?"

"You mean aside from the fact that I love you?"

Crap! Another thing they hadn't had time to discuss. He'd almost forgotten it; he'd tried to, but hadn't succeeded. He also hadn't found a way to talk about anything else that he found to be less intimidating while that topic remained untouched all morning.

"Yeah." He cleared his throat as he followed her up a ladderway to the deck above, trying not to let his hormones dwell too much on his butt-level view of her. "Aside from that."

"The way you see things. And the way you stick to your guns. I'd have totally caved when I saw how ticked off Mark was, but you just breezed right over him. Even Emily can't do that."

"Mark wasn't pissed." Well, not at them. He was pissed at being trapped in a nonmilitary job. But Cal wasn't sure that was his to share. He'd want to check in with Mark before letting that one spread any wider. Especially not to Jeannie who was so cozy with Mark's wife…

Cal stopped on the top step of the ladderway where it came up into the hangar. He'd said he wouldn't lie to Jeannie. But this had that same pinch. Not only did it feel wrong not telling her, but he wanted her view. He wanted her take on the situation. She took on yet another type of importance that no other woman ever had. He valued her opinion as much as his own. Maybe even more.

"Jeannie?"

She stopped at the question in his voice.

He finished climbing the ladder and met her in the cool darkness of the empty hangar. This time he kissed her. Long and slow, appreciating the soft moan as she flowed against him. As his pulse sped, then pounded in his ears. He pulled back and studied her face. Such an amazing face, beautiful and expressive and…and something else he could never tire of.

"Look, beautiful. I know there are about a hundred things we need to talk about. As I said, I'll do my best. But right now, we need to figure out how to help Henderson."

"Help him? What kind of help does he need?"

"I was hoping you could figure that out. All I know is that he's hurting. This assignment is hurting him: seeing Connie in charge, not being able to wander the ship at will, leaving the military. He doesn't strike me as a guy who gets angry about things."

"He isn't." Jeannie glanced back toward the darkened ladderway, thinking hard. "Except these last few days."

"Do you think he and Emily…" He didn't want to ask the question. He'd come to like them.

"No," Connie said, climbing up out of the ladderway

and joining their conversation as if she'd always been a part of it. "Something else is bothering him. Major Henderson is the savviest commander ever to fly for the Night Stalkers. And he and Emily—you can't imagine what they're really like together. If I could figure out how to be more like them, I would be. It's something else that's bothering him. Come, give me a hand." And the enigmatic sergeant walked over to the equipment rack at the rear of the hangar, leaving the conversation just as abruptly as she'd entered it.

Jeannie offered a whispered, "I'll think about it." Then they followed along.

Connie handed Cal two small, heavy steel cases. One was labeled "7.62x51," while the other bore several labels including a yellow triangle with bold, black letters inside: "EX kit." He thought about asking what they were, then thought better of it. After that, Connie pulled a long, heavy case off the shelf, one of a half dozen there, and herded them back into the sunshine. Cal had a bad feeling about that when he saw the FN-SCAR label; he was fairly sure the last three letters stood for combat assault rifle.

Chapter 16

THE SUN BATTERED JEANNIE LIKE A SLEDGEHAMMER after the cool interior of the ship. She started to preflight her chopper and literally ran into Connie. The woman was on the same quest.

"Sorry, force of habit," Connie apologized. "I was Emily's chief mechanic for her last year in the Night Stalkers. I still take care of her helicopter, though Chief Warrant Lola Maloney now flies the *Vengeance*."

Jeannie did her best not to feel daunted by Connie's obvious competence, especially since she was learning to see her own skills as far less meager than she'd thought only a week or so before. Actually Cal did a fairly good job of convincing her she was capable. That a man that competent kept seeing her as so much better than he was; it certainly elevated her self-esteem a bit. They had quite the little mutual admiration society going on. Now if they could each just acknowledge their own strengths.

Well, it was time she started. This chopper was her baby. She felt a hesitation at letting a super-professional mechanic critique her maintenance and care. Then she decided that as part of her new trust-yourself campaign, she would simply decide she was good enough, let Connie say what she would, and learn from that.

Jeannie waved for Connie to go ahead. It would also be an interesting lesson to see exactly what a Night Stalkers master mechanic did, even with something as simple as a preflight. It wasn't until they had both climbed up to inspect the starboard side engine that Connie made any comment.

"I worked on this airframe."

"You did?" She had known it was a rebuild of an Army chopper.

"It was a transport bird, got shot up lifting a load out of Kandahar for the 101st. Came down in a little village called Gereshk about twenty kilometers to the west. They flew me out from Kandahar to fix it, didn't have a lot of spare parts with me. See that clamp?" She pointed down inside the system into the nest of control lines running to the engine. One of them was a different size than the others.

"Yeah…" Was it the sort of thing she should have noticed? No, that was ridiculous.

"That's a Bell helicopter clamp on a Sikorsky aircraft. Did the job when I needed it to."

"When was this repair?"

"May 14, 2008, at about ten thirty-five local time."

"How did you remember that?"

Connie turned to her and tried to change the subject. "You keep a really clean aircraft. Good job."

Jeannie appreciated the comment, but wasn't so easily knocked off her question.

"Sorry." Connie sighed, then spoke reluctantly. "I try not to do that in front of people."

"No, it doesn't bother me. I just want to know how or I'm going to feel less competent than I already do." They climbed back down and continued the inspection of wheels, brake hydraulics, nose cone, and on around to where they started.

"Eidetic memory. Freaks out most people." Then she smiled for the first time. Connie went from quiet girl next door to a total knockout. She'd better not shine that smile at Cal or he'd be a goner. "My husband likes it, though. Keeps telling me how good I am. He's the best mechanic in the Night Stalkers. Says I'm better than he is, but he's just besotted."

They finished the preflight and Jeannie wondered if that was what was going on. Was Cal "besotted" with her? Surprising, but it fit. And Connie didn't seem to mind that her husband kept complimenting her.

Connie insisted on climbing in back. "I don't like being up front on a mission. Not of any kind. Last time I did that, we were in it deep and Emily was bleeding out. I'm not a pilot." She actually loosened up enough to shudder at the memory. "I'll be a backender any day."

No wonder Emily saluted her the way she did. This was a woman who had saved Emily's life, who got it done when it counted no matter how much out of her comfort zone.

"Glad to have you along."

Connie glanced briefly toward the coast, thinking hard before answering.

"Let's hope you still think that when this is all over."

—∿—

Cal moved to the front seat. All he could think about were the three ignition points. There had to be some clue out there as to what was going on. As a hotshot, he'd often ended up being sent to the ignition point of a fire when no fire investigator was available.

"Hey, Cal," they'd say, "you're good at seeing shit. Go check it out."

Well, more than half the time he could send back photos to the local marshal, who often could declare probable cause right away. It helped accelerate tracking down the culprits quite a bit. He'd go and see if there was an obvious lightning strike—about ten percent of wildfires. More than half were unintentional human cause: runaway campfires, logging operations, discarded cigarette butts, that sort of thing. The rest were arson. Most estimates placed arson at around a third of all wildfires. This first one here in East Timor obviously was. He dreaded what he'd find at the next three. Arson always gave him the chills.

With Connie on the intercom, he felt awkward discussing any of the topics rattling around in his mind. But Connie's single comment had stuck there and stuck hard: "You can't imagine what they're like together. It's something else."

Maybe he couldn't. But he could imagine what he and Jeannie were like together. Not just the sex either, though the level of sheer spectacularity was new for him. Also, he could imagine what she looked like when she was happy and when sad. He couldn't get enough of seeing her awake or asleep. When she curled against him, seeking him even in her sleep, Jeannie made him feel more male and more capable than any woman ever had before.

The images in his head were overwhelming. He'd often see a picture forming in his mind's eye before it came together through the lens. That was how he found so many of his photographs. He'd see the image taking shape, and he'd shift his camera to be at the best angle when it showed up.

With Jeannie, every angle formed an amazing image born fully complete. She and Connie clambering over the Firehawk, two beautiful and smart women. He felt the passion and determination that drove Jeannie ahead as hard as she now drove the Firehawk back across the water to the East Timor coast.

He could see her as a woman grown: family, children, joyful. And, strangest of all, he could see himself there as well. He'd never thought much about the future. Mostly he just ran his life from one fire season to the next. He could see them together, feel them together as clearly as he could see what he would find at the other three ignition points.

Reaching across to her, he brushed his fingertips along her cheek, earning a smile he'd never before deserved. Now, in this moment, he'd found a higher calling. Living up to the way Jeannie saw him.

They flashed over the beach and arrowed in on the first fire start, just east of the quiet southern border crossing. With the fiery destruction of the town of Tilomar, the little traffic that used the southern road between Indonesia and East Timor had entirely ceased. The fire had begun down on the coast and quickly climbed up and into the steep hills, chasing out everyone ahead of the flames.

They had to circle twice before Cal could spot the actual point of origin. Carly's estimate had only been approximate. They landed a few hundred yards away, well into the black.

With Connie's assistance, he identified the exact

ignition point and soon had a set of photos depressingly similar to the first set.

"Different boot, same make." She didn't even ask to see his old photo, which was weird.

He had a good memory for images, but not that good. "What…"

"This one has two treads that were torn off near the toe." She shared a smile with Jeannie, but he had no idea what about. "Probably uncomfortable to walk in."

Jeannie nodded her agreement.

Women had to be the most confusing creatures on the planet.

Aloft, they climbed up into the steep hills. The two Bombardiers were working this fire, trying to keep it from overrunning Maliana and Bobonaro.

"This feels wrong," Jeannie said over the intercom as they turned away from the fire and cruised westward over the black.

He reached out a hand and rested it on her left thigh. Her instincts were good, so he began scanning the area more carefully. But he remained aware of their connection, of the little shifts in her thigh as her muscles flexed and relaxed. He also had his feet resting lightly on the pedals, could feel her constant tap dance guiding the chopper.

So in contact with her, so connected. He felt…happy. Could it all be so simple?

"There," Connie called over the intercom. Eleven o'clock low.

This time there was nowhere for Jeannie to land. She hovered close against a steep slope, allowing Cal and Connie to jump down. She moved back aloft above them as they scrambled downslope to the origin point of the middle fire.

They were ten miles from the first fire's origin over rugged ground. It would have taken a significant part of a day to make the hike. Yet similar boot prints were here as well. Not a single arsonist, but rather a planned attack. The tiny town of Taz had once stood here where a dry creek entered a small river, but no more. The town was gone.

"No warning."

"Why do you say that?"

Connie pointed. And that was the moment he was glad Jeannie was still aloft. His mind had been ignoring the smell, charred meat. His gorge rose, but he fought it back as he identified the burned corpses. Two people struck down in mid-flight, three huddled together in the corner of what must once have been a hut, one still sprawled as if they'd never woken from their sleep. He forced himself to take the images. Record the event. Step back behind the camera and not let it touch him. He'd do his damnedest to make sure Jeannie never saw these. She didn't need these images lodged forever in her mind.

"Over here." Connie's voice was cold, almost mechanical. But he was starting to learn to read the quiet woman. It wasn't lack of emotion or revulsion, it was anger. Her job was to protect, and here were innocents dead from arson. He had a sneaking suspicion that despite her demure exterior, this was not a good woman to have as your enemy.

Cal followed to where she'd indicated. No boot prints this time, but the same incendiary. The difference this time was that there were no mud-brick houses to resist burning any stray accelerant. Any back spray from the igniter caused the buildings behind to burn as well. This time they found the remains of the safety fuse housing.

"Military grade," Connie declared. "United States manufacture."

Cal flinched. "Which means—"

"Nothing. We supply military-grade materials to well over a hundred countries including Indonesia, Australia, and East Timor, all of whom have interests in this area."

"Damn it! What have you gotten us into?"

"I'm not sure. We need to move. Call Jeannie back down."

There was no need to call. She was already hovering as close as she could get to the bluff by the time they reached it.

Cal didn't like the reminiscent feel of the jump to get on board. It wasn't a leap off a cliff to escape a lethal flame; it was only a gap of a couple feet over what had once been a grassy slope. But he still didn't like it.

At Connie's refusal of his offer to let her sit up front, he once again clambered forward and buckled in beside Jeannie. Once there, he inspected the third point on the map. It was down near the northern coast. The fourth point of origin was somewhere under the third, now that the wildfire had crossed over it.

"I can't fly direct line to the Mota'ain crossing," Jeannie informed him.

Cal looked up at the wall of fire towering ahead of them. It was a staggering sight. Between beating the Suai fire and refocusing their attention on the origin points, they'd only been flying over the black. The black was a world of blacks and grays, of ash and scorch. Small, often inexplicable patches of green survived, but it was a muted world wrapped in thin tendrils of smoke clawing its way up blackened stumps. Where the fires had burned low, due to thinning fuel on the forest floor, green-tufted tree crowns often bobbed lightly in the thin breeze.

But between them and the coast they were once again confronting the heart of the fire. The smoke towered thundercloud tall above them, a study in whites and grays. For moments, some fire-driven wind current would tear open the smoke curtain and a view of flame would flash forth. A Bombardier slashed across Cal's sight line, tiny against such flames.

He'd seen many hundreds of forest fires over the last ten years and thirty or so that truly deserved the title of wildfire. There was no such distinction really, but that was how they talked about them on the crews. This particular beast was a major player in the "wildfire" category of hotshot-speak. The chaotic winds were tearing trees from the ground and heaving them skyward, rather than merely tossing them aside as the Santa Barbara blaze had done. The fixed-wing water tankers would be avoiding this worst edge. Flame ripped into the sky in sheets, reaching hundreds of feet aloft before finally fading when there was nothing else to burn.

"Indonesia has offered aid," Connie told them, "so passage over their territory shouldn't be an issue. Besides, there won't be anyone but villagers up in these hills on either side of the border to write us a customs violation. Cut west over Indonesia to get around this.

We need to see what's at that third ignition point. Let's get this done and then get back to the firefight."

Jeannie swung them due north and laid down the hammer.

Cal inspected Indonesian West Timor as they crossed over the sparse jungle. It was a lowland of valleys and small-scale agriculture. He snapped a few photos; nothing much there, but it gave him something to do while they were in transit. There was just—

"Connie. Look out the port side, quick."

"What am I looking at?"

"Doesn't the jungle look wrong there? Jeannie, circle back." He leaned out again and shot a series of images as he did so. "The greens don't match. And it looks denser." He slid his zoom all the way out and studied the viewer.

"It's not jungle. That's jungle camo netting."

Something caught his eye and he snapped the image, then scrolled back to it. "I have some sort of an emblem. Golden eagle. Looks like it has a red and white shield over its chest."

"Jeannie! Get us out of here!" Connie's order was cut off by an abrupt pounding against the Firehawk's airframe.

Moments later, Cal heard a sound he'd never heard outside of a movie, a machine gun firing. Really close. He spun around to see Connie squatting in the open cargo-bay door. The case she'd loaded aboard was open beside her, and a nasty-looking weapon was raised to her shoulder. A stream of brass casings was arcing into the back of the chopper as everything shifted into slow motion.

Jeannie turning the chopper back toward East Timor, the deck tilting sharply.

Connie hooking a leg over the edge of the cargo-bay deck to hold herself in place as she continued firing.

He tried searching for the source, even as the chopper spun. There! Someone had thrown back some of the camouflage exposing a military crawler of some sort, though it didn't look like a tank. He managed several shots of it and the dual machine guns on its back before it disappeared from view.

"Cal!"

He barely heard Jeannie's call over the scream of Connie's weapon and more bullets thwacking against the chopper from the ground.

"Yeah?"

"Take the cyclic."

He jammed his camera into his case and grabbed the controls. They jerked abruptly in the air as he did so. He didn't think he'd jarred them, but his adrenaline was running so high he wasn't sure of anything anymore.

"You have control."

"I what?" Cal looked over in time to see Jeannie take her hands off the controls.

Then she reached her left hand to her right arm and it came away red. She reached her bloodstained left hand out toward him practically in supplication.

"Okay. I've got the controls." He had no idea what he was doing. But he'd seen enough injuries on fires to know that it was up to the uninjured to keep their heads. "Clamp your hand over where you were…hit." He couldn't say shot.

The pounding and Connie's firing cut off simultaneously.

"Keep driving ahead," Connie shouted.

"Uh…sure." He pushed the cyclic farther forward, tipping the nose down. Then he slowly raised the collective, making the rotor blades twist to bite more air, create more lift. He watched the airspeed, and they accelerated without getting any closer to the ground.

"That's good, Cal."

He almost cried out in relief at hearing Jeannie's words.

"Cal?" Connie stuck her head up between the seats.

"That's Captain Cal to you." If he didn't make a joke about it, he'd lose what little grip he had on what was happening.

"What the hell?" Connie's question came out with a military snap, a side she hadn't revealed before.

"Jeannie's hit." Cal had a sudden desire to turn around and ram the chopper down the throat of whoever had done that to her. Might have considered it, if he'd thought they had a chance of surviving him actually making a turn. Straight and level was freaking him out badly enough.

"Where and how bad?" Connie was leaning way forward.

"My arm," Jeannie gasped out. "No pumping blood, but I think the bone's broken. Oh my God, but it hurts. Cal!"

Her cry tore at him. He'd seen Jeannie in dozens of moods and imagined a hundred others. Fear was not one he'd ever contemplated. He almost panicked when he heard it. Almost reached for her. But he couldn't and he'd never felt so helpless. He wanted to howl himself.

Sweat was pouring off him, blinding his eyes, but he
didn't dare wipe them. The sweat made his hands slick
on the controls. He instinctively wanted to grip the controls tighter to make sure they didn't slip, but Jeannie
had taught him that was bad.

The few gauges he thought he'd understood now
blurred into the dozens he didn't until he could make
sense of none of them. The fear was right on the cusp
of overwhelming him. He knew that feeling. Knew he'd
walked that line before, every time he'd gone past that
second step and out toward the third.

Fear. He'd been trained. There were ways to turn
fear. When a rookie faced his first inferno or, worse,
his first burnover. When you faced the trap, just like he
had up on that ridge above Santa Barbara where Jeannie
had rescued him. Where Jeannie—that was the answer.

"Okay, Helitack. I need you to focus. If we're gonna
get through this, you better start telling me what to do."
Focus on the job if you want a chance to get through it.
The only way out of fear was also their one chance of
survival: take action.

"Come on, Jeannie," he coaxed her, doing the best he
could to keep his voice light despite what was going on
inside him. "You got me out on this limb. Don't leave
me out here."

They were about halfway back to the fire. It couldn't
have been more than a minute.

"Commun-i-cate." It came out between three gasping breaths.

Right, he had the radio as well. He pushed the radio
button on the back side of the cyclic with his index finger.

"Base, this is Cal."

"Remember to watch what you say," Connie reminded him from her perch close beside him.

"This is Mark, go ahead."

"Hey, boss, we've got, uh, a bit of a problem here. Found what we were looking for, and it, uh…" Then he remembered his very first talk with Henderson. "It went about as well as the first time you kissed your wife." When she'd pummeled his face into a table on an aircraft carrier.

That earned him a respectful silence. "What do you need?"

A miracle if they were going to survive with him at the controls.

"We've got"—Jeannie gulped for air—"about two more minutes aloft."

Cal glanced over and she nodded down toward something on the console. He looked down, but the amount of information was overwhelming. He did spot something flashing red, but didn't know what it meant.

"Put me on," Connie called over the intercom.

Cal keyed the mic and nodded for Connie to speak.

"Hey, boss, we're back in it again, just like last time I flew. And going about as well as last time I flew with you."

Cal clicked off the mic. "What did that mean?"

"He knows I'm an inexperienced pilot. And that I had to finish a flight after his wife had been shot."

"Who's flying?" was Henderson's tight response.

"First time I flew with him"—Connie sounded almost nostalgic—"we were shot out of the sky. A guy named Dusty James took several rounds." Maybe not such a happy memory.

"This…" Cal triggered the mic and tried to ignore the console as a second something started blinking red. He had to clear his throat before he could continue. "This is Captain Cal Jackson. I'm in charge of the remainder of today's flight. We're at…" He had to look around the console display to identify the coordinate readout of their present location, then read them off.

"Roger that. We're—" Something above his head sparked brightly and the radio cut out.

"Well, that was fun. Is the cyclic supposed to be vibrating like this?" It felt like he was holding a hand mixer.

Jeannie squeezed her knees together on either side of the cyclic. "Not good. Really, really, not good."

Cal returned his attention to outside the aircraft. So, if he was going to land, he wanted somewhere wide, no trees, and preferably very soft. The mountainous terrain of East Timor that greeted him through the windscreen told him he wasn't going to be finding that any time soon.

And the fire was too damned close.

"I need you to climb."

"Climb? Did that bullet hit you in the head?"

"Shut up, Cal, and listen. Pull up on the collective and slow down to a hundred and ten knots airspeed by pulling back on the cyclic."

He looked forward at the approaching wall of smoke and fire. Either you were going to trust the woman all the way or not at all. Taking a deep breath, he eased up on the collective. Their heading started to drift and he tapped on the pedals.

"Don't do that. Gentle, easy motions. They damaged

the tail, and I don't know how bad it is. We're in the
death zone right now. We either need to be under fifty
feet or over four hundred."

"I vote for fifty."

"Do you? Look down."

Cal did, gasped, and continued climbing the chopper.
They were on the rugged front slopes of the mountains
that defined the country's border in this area. If they
crashed here, they'd tumble down a long way back into
Indonesia. Back toward the people in the valley who just
shot Jeannie.

—◦◦◦—

Jeannie breathed through the fog of pain. Her poor
Firehawk. It was crying with so many voices. Hydraulic
pressure falling, a fuel leak, though not a dangerous
one—they'd be down, one way or another, before they
ran out of fuel at this rate. The out-of-balance indicator
on the main rotors worried her the most; that was what
was making the cyclic vibrate. Some part or parts had
been shot away. For now the main rotor was holding up
to the imbalance, but for how long?

Black Hawks were built tough. This was a machine
designed for war, and one that had actually served. For
now, she'd have to trust the machine to do what it was
designed to do.

She wanted to beg Connie for a painkiller—there had
to be something in the med kit—but she needed to stay
sharp. And there was no way for Connie to reach around
to help with her wounded arm; the high chair back and
narrow space precluded that.

And Cal. He was magnificent. She could hear the

strain, but she could also hear him keeping it under control. She'd told him to take over, and he'd done it without question. And he just might get them down. He'd better—he was their only hope.

"You're doing great, Cal."

"Tell me that after we get out of this, Helitack."

"Watch your airspeed, Hotshot." It helped her ignore the pain if she kept up the tease.

"One-ten. Why one-ten?"

"Best rate of glide," Connie answered for her. "At our current altitude, it provides almost a half mile to find a safe place to land once we have engine failure."

"Is that what's happening?"

"Well—" Jeannie hesitated. She really didn't want to scare him. He was in so far past his comfort lev—

"It's a race," Connie informed him in a calm voice. "At this point it's between engine failure and rotor failure. If rotor failure wins, we die. With engine failure, our chances improve with more altitude at the moment."

Jeannie could see that Cal was really sorry he'd asked.

"Yeah, this is as good as it gets," she teased him. Except it came out more like a moan than a tease. She reached deep, looking for reserves, and wasn't having a lot of luck finding them.

"We need a new definition of good," he stated definitively, bless the man. The fire lay before them. The black was too far away. They had a choice between level and clear. The clear areas were too vertical and the level areas were... Cal whimpered aloud like a mad cartoon character, almost adding a smile, and then his face sobered. "We're going into the trees, aren't we?"

"Smart, Hotshot. Always said you were." Jeannie hissed as the chopper jarred in an air current.

"Sorry, Jeannie."

"Just get us down. Then you can be sorry all you want."

"Deal. How do I do that?"

"That fire is really squeezing our options."

The smoke was squeezing them worse. They were already past any smoke density Jeannie was allowed to fly into short of a life-and-death emergency. Well, this definitely counted for that, but she doubted Emily would be following them in for a rescue. According to the instrument panel, Emily was back at Suai for refueling—thirty miles and too many minutes away, at least ten, maybe more depending on her fuel status. This would be over in two…if they were lucky. One minute if they weren't.

Steve's drone zipped into view and circled them once before waggling its wings.

"Don't answer!" Jeannie snapped just as Cal was about to wiggle the cyclic back and forth. "It just might be the last gesture we ever make."

His look of alarm made her smile. He smiled back. In the midst of all this hell, he smiled at her.

"There!" She pointed and immediately wished she hadn't. The sudden easing of pressure on her wound sent a wave of pain racing up from her injured arm, making her head spin with nausea. She bit down on her cheek. She was not going to be sick all over herself. She wrapped her hand once more about her arm and made herself a promise not to remove it again until she had some really good drugs in her.

Steve's drone circled around them again. She

wondered how bad they looked. There'd definitely be a black smoke contrail, maybe—

The drone exploded right in front of them in a bright flash. She and Cal cursed in unison. Even the unflappable Connie made an unhappy sound.

"RPG!" Connie announced. "Rocket-propelled grenade. We've got to get down now!"

Jeannie could have avoided the cloud of debris, maybe, but Cal didn't stand a chance and flew right into it. Her front windscreen star-cracked as a chunk of the drone's wing bounced off the Plexiglas and disappeared upward.

Then she heard the cry of metal. The number two engine had just eaten a chunk of Steve's drone.

"Connie. Can you pull the number two T-handle?"

The woman reached forward, whispering a sorry before she leaned on Jeannie's good shoulder. The pain transmitted sideways, but it was better than the risk of jarring an under-qualified pilot. It was awkward but Connie pulled down on the number two shutdown-and-fire T-handle.

Jeannie had never had to do that outside of a simulator. Immediately, fuel flow to the number two engine cut off, the loud clanking of the damaged engine began to slow rapidly, and a sharp hiss announced the release of the extinguishing fluid. And they started to drop.

"Up on the collective, Cal. Connie, strap in. This is it."

"This is what?" Cal yanked up on the collective and the chopper jerked. Then he eased it off. He was overreacting, but he didn't understand what had just happened.

"We now are flying on one engine. Head for that opening at about two o'clock. We have enough altitude. Pull back on the cyclic until we're only going eighty knots." Jeannie's voice was rasping against the pain.

"Lost an engine." "RPG." Steve's drone exploding. He was not ready for any of this.

"C'mon, Hotshot. Ease the cyclic to the right."

To the right. What idiot had put him in charge of a crashing helicopter? "Two o'clock." All he saw was forest. Finally he spotted a clearing coming around in front of the nose from Jeannie's side.

Something on the panel started beeping for attention. When he looked down, he saw a whole lot of red on the displays.

"Don't look down!" Jeannie shouted at him, then groaned. "I'll take care of that."

Cal gave up and let go. Let himself become a vehicle for Jeannie's orders. "A shade forward on the cyclic. A little more left pedal."

Any emergency he'd ever been in, he'd always been the go-to guy. He'd never liked it when it was someone else. Following a crew boss's orders was what you did, but he'd never enjoyed it. One of the many reasons he'd gone freelance. In control of his own destiny.

But he trusted Jeannie Clark, trusted her with his life. So she commanded and he flew.

"Cal, see the other T-handle in the overhead console?"

"The one that isn't flashing."

"Right. Once we hit the ground or the first tree, the controls will be meaningless. I want you to do two things the instant before we hit. Number one, most important, pull that handle. Number two, tuck in your knees and grab your crossed-shoulder harness with both hands. You got that?"

"T-handle. Go fetal." He struggled to keep his mind working. "Can't I just go fetal now? It would make me much happier, Helitack."

She laughed, groaned, and told him to pull the cyclic back a little.

There were so many things to say. But the ground was approaching, fast. They were only seconds above the trees. There were far too many things to say, all of them important.

"Full up on collective! Full back on cyclic!"

He did. They slowed abruptly, then with an awful crunch, he watched one of the rotor blades snap in half as it spun by the forward windscreen.

The most important thing to say rose to the surface just as the remains of the main rotor blades caught the top of the first tree. Way too far past that second step already, but it was what needed saying.

"Love you, Jeannie!"

Then they fell from the sky.

Chapter 17

THE CHOPPER WRENCHED SIDEWAYS AS THE ROTOR caught the sandalwood tree. Then wrenched again as it caught a eucalyptus. Jeannie kept her focus on holding her shattered arm tightly in place and praying they hit upright.

Close enough. They hammered into the ground, utterly destroying the wheels and their shock absorbers. Then the crash-worthy seats came into play.

The land wasn't as flat as it looked and the damaged chopper tumbled sideways into the trees, the rotor blades flailing, shattering against trees and ground, and firing large chunks of metal and composite off in all directions. They rolled sideways down the hill once or twice, flattening trees as they went. One more roll through a short open section and they slammed into a stand of trees that brought the Firehawk to a rest.

Jeannie hung sideways in her harness looking down at Cal.

Slowly, the event unraveled itself in her mind. Then the pain slammed her and she blacked out for a moment while someone was screaming.

She came to before the scream even had a chance to fully fade from her throat. She swallowed hard and blinked to focus.

"We're alive!" That was unexpected. "You're alive, aren't you, Cal?"

He twisted from where he lay mostly on the door that looked down into the soil. "Remember when I said I wanted to do an autorotation landing someday?"

"Yeah."

"I take it back." He began working his way out of his harness.

"Connie?"

The woman pulled open Jeannie's door from above. She was already out and kneeling on the outside of the chopper. "We need to get you out of there."

Jeannie inspected the chopper, which was mostly upside down. "Hotshot, you pulled the T-handle." It too now blinked red and she could hear the number one engine winding down.

"You told me to, Helitack. So I did."

"You do everything I say?"

He aimed one of those lovely smiles at her. "You bet. You found a way to get us out of the sky alive. That puts you number one on my list of people worth paying attention to. I'd have put good money on this going the other way." He stood and supported her in his arms as Connie reached down and sliced away the harness with her knife. The earlier scream tried to resurface, but Jeannie managed to downgrade it to a groan through sheer willpower. Also, that scream had frightened her with its complete lack of control.

With their careful handling, she managed to get out of the Firehawk without passing out, though her vision definitely tunneled a few times. They set her on the grass, and she stared at her chopper. Mark was gonna be pissed. She'd really messed up her machine. Denise could put a lot of things right on a helicopter, but this one was a bit extreme. The rotor blades were gone, of course, no more than broken stubs. The tail boom lay twisted to the side. The tree that had ultimately stopped them had ripped up both engines and knocked the rotor shaft well back out of alignment.

She sniffed the air, half expecting the smell of eucalyptus or the smoke of the nearby fire. Instead she sneezed. The sharp bite of kerosene. Jet A was leaking out of the chopper despite the crash-rated fuel tanks.

"Hey," she shouted, then wished she hadn't for it jostled her shoulder which… "We need to get out of here now. It's leaking fuel."

Connie and Cal were tossing out gear. An emergency backpack that would have food and water. Several of the wildfire emergency shelters arced out onto the grass. Connie tossed down a rifle and box of ammo. A pair of first-aid kits were tossed out next. A couple of Pulaskis. Three hard hats. Then they both disappeared inside for most of a minute.

"Hey!" Jeannie shouted again, and her head spun as the pain washed through her. Moments later they both clambered up out of the cargo-bay door, which now opened upward, and jumped down to the ground. They stuffed everything into the packs and each slung one on. Cal draped on his precious camera bag over that.

He came up beside Jeannie, knelt down, and opened a first-aid kit he'd kept with him. Connie disappeared into the woods on the far side of the chopper. He gave Jeannie a couple of painkillers.

"These aren't the heavy-duty ones, but we need you mobile, okay?"

"Okay." At least until they were safely away from her broken chopper. "We have to move first."

"Connie said we're okay for the moment. Give me your arm, Helitack."

He was fast and neat: well-trained or well-practiced. She tried not to think about the latter.

"I'm leaving the bullet in because I'm squeamish. No more bleeding, Helitack. I might faint."

The man actually made her smile despite the pain he was causing. The antiseptic stung, but not nearly as much as the stretch bandage he wrapped over the gauze pad. He was very gentle as he positioned the sling. Then he helped her into a Nomex fire jacket, trapping her slung arm inside, and patted a hard hat onto her head.

"There, now you look like a real firefighter." His kiss was sweet, tender, and unhurried. It promised so much. The man had so much to give if he would only let himself.

Just as he finished, Connie came back. "We have a problem."

"Worse than a helicopter crash?"

Connie nodded. "We came down on the west slope. If they have armored vehicles, we have at least a company, probably a battalion strength unit of the Indonesian Army, down below and a couple of squads or a company climbing up toward us on three sides under cover of smoke. Fast, hard to spot if I didn't have this scope." She raised the rifle with a long scope mounted on top in explanation. "Army Special Forces on foot unless I miss my guess, probably their Group 2 Para-commandos."

"Are they good?" Cal asked as if he was ready to take them on himself.

"At least ten of them that I spotted, which means twenty. Plenty good enough to take out the three of us. Without the drone, command won't know what's happening, which these guys will know. I don't want to risk any more comm traffic. First, it will give the bad guys something to triangulate on. Second, it would be better if they thought we died in the crash."

"Fine." Jeannie joined the conversation to show the painkiller was kicking in, which it wasn't really. "Who's on the fourth side?" When neither one answered her, she looked up at them. They were both facing back behind where Jeannie was sitting. Then she remembered. There wasn't a "who" on the fourth side of their personal box, it was a "what."

Wildfire.

They had trudged a hundred yards upslope when Connie called a hold.

Cal pulled Jeannie behind the stoutest tree he could find and wrapped his arms around her.

"What the—"

"Shh." He clamped his hands over her ears, not knowing what to expect.

Connie spoke quietly, "In three, two…"

A roar erupted from the chopper. The C4 charges that he and Connie had planted throughout the machine blew it apart. Chunks of it fell to either side of their narrow shelter. They weren't incendiaries, they were explosives, so they simply shredded the machine. But the blast did catch the leaking Jet A fuel on fire. With the prevailing winds, that new fire would only burn a few additional acres before it merged with the main fire. The problem was, those few acres were their safety zone unless Cal could find a safe path for them into the black.

"My chopper!" Jeannie stepped out from behind the tree and stared downslope in horror.

"We're hoping they'll think we were still inside and won't look any further."

"My chopper!"

What was it with her? It was a machine. It could be replaced. If his favorite old camera died or was lost, he'd buy another. Granted it would be roughly ten thousand times cheaper than a Firehawk, but that wouldn't be Jeannie's concern. She sounded as if she'd just lost a child or something.

He wasn't used to being around people who cared so deeply about things. Most hotshots were single and cared more about their cars than people. The people on the team itself were close. They had your back when it got tight. While you were with them, they were the best people on the planet. But when you moved to another team, especially in another state as Cal had done any number of times, there wasn't any real draw to get back together—glad to see them in a bar and catch up on old times if you ended up on the same fire someday, but that was the limit of it.

When you were in the field six months a year, year-round if you were lucky enough to be full-time, it didn't leave a whole lot of room for family. He'd seen enough married hotshots—pumped on fire—hitting on the groupies in some out-of-area bar just as hard as any solo fire jock did. There were straight aces, but they were the rare breed.

When Jeannie cared, she did it with her whole heart. The same way she did everything. The same way she loved him... *Later*, he ordered himself. But that later better come soon.

"Emily's gonna be so pissed at me," she complained. He considered teasing her about whining, but thought better of it when he saw her eyes. She was going shocky, but there was no time to deal with that.

He got her turned around, and they began moving upslope. The fire was definitely on the move—both of them: the main one ahead and the one they'd just lit by using an exploding helicopter as a match. He wished he could call out for a report, but he didn't see that happening anytime soon. They were now officially dead. And the evidence in his camera of just who had started these fires had to survive to get out.

He also knew that no one on the outside would be able to give them a useful report. They were inside the smoke pall, and worse, with the second fire they'd just started, they were inside the heart of the fire. No one on the outside would be able to give them useful information on what was going on in here.

It was hard to see through the gathering smoke. They all pulled on simple carbon filter masks, no way Jeannie could have worn a full breather bottle even if they had them. She was barely remaining upright as it was, though she did stagger gamely onward.

He loved this woman so much. He really did, which he still found rather startling. And he'd said it aloud, even if she hadn't heard him. If he took the next step and connected that he only spoke truth to her, that meant it must be true. Wasn't that a shocker?

Now he just had to get them both out of this alive so that he could tell her again.

The main fire ahead wasn't hard to locate, despite the smoke. Like any wildfire, it ate forest and ate it cooked well-done, then roared for more. Ahead and to the left it was in full, deep-throated howl. He'd heard that pitch before, but not often. It was too hot. If they got caught in that main fire, they'd be in deep trouble. Twenty-five hundred degrees or more.

He turned them upslope and to the right. They were now paralleling the main blaze even if he couldn't see it. He couldn't see the one started by the chopper explosion either, but he knew it was there. Knew it was coming for them.

"Wait a sec." Cal stopped and let himself feel the fire-torn winds, listen to the sounds of the dying forest. He knew this place. He'd stood once before in the heart of the maelstrom.

Jeannie stumbled into him and ground to a halt, blinking hard to keep her focus. Connie came up close enough to hear him over the fire's roar.

"We've got two choices," he shouted to her. "One bad, the other worse."

Connie nodded for him to continue. He pulled Jeannie close, careful of her arm, and kissed her on the temple while he was thinking. It calmed him, holding her, made his world clearer.

"We could keep looking for a way through. Visibility is negligible. But the lower fire is coming and the main fire is too hot. Our chances of slipping out between them is pretty close to zero."

"I'm hoping that's the 'worse' choice," Connie said. "What's the 'bad' one?"

But it wasn't. That was the *bad* choice. The problem was, the *worse* choice was probably their only option.

Jeannie just lay against him, completely past her limits. It would have to be the *worse* one. He swore he'd never again do this. Not after losing Jacob in that Montana fire four years ago. He would never let himself be so trapped that he had to hide and hope under a flimsy foil shelter.

"They say it's last resort." He closed his eyes, trying not to see anything as he said it, but his friend's face shone before him: clean and laughing in a bar, exhausted, sooty, and sacked out in the black…and crisp beneath a burned-through shelter while Cal had stood back and taken the picture. A picture that shamed him to this day because he'd never directly looked one last time upon his friend's face.

"Where?" Connie was a hundred percent business. Something they did to SOAR people? Somehow removed their emotions? She was as straight ahead as Beale. No, it was training. Henderson was a hundred percent squared away on a fire, even if he was unhappy with his chosen role in the quiet times.

Cal looked around, and from what he could see, they were roughly in the center of a small clearing. It was thick with grasses but—"We need to scrape the grass down to dirt. As big a circle as we can."

He sat Jeannie down and piled the gear around her. She was past protesting. He forced a water bottle into her hand and tipped it for her to drink so her dazed mind would get the idea.

"We have ten minutes, fifteen at most," he told Connie. He grabbed a Pulaski and didn't have to say

anything more. Fire ax on one side, the cutting hoe
of an adze on the other. He swung it into the sod and
gave a pull. Thankfully, the grass pulled up in fairly
easy clumps. Soil beneath, not rock. Maybe their luck
was turning.

He began cutting a line in the low, fast, repeated
motion that he'd perfected as a hotshot. No one could
rid the ground of burnable material to make a firebreak
faster than a trained hotshot. In moments he'd cut a
swath a yard wide and four long across the slope. Connie
had covered about half that.

"I'm faster. I'll cut, you swamp."

Connie didn't waste time on words. She just looked
at him like he was speaking a foreign language.

"Swamper clears the material that the lead cuts. Drag
the grass upslope into those trees. When the fire climbs
from below us, we want it to have as little fuel to work
with as possible until after it's past us."

Without a word, she tossed aside her Pulaski and
gathered up an armful of the long, dry grass and trotted upslope. A woman of action, just what he needed at
the moment.

So he cut. He put his head down and cut and pulled.
He didn't have enough oxygen through the breather
mask and tore it off and chucked it aside. The smoke was
thick, but nothing he hadn't eaten before. When he had a
four-yard square, he focused on cutting the swath longer
toward his best guess on the direction of the oncoming
blaze. If it had less to burn before it reached them, it
might be a few crucial degrees cooler when it hit them.

Sweat was streaming down his face when
Connie yelled.

He couldn't make out her words, but he didn't need to. Despite the thick smoke, he could see the orange glow coming toward them from downslope, could feel the heat, could hear it gathering its angry breath.

After a quick glance around to judge the final angle of attack, he moved toward the upper edge of the cleared area he'd created and hacked out three small holes, each about a foot deep.

Connie looked at him strangely.

"Face holes. We lie face down and put our faces in the hole. The air will be cooler down there." Then he spotted the rifle slung across her back. "Bury that."

"Why? Rounds don't cook off until well over two hundred degrees."

"Bury that. And your sidearm and the rounds. Don't miss any. It will probably be way over two hundred inside the shelter; more like fifteen hundred to two thousand outside."

Her look of horror only lasted a second before she sprinted for her Pulaski and began chopping a hole well to the side of the clearing.

Cal cut a hole for his camera bag that would be right under his belly. He had to protect those images of the invading and arsonist Indonesian Army. If the good guys found his body, alive or not, they'd find the images. Then he went to fetch Jeannie and the pack with the fire shelters in them. She was having trouble standing, so he simply swept her up into his arms, though they were shaking with the unaccustomed strain of wielding the Pulaski as fast and long as he had.

"Carrying me over the threshold?"

"Sure, Helitack. Whatever you say." He checked

her eyes to see if they were shocky, but they looked coherent. He was just setting her down when she continued.

"I seem to recall you saying something about loving me just before we crashed. It took some considering, but I don't think I imagined it."

He managed not to drop her. "Might have."

"Bit of a surprise?" she teased him.

"Everything about you is a surprise to me, Helitack. Now, lie down and put your face in that hole. Then don't move."

"Yes sir, Mr. Hotshot, sir."

He couldn't help himself. He kissed her. He was afraid it would feel as if he was saying good-bye. But it didn't. It felt as if he was saying hello to a whole new world.

Jeannie did everything Cal said. He hooked her feet into the lower end of the shelter.

"Feet toward the fire. If I shout for you to turn, you find a way to do it, but do not, *do not* come up out of that shelter."

Then he tucked it under her hips. Slid a handle up her good arm to the elbow. He tugged a heavy glove on her good hand.

"That arm goes up over your head to pin down the shelter. The fire will create updrafts trying to tear the shelter off. You keep it pinned in place."

"What about my other side?" She had to shout to be heard above the climbing roar of flame. Already it was as loud as her Firehawk right before takeoff.

"I'll pin that down with my shelter."

"I'll be right beside you on this side," Connie told her as she was clambering into hers on Jeannie's other side.

"Both of you," Cal said. "Do not come out of the shelter no matter what you feel, no matter what you hear. Not until I tell you. You'll think you're burning alive, but if you come out too soon, you will be."

Jeannie couldn't stop looking at Cal. He snapped out his own shelter with the ease of too much experience. He didn't even lie down first, he stepped into it, pulling it up and over his fire gear and deftly hooking it over his hard hat, reminding her of a weird kind of silver caterpillar with a firefighter underbelly. He inspected them both carefully.

"Connie, make sure you keep your boots and knees on the ground, that's what's holding the shelter in place."

She saw him make a quick scan downslope.

"Our orientation is good." Then he looked upslope and swore quietly, his hands scrambling for his camera even as he stood there in his silvery caterpillar cocoon.

Jeannie looked upslope. The smoke had blown clear for a moment, exposing the main fire to view. It was closer than she'd thought, closer than she'd ever been. Though she lay hundreds of yards away, she could feel the heat of the wall of brilliant orange flame on her face. The heart of the inferno towered far above them. It flung aside trees as if they were weightless. And in the heart of the flame was something she'd heard about but never seen.

Cal was wielding his camera with the same skill he'd used minutes before with his Pulaski. In her half-dream state, she'd enjoyed watching the man work, imagining his flowing muscles beneath the heavy protective gear. Comforted, knowing that if anyone could save them, it would be Cal Jackson.

He was photographing the heart of the fire. And in its midst, the winds were so strong, that they'd created a flaming tornado of blood-red flame. She'd always wondered if the streak in her hair was too dark, too red, but she could see that it wasn't. That she'd nailed it perfectly. The fire whirl was beautiful and simultaneously terrifying as it spun and climbed into the darkness of the smoke-shrouded sky. It wasn't some distant phenomenon, safely placed on a *National Geographic* cover. This was a monster that howled to the heavens right above their heads.

Cal stood a few steps downslope of them and, for just a moment, Jeannie could see the image as he must see it. Both her and Connie's shelters would show the firefighters peeking out to see the towering fire whirl that could destroy them with the merest flick of its tornado-strength winds. That was the award-winning photograph he was always talking about, and she saw why. It was magnificent, horrible, and with her and Connie's shelters visible, it would be very human as well.

She also remembered him on a Santa Barbara cliff edge, so lost in his photographs that he'd almost been caught by the flames.

"Cal. Cal!" At her second shout, he looked down at her.

Then he came back from wherever he'd gone behind his camera. "All the way under now, Helitack." He stuffed the camera into the bag.

Jeannie pulled the foil over her head and felt his

hands, sure and strong, making sure she was in the best position.

"Face in the hole. It's almost here," he shouted. She tried to peek over at him, but he already had the edge of her shelter pinned under his. He moved tight against her, his left arm against her broken one. It hurt like mad, and she was so glad for the pain that she wanted to weep with relief.

"Hang on!"

Then it was upon them.

The roar was deafening. Well past anything she'd ever experienced in her Firehawk. On top of the fire's roar, the shelter snapped back and forth in the powerful winds, like a thousand champagne corks popping.

Then the heat hit and all she could do was scream down into her hole in the ground. It was so painful that there was nothing else she could do.

Cal was shouting something on one side. She didn't understand, but it sounded encouraging. The only thing she could feel other than the searing heat was his shoulder against hers where he'd pinned down her own shelter.

To the other side, Connie was also yelling. At first it sounded like repeats of "I'm okay." But finally, like her own cry, it just became a constant yell, as if they could beat back the wildfire with the release of their own pain and fear.

Finally the roar was so loud that she could hear no one. She was alone and her body was on fire. A thousand nightmares were visited down on her. Her helicopter exploding and burning, except this time it felt as if she still lay inside it. She imagined emerging from the shelter to find Cal hadn't survived. Or the pain on Cal's face when he emerged and found she was the one who'd died.

That, oddly, was the image that sustained her as she lay in the darkness under the foil and screamed out her pain, down into her hole in the dirt. Cal loved her. And even though he might not know it yet, his kiss had said it all—he loved her so much that it might destroy him if she died. So she would have to live. All it took was holding on and riding it out.

She could do that.

Chapter 18

"HEY, HELITACK. YOU STILL WITH US?"

The voice came out of a dream and slid around Jeannie's thoughts like a caress. She tried to turn toward it.

"Not yet, Helitack. Just lie still."

And she did. Lying there in the dark cocoon of…her fire shelter. The roar was gone. The searing heat had passed as well. The occasional gust snapped her shelter loudly, but it wasn't the constant tearing and tugging that had made her fear its loss at the height of the fire.

Connie said something from the far side.

"We made it," Jeannie repeated for her.

"We did, Helitack." Cal's voice sounded just inches away through the two thin shelters.

She let herself wallow in the sound as his deep voice soothed her.

"We need to let the area cool down. Maybe five or ten more minutes, but we did it."

"And you love me."

A brief silence stretched out, followed by one of his wonderful low chuckles. "You're not going to let me live that one down, are you?"

"Never. Not even after you marry me."

She wished she could see his face. Jeannie could certainly picture it well enough: that stunned puppy look each time she'd surprised him with something he hadn't had time to think through before.

"Damn, Helitack. I, uh, hadn't gotten that far."

"That's okay. You said you wanted to follow where I'm leading." He'd said it while they were wallowing in a cool river in the Outback above Katherine Gorge, which sounded wonderful right at the moment.

"I did," he admitted a little reluctantly as if he'd swum out into deeper waters than he'd intended.

She wanted to reach out to him, touch him to comfort the nerves of the man who'd become far too good at being alone. She couldn't. All she could do was lean her shoulder a little more tightly against his and try to ignore the pain of the bullet wound.

"I love you, Calvin Hobbes Jackson, and whatever that poor, angry young boy was called."

He spoke after a long silence. "Francis Bernard, for Francis of Assisi."

"Thank you, Cal." He'd told her. It didn't matter at all, and it also meant the world. How hard had that been for him? She couldn't see his face to tell. She took a deep breath to still her driving pulse. It was another big step for him, for both of them.

"Let that be enough for now," she offered him.

"I love you, Helitack," his voice soft.

She wrapped the words around her tighter than the foil shelter. Last time he'd said the words moments before they were expected to die. This time he'd said them after they'd known they were going to live.

Enough time had passed that they should be safe to crawl out, but Cal didn't want to move from beside Jeannie. As close together as if they shared a bed.

A sharp buzzing sound built from nearby. It Dopplered by close above them, fast. Friendly or not?

He cracked the edge of the shelter off the ground and took a careful breath. No blast of heat in the face. He pulled back the top of the shelter and spotted Steve's black-and-flame painted MHA drone circling back for another pass. He raised a hand and received a wing waggle in response.

Then he looked downslope, into the black. They'd left the remains of the chopper five hundred feet below and perhaps a half mile behind. The vegetation was now sparse enough, mostly just the trunks of burned trees and spirals of lazy smoke climbing upward. He'd have easily spotted anyone moving upslope. They were safe, at least for the moment.

"Okay to come out now." He began to help Jeannie up.

Connie jumped up and sprinted over to grab a charred but intact Pulaski and, after a little fishing around, dug up her rifle and ammo. She scrambled back and placed herself downslope of himself and Jeannie. Crouching, she shouldered her rifle and aimed it downslope toward the chopper.

"Is that really necessary?"

The drone flashed over again, then another wing waggle and it was gone.

Connie relaxed. "Easiest way to tell Mark not to let Emily come and get us. At least not without backup."

That sobered Cal. He retrieved his camera case and checked inside. Everything looked okay, both the proof of arson he needed and the photo like none he'd ever taken before. Both safe.

"Can we keep moving upslope?"

Jeannie nodded, and Cal helped her to her feet.

"Everyone drain a canteen; we've just sweated out a lot of water. Then let's get out of here."

They followed the black up into the hills of East Timor.

———※———

Cal's radio squawked to life, startling Jeannie back to consciousness. She had descended into a fog, wholly focused on putting one foot in front of the other.

"What was that?"

"Emily found a landing just a hundred yards to the south." He turned her, and even that change was enough to make her stumble badly.

Cal stopped her, then squatted in front of her, presenting his back.

She wrapped her good arm around his neck and hooked her legs over his hips as he locked his arms under them. Her right arm was in such pain that having it squeezed between them didn't make it all that much worse. Maybe she'd be lucky and pass out for real this time.

He lifted her as easily as if she weighed no more than his camera, and they were off again. She laid her head on his shoulder despite the jouncing. A soot-stained ear showed from beneath his soft brown hair. She nipped it with her teeth.

"Hey!" But he laughed.

Then she heard it. The best sound ever. A Black Hawk helicopter on the descent. She looked up to MHA's Firehawk Oh-one, her black-and-fire paint shining where the sun hit on it. Two more choppers hovered in close formation.

Cal turned her so that their backs were toward the rotor's downblast and the swirling ash, but he didn't stumble, didn't falter. The man was as solid as a rock. Just like his heart.

In moments they were aboard.

A medic who she didn't know, a pretty young woman in an Army uniform with a single gold bar on her lapel and that sword-and-twined-snakes patch on the arm, helped ease Jeannie down onto the cargo deck.

Connie saluted her. "Greetings, Lieutenant Wallace."

The woman saluted back just as neatly with a disarming smile. "Greetings, Sis. Damn but we're glad to see you."

There was no way the two were related; they looked nothing alike. The woman must have seen her confusion.

"Sister-in-law. She married my big brother. My name's Noreen. Now, let's look at that arm."

With a deep roar, one that had always sounded so big and powerful until she'd stood in the middle of a wildfire, the Firehawk lifted back into the sky.

When Noreen exposed the bloody bandage, Jeannie looked away. When she felt the sharp prick of a needle, she concentrated on what was going on around her, even as the screaming nerves were drugged into sleep. Emily was at the controls. Over the noise of the helicopter, Jeannie couldn't make out what anyone was saying, but she could see Cal do something with his computer and then hold it forward between the seats for Emily to see.

"Where's Mark?" Jeannie asked the medic. "If he's stuck back with the baby, he'll—"

"He's up with my brother." She pointed out the open cargo-bay door at one of the other helicopters that had come in with Emily's Firehawk. "We're perfectly safe with them here. Tessa's with Carly and Steve on the *Freedom*."

Jeannie looked out at the other two choppers. They were painted pitch black. Not glossy, like MHA's job, but matte black, like stealth stuff. And they had the strange angular shapes that she associated with that kind of modern technology. They also had stub wings that stuck out to either side and from which hung an alarming array of missiles and guns.

"That's Major Beale's old bird, the *Vengeance*. Lola Maloney is awesome, but I wish I'd had a chance to fly with Emily. Major Henderson is up in his old *Viper*. Copilot only, but there was no stopping him, and he is the best pilot SOAR ever had other than Major Beale." Noreen spoke with such intense pride. The Night Stalkers were obviously deep in her blood. "My brother's up on the *Viper* as well."

Cal, apparently done up forward, came back to sit with her and hold her good hand.

"Beale has an encrypted radio and is already talking to Mark who is talking to Lola who is... Aw, hell. I don't know. They're fixing it all, somehow. How you doing, Helitack?"

Now Jeannie could see his face. See the worry, the fear for her despite the heavy soot smears. She also saw the exhaustion. These last hours had been much harder on him than she could ever imagine.

"Not sure. Let's ask the doc."

"Not a doc yet," Noreen replied cheerfully. "Just

an Army medic. Army assigned me to the USS *Independence* when all this came up."

"The *Independence*?"

"Sure. It's the sister ship to the one you've been on. We've been parked just over the horizon with Lola's unit in case things got ugly."

"Ugly!" Cal's bark of laughter was thick with pain. He squeezed her good hand so hard it would have hurt at any other time. He was being so careful to avoid looking at her other arm.

"Apparently even the most pessimistic projections never anticipated an attack against civilian aircraft, especially not by trained military units. At last, your wife's arm is fine."

Jeannie looked down at the deck to hide her smile while Cal sputtered.

"Okay, not your wife." Noreen said it like an insult, questioning Cal's intelligence. Then she switched instantly back to her former cheerful manner. "We'll get X-rays when we're back aboard ship, but I think it's only a fracture. I pulled the bullet out, and there were no bone fragments with it. The round appears to be intact. Right up against a nerve cluster; bet it hurt like hell to move, but not much damage because I see you moving all your fingers and joints. The round must have been mostly spent."

"It went through the chopper's door first."

"That explains it. That's why it did so little damage."

Jeannie shivered. "You mean a real gunshot would…"

"Be way messier and would hurt about ten times as much."

"I'll pass."

"Me too."

Jeannie looked up at Cal as Noreen finished her bandaging. Despite the grime, he'd gone sheet white.

"Hey, Hotshot?"

"Huh?"

"What say we don't do this again? Okay?"

That woke up his slow smile and some of the color returned to his face.

"That, Helitack, is a deal."

Chapter 19

THE DALY WATERS PUB IN THE MIDDLE OF AUSTRALIA'S Northern Territory was one of Jeannie's favorites anywhere on the planet. If they were going to make her convalesce for a month, she'd be damned but she was going to do it in style. And that Cal had the same idea of what defined style just made it all the better.

They'd rented a small caravan in Darwin and a car stout enough to tow the little camper. It boasted a tiny kitchen and table, and a shower and dunny that was definitely too small to share, though they'd tried on the shower. Which didn't really matter because most of the rest of the camper was a very comfy bed.

She'd taken him swimming in the Wangi Falls of Litchfield National Park. It was a twenty-meter waterfall that seemed to appear out of nowhere atop a cliff and disappear to nowhere after languishing for a while in a wide pool a few hundred meters across. After a couple days soaking there, she'd been able to lose the sling, which had opened up several more options.

They'd stayed for most of a week with Dale and Kalinda. They'd gone on several walks together, but not back up the gorges. The Wet had come to Arnhem Land and the river levels were on the rise, along with the salties working their way upriver.

Cal had grown a little shy on her, reluctant to talk about what was happening between them. She could

see that "processing internally" sign flashing behind his
eyes whenever she brought up the things they'd said to
each other during the fire.

She bit her tongue for patience and focused on being
thankful for the pieces he did show her. He talked about
his childhood enough for her to agree with him that it
was indeed best left in the past. Let Calvin Hobbes be
born at sixteen on an Alaskan fire line. That worked for
both of them.

The long hours rolling down the Alice towing their
little caravan and watching the Outback had been filled
equally with tales of fires past and present, and comfortable silences. They'd crest a low rise, just meters tall,
and the two tar-and-gravel-sealed lanes of the Stuart
Highway would stretch straight ahead to the next rise a
half-dozen kilometers off.

"What are those?" At the midway point between two
rises, Cal had pointed to a man-high white post with the
numbers "1" at waist height and "2" near the top.

She'd teased him for a while, but no outsider was
likely to unravel the code, so she finally gave in. "That's
how many meters deep the water is during a flash
flood in the Wet season. They don't happen much, but
it happens."

He'd refused to believe her, that two meters of water
could cover the vast area between the two rises. So, she
stopped them at a stout bridge stretching over a deep dry
gully a hundred meters across. Out of the car, she pointed
to the markings along the side of the bridge's very stout
pilings. They counted up to eighteen meters, the depth of
the gorge. "Water's been over this bridge's deck twice
in the last century. Gully will be dry within a day after."

On their trip, they'd also thrashed over the results of the East Timor mission. SOAR had reported to the UN Security Council, and the council had landed hard on Indonesia's doorstep. The Grup 2 Para Commandos' entire command structure had been arrested. The orders probably went higher up the ranks, but that was denied. The Grup 2 commanders were labeled as "rogue," and international face was saved.

Indonesia had instantly supplied massive firefighting aid and rebuilding grants to East Timor. Apparently they'd initially tried to make the grants be loans, but with the supporting evidence of Cal's photos, the Security Council had quashed that and the grants became outright gifts to the struggling country. MHA had also received forty million dollars for a pair of factory-new Firehawks, one as a replacement and one brand-new. Mark had been given a free hand with the specifications, and Jeannie had already been booked for simulator time to get up to speed on the new equipment.

Cal told her about getting Mark aside and actually getting the man good and drunk—a state even Emily had never witnessed. Mark had confessed to finally accepting just how critical an operation he was running for MHA. He hadn't minded not flying the attack choppers anymore; he'd missed the feeling of doing good deeds against bad intentions. This latest mission had proven that Mount Hood Aviation was doing exactly the kind of work he believed in so deeply. Of course both of their hangovers the next morning had put paid on them ever doing something quite that stupid again.

So now she and Cal sat in Jeannie's favorite pub. Daly Waters traced its origin back to 1862, named after the first white man to cross the continent from south to north. It had headquartered the Australian Pony Express, become a telegraph station, been the first international airport in the country, and was now a near-forgotten wayside in the center of the Northern Territory.

The pub sported a wall covered layers deep with banknotes from different currencies signed and tacked up by different travelers. For reasons that still amazed her, her bra now dangled with hundreds of others from the rafters in the main room. She'd been here dozens of times and had avoided paying that particular tribute, but Cal was a bad influence.

Now they sat out in the beer garden that was shaded in equal portions by a trellis of lush bougainvillea and a colorful tree dangling with thousands of travelers' thongs. Cal kept making lame jokes about them, but no self-respected Ozzie would call them flip-flops no matter what some women wore under their clothes.

Evening had settled while they sat at one of the long picnic tables under the bougainvillea and the thong tree. She'd been nursing a stubby, but Cal had a full schooner of Four-X. This was definitely going to be a fun night; he obviously didn't have a clue about the mule kick delivered by Aussie beer. Or he did and didn't care. It wasn't as if they had to be anywhere in the morning. Or even the next day. They'd been told to get lost for a month and heal on full pay, and that was exactly what they were doing.

They finished their "beef and barra" dinner with hot damper, a bread she'd sorely been missing, and the evening sing that was tradition at the Daly Waters kicked into gear. The leader had opened with a "classic from the last century," which was at least partly true. After all, Men at Work's "Down Under" had been released before she was born.

"I liked our barramundi over the campfire better." Cal leaned in close so that she could hear him as a fifty or so people all swung into slightly different versions of "Waltzing Matilda."

She nodded her agreement.

"Jeannie of the dark red hair that was never bright blue," he whispered so close it tickled.

She really wanted to stay for the singing and drinking; it was always a fun night here. But when he spoke to her like that, she wanted to take him somewhere private, wrap herself around him for the rest of the night, and hold on as hard as she could.

"I've been trying to get up the nerve to ask this for two weeks now. I was wondering if you'd do something for me?" He followed his whisper with a kiss and a light tug on her ear.

"Anything, as long as you don't stop that." She had to raise her voice to be heard over the chorus about the itinerant ranch hand stealing and cooking a sheep. Sufficient beer had been consumed that the chorus was loud and merry, even if it was nowhere near on key.

"Would you consider wearing this? You know I wouldn't ask if I didn't mean it."

He held up a beautiful ring. A large garnet caught the last of the sunset and glittered like the dark red of a fire's heart.

"Cal, it's beautiful. I'd love to wear it."

She held up her hand.

"No. The other one, Helitack." His smile was laughing at her even as his eyes remained wary.

Unsure of what he was about, she raised her left hand.

He clambered off the bench and knelt on the red dirt of her homeland.

Then her slow brain caught up with what was happening, and all the sounds of the pub fell away. She could see people singing. Could see the blue, gold, and green lorikeets calling aloud as they ducked and swooped, hoping for a morsel from an unguarded plate. But she could only hear two things: the pounding of her own heart and Cal's words.

"Marry me, Jeannie. My life wouldn't be worth fighting for if it weren't for you. You make me my best self. I want to spend a lifetime trying to prove that to you."

And no matter how hard the going was, she was certain that Cal spoke truth. He'd be there, always being his best, incredible self.

She knew her answer. Knew because it filled her near to bursting until she wanted to explode forth like a wildfire.

But she couldn't say it.

A "yes" was too small.

A cry of joy to the heavens too lame, for it could never be big enough to express her joy.

Instead, she kept it simple.

"I'd love to, Hotshot."

*In case you missed it,
read on for an excerpt from* **Pure Heat,**
the first book in the Firehawks series

STEVE "MERKS" MERCER HAMMERED DOWN THE LAST HALF mile into the Goonies' Hoodie One camp. The Oregon-based Mount Hood Aviation always named its operation bases that way. Hood River, Oregon—hell and gone from everything except a whole lot of wildfires.

Foo Fighters roared out of the speakers, a piece from his niece's latest mix to try and get him out of his standard eighties "too retro" rock and roll. With the convertible top open, his hair whipped in the wind a bit. Hell, today it could be pouring rain until his hair was even darker than its normal black and he wouldn't care. It felt so damn good to be roaring into a helibase for the first time in a year.

Instead of rain, the sun shone down from a sky so crystalline blue that it was hard to credit. High up, he spotted several choppers swooping down toward the camp. A pair of Bell 212 Twin Hueys and a little MD500, all painted the lurid black with red flames of Mount Hood Aviation, just like his car. He'd take that as a good omen.

He let the tail of his classic Firebird Trans Am break loose on the twisting dirt road that climbed through the dense pine woods from the town of Hood River, perched on the banks of the mighty Columbia and staring up at Mount Hood.

This was gonna be a damn fine summer.

Helibase in the Oregon woods. Nice little town at the foot of the mountain. Hood River was big enough to boast several bars and a pair of breweries. It was also a big windsurfing spot down in the Gorge, which meant the tourists would be young, fit, and primed for some fun. The promise of some serious sport for a footloose and fancy-free guy.

And fire.

He'd missed the bulk of last summer.

He hammered in the clutch, downshifted to regain control of his fishtail, and did his best to ignore the twinge in his new left knee.

Steve had spent last summer on the surgeon's table. And hated every goddamn second he'd been away from the fight. It sure hadn't helped him score much, either. "I used to be a smokejumper until I blew out my knee." Blew up his knee would be more accurate since they'd barely saved the leg. Either way, the pickup line just didn't sweep 'em off their feet the way you'd like. Compare that with, "I parachute into forest fires for the fun of it." Way, way better.

And never again.

He fouled that thought into the bleachers with all the force he could muster and punched the accelerator hard.

Folks would be milling around at the camp if those choppers meant there was an active fire today. As any entrance made was worth making properly, Steve cranked the wheel and jerked up on the emergency brake as he flew into the gravel parking lot.

A dozen heads turned.

He planted a full, four-wheel drift across the lot and

fired a broad spray of gravel at a battered old blue-and-
rust Jeep as he slid in beside it. Ground to a perfect
parallel-parked stop. Bummer that whatever sucker
owned the Jeep had taken off the cloth covers and doors.
Steve had managed to spray the gravel high enough to
land some on the seats. Excellent.

He settled his wrap-around Porsche Design sunglasses solidly on the bridge of his nose and pulled on
his autographed San Francisco Giants cap. The four
winning pitchers of the 2012 World Series had signed
it. He only wore it when appearances really mattered.
Wouldn't do at all to sweat it up.

He hopped out of the car.

Okay, his brain imagined that he hopped out of
the car.

His body opened the door, and he managed to swing
his left leg out without having to cup a hand behind the
knee. Pretty good when you considered he wasn't even
supposed to be driving a manual transmission yet. And
he'd "accidentally" left his cane at the roadside motel
room back in Grants Pass where he'd crashed into bed
last night.

So done with that.

Now he stood, that itself the better part of a miracle,
on a helibase and felt ready to go.

He debated between tracking down a cup of coffee or
finding the base commander to check in. Then he opted
for the third choice, the radio shack. The heartbeat of
any firebase was its radio tower, and this one actually
had a tower. It looked like a very short fire watchtower.
Crisscrossed braces and a set of stairs led up to a second-
story radio shack with windows and a narrow walkway

all around the outside. All of the action would funnel through there for both air and ground crews.

An exterior wooden staircase led in switchbacks up to the shack. The staircase had a broad landing midway that gave him an excuse to stop and survey the scene. And rest his knee.

He could have done worse. Much worse.

Hoodie One helibase was nestled deep in the Cascade Mountains just north of Mount Hood. From here, he could see the icy cap of the eleven-thousand-foot-high dormant volcano towering above everything else in the neighborhood. A long, lenticular cloud shadowed the peak, a jaunty blemish in the otherwise perfect blue sky.

The air smelled both odd and right at the same time. The dry oak and sage smell of his native California had been replaced with wet and pine. You could smell the wet despite the hot summer sun. At least he supposed it was hot. Even in early summer, Oregon was fifteen to twenty degrees cooler than Sacramento in the spring. Sometimes the California air was so parched that it hurt to breathe, but here the air was a balm as he inhaled again.

Ah, there.

He inhaled again deeply.

Every wildfire airbase had it, the sting of aviation fuel and the tang of retardant overridden with a sheen that might be hard work and sweat. It let him know he'd come home.

The firebase had been carved into a high meadow bordered by towering conifers. Only the one dirt road climbing up the hills from the town a half-dozen miles below. A line of scrungy metal huts, a rough wooden barracks, and a mess hall that might have been left over from a summer camp for kids a couple decades back. You certainly didn't visit firefighting bases for the luxury of it all.

You came here for the fire. And for what lay between the radio tower on which he perched and the grass-strip runway.

A couple of small fixed-wing Cessnas and a twin-prop Beech Baron were parked along the edge. They'd be used for spotter and lead planes. These planes would fly lead for each run of the big fixed-wing air tankers parked down at the Hood River airport or flying in from other states for the truly big fires.

Then there was the line of helicopters.

The 212s and the MD500 he'd spotted coming in were clearly new arrivals. Crews were pulling the big, orange Bambi Buckets from the cargo bays and running out the lines for the 212s. The MD500 had a built-in tank. Someone crawled under the belly of each of the 212s and hooked up the head of the long lead line used to carry the bucket two hundred feet below the bird and the controls to release the valve from inside the helicopter.

There must be a fire in action. Sure enough. He could see the refueling truck headed their way, and it was not moving at some leisurely pace. Not just in action, but somewhere nearby.

With a start, he realized that he wouldn't have to go trolling off base for company. He'd always been careful not to fraternize with the jump crews, because that made for a mess when it went south. But if he wasn't jumping anymore… Some very fit women would be coming into this camp as well.

He breathed the air deeply again, trying to taste just a bit of smoke, and found it. Damn, but this was gonna be a fine summer. .

---~~~---

"Climb and left twenty degrees."

As the pilot turned, Carly Thomas leaned until the restraint harness dug into her shoulders so that she could see as much as possible. The front windscreen of the helicopter was sectioned off by instrument panels. She could look over them, under them, or out the side windows of her door, but she still felt like she couldn't see.

She really needed to get her head outside in the air to follow what the fire was doing. Taste it, feel the heat on her face as it climbed the ridge. Could they stop the burn, or would the conflagration jump the craggy barrier and begin its destruction of the next valley?

She needed the air. But the doors on this thing didn't open in flight, so she couldn't get her face out in the wind. In the little MD500s she could do that; they flew without the doors all the time.

This was her first flight in Mount Hood Aviation's brand-new Firehawk. It might rank as a critical addition to MHA's firefighting fleet, but she was far from liking it yet. The fire-rigged Sikorsky Black Hawk felt heavy. The MD500 could carry four people at its limit, and this bird could carry a dozen without noticing. The heavy beat of the rotors was well muffled by the radio headset, but she could feel the pulse against her body.

And she couldn't smell anything except new plastic and paint job.

When she'd suggested removing the doors, the pilot

had laughed at Carly. Well, not laughed; the woman looked like she didn't laugh much. But she certainly implied that Carly could never get her to do that. Whoever she was, the pilot was new to the MHA outfit and Carly didn't appreciate the brush-off. When she'd insisted, she was told she could sit in the cargo bay, which had a great view with the doors open, but only to the sides. At least the Firehawk doors, on both sides of the craft, had a large, rounded bulge in the Plexiglas window. That allowed Carly to lean over enough to see straight down, which would help once they were dropping loads over the fire.

Carly wanted the wide view through the forward windscreen, in addition to the smoky air stinging her eyes and clogging her lungs. Well, she wasn't going to get it, so she'd better focus on what she could have. She shoved her hair aside and leaned her head into the Plexiglas bulge in the door and stared down.

At her command, the pilot lifted the Firehawk another five hundred feet and tipped them left. As they topped the last of the ridge, the vista opened before her. The morning sun shone down as if it were another peaceful day in the forests of Oregon. Everything was quiet on the yet unburned west side of the ridge. Stately conifers climbed, stacked like pillioned soldiers, rank upon rank of forest dripping with intensely flammable pitch. The mid-July sun baking the stands of bone-dry timber didn't help matters at all.

Mount Hood towered to the east, its glacier-wrapped head glared in the morning sun and looked so close she could touch it. This fire was still reported as small, but it was in a remote and inaccessible corner of the Mount

Hood National Forest. MHA had no other fire calls, so the Forest Service had dropped this one into their laps to snuff before it got too big.

Carly waited to see what the pilot did when they crossed the ridgeline. Some retired Army major suddenly flying fire. This should be interesting.

"You fly much?" Major was some kind of high rank. Carly wasn't sure how high, but definitely senior officer. The woman had probably been a desk jockey who only touched a machine once a year to keep her certification.

"First time in a year."

Ka-ching, nailed that in one.

But the woman's voice had been dry. Or perhaps it was droll? Was she making some kind of joke?

"Ever flown fire?"

That almost earned Carly a laugh. "Not the way you're talking about it. Had to have a kid to do that." Her age was hard to tell. The woman had a sort of ageless blond beauty. Thirty maybe. But how had she made senior officer by that age?

"What was your last flight?"

"Oil rig." The way she said it was obviously a conversation ender so Carly let it die.

Maybe this Major had been thrown out of the Army for being hopeless. So bad that she'd even been chucked off the relatively mundane task of flying oil workers back and forth to their offshore rigs. If she was a Major and any damn good, rather than just having passed on her good looks, what was the woman doing in a Sikorsky Firehawk over a forest fire?

Though Carly had to remember that she'd often been discounted for being too pretty to know anything. Tall, slender, and bright blond hair, unlike the ex-Major's darker blond, always made guys assume she was an idiot, though even the densest ones soon learned she was way smarter, at least about fire, than all of them put together.

Carly had been up on a thousand flights over hundreds of fires. She'd seen them scorching across the hillsides from firebases since before her first toddling steps. She'd spent every summer of her life at air base camps. In her late teens, she'd gotten her red card and joined the mop-up teams—endless hours trudging through clouds of ash and charcoal seeking any stray heat or scent of smoke.

Her college summers were spent hiking the burning hills with hotshot crews, chasing the active fire up close enough that the heat was a continual prickling wash across her skin despite the Nomex suits. She'd worked her way up the ranks, and now she lived at the helibases during the fire season.

Lead spotter. Senior fire-reader for Mount Hood Aviation, the contracted flying arm of the Goonies, the Oregon wildland firefighters. The Flame Witch. She rather liked the last one. Never reacted when someone called her that behind her back, but she'd considered it more than once for a bumper sticker on her old Jeep.

At the crest of the ridge, the entire vista changed. The clean green of comfortably resting Douglas firs and larch spreading across rolling hills to the horizon was replaced by the fire giants of lore and legend. The quiet legions on the western face of Saddlebag Gap had been transformed into towering infernos, shooting flames to twice their majestic height. Eighty-foot trees had been turned into two-hundred-foot-tall blowtorches.

The pilot didn't flinch. That was a good sign. More than one rookie flyboy—or flygirl, in this case—had simply lost it and returned them to base before Carly could even get a sense of the fire. They'd land with a full load of retardant still in the belly of the aircraft.

A complete waste.

At least something like that usually happened early enough in the season that it didn't cause too much trouble. When the late-summer monster burns rolled across the Cascade and Coast Range, a lost minute could mean success or failure in the firefight, even life or death for the ground crews.

She'd only been at the helibase for a day, but there was already a rumor mill about the woman sitting in the pilot's seat. Carly didn't care. As long as the pilot didn't bank and run away, they were good. Now Carly could see the fire, and that was all that really mattered. Ground chatter on the radio had told her that the smokejumpers were fighting a losing battle against the head of the flame. Against one head. She could see that the flanking line they were trying to clear wouldn't be ready before the fire climbed up to them.

The fire had started with a wilderness camper who'd had the good sense to call it in as soon as they lost control of it. They wouldn't be so happy when the Forest Service sent them the bill to fight the fire. The entire forest was posted with the USFS's highest warning: all burning forbidden. Every pointer on every warning sign had been swung over to the far end of the "extreme danger" red zone.

This was an easy hundred-thousand-dollar blaze. If they didn't kill it fast, it would be many times that by tomorrow. One saving grace was that there were no homesteads out here to burn. When you started burning million-dollar homes perched on scenic hillsides, then costs started adding up quickly.

The fire was still just a Type III, so she could work as Incident Commander—Air on this one. She radioed Rick that she'd be coordinating directly with the Incident Commander—Ground at base. She was trained and authorized to serve as ICA on fires right up to a monstrous Type I response, but she found it incredibly distracting to set up each little aircraft run and her bosses at MHA agreed. Her skills on the big fires were best used as a Fire Behavior Analyst. As an FBAN, her job was about predicting the shifts and changes of a fire rather than the hundreds of tiny details of fighting them minute by minute.

This fire had climbed the western face of Saddlebag Gap, splitting from a single tail at the campfire into a dozen different heads, each fire front chasing up a deep-cut valley etched into the landscape, carved by ten thousand years of trickling streams.

Most of the heads were dying against a cliff wall at the upper end of their little valleys, leaving long trails of black behind them. Smoldering black tree trunks denuded of all branches and foliage were all that remained. Their shoulders were yet wrapped in the lingering smoke of dead and dying fires. They'd need heavy mop-up crews to check it all out, but there shouldn't be any real problems.

Three separate heads were still running hot, finding more fuel as they climbed to the ridge, not less. They fired showers of shining sparks upward into the climbing smoke plume that darkened the sky ahead of them.

The pilot tipped the Firehawk helicopter and headed toward the embattled smokejumper crew on the ground.

"No, wait." Carly hadn't finished understanding the fire from their vantage point five hundred feet above the ridge crest. Most Army hot-rodders thought you fought fires down between the branches. It was a relief that this one didn't, but would she get close enough when it mattered?

The pilot pulled back to a hover, and Carly could feel the woman inspect her. Rumor was that the pilot almost never spoke, except to her husband and her newborn girl. Carly could appreciate that. She tried to recall the silent woman's name but decided it wasn't important. Time enough to learn names if the new pilot lasted.

The flames climbing toward the fire crew were bad, but the crew had an escape. They could forge a path through that notch in the ridge and down the other side, ahead of the fire.

The number two head from the north was clawing up the ridge with no one to stop it yet. It radiated a malevolent, deep orange, as if saying, "I'm going this way, and just try and stop me. I dare you." The next sticks of smokejumpers would be here shortly. That's where they needed to jump.

"Base, this is ICA Thomas. How many smokies in your next load?"

"Three sticks, Carly."

"Roger, jump all six of them on the number two head. Out."

The number three head...

"That's the one." Carly pointed for the pilot. "That's the bitch. Hit her. Hit her hard."

The pilot didn't move. She was just looking toward Carly again, her face unreadable behind silver shades.

They simply hovered five hundred feet above the ridge, dancing on that margin between enshrouding smoke ahead and below, and sunlight above and behind.

Had she nerved out?

"The crew's okay for now. We'll drop more smokies on number two. Number three is going to cross the ridge and burn into the southern slope. Then we're in a whole new world of hurt."

No nod. No acknowledgment. Frozen for half a moment longer. No waver in the hover, a good trick in the jumpy gusts that heat-blasted first one way and then another above a fire. Carly now felt as if she were the target of study. As if she were the one being assessed, analyzed, and mapped instead of the fire.

"Drop in twenty seconds, chief." The pilot spoke over the intercom with absolute surety, warning the crew chief in the back to be ready on his fire-dump controls. "Fifty percent drop in three hundred feet of flow, so give me a dial setting of two for two and a half seconds. Eight-second hold and then the second half of load."

Evans Fitch, who'd been silent so far, acknowl-edged with a simple "Ready." That was weird because normally Evans was one of those guys who couldn't shut up.

He had flown a training run with the woman and had simply described the flight as "Serious, man. Real serious."—whatever that meant—in his atypically abbreviated speech, as if the pilot had stripped him of his voluble word supply.

Not counting Carly as spotter, there would normally

only be one person flying in the Sikorsky Firehawk, but with a newbie pilot, even one who came with helitack certification, they were overstaffing. Evans was manning the duplicate set of drop controls, which connected back to a console in the helicopter's cargo area where everyone except the pilot and copilot rode. Carly would have to decide how long they needed to have Evans at the backup controls.

The woman's numbers were wrong. The drop length was okay, but the turn couldn't happen that fast. Before Carly could protest, the helicopter dipped and turned so sharply that Carly found herself hanging on to the edges of her seat so she wouldn't be thrown against the harness. The rotors beat harder through Carly's headset as they dug into the air, thrusting the Firehawk toward the third head of the blaze.

"Winds?" the pilot asked.

Carly blinked as they dove into the smoke. Visibility alternated from a hundred yards to a hundred inches and back as they plunged toward the maelstrom. The heat in the cabin jumped ten, then twenty, degrees as they flew into the hot smoke over the fire.

"Pretty mellow, steady at fifteen from the west-northwest." She could tell by the shape of the smoke plume and the slight movement in the droopy-topped hemlocks still outside of the fire.

The pilot simply left a long enough silence to remind Carly that she wasn't stupid and had known that. Of course, any decent pilot knew how to read the winds at altitude. The woman was asking about the real-world winds, a hundred feet over the treetops. That was a whole different question. As a pretest for planning a parachute jump, the smokejumpers would spill out weighted crepe-paper streamers that would twist and curl in the thousand conflicting air currents that battered above a raging fire.

"Chaotic. Winds can microburst from forty knots to zero and back in a couple seconds, and the worst of that occurs vertically. Horizontally, the winds will carry more or less up the slope, probably about thirty knots and chaotic at the moment. The winds are better at two hundred feet, much more stable." She offered the woman an out.

"But the retardant is best at a hundred feet."

Carly considered. "In these tight canyons, yes, if you can get it in the right place." The accuracy would be better, and the tighter spread would provide heavier coverage per acre. That would be an advantage right now.

Through the next visibility break, Carly could see they were already at the hundred-foot mark and moving fast. She glanced down at the unfamiliar console, needing a moment to spot their airspeed. Damn, but they were moving fast.

The pilot returned to her silent mode, and Carly worked the numbers in her head while she held on. Dial setting of two would be about right at this speed, if the flame retardant landed in the right place.

A loud bang could be heard even over the heavy beat of the Firehawk's rotors. A tree had just gone off like a bomb. Superheated until the pitch didn't ignite, it exploded. A thousand shards of tree in every direction. But the pilot had them moving fast enough that they were in the clear on this one. Not even the bright patter of wood chips against the fuselage.

"Drop in five, four, three, two, one. Drop now. Now. Now."

Carly more felt than heard the mechanical door opening on the thousand-gallon tank of flame retardant mounted under the belly of the helicopter. Most pilots drifted higher as the load lightened. This pilot was good enough that their altitude remained steady. Even better, the pilot held the same height above the treetops as they dipped into the valley, then climbed up the other side. She'd seen pilots who tried to hold stable to elevation above sea level. They either learned fast or were thrown out of the service. It was fine in a chaparral fire, but up here in the mountains, firefighting altitudes always had to be referenced from the terrain or you could fly straight into a mountain.

Leaning into the curved side window and twisting to see what she could, Carly pictured the pattern of the red mud. With a slight arc, half of the mud landed just at the very leading edge of the fire, and half on the trees just ahead of the flames. Textbook perfect. Normally, you'd attack the flank, narrowing the fire to extinction. But here they didn't have that luxury. By the time they flanked it, the fire would be over the ridge. It was still small enough now that maybe they could just cut its throat.

She'd counted to two and half, then again felt the slight vibration through her seat as the dump hatch's hydraulics slammed shut. The Firehawk helicopter somehow went from a hundred and twenty knots in one direction to a hundred and twenty in the other.

Carly couldn't quite tell how they'd done it so abruptly, though her eyes did momentarily cross from the g-force that knocked the air out of her lungs like a punch.

Some part of her mind had continued to count seconds. At eight seconds, Evans popped the retardant hatch again even as the pilot repeated her call of "Now. Now. Now." Somehow, impossibly, they were lined back up on the fire. It had taken a hard-climbing turn to avoid slamming into the wall of the valley that they had been crossing laterally. But again, they were just above the top edge of the flames, bouncing through the rough edge of superheated air currents bolting for the skies.

Carly sat on the uphill side, making it so that she couldn't see exactly where the pilot placed the drop. That was a good sign. Beginners thought that dumping the retardant directly on a fire did something. It really didn't. Retardant had to be dropped ahead of the fire. It was a sticky, nasty goo that clung to branches and bark like heavy glue, tinted bright red so that you could see where it lay. It cooled the unburned fuel that the fire sought and trapped the oxygen-laden air away from the wood so that it couldn't burn. No oxygen, no fire.

So this second pass, if the pilot did it right, should be laid just upslope from the first pass, overlapping to allow for the different direction of flight to coat the back side of some of the unburned trees and branches that had been coated in the first pass. But mostly the second pass would be targeted on the untouched and yet unburned trees. All to create a wider swath of protected fuel.

This one drop of retardant wouldn't be enough. Carly could tell that by the rough ride of the Firehawk helicopter through the air pockets as they hammered down into the valley and back up the opposite slope.

They'd need another load right away, and probably two or three after that, to cut this head. The fire-heated wind roared up the valley too hard, too fast. Even the wide barrier laid down by the near-perfect drop wouldn't stop this beast.

But they'd sure slowed it down.

The ex-Army pilot hovered once again over the point of the ridge, turned so Carly had the best view of the fire below.

Carly keyed the radio.

"Tanker base. This is Firehawk Zero-one. Come back."

"Tanker base. Go ahead."

"Three heads. We hit north hard. You'll need two flanking loads to trap it. But first load we need water and foam on top of the crew on the south head. They're jumping the next couple sticks of smokies into middle head. Over."

"Roger that. Out."

"Out."

Even as she took her hand off the mike switch, she saw the jump plane, MHA's beautiful old DC-3 twin-engine, with the next round of smokejumpers. The plane was swinging above a high meadow not far from the middle head of fire. Two brightly colored paper streamers spilled out into the wind. They fluttered and twisted, showing a strong draft up the valley but no chaotic crosswinds. She'd seen the winds tie smokie streamers in knots while they still turned in the air. The smokies would be watching them intently to decide their best approach.

The plane turned again, and on the next pass, four jumpers spilled out, two sticks. The smokies' rectangular parachutes popping open in a bright array of Crayola red, white, and blues. In contrast, their heavily padded and pocketed jumpsuits were a dusky, dirty, soot-stained yellow.

As the plane circled to drop the next stick of jumpers, the pilot spoke, breaking Carly's reverie as she watched the choreographed ballet of a coordinated fire attack.

"Seen enough?"

"Roger that. Let's get another load."

The nose of the chopper pulled up sharply. In some kind of crazy compound maneuver that Carly had never experienced before, the body of the helicopter spun on its axis. Now they were equally abruptly nose down and moving fast back toward the firebase. Not one wasted moment of motion.

"Where did you learn to fly like that?"

Again that long, silent moment of assessment from the pilot.

"Army."

"I've flown with plenty of Army jocks. They don't fly like you. I've been up with enough of them to know that the Army doesn't teach this."

"I flew for the 160th SOAR, Airborne. Major Emily Beale." Then a note of deep chagrin entered her voice. "Retired, I guess."

It was now Carly's turn to remain silent as they roared back toward the helibase for the next load of retardant. SOAR. The Army's secret Special Operations Aviation Regiment. The best and scariest helicopter pilots on the planet. Well, they certainly wouldn't need Evans as a backup on any future flights.

"Why are you flying fire?"

"As I said, had a kid. Didn't seem fair to her if I kept flying military."

"Oh, like flying fire is so much safer."

Emily Beale again answered with silence.

Take Over at Midnight

The Night Stalkers
by M.L. Buchman

NAME: Lola LaRue

RANK: Chief Warrant Officer 3

MISSION: Copilot deadly choppers on the world's most dangerous missions

NAME: Tim Maloney

RANK: Sergeant

MISSION: Man the guns and charm the ladies

The past doesn't matter, when their future is doomed

Nothing sticks to "Crazy" Tim Maloney, until he falls hard for a tall Creole beauty with a haunted past and a penchant for reckless flying. Lola LaRue never thought she'd be susceptible to a man's desire, but even with Tim igniting her deepest passions, it may be too late now…With the nation under an imminent threat of biological warfare, Tim and Lola are the only ones who can stop the madness—and to do that, they're going to have to trust each other way beyond their limits…

"Quite simply a great read. Once again Buchman takes the military romance to a new standard of excellence."—*Booklist*

"Buchman continues to serve up nonstop action that will keep readers on the edge of their seats."—*Library Journal Xpress*

For more M.L. Buchman, visit:

www.sourcebooks.com

Light Up the Night

The Night Stalkers
by M.L. Buchman

—◦◦◦—

NAME: Trisha O'Malley

RANK: Second Lieutenant and AH-6M "Little Bird" Pilot

MISSION: Take down Somali pirates, and deny her past

NAME: William Bruce

RANK: Navy SEAL Lieutenant

MISSION: Rescue hostages, and protect his past—against all comers

They both have something to hide

When hotshot SOAR helicopter pilot Trisha O'Malley rescues Navy SEAL Bill Bruce from his undercover mission in Somalia, it ignites his fury. Everything about Trisha triggers his mistrust: her elusive past, her wild energy, and her habit of flying past safety's edge. Even as the heat between them turns into passion's fire, Bill and Trisha must team up to confront their pasts and survive Somalia's pirate lords.

—◦◦◦—

"The perfect blend of riveting, high-octane military action interspersed with tender, heartfelt moments. With a sigh-worthy scarred hero and a strong Irish redhead heroine, Buchman might just be at the top of the game in terms of relationship development." —*RT Book Reviews*

For more M.L. Buchman, visit:

www.sourcebooks.com

Hell for Leather

Black Knights Inc.
by Julie Ann Walker

New York Times and *USA Today* Bestselling Author

———

Unlimited Drive

Only a crisis could persuade Delilah Fairchild to abandon her beloved biker bar, let alone ask Black Knights Inc. operator Bryan "Mac" McMillan for help. But her uncle has vanished into thin air, and sexy, surly Mac has the connections to help her find him. What the big, blue-eyed Texan has against her is a mystery…but when the bullets start to fly, Mac becomes her only hope of survival, and her only chance of finding her uncle alive.

Unstoppable Passion

Mac knows a thing or two about beautiful women—mainly that they can't be trusted. Throw in a ticking clock, a deadly terrorist, and some missing nuclear weapons, and a man just might find himself on the wrong end of the gun. But facing down danger with Delilah is one passion-filled thrill ride…

———

"The heat between the hero and heroine is hotter than a firecracker lit on both ends… Readers are in for one hell of ride!" —*RT Book Reviews*, 4.5 Stars

For more Julie Ann Walker, visit:

www.sourcebooks.com

Full Throttle

Black Knights Inc.
by Julie Ann Walker

New York Times and *USA Today* Bestselling Author

Steady hands, cool head...

Carlos "Steady" Soto's nerves of steel have served him well at the covert government defense firm of Black Knights Inc. But nothing has prepared him for the emotional roller coaster of guarding the woman he once loved and lost.

Will all he's got be enough?

Abby Thompson is content to leave politics and international intrigue to her father—the President of the United States—until she's taken hostage half a world away, and she fears her father's policy of not negotiating with terrorists will be her death sentence. There's one glimmer of hope: the man whose heart she broke, but she can never tell him why...

As they race through the jungle in a bid for safety, the heat simmering between Steady and Abby could mean a second chance for them—if they make it out alive...

Praise for Julie Ann Walker:

"Julie Ann Walker is one of those authors to be put on a keeper shelf along with Nora Roberts, Suzanne Brockmann, and Allison Brennan." —*Kirkus*

For more Julie Ann Walker, visit:

www.sourcebooks.com

Bad Nights

by Rebecca York

New York Times Bestselling Author

———

You only get a second chance...

Private operative and former Navy SEAL Jack Brandt barely escapes a disastrous undercover assignment, thanks to the most intriguing woman he's ever met. When his enemies track him to her doorstep, he'll do anything to protect Morgan from the danger closing in on them both...

If you stay alive...

Since her husband's death, Morgan Rains has only been going through the motions. She didn't think anything could shock her—until she finds a gorgeous man stumbling naked and injured through the woods behind her house. He's mysterious, intimidating—and undeniably compelling.

Thrown together into a pressure cooker of danger and intrigue, Jack and Morgan are finding in each other a reason to live—if they can survive.

———

"[Rebecca York] turned the tables in a brilliant stroke of genius. It's a page-turner for sure." —*Night Owl Reviews* Top Pick

"A heart-in-throat thriller and a soul-satisfying romance—a fantastic read!"—*Long and Short Reviews*

For more Rebecca York, visit:

www.sourcebooks.com

Betrayed

Rockfort Security Book 2
by Rebecca York

New York Times and *USA Today* Bestselling Author

———

To trust

Rockfort Security operative Shane Gallagher has been brought into S&D Systems to find a security leak. Confidential information has been stolen, and Shane suspects Elena Reyes, a systems analyst with the access and know-how to pull it off. As he finds excuses to get close to her, their attraction is too strong to ignore, but how can Shane trust the very woman he's investigating?

Or not to trust

Elena has spent her life proving herself, but now she's risking it all: everything she's worked for, and her growing feelings for Shane. Much as she wants to trust the devastatingly sexy, hard-as-nails investigator, she can't let herself fall for him…the stakes are too high.

———

"Rebecca York delivers page-turning suspense." —Nora Roberts

"Rebecca York's writing is fast paced, suspenseful, and loaded with tension." —Jayne Ann Krentz

For more Rebecca York, visit:

www.sourcebooks.com

Her Perfect Mate

X-Ops Series
by Paige Tyler

USA Today Bestselling Author

He's a high-octane Special Ops pro

When Special Forces Captain Landon Donovan is pulled from an op in Afghanistan, he is surprised to discover he's been hand-picked for a special assignment with the Department of Covert Operations (DCO), a secret division he's never heard of. Terrorists are kidnapping biologists and he and his partner have to stop them. But his new partner is a beautiful, sexy woman who looks like she couldn't hurt a fly—never mind take down a terrorist.

She's not your average Covert Operative

Ivy Halliwell is no kitten. She's a feline shifter, and more dangerous than she looks. She's worked with a string of hotheaded military guys who've underestimated her special skills in the past. But when she's partnered with special agent Donovan, a man sexy enough to make any girl purr, things begin to heat up...

"An absolutely perfect story—one I honestly couldn't put down. I definitely want more of Paige Tyler's shifters." —Kate Douglas, author of the bestselling Wolf Tales and Spirit Wild series

For more Paige Tyler, visit:

www.sourcebooks.com

Her Lone Wolf

X-Ops Series
by Paige Tyler

USA Today Bestselling Author

Leaving him was impossible...

It took everything she had for FBI Special Agent Danica Beckett to walk away from the man she loved. But if she wants to save his life, she has to keep her distance. Now, with a killer on the loose and the stakes higher than ever, the Department of Covert Ops is forcing these former lovers into an uneasy alliance...whether they like it or not.

Seeing her again is even worse

The last thing Clayne Buchanan wants is to be shackled to the woman who broke his heart. She gets under his skin in a way no one ever has and makes him want things he has no right to anymore. All he has to do is suffer through this case and he can be free of her for good. But when Clayne finds out why Danica left in the first place, everything he's tried to bury comes roaring back—and there's no way this wolf shifter is going to let her get away this time.

"Dangerously sexy and satisfying." —Virna DePaul, *New York Times* bestselling author of the Belladonna Agency series

For more Paige Tyler, visit:

www.sourcebooks.com

About the Author

M. L. Buchman has over twenty-five novels in print. His military romantic suspense books have been named NPR and Barnes & Noble "Top 5 Romance of the Year" and *Booklist*'s "Top 10 of the Year." In addition to romance, he also writes thrillers, fantasy, and science fiction. In among his career as a corporate project manager he has: rebuilt and single-handed a fifty-foot sailboat, both flown and jumped out of airplanes, designed and built two houses, and bicycled solo around the world. He is now making his living full-time as a writer, living on the Oregon Coast with his beloved wife and telling any who will listen about his awesome kid. He is constantly amazed at what you can do with a degree in geophysics. You may keep up with his writing at www.mlbuchman.com.